"I WILL NOT WED A MAN
WHO THINKS TO OWN ME."

Bayard smiled slowly. "I shall change your thinking," he purred, and his hand rose to cup her breast. "I shall teach you what prize can be yours, my Esmeraude, and you shall be powerless to refuse."

"I invite you to try," she said, her voice breathless though she tried to sound bold.

"Oh, I shall," Bayard whispered. He bent and nuzzled her ear, his expert touch making Esmeraude dizzy. "And I shall begin this very night."

Esmeraude returned his ardent kiss, welcoming the heat of his touch. Though he might seek to conquer her with a kiss, she would begin her own conquest of his heart. On the morrow they would reach Airdfinnan and she would have Jacqueline's counsel.

In the interim, she saw no reason to deny herself such pleasure as this. Aye, this man could be shaped to her expectation. Esmeraude knew it well.

Indeed, she looked forward to the challenge. . . .

Dell Books by Claire Delacroix

The Bride Quest series:

The Bride Quest

The Temptress

Claire Delacroix

A Dell Book

Published by
Dell Publishing
a division of
Random House, Inc.
1540 Broadway
New York, New York 10036

ISBN: 0-440-23640-1

Printed in the United States of America

Published simultaneously in Canada

December 2001

10   9   8   7   6   5   4   3   2   1

OPM

For Kara Cesare
and
Liz Scheier,
with thanks.

Prologue

THE OLD FORTRESS WAS SHROUDED IN FOG WHEN Bayard arrived at its gates. If anything, the cloak of mist and fine rain made it look even more formidable and ancient than he recalled.

Montvieux had stood since the dawn of time, or at least for as long as anyone could remember. Its stone walls had been smoothed by expert craftsmen and polished by years of rain, stained by the blood of would-be conquerors. They seemed to be one with the earth of the holding, soil that had been tilled in the name of the lords of Montvieux for centuries.

For the lords of Montvieux had been in this place longer than even the château itself. 'Twas said that their line was older than the lineage of the kings of France, or even of the kings before these. They had been among Charlemagne's hosts, they had proven themselves even in those days to be bolder, stronger, and more valiant than any other warriors.

And their noble seed sprang from here, was nurtured here, was rooted here no matter how far any one of them wandered. Bayard halted his destrier and stared, struck by the vigor of the resonance this place awakened within him.

He had been certain that his origins were of import to him no longer. He had known that he was naught but the sum of what he had done since his departure. He had believed that he was a man who needed only his blade and his steed. Montvieux proved him wrong. The truth shook him to his core.

He loved this place.

He had missed this place.

And not just the cold stones themselves. He had missed the family that drew their power from within it. Bayard was of this place, as he would never be of any other place he conquered or defended. He carried Montvieux's blood, he bore the burden of its legacy. And the very sight of it made his heart beat faster with what might have been pride.

Pride. Yearning. Two sentimental traits Bayard thought long behind him.

But truly, was it not sentimentality that brought him back here now?

"'Tis a remarkable holding, sir," said Michael, the elder of his two squires, with the prim conviction he oft thought fitting of his role. 'Twas five years that the boy had ridden with Bayard and soon now he would gain his own spurs. That pride flared in Bayard's chest again, though for a different reason.

"'Tis incredible! I have never seen the like!" crowed Andrew, who, truth be told, found much of the world astounding. His very manner oft prompted a man to look again at what he might otherwise have missed.

Bayard remained silent, caught in the turmoil of his own response. His gaze slipped over the wet walls and gates and turrets, the bedraggled pennants, the fields beyond the château, the river and the forests. Memories deluged him, happy memories of a surprisingly joyous boyhood spent here in these fields and gardens and halls and riverbanks.

His grandmother's proud voice, so long unheard that he would have thought it forgotten, now echoed in his thoughts so clearly that she might have sat beside him:

Never conquered.

Envied by many but entrusted to few.
And of course, her most favored claim of them all:
The prized seat of warrior-kings.
Warrior-kings of which Bayard was one. 'Twas a fact that
his grandmother had always underscored to him, evidently
unaware or uninterested in the existence of Bayard's younger
brother, Amaury. Montvieux should be Bayard's, by virtue of
blood and of battle, at least by Margaux's reckoning.

Even if she had granted its seal elsewhere. In the wake of
her battle of wills with Bayard's own father—the battle
Margaux had lost—she had cast the seal to Bayard's uncle.
Bastard-born Rowan carried not a drop of the blood of
Montvieux, being the product of Margaux's husband and
a dancer, but Margaux had raised Rowan as her own.
Montvieux's seal was now destined for the hand of Bayard's
cousin and Rowan's son, Nicholas.

Bayard had never cared particularly. It had been enough
for him that Montvieux was held in the family, that 'twas
tended and respected. Now, the competition between kings
had changed his perspective.

Whatever the disputes that had parted him from his family,
they were his family, all the same. Bayard's liege lord, King
Richard of England, had defined Montvieux as a key asset in
his conflict with the King of France. Richard had been prepared to besiege it.

Richard, of course, had been delighted by Bayard's kinship
link. He had not realized Bayard's association with Montvieux,
since Bayard used his mother's estate in his name. Thirsty for
blood, Richard had even proposed to make Bayard lord of
Montvieux in his uncle's stead, once the keep was captured.

Had Bayard been a more ambitious man, or even a man as
cold as he preferred others to believe, he might have accepted the king's offer. Instead he argued the matter, at not
inconsiderable risk to his position in the royal household.

Instead he advised diplomacy to Richard. He appointed himself to persuade his uncle Rowan to surrender the allegiance of Montvieux to Richard's hand. He had insisted 'twould be less costly in terms of manpower, denying the suggestion that he felt any tenderness for his estranged family.

Tenderness was a weakness. Sentimentality was a weakness. And weaknesses, as Bayard had seen time and time again, could be readily exploited and cost a man dearly. A wise man hid any sentiment he was fool enough to feel, locking it away from those who coveted whatsoever he held.

Bayard clicked his tongue decisively and the destrier trotted proudly forward, tossing its mane so that the myriad silver bells upon its bridle jingled. Bayard blew his horn and the sound echoed off the stone, then he blew it again, as if impatient with the waiting.

"Who comes to the gates of Montvieux?" bellowed an unseen sentry. Bayard knew where the guard's hole was secreted, for he had played there as a boy. He turned toward the opening that was only the barest shadow from this side of the moat.

"I am Bayard de Villonne," he roared, "son of Burke de Villonne and nephew of your lord Rowan de Montvieux."

"What business have you here?"

"I come to visit my kin."

There was a delay. 'Twas a considerable delay and Bayard did not doubt that his name was known and that the lord had been consulted. The boys exchanged a glance. The rain fell more steadily, a drizzle that soaked through their clothes and chilled their flesh.

Bayard did not move, he did not flinch. He stared unswervingly at the shadow, daring his uncle to deny him entry. He showed only impatience and expectation, nary a doubt that his request would be granted.

And it worked, as so oft it did. Andrew sighed with relief

when the hinges on the great gates groaned. They opened slowly, revealing a formidable portcullis.

Rowan was silhouetted behind it, hands propped on his hips. Typically, Bayard's uncle was not garbed for war. He wore naught but a chemise, cut full of white linen, dark chausses and tall boots. His russet hair was shot with silver and there were lines in his tanned face that had not been there all those years before. His gaze held a new shrewdness though, or perhaps Bayard had been too young to see that his uncle possessed more than a playful side.

Bayard urged his steed forward, and the beast tossed its head with disdain as it trotted along the muddied road to the gates. He halted before the portcullis, closer than many a man would have come, the steam of the steed's breath nigh dampening Rowan's chemise. "Greetings, Uncle."

"So, you have returned." Rowan's tone was harsh. "Does your father know of it?"

"I have naught to say to my father and I doubt he would welcome any news of me." Bayard spoke dispassionately, that part of his life far behind him. "Will you grant me entry or nay?"

Rowan studied him warily. "What do you want here?"

"Can a man not visit his family without suspicion?"

"Nay, he cannot, not if he is you. What do you want of us?"

"I would speak with you," Bayard said carefully.

"So that you might sway me to your view against your sire? 'Twill not work, Bayard."

Anger crackled within Bayard though he strove to hide it. "Are you so enamored of my father in these days then? Time was you defied your own father, or so I have heard told."

"My father was a bloodthirsty wretch devoid of decency." Rowan lifted one brow. "Time was you remembered as much."

"So, if a man is good and honorable, 'tis impossible that he might err?"

"If a son is bent upon irresponsibility, 'tis impossible that any father might bend such a wayward will."

Bayard had not expected such indomitability from his uncle. Rowan had always been the rebel and the rogue, the son who had defied expectations. "I see you are resolved in this, then."

Rowan shrugged. "You left. 'Tis as good a sign that you knew yourself mistaken as any."

"Or a sign that a battle cannot be won by honorable tactics."

Rowan waved him off. "You have always been one who loved dearly to win. Do not pretend otherwise, Bayard. You lost this. You were wrong and your father was right. Have the grace to grant him that much, if not your obedience."

Anger boiled hot within Bayard and he kept his expression impassive only with the greatest of efforts. They knew naught of what faced a knight in these days, naught of what he had seen, naught of what he had been compelled to do and to witness. They were innocent and ignorant, these lords who lived in deceptive peace, these lords whom he had defended from the infidel encroaching upon Christendom from the east.

Worse, they were ignorant of the ambitions of a foreign king. He saw now that Rowan would not listen to him, not about his father, and not about King Richard.

Yet that changed naught. Bayard still would not see Montvieux besieged and its defenders slaughtered.

Perhaps one matter changed—his tactic. He would protect them from the fullness of the threat against them, but he would do so without them even realizing what he did. Let them think him wicked, if it assuaged their fears.

They knew naught of true fear—and the truth of it was that he preferred to not have them learn.

"Why are you here?" Rowan demanded.

"I came to see my grandmother, of course," Bayard said smoothly, and managed a thin smile.

Rowan snorted. "You seek out Margaux, of all people? Is it true, then, that like appeals to like?"

"She was always good to me."

"You mean that she always favored you. Do you think to persuade her to take your cause? If so, know that none will agree with her, regardless of the respect her age calls as its due."

Bayard stiffened. "I know Margaux is aged and I would see her once again while yet I can. Is there aught amiss with that?"

"Naught save that it is unanticipated. Sentiment is not what I would have expected of you."

Bayard was unwilling to argue this perception of him. "But then, you know so little of me, do you not?"

Rowan frowned. "That was your choice, Bayard."

"Was it?"

"You *left*."

"I believed then that I had no choice."

"And now?"

Bayard almost smiled. "I know that I had no choice."

Rowan's expression tightened and Bayard knew 'twas not the answer for which his uncle had hoped. But 'twas the truth and the truth was not always comforting. Bayard had no regrets and doubted that he ever would.

Rowan's gaze danced over him and Bayard knew what his uncle saw. He was a knight and a crusader, a champion and the companion of a king. He was larger and stronger and more hardened than he had been when last he saw his family, and he had no doubt that his experiences had left their mark upon him. He had waged war and won, he could afford the finest weaponry and steeds, and he had them.

Rowan looked, but said naught for the longest time.

The rain began to fall in earnest, slanting coldly against the trio outside the gates, splattering against the stone. The destrier did not move, but the palfreys ridden by Bayard's two squires began to flick their ears restlessly.

Then Rowan stepped abruptly away, gesturing to the sentry. "'Tis in good faith that I take you at your word and grant you admission—take care that you do not forget as much."

"And what is that to mean?"

"Have the courtesy not to turn Margaux against me," Rowan said harshly, then strode away.

He did not wait for Bayard to pass beneath the gates, but disappeared into a side entry. 'Twas one that Bayard knew entered the great hall itself.

The sentries stood back, wary, weapons at the ready, as the horses passed beneath the arch and through the tunnel of stone behind the gates. No ostler ran to take their reins, not so much as a stablehand came to tend them.

And if Bayard had been angry before, now he was furious. 'Twas unspeakably rude that he had not been invited to the board, that he was offered no cup of greeting, that his uncle chose to blame him alone for his estrangement from his father.

He had expected more from Rowan than this, far more. Rowan, after all, had always been the rebel, the one who confounded expectation. Bayard had expected at least a hearing from his uncle. Clearly it had been too much to hope that someone in his family would hear aught against his august father, or at least grant him a chance to discuss the matter. Instead they had closed ranks against him so surely that even Rowan—*Rowan!*—offered him little.

And this when he had come to aid them. Though he might have been prepared to soften, to be swayed by sentiment, now his resolve hardened. Bayard brushed down his destrier himself, his strokes vigorous in his fury. The boys hung back, sensing his mood. They stayed silent as they tended their own steeds with diligence.

Aye, the king demanded Montvieux of Bayard.

The king would have it.

For there was one person who could grant it to Bayard, and grant it without the shedding of so much as a drop of blood. So it was that Bayard had told no lie—he truly desired to see his grandmother and none other.

Perhaps the end result would be that she turned against Rowan, but for that, Bayard would not apologize. His uncle had chosen to spurn Bayard, and thus had spurned the opportunity he offered.

Winning Montvieux from Margaux was the next best possible scenario. Let them think him selfish and malicious—let them never know the fate from which Bayard had saved them. He cared naught and he would care naught, for caring was a weakness that could readily be exploited.

And once he held Montvieux, Bayard de Villonne would not tolerate a vulnerability of any kind.

His forebears would have demanded no less.

❧

Bayard's grandmother, however, demanded a price both heavy and light. Her chamber was shrouded in shadows and thick with the smell of unguents and healing potions.

"My lady has taken to her bed," her maid whispered as they stood upon the threshold of the chamber. "She is despondent and weakened by age." The maid cast Bayard a shrewd glance. "Perhaps she will be cheered by your visit."

'Twas impossible to think of his grandmother ceding to any weakness, and Bayard tried to make sense of what he had been told. He doffed his gloves and slapped the leather against his palm, eyeing the curtains pulled tight around her pillared bed. They were wrought of sapphire samite trimmed with white, their hems adorned with the fleur-de-lis of Montvieux.

"Who admits a draft to my chamber?" Margaux demanded, as querulous as ever.

" 'Tis I, *Grandmaman*, Bayard." He strode into the room as the curtains rustled, then Margaux hauled open the fabric with surprising vigor.

She stared him up and down, her gaze bright with challenge, then her lips curved slightly. "If you came for a funeral, I am not dead as yet."

"For which I am grateful." He bowed his head. "I came to visit you and expect your conversation will be finer while you draw breath."

"You have taken your own time about it," she snapped. She sat up and the maid rushed to plump cushions behind her lady's back. Margaux ignored the younger woman, her bearing imperial and not the slightest bit despondent. Indeed, she looked prepared to argue any matter.

" 'Tis not so readily done to visit from Outremer."

"So you have been on crusade, as 'twas rumored."

"With Richard of England."

"Ah." She studied him more leisurely, her gaze lingering upon his blade and his boots, his armor, the trappings of his wealth. " 'Tis not the weaponry granted upon your knighthood."

Bayard smiled. "I have seen fit to indulge myself."

"And you have the coin to do it." She met his gaze so suddenly that he nigh jumped. "Or the plunder."

"Those in France know little of Outremer and her ways," Bayard spoke mildly, knowing that the maid attended every word avidly. He gestured to a stool and Margaux nodded once crisply. "I am sorrowed to hear that you are ill, *Grandmaman*, and had thought you might find entertainment in the tales of my adventures."

Margaux smiled a calculating smile. She waved abruptly to the maid. "Fetch wine for my guest and myself. A man of such experience must have missed the pleasures of hearth and home, and surely a man so successful deserves some acknowledgment of his triumphs."

The maid bobbed her head and scurried away as Margaux held Bayard's gaze. Only when the footsteps had faded beyond earshot did the crone lean forward. "You have come for a prize, a prize that only I can grant. I know this."

Bayard said naught, merely smiled in his turn.

Margaux glanced across the chamber. "Your father is the sole fruit of my own womb. I only surrendered Montvieux to Rowan because your father would not have it. Who was to know that your mother would bear a worthy child?"

Bayard knew this was not strictly true—his father had refused to spurn his love at Margaux's bidding and she had taken the promise of Montvieux from him in an effort to force him to her will. When Burke had wed his lady love despite the price, for the sake of pride, Margaux had had no choice but to be true to her own pledge.

Indeed, Bayard's hopes relied upon Margaux's dissatisfaction with that outcome. He waited, as all hunters wait, for the moment of opportunity.

She looked at him, her eyes narrowed. "And now you would ask of me what he has spurned."

"I am the eldest of your blood grandsons."

"And you are the most like mine own father. The blood runs true in your veins. Perhaps that is an omen that the legacy belongs in your hands." She tilted her head suddenly. "But perhaps I should prefer greater proof of your desire than a fine new coat of mail."

Bayard frowned, but his grandmother conjured a scroll of vellum, then fairly threw it at him. 'Twas hung with wax seals and ribbons, and clearly a pronouncement of some kind.

To his astonishment, 'twas an invitation.

Greetings to Burke, lord of Villonne, & Alys his lady
wife, once of Kiltorren; to Luc of Llanvelyn & his lady
wife Brianna of Tullymullagh; to Rowan, Lord of
Montvieux & his lady wife Bronwyn of Ballyroyal. May
the blessings of good health and God's favor be upon
all of the brothers Fitzgavin and their children.

Your sons are cordially invited to partake in a contest
for the hand of our daughter Esmeraude, held in the
tradition of your own Bride Quest, launched some
twenty-three years ago from Tullymullagh Castle in
Ireland. Those sons of whom we speak are Bayard of
Villonne, Amaury of Villonne, Connor of Tullymullagh,
and Nicholas of Montvieux.

Esmeraude is twenty summers of age, innocent, and
well known for her wit and beauty. In addition to the
prize of the lady's hand itself, there is a dowry to be
won, including the title of Ceinn-beithe itself, now a
prosperous estate in addition to being of much
traditional value. Esmeraude will decree both the terms
of competition and declare the winner of her heart.

We request that all men who would compete gather
here at Ceinn-beithe on or before the first of May of this
year, and welcome their families to enjoy our hospitality.

May this missive find you well—

Duncan MacLaren, chieftain of Clan MacQuarrie,
defender of Ceinn-beithe

& Lady Eglantine, formerly of Crevy-sur-Seine and
Arnelaine

Dated February 20, in the year of Our Lord 1194

Margaux leaned forward and tapped a gnarled finger upon
the coverlet. "Your father declined my advice in matters of
marriage and defied my will in wedding unsuitably. Whomsoever I endow with the sole prize I possess will obey my will."

Bayard blinked, surprised despite himself by this test. "You will grant me Montvieux if I wed this maiden?"

"You must win her. 'Tis both a quest and a test."

"But why this damsel?"

"Because you must defeat your own cousins and brother to prove your obedience to me. Because her lineage is adequate, because she may not be readily won with so many suitors competing for her hand."

Bayard handed back the scroll, its contents already committed to memory, then met Margaux's gaze steadily. "You would be unwise to doubt me in this," he counselled. " 'Tis my habit to win."

She smiled coyly, clearly believing that she had turned him to her own will. "Then you will have need of a fitting weapon for such an adventure. In the chapel of Montvieux, there is a staircase hidden beside the altar."

" 'Tis not hidden so well as that. I recall it."

"Aye and did you ever descend it?"

"It leads to the crypt."

Margaux leaned forward. "Seven forebears lie there in eternal slumber, most recently mine own father. Go there, to the father of his father, the third sarcophagus. 'Tis said that the son who can lift the lid of that stone coffin and who can seize the blade that defended Montvieux against the barbarians is the one destined to rule."

"You think I cannot do this?"

"I think I should like to know."

Bayard made to rise, but Margaux lifted a hand. "None should witness this. 'Twill prompt suspicion. Go this night, and in the morn, show me your blade at the board with the tale that 'tis one plundered from a Saracen. If 'tis truly the blade of my great-grandfather, then I shall kiss it to seal our bargain. You will depart immediately and none shall be the wiser."

"Until I win the bride."

Margaux smiled. The maid scurried into the chamber, two chalices and a pitcher of wine in her grip. Margaux nodded and the girl poured the red wine, her curiosity evident. "But how would a Saracen know of your plan to aid the king?" Margaux asked, as if they had been interrupted in the midst of a tale.

"Ah, there was a spy within our ranks, as you most certainly have already guessed." Bayard lifted the chalice and saluted Margaux. "To your health, *Grandmaman*, and may you live many years yet to hear tales of chivalry and conquest."

She cackled before she sipped. "Or at least till the end of this one." Margaux lifted her chalice to her grandson, then drank heartily of the wine.

Chapter One

I THINK 'TIS A TERRIBLE IDEA," ESMERAUDE COM-plained.

The woman who had been Esmeraude's nurse-maid and later her maid grimaced, though she said naught more.

"'Tis terrible to petition for a spouse for me in this way and you know it well!" Esmeraude repeated the complaint she had made since her parents had sent their missive to France. "Why, for the love of God, should I choose a husband in such a manner?"

"Because you will adore it," Célie said tartly.

The two were in Esmeraude's chamber, making the bed ready for the night. *"Moi?"*

Célie laughed and shook her head with affection. "Indeed, I can scarce imagine what you would enjoy more than to have several dozen men competing for the favor of your hand." She wagged a finger at her charge. "You shall be in your glory when your suitors arrive."

"Men competed before and I did not enjoy it." Esmeraude plumped a pillow, challenging the other woman to convince her otherwise.

"They brought you gifts, which you liked well enough."

Esmeraude shrugged. "Fripperies that they would take to any woman they wooed. 'Tis my face and the promise of my womb they court, no more than that. Now they may add Ceinn-beithe itself to the prize, so 'twill only be worse."

"Esmeraude! 'Tis vulgar to speak thus!"

" 'Tis true and you know it."

"Perhaps so. Still, you should not say as much." The pair shared a smile of understanding, wrought of years of similar such exchanges.

"If you had wished to avoid this contest, you might have chosen Robert," Célie said finally, though her casual mention of a suitor's name did not fool Esmeraude. "He seems different from the others who would court you."

"Aye, he does whatsoever I ask of him."

Célie's quick sidelong glance was wry. "I should think you would like that."

"And you would be mistaken." Esmeraude rolled her eyes. "The man has no wits of his own, Célie, and I am certain that he would pursue any folly I commanded of him. No woman should wed a man so devoid of sense!"

"What of Douglas?"

Esmeraude grimaced. "Why, he is intent upon telling me what to do and what to say at every moment, though we are barely acquainted! Why does he court me if he so disapproves? What manner of spouse would he make?"

"Not the one for you, 'tis clear, when you are so certain of your own thinking."

Esmeraude lifted her chin, knowing full well that she was with a strong ally. "And is that so wicked?"

Célie chuckled. "Nay, child, not so wicked as that. Indeed, it makes sense to consider this matter of marriage carefully. You show your usual good sense, even if 'tis wrapped in your need to have the eyes of all upon you." Célie stroked the linens smooth. "What of Seamus?"

"Too tall. I should never be able to kiss him, *if* I desired to."

"Ah, but you must favor Alasdair."

"He is too short."

"But you always laugh so in his company."

"Because he is amusing." Esmeraude propped a hand upon her hip. "But truly, Célie, the man considers all of life to be a merry jest. He is serious about naught and 'twould undoubtedly become a tedious trait all too soon."

"Lars?"

"Too dour! That man has no ability to smile at all."

"Calum? Now, there is a handsome man, neither too tall nor too short, too amused or too somber."

"He has no holding to his name." Esmeraude thumped a pillow. She had an alternative scheme and simply had to find a way to best present it to her maid. "I have no fancy to starve and one cannot live upon the sight of a handsome man's visage."

"What of Ceinn-beithe? The legacy would come to Calum's name upon your nuptials, for Duncan has decreed as much."

"Aye, and what experience has *Calum* of ensuring it prospered? He has never administered an estate and indeed I believe his every thought is bent upon the pursuit of pleasure alone. Nay, I owe better to those so used to Duncan's steady hand."

Célie smiled with approval of this concern for responsibilities. "Then you can have no quibble with Hamish. He has more wealth than any man I have ever met and is responsible beyond all else."

"And is concerned with the maintenance of that wealth to the exclusion of all else!" Esmeraude jumped onto the bed, ruining the perfect arrangement of the linens, and appealed to her exasperated maid. "Do you not see, Célie? If I am to wed a man, I wish to love him with all my heart."

" 'Tis what your parents desire for you. 'Tis why they summon these men, to win your heart."

"Aye, but I fear that men embarking upon such a quest are men concerned with material reward alone. The men who have come thus far have but one trait in common, Célie— they show no passion."

"Passion?"

"Aye!" Esmeraude closed her eyes and leaned back. "I would have a man with a heart, a man who feels great ardor for his beliefs yet will listen to other views. I would wed a man keen of wit but trusting of heart, neither too tall nor too short, neither too rich nor too poor, neither too amusing nor too dour." She smiled confidently. "A man exactly perfect for me."

Célie shook her head and began to chuckle. In a trio of heartbeats, she was laughing right from her toes and had to brace one hand against the bed to steady herself.

Esmeraude did not share her amusement. "And what makes you laugh at that?"

"I suppose your man must be handsome, and well wrought too."

"Of course!"

"And where would you find this man? You and all the other demoiselles who seek a perfect spouse?"

Esmeraude smiled. "I intend to seek him out."

"What madness is this?"

Esmeraude's smile broadened even as her maid's disappeared. "I shall find the man I wed. 'Twould be only fitting, particularly as you suggest my expectations are too high."

The maid propped her hands on her hips, her amusement gone. "Fitting in whose terms? 'Tis *fitting* for a man to seek a bride, as the men summoned by your parents will seek you out, not back ways round! No bride seeks her spouse and no man of honor finds such boldness fitting at all."

Esmeraude wrinkled her nose. "And most, if not all, of the

men who compete will prove to be exactly like the ones who already come to Ceinn-beithe to win me. Nay, Célie, I am convinced that the man I desire does not even know he needs a bride, much less that he has need of *me*."

"Then how will you know he is the man for you?"

"I will know him." Esmeraude leaned back and closed her eyes. "My heart will tell me the truth of it." She peeked through her lashes and found the maid looking skeptical.

"And where do you intend to seek him out, if this man is disinclined to find a bride or even dubious that he has need of one?"

Esmeraude grinned. "But that is the exciting part, Célie! I must embark upon a quest to find the man who will hold my heart captive. There is naught else for it."

Célie responded with perfectly predictable outrage. "You will do no such thing! I forbid it!"

"I will do exactly thus!" Esmeraude knew that her determination was apparent for her maid regarded her warily. "I will leave this very night, and be gone before any are the wiser."

"I shall barricade the door!" Célie thundered. "Why, I shall go to your mother this very moment and tell her of your scheme."

Esmeraude immediately grasped the maid's hands in her own and begged. "Célie, you would not, you *could* not! I thought we were friends."

The older woman's eyes narrowed. "Even if we were friends," she said carefully, "friends do not let each other commit such folly as this."

"But Célie, this is my future and my life, my *dream*. Surely you would not condemn me to a loveless match?"

Célie pulled her hands from Esmeraude's grip and shook a finger at her charge. "Do you realize what might happen to you, if you left unprotected? There are wolves beyond these walls and unscrupulous men and countless dangers . . ."

"And adventure!" Esmeraude flung out her hands and rolled to her back. "Imagine, Célie, all the marvelous places I might see! Oh, 'twould be worth any risk to live unfettered, even if 'twas not destined to last."

"Where would your fetters be, lass? You are fortunate in your life, make no mistake."

"But why must I wed a dull man and move from this household to his household, only to bear sons and manage accounts and see to it that his mother is happy? 'Tis too dreadful a fate to be embraced willingly."

The maid sat on the edge of the mattress and patted Esmeraude's hand. "And what makes you imagine that a man of passion will not have such expectations of his wife?" she asked gently.

"'Twill be easier to fulfill them with a heart filled with love." Esmeraude ignored the way her maid snorted at that. "And even if I am doomed to such a fate, why can I not have but one small adventure first?"

"Because you are the daughter of a respectable house."

Esmeraude closed her eyes and smiled, her hands clasped in her lap. "Would it not make a fine tale? How Esmeraude of Ceinn-beithe ventured boldly into the world to seek her one true love?"

"Aye, if she did not die ignobly instead."

"I would not be so foolish as that!" Esmeraude held her maid's skeptical gaze. "I have a scheme."

Célie's eyes narrowed. "Some mischief no doubt, in which I suspect I am shortly to find myself embroiled."

"Of course, 'twould be far better if I ventured forth with a loyal companion. All those in tales do as much." Esmeraude rolled abruptly across the mattress, catching the maid's hands in her own. She saw the gleam in the older woman's eyes and knew its import. "Will you accompany me? We could flee this very night, before *Maman* begins her competition for my hand, then none could say I acted unfairly."

"I will not let you abandon your duties so readily as you desire, mademoiselle, regardless of your opinion upon the matter." Célie huffed. "I have not been entrusted within your mother's employ all these twenty years and enjoyed her care to betray that trust readily, however great your desire for adventure." She spat the last word, as though 'twas an obscenity.

"Please, Célie? Would you deny me my very last chance, nay, my *sole* chance, to win my heart's desire? Will you not see that I do not pay a dire price for daring to dream of a great love?"

The maid considered her for a long moment. "I should not so indulge you," she said finally. Célie shook off Esmeraude's grip and rose to her feet. "Indeed, you should not ask me to do so!"

Esmeraude smiled impishly. "But when have I been concerned with what I should and should not do?"

Célie chuckled. "Vexing child. You have always known your own intent too well to be biddable." She smiled and Esmeraude smiled back, the fondness between them undisguised.

"You must come with me, Célie, you simply must. I cannot imagine being without you and your splendid good sense."

The maid eyed her charge. "Where will you go?"

Esmeraude shook a finger at her. "Nay, nay, nay. You must pledge to accompany me in good faith before I will tell you."

"Then you must pledge to at least look upon the men who arrive to compete for your hand before you flee."

"But why?"

Célie's expression turned arch. "'Twas you who said your heart would recognize the man for you."

"I did look," Esmeraude reminded her maid. "And the man for me was not there."

"They have not all gathered as yet, and surely the one less intent upon winning a bride would not arrive first, like an anxious pup?"

Esmeraude nibbled her lip as she considered that.

Célie folded her arms across her chest, clearly prepared to argue her own side. "And 'twould be rude to depart so abruptly and condemn those men who did arrive to no reward. 'Twould make Duncan look to be a poor host, which surely is not your intent. Your parents might not forgive such a dishonor readily, even from you."

"But I cannot stay!"

"Even if the man you seek might arrive yet? Or might even be here but as yet unnoted by you? Can you truly see to the heart of a man so readily as that?" Célie leaned closer. "Indeed, the man of whom you dream might already be in this hall. Would you risk losing him when he is so close?"

"Do not make me choose betwixt adventure and love! I would have both."

"Aye, I know." The maid leaned forward, her eyes gleaming with mischief. "What if you left a clue, that a stalwart man might pursue you?"

Esmeraude's dismay vanished at the suggestion. "A riddle!" She laughed, well pleased with this scheme. "I shall leave a devious riddle as a test, for only the man destined for me would both solve it and act upon its import. 'Tis a perfect compromise, Célie."

But the maid shook her head. "Nay, you should leave a simple riddle."

"Why?"

"Of what merit is a chase without competitors? And men

are at their most valiant when they are threatened by the per-
formance of others. If you wish to be pursued, you must
leave a simple riddle." Célie nodded confidently. "Indeed,
you might find that your more familiar suitors show unexpected qualities when faced with such a challenge. 'Twould
be a fine test of a man's mettle, or of his determination to win
you. I do not believe in your quest for this great love, nor do I
approve of your desire to live as a maiden in a song, but it
makes good sense to know the truth of a man's character before pledging to him forever."

Esmeraude tapped her lip with her fingertip and nodded.
" 'Tis a fine scheme. I shall do it."

"Then I shall pledge to accompany you and to protect you
from harm as best I am able. I have little doubt that you will
do whatsoever you will, with or without me." The older
woman smiled. "And I have a strange thought that your
chances of emerging unscathed from your adventure are
somewhat better with me in your company."

"Thank you, Célie!" Esmeraude leapt from the bed and
hugged her maid with enthusiasm.

"Know that I am persuaded to this course solely to ensure
your happiness." Célie's words were spoken with gruff affection, and she touched her charge's cheek.

"Oh, and I will be happy, I know it well." Esmeraude fell
back upon the mattress and leaned against the pillows. "The
King of the Isles will no doubt ensure it."

The older woman paled. "What nonsense is this?"

"He will not approve of *Maman* inviting foreign knights to
compete for my hand. Nay, not he. Indeed, he has lost too
much land to the Scottish king by way of the Norman knights
who have settled holdings."

"But—"

"But naught, Célie. Those holdings are carved from the
King of the Isles' territory yet surrendered to foreigners by

the Scottish king. Though the King of the Isles does not approve, he has few means of ousting foreign knights once their households are established here."

"Like your *Maman* and her household."

"Aye. And truly, now that the Scottish king is returned to the graces of the King of England, the King of the Isles must be uncertain of his territories indeed."

"Where did you learn so much of these matters of men?"

Esmeraude spared the older woman a devilish grin. "I listened when I was not supposed to." She tapped her chin with a fingertip, frowning slightly as she continued. "Nay, the King of the Isles is the only one who will save me from the invitations *Maman* sent to Norman knights. We shall go directly to him and entreat his aid."

"God in heaven." Célie sank to a chest and crossed herself. "Never let it be said that you are timid of heart, child."

"Oh, Célie, you worry overmuch. The King of the Isles *likes* me."

The maid's eyes narrowed. "In what manner does he like you?"

Esmeraude scoffed. "He is ancient, Célie, you have naught to fear of his amorous intent. We had a pleasant conversation when last he visited Ceinn-beithe, not more than that. He oft has told me tales and brought me fripperies from afar. Perhaps he even has heard tell of a fitting man. Do not scowl at me so." Esmeraude smiled confidently. "I am certain that I can charm him into supporting my quest."

"As am I," the maid agreed darkly. "You could charm the birds from the trees, child, and that with scarcely any effort at all. My concern is only what he will demand in return for granting your wish."

Esmeraude waved off this reservation. "Some trinket or other. A lock of my hair. Perhaps the favor of a kiss."

Célie looked less persuaded of this than she, but Esmeraude was undaunted.

She patted the plump mattress, well pleased that all was resolved to her satisfaction. "Come, Célie, and slumber with me this night. Adventures, I am given to understand, require considerable planning and a measure of foresight."

Célie granted her a hard look. "You are determined in this?"

"Aye! I can barely wait to begin. 'Tis all so exciting." Esmeraude bounced in anticipation, making the ropes that held the mattress creak. "Do you think some minstrel will compose an ode of my adventure? I should dearly love to be so heralded, to know that I have not lived a common life."

The maid harumphed, clearly not seeing the marvel of the adventure or any immortality among the bards.

"Get yourself onto your knees, child," she said in the tone she reserved for matters that were not to be argued. "We shall also have need of all the prayers we can say. Adventures, *I* am given to understand, oft require divine intervention to end merrily."

Excitement bubbled within Esmeraude even as her prayers fell dutifully from her lips. She would have an adventure of her own. A *quest*, like one of Duncan's tales.

She could imagine naught better.

Bayard de Villonne was certain of his pending triumph. He had crossed to England to attend the Wearing of the Crown by Richard and to present the good news. Richard was not readily swayed from his plan to beseige Montvieux, but Bayard had prevailed.

To win the hand of a rural maid in a barbarian contest had seemed so simple that both Richard and Bayard had enjoyed a hearty laugh over the matter. Bayard, after all, was handsome

and well mannered, a knight and a champion. There could
be none of his ilk gathered at this remote holding—Richard
had jested that the maiden would fairly leap into Bayard's
bed. 'Twas that, in the end, which convinced the king to stay
his hand.

For now.

Bayard guessed that 'twas seldom, indeed, that a man like
him ventured this way. He had been to Outremer and back,
he had been to Corsica and Sicily, he had fought at the right
hand of the King of England, sampled women of nigh every
hue, met royal princesses, dined with princes and potentates.
He had foiled assassination attempts against his liege lord, he
had plunged into battle against the Saracens, he had been entrusted upon diplomatic missions.

Perhaps Richard guessed aright when he suggested that
this northern demoiselle would not be able to resist Bayard.

'Twould be moot, of course, if she chose another spouse
before he arrived; 'twas the only way Bayard might lose this
contest. And his discussions with the king had made him
sorely late, which did little to ease his concern. Bayard encouraged his palfrey to greater speed, fearing that the battle
would be lost before he entered the fray.

He had to win Esmeraude, for the sake of his family.

So, on this morn, he made unholy haste. His squires raced
their palfreys to keep up with his own; his destrier galloped
at his right hand, breathing noisy displeasure all the while.

Finally, they crested a rise and Bayard spied the palisaded
walls of Ceinn-beithe. The village buildings and the surrounding camp of tents were touched with the gilt of an early
sun. Beyond the coast, the sun also touched the shimmering
surface of the sea and pierced the mist enveloping distant isles.

Bayard, though, studied the scene before him for hints that

he had arrived in time. The fields were still and devoid of so much as a sheep, a poor portent indeed. His heart leapt as he spied the last of a small party disappearing into the village gates.

Perhaps just in time.

Bayard slipped from the palfrey's saddle, donned his helm, then flung his fur-lined cloak over his shoulder. Andrew straightened Bayard's tabard and gave his knight's scabbard a last buff. Truly, Bayard's arsenal gleamed after the boy's efforts and the knight thanked him with sincerity.

Michael held the destrier's leads, a position of considerable responsibility. He stroked the beast's nose even as he adjusted the caparisons hanging from the fine saddle. Argent stamped, impatient for a run. Bayard leapt into his saddle as he had on the day of his dubbing and the boys cheered.

"I shall meet you at the village gates. Ensure that the palfrey is prepared for a lady."

"Aye, sir."

"May Dame Fortune smile upon you, sir."

"Aye, Michael." Bayard smiled himself. "May she always continue to do so." He winked at the boys, whistled to Argent and gave the destrier his spurs. The boys shouted encouragement as Argent galloped down the path to Ceinn-beithe.

'Twas good to ride the great stallion again, to feel his strength and vitality. The blue caparisons flew out behind him, the white edges flickering. The silver bells upon the harness jingled madly, their peal not unlike a thousand fairy bells.

Argent had not borne his master since Winchester and it showed in his vigorous run. His hooves were polished to a gleam and his coat was so thoroughly brushed that he seemed wrought of polished silver himself. His mane and tail, a darker hue of grey, streamed like silky feathers as he ran.

The blue leather saddle was the beast's pride, for he was more vain than any Bayard had known. Argent pranced high as Bayard slowed him before the village gates, snorting and fighting the bit, clearly pleased with his fine appearance. Two young men hovered at the gates, but stepped back at the sight of Bayard and his steed.

Bayard gave Argent his spurs, not waiting for approval to enter. The men stared after him, astounded. Aye, 'twas much as he had expected—none had seen the likes of him or his finery here before. His bride would be claimed by midday at the latest. He would be most glad to see this matter resolved.

He galloped through the narrow streets, letting the clatter of heavy hooves announce his presence. The village was quiet, most clearly having gone to watch the festivities in the hall, but those who were yet in the village halted their labors to stare.

Bayard dismounted with a flourish and cast the reins to the astonished stableboy. Bayard noted one richly hung destrier in the group, as well as three other fine beasts less ornately outfitted. He headed for the hall, his pulse quickening at the prospect of competition.

The hall was squat and square, its perimeter hung with tapestries that appeared rough to Bayard's worldly eye, and its floor jammed with onlookers. They were primarily peasants, simply dressed, though a line of nobles stood at the front. On the dais stood a man and a woman, the man garbed in the manner of the Scots with his legs bare and a length of cloth cast over his yellow chemise. The woman was garbed in a kirtle which was devoid of embellishment and her flesh was tanned to a golden hue. Her patrician features and serene expression revealed her upbringing as a noblewoman even though her garb did not.

They were his host and hostess, no doubt. A fair maid

stood between them, rather too young and slender to be interesting, but Bayard was prepared to wed and bed whomsoever he must.

No price could be too high.

"Greetings, Duncan MacLaren and Eglantine de Crevy," he cried, deliberately disrupting whatever ensued in the hall that he might not be deemed too late. The assembly turned and he bowed low. "Bayard de Villonne, knight, crusader, and champion, at your service."

He strode forward and the crowd parted before him. He expected the whispers, but he ignored them and smiled for his host and hostess with all his charm.

They smiled in return and he was reassured.

'Twas in his recent training to note pertinent details of the hall, the number of entrances and windows, the number of people therein, the number of weapons worn openly. 'Twas truly one of the safest halls he had entered in years, and though there was excitement, 'twas due to anticipation of festivities and entertainment, not the darker tension that he knew too well. Bayard noted precisely where his parents stood, yet did not glance their way.

He most certainly did not look at the cousin whose inheritance he would shortly steal for his own, however noble the cause.

Eglantine inclined her head. "Greetings, Bayard de Villonne. Your reputation has long preceded you. 'Tis many years since once we met and perhaps you do not recall. I would not have known you, for you have changed indeed."

"How could I forget such grace as your own, Lady Eglantine?" Bayard kissed her hand as Duncan bristled slightly. He smiled at the older man. "'Tis clear your companionship well suits the lady, for she blossomed into even greater loveliness in your company."

"I thank you," Duncan said gruffly, then reclaimed his

wife's hand. "Though a woman's merit should be measured by more than the loveliness of her features."

"Of course, though the state of a lovely woman's happiness can always be read in her eyes. I salute you, Duncan MacLaren, for 'tis clear you have achieved that rare prize of a wife well pleased with her spouse."

The pair exchanged a warm glance, the lady coloring slightly that her happiness was so evident as that. Bayard cleared his throat, then gestured to the shy flaxen-haired maiden who hovered behind them. He doffed his gloves. "And this would be fair Esmeraude?"

"Nay! This is Mhairi, our daughter." Eglantine caught the girl's shoulders in her hands and urged her forward. "She is but fourteen summers of age."

"Indeed?" Bayard expressed polite surprise. "And so lovely as this, already." He winked for the shy maiden and pink blossomed in her cheeks. "Mademoiselle, you will have many suitors, indeed, seeking your fair hand." He kissed the back of her hand and Mhairi flushed crimson.

When she stepped back behind her mother, Bayard slapped his gloves against his palm, glancing pointedly about the room. He met the accusation in his father's glare coolly, having no intention of answering anger in kind again, then turned back to his host and hostess with a smile. "And where is Esmeraude? I should enjoy making the acquaintance of the woman whose hand I intend to win."

" 'Tis I who will win her!" insisted another man.

Bayard looked back and started slightly in recognition. He had thought the other large destrier looked familiar. "Simon! How strange to find you so far from home."

"Too far from home," Eglantine murmured hotly. Bayard noted the dark glance that Duncan cast his wife's way and wondered what she knew of Simon de Leyrossire.

Simon showed no unease as he sauntered to Bayard's side,

nor certainly when he looked Bayard up and down. Bayard hid his lingering annoyance with only the greatest of effort. There were few things that truly angered Bayard de Villonne— cheating in a tourney was one of them. Simon cheated and cheated often, and had done so once at Bayard's expense.

'Twas not a matter easily forgotten.

"I did not realize you had deigned to grace these shores once more," Simon said.

"But of course." Bayard smiled more broadly. "Where Richard rides, so do I. Who is your liege lord these days?"

"Philip, King of France, as always."

"Yet strangely, you were not in his company when I met him in the east. I wondered at that, for all his great vassals rode in his company. Were you elsewhere in the party, rather than riding with the king himself?"

Simon's eyes narrowed. "I had duties to attend which did not permit me to join the crusade at that time."

"Ah, but if the King of England can be absent from his newly claimed dominion for near five years for the service of Christ, what mere noble among us can make an argument for the weight of our burdens?"

The men exchanged cold smiles, then Simon forced a laugh. "I could never expect a man devoid of a holding to understand." Simon gasped, feigning surprise. "But nay, I see that you wear the colors of Montvieux. Surely you are not suzerain of that holding?"

"Nay, not I." Bayard wore the blue and white of his lineage, though he did not embellish his garb with the fleur-de-lis of the house. 'Twas a nod to his ancestry, though a man like Simon sought an excuse for argument and divisiveness in all before him.

"Nor heir?" Simon glanced pointedly at Bayard's cousin and uncle, both garbed in Montvieux's colors with the fleur-de-lis.

"The lineage of Montvieux is my legacy, not the holding itself. I wear its colors as a tribute to the considerable history of the holding and the valor of my forebears."

'Twas a reasonable answer, though Bayard saw that none believed him. His father's eyes were narrowed in suspicion and his cousin, Rowan's son Nicholas, folded his arms across his chest and glared at Bayard.

Simon smiled, baring his teeth as he did so. "Perhaps 'tis just as well, for Philip would be concerned if the lord of Montvieux were a man who pledged his blade to England."

"'Tis to Richard I am pledged, and he is no less French than you or I."

"If from the south."

"Aquitaine is an old holding, a large one and a prosperous one. 'Tis only a fool who would mock a king who holds territories some ten times the size and the value of those held by the King of France."

"No less one who demands tithes of equally onerous measure," Duncan interjected, sparing the knights a censorious glance. "Perhaps we have forgotten our intent here this day."

"I apologize," Bayard said, bowing low once more.

"Aye, 'tis the mark of friends well met to forget themselves," Simon agreed, too silkily for Bayard's taste. "Let the contest begin!"

"If there is to be a tourney," Bayard began, choosing his words of warning carefully, but Duncan shook his head.

"'Tis to Esmeraude to decide and doubtless she has wrought some plan. Esmeraude!" Their host lifted his voice and everyone in the hall straightened in anticipation. "Esmeraude, come meet the men who would compete for your hand!"

Applause broke out and the musicians began a merry tune. People clapped along with the music, craning their necks to see the lady in question.

But no lady appeared.

"Esmeraude!" Duncan cried once more, when she did not appear.

The musicians began their tune again, evidently untroubled by the tardy appearance of the guest of honor. But Eglantine and Duncan exchanged a glance. Eglantine strode from the dais and disappeared while Duncan endeavored to look as if naught were amiss.

Bayard wondered whether Simon had wrought some dark scheme to ensure that he won the lady and shot a sidelong glance at the other knight. He caught Simon in the midst of making the same gesture, though he could not guess whether 'twas an honest one or a ploy to hide that knight's true objectives.

All in the hall were clearly surprised when Eglantine returned with no more than a roll of vellum. The music fell silent as she turned to Duncan in evident dismay. "She is gone. There is naught but this."

Duncan frowned. "Nay."

"Aye." Eglantine proffered the scroll, then clutched her spouse's sleeve. Duncan slid an arm around his wife's waist and whispered something to her that made her nod and clamp her lips tightly together. The company held their breath, in anticipation of a delightful surprise.

But Bayard knew 'twas no ruse. The parents were too embarrassed that all had gone awry and their concern for their child was obvious to any who cared to look.

Bayard leapt to the dais and plucked the scroll from the lady's hands. "A jest, no doubt," he said loudly and in good humor. Eglantine smiled gratefully. He unfurled the scroll and glanced to the parents.

"She writes?"

Eglantine nodded. "She speaks French as well, both langue oil and langue d'oc."

"She speaks, but does not write, Gael," Duncan added. "For 'tis not readily committed to the parchment."

Bayard was impressed despite himself. Truly his intended had unexpected talents! Indeed, he had given little consideration to what manner of woman this Esmeraude might be and was momentarily startled by this hint of her assets. But then, there was no shame in having a clever wife.

He cleared his throat to read what she had written, noting as he did so that she had a fine, careful hand.

> *One by land after one by sea*
> *Is the distance to follow me.*
> *The home of one I do now choose*
> *He is the one with most to lose.*

Bayard finished and glanced across the hall. The men looked puzzled, then turned to him again in anticipation.

"What else, what else?" Simon demanded.

"It says naught else."

Chaos erupted in the hall when Bayard rolled the missive once again. His own thoughts flew, reviewing all his father had ever told him of the holding that came by right with Esmeraude's hand.

"Whose claim to Ceinn-beithe might be lost by Esmeraude wedding a man not of these parts?" he asked Duncan in an undertone.

"Only the King of the Isles. 'Tis he who believes Ceinn-beithe to be within his suzerainty, and he to whom I am pledged."

"But are there not Norman knights in these parts? Are they allied with him?"

"Nay, they oft choose to ally with the King of Scotland, who was raised in the Angevin court and seems thus of a kin with them."

Bayard fingered the missive, very aware of Simon's gaze fixed upon him, and spoke low. "Where is the abode of this King of the Isles?"

"He holds court upon the Isle of Mull."

"A day by sea and a day by land?" Bayard guessed.

Duncan grinned. "If a man were leisurely about it." He shrugged. "Or a woman might make slightly worse time against the tide."

Bayard nodded and might have stepped away to make his plans to depart, but Eglantine caught at his arm. "Sir, if you mean to pursue my daughter, I would have your word that you will not see her harmed for her bold choice. She can be"—the lady hesitated—"impulsive, but her intent is not malicious. I fear for her fate in this foolery."

Worry lit the lady's eyes and Bayard took her hand. "I am a man of honor, Lady Eglantine, and have pledged to protect those weaker than myself. I have no desire to see my intended injured in any way. Should I find her, she will be safe with me. I cannot speak for her fate otherwise, but I grant you my word that I shall endeavor to find her first."

Eglantine was not as reassured as he might have expected. "You look so much like your father when he was of your age that 'tis surprising to hear you speak this way of Esmeraude."

"How so?"

Eglantine tilted her head to regard him. "You call her your intended though, indeed, you have yet to see her, let alone to come to know her." She stepped back, her shrewd gaze bright. "Your father would never have said such a thing."

Bayard smiled thinly. "My father and I are not the same man, though, indeed, we share the same code of honor."

"Is that then the reason you do not wear Villonne's colors?" Eglantine asked softly. "Your father's legacy is not inconsiderable."

Bayard held her gaze for a moment, but said naught. He was not a man who shared the details of his life with any who simply cared to ask. Eglantine stared back at him steadily, then her lips tightened and she looked to her spouse.

Duncan leaned closer, his expression intent. "Why are you so eager to win the hand of Esmeraude?"

"Perhaps I enjoy a challenge, sir."

The older man chuckled ruefully. "Then, indeed, Bayard de Villonne, you and Esmeraude may be well suited. She is naught if not a challenge." He shoved a hand through his hair and frowned at the scroll once again. "This quest for her hand is a fitting test in my estimation of any man who would take her to his side, though I wish she had not embarked upon it so impulsively." He shook Bayard's hand. "Godspeed to you." Then he raised his voice and addressed the assembly. "Godspeed to all of you who accept Esmeraude's challenge. Ride forth and see my daughter safely returned!"

A loud cheer fairly rent the hall but Bayard was already leaving, his thoughts spinning as he made a list of what to do and sorted it in order of necessity. He did not even notice Simon by his elbow, until that man snatched his sleeve.

This time, Simon's antagonism shone in his eyes. "I always said you were a fool, Bayard de Villonne. You have lost a great chance by telling the entire company the contents of the note."

Bayard halted, insulted. "Are you suggesting that I should have lied?"

"A thinking man would have guaranteed his advantage."

"An honorable man does not feel the compulsion to cheat." Bayard paused to meet Simon's gaze squarely. "And unlike you, I know I have no need to cheat to win."

With that, Bayard turned on the heel of his finely wrought boot and left Simon behind him. He was sufficiently honest with himself to admit that his intended had just made herself far more interesting than he had dared to hope.

Which merely redoubled his determination to win her.

Chapter Two

ESMERAUDE'S ADVENTURE WAS NOT PROCEEDING PRE-cisely to plan.

'Twas two nights since her departure from Ceinn-beithe. The King of the Isles had not been pleased with her news, as she had expected, and he had refused to be charmed. Indeed, his course of action had been somewhat different than Esmeraude had hoped.

"A wise man seizes what opportunities present themselves," he had declared after Esmeraude shared her tale with him. For a heartbeat she had felt triumphant, until he shattered her hopes with his next words. " 'Tis a perfect opportunity to see Ceinn-beithe secured as mine own."

And despite Esmeraude's vehement protest, she had been handfasted immediately to the king's most loyal man.

Indeed, the king had laughed—*laughed!*—at her protest that she would wed for love alone. Her consent to this match had not been deemed necessary, nor even her repetition of the binding vow. The king decreed that once this man bedded her, she and Ceinn-beithe would be his own.

And if he planted his seed in her belly, then her handfast would endure beyond the traditional year and a day.

Esmeraude was furious. She had never been treated as a mere means to an end in all her days, and she cared for the sensation not a whit. These men desired her dowry alone, a situation far worse than being courted by ambitious fools. She knew now, belatedly, that the King of the Isles had only indulged her whims previously because there was naught at stake. Esmeraude knew that when she had the time, she would appreciate how favored her life with Eglantine and Duncan had been.

But first she had to escape.

Her new spouse was a massive Norseman, the largest man Esmeraude had ever seen. His flesh was tanned to a deep gold, that hue matching both the straight hair that hung past his shoulders and what few teeth he had. There was a gold band around his wrist and some small talisman on a leather cord around his neck. He had a scent about him that told much of his personal habits and none of it good.

He dropped the latch on the door behind himself after fairly dragging her to a small chamber and smiled with satisfaction. 'Twas clear he had taken the king's challenge to heart. Esmeraude understood that the latch was fastened to ensure that none might intervene, even if she screamed. Célie might be outside the door, but she could do naught. The din of the celebrants in the hall was faint with distance and she knew she could rely only upon herself for salvation.

The flickering light from the lamp in the chamber accentuated his size and his every muscle when he turned to face her. She supposed his expression might be considered a smile of invitation.

Esmeraude was not inclined to accept. Aye, there was no mistaking the glint of avarice in his pale eyes. Clearly he knew what wealth would come to his hand with this deed.

If he could do it.

He peeled off his shirt, kicked off his chausses, and approached her in a state of expectation. Esmeraude backed away and his smile faded at her defiance.

He lunged for her but Esmeraude ducked out of his way

just in time. He fell heavily against the wall, muttered a curse in Norse that had no need of translation, then came after her once again. A new flame burned in his eyes and he scowled. Her mouth dry with fear, Esmeraude evaded him once more by dodging at the last moment.

He roared fit to shake the roof, then moved with lightning speed. He caught her around the waist and flung her over his shoulder. Esmeraude bit and kicked, but he barely acknowledged the blow of her heel slamming into his calf. He was as hard as a rock and as strong as a bear.

When he flung her onto the hard pallet, the breath was momentarily knocked from her. Esmeraude tasted terror, for she knew that she would not survive a year and a day of bedding with this man.

'Twas then she began fighting for more than her maidenhead.

She wrestled and bit, struggled and tried to escape from the bed with unholy vigor. He caught her easily every time, chuckling to himself at the futility of her efforts, and she hated him more than she had ever hated another in her life.

Esmeraude suddenly recalled a saying of Duncan's. *A foe greater in size is seldom greater in wits.*

Aye, she could outwit this oaf, she knew it well.

Esmeraude smiled at her new spouse when he cast her again onto the pallet. He halted, puzzled. She sighed as if happily surrendered and touched his face with her fingertips. He stared at her, eyes narrowed.

She lay back on the pallet as if prepared to accept his touch. He watched warily and she smiled a welcome. She stretched her arms over her head, noting how he fairly devoured the sight of her. She smiled anew and crooked a finger, which finally won her a wide smile and a growl in response. He shed his loincloth with a smile, then seized the hem of her kirtle to push it over her waist.

Esmeraude struggled not to flinch. His hand moved heavily over her legs, and he grasped her thigh with the strength of one accustomed to winning his way with force. She caught her breath but did not draw away, which seemed to please him well. He crawled over her and Esmeraude knew she had to keep him from settling atop her. She would never shift his weight once he had done so!

She sat up abruptly, clasped her hands behind his neck, and pulled him down onto the pallet beside her, echoing his rough play. His eyes glinted and he smiled. His hand landed assessingly upon her breast, as if assuring himself that he had been paid his due in full. He squeezed none too gently and she wondered whether he intended to milk her like a goat.

Esmeraude forced herself to breathe in a normal fashion. He began to utter some encouragement as his hands roved over her, his voice low and rough. Clearly, he thought her shy. He stretched out beside her, at ease and evidently convinced that she had no inclination to avoid him any longer.

But when he bent down to nuzzle her neck, Esmeraude, in her turn, moved with startling haste. She jabbed her fingers at his eyes, drove her elbow into his ribs, and slammed her knee into his crotch.

He howled in mingled pain and outrage as he rolled away. Esmeraude did not waste her chance. She bounced to her feet and ran to the door. He roared with frustration, his foot landing heavily on the floor, and she knew she had not long to flee.

And even then, he might catch her. Esmeraude refused to think about what he might do after that.

Her cursed fingers shook so much in her desperation that she dropped the latch, losing precious time. She glanced back to find him diving after her.

Esmeraude impulsively snatched up the lantern and waved it before his face. He yelled and fell back, raising his arms against the flame, then tripped over the tangled garments on the floor. He bellowed in fury and fell slowly, like a great tree toppling. His head made a thunk as it hit the floor.

He moved no more.

Esmeraude stood and stared, her heart hammering in her throat, her breath echoing loudly in the chamber. Was he dead? She did not know. Perhaps he feigned his state to lure her closer, the better to pounce upon her once more. Esmeraude swallowed as she considered the response of the king if she had, indeed, killed his trusted man.

The latch jiggled and she nigh jumped through the roof. Surely they could not know her crime so soon!

"Esmeraude!" Célie hissed and Esmeraude steadied herself against the wall in relief. "Is this where they have taken you, child?"

"Aye, Célie! I am here." Esmeraude put down the lamp and opened the latch.

The maid took one look at her face and hugged her tightly. "Did he . . ." she began fiercely, but her gaze slipped past Esmeraude to the fallen man and she gasped. "What have you done, child?" she whispered.

"He would have forced me. I fought him and he fell."

Célie leaned closer to peer at him. "Is he dead?"

"I do not know."

"Then we had best discover the truth." Célie stomped over to the large man, surveyed him thoroughly, then bent down to listen for his breath. "He yet lives," she said as if disappointed, and poked him with her toe. He stirred, much to Esmeraude's relief. "Though he will not be pleased when he awakens."

"Nor will the king be pleased with what I have done." Esmeraude eyed the open door, easing closer to listen to the distant sounds of revelry. "We could escape, Célie, and none would know the truth of it soon."

"Save this one. He stirs even now."

"We can ensure he does not stir far." Esmeraude unfastened her girdle, and used it to knot his wrists securely together. Célie rummaged through the satchel she carried, examining the few things they had brought. She produced a short length of rope. The two women exchanged a smile, and Esmeraude bound the man's ankles together.

He stirred, groaned, and was still once more.

"The beauty of a handfasting," Esmeraude said with quiet resolve as she stared at her would-be spouse, "is that either party has the right to leave the match if it proves unsatisfactory. I find you an unsatisfactory partner, sir, and thus I leave you."

Célie clicked her tongue. "He may insist otherwise. If you are not present to defend yourself, who knows what will be said of you? Are you yet a maid?"

"Aye!"

"But he may lie. There is much at stake in this."

Esmeraude had to think for a mere moment. "Then I shall leave a note, one that will make the truth clear. Aye, I shall leave a riddle so that those men who pursue me know the fullness of the truth on their arrival."

Célie sat down heavily and crossed herself. "Esmeraude, you have no lack of audacity. What if the King of the Isles follows you?"

"Then I shall tell him before all that he has treated me poorly." She dug through the satchel's contents grimly. "Either way, I shall insist that whoever weds me pledges himself to any king other than the King of the Isles."

" 'Tis not your place!"

"I do not care! I have been poorly served, Célie, used as no more than a means to an end by a king I came to in trust. I was his *guest*!"

"Your trust was poorly rewarded."

"Indeed 'twas! I did not agree to handfast with this one, yet I was forced. We both know 'tis not customary to do such a thing." She gestured to the Norseman with disgust, her anger now replacing her fear. "He would have injured me without remorse. The king wants Ceinn-beithe secured for all time, regardless of the price to me, even though 'tis through me he would win it. 'Tis unfair! I shall make sure Ceinn-beithe is never his again."

"God in heaven!" The maid regarded Esmeraude in shock.

"I know my words are uncommonly bold, Célie. But I am vexed and I am right. A *man* would see blood shed over such an indignity."

"A man has the right to mete justice."

"If the suzerainty of Ceinn-beithe is so coupled with my maidenhead, then I should have some right to say what shall be done." Esmeraude smiled for her aghast maid. "I think my response quite temperate, under the circumstances."

Célie blinked and protested no more. In the satchel, Esmeraude found the nib and the stoppered vial of ink, drew out a snippet of used vellum that had been carefully cleaned, and began to write.

"What shall we do now?"

"We shall do what I should have done in the first place. We shall visit my sister Jacqueline, for she will defend my right to choose the man I should wed. A *woman* will understand, as the King of the Isles did not."

The maid shook her head. "But Airdfinnan is so far away!"

"All the more time to be rid of the one encumbrance to my quest," Esmeraude said firmly.

"And what might that encumbrance be?" the maid asked faintly.

Esmeraude did not answer immediately, for she knew that Célie would not approve. She blew on the ink, then tucked the missive into the lace of the Norseman's boots. As an afterthought, she removed the lace from about his neck, though she placed the talisman on the floor beside him.

She scooped up the lamp and beckoned to Célie, pausing to loop the lace over the latch. She drew it through the door as 'twas closed, used the lace to drop the latch, then flicked the lace so that it came free. The door had no means to lift the latch from the outside.

She grinned triumphantly at her maid, who shook her head. "Now, let him learn what it is like to be helpless at the will of another."

Before her maid could chastise her, Esmeraude scooped up the satchel and headed away from the clamor of the hall. The two slipped as quietly as shadows from the hall, then ran as quickly as they could.

The night was black, the moon high, and Esmeraude knew they had much distance to put behind themselves this night. They ran toward the rocky outcropping on the shore where they had hidden their small boat.

"Did I not ask what this encumbrance might be?" Célie asked when they slowed to a fast walk.

Esmeraude granted her maid a sparkling smile. "My maidenhead, of course."

"What nonsense is this?"

Esmeraude had not expected ready agreement to her scheme, although it made perfect sense to her. She tried to explain in a reasonable manner. " 'Tis my maidenhead alone that is responsible for the events of this eve. I think it only sensible to be rid of it."

Célie made a choking sound.

" 'Tis perfectly clear—a maiden can be forced to couple with any man who happens to be stronger than she. 'Tis an unfair advantage, for most men are stronger than most women."

"But still . . ."

"If men mean to use me as a pawn to win Ceinn-beithe, then I dare not allow them such an advantage," Esmeraude said firmly. "Nay, I shall surrender my maidenhead to the first stranger of promise, and then no man can compel me to wed him because he has seized the prize of my virginity."

"Esmeraude, this is too bold by far!"

"'Tis but a small price to pay for the surety of wedding whomsoever I desire."

Célie shook her head again. "But Esmeraude, in your innocence, you underestimate the obsessions of men. You may have *no* spouse as a result of this folly. What if the man you desire wishes only a virginal bride?"

Esmeraude smiled, and dismissed her maid's well-intentioned concerns. "The man I wed will love me sufficiently to forgive such a small detail."

"'Tis not a small—" Célie began, then shook her head anew. "'Tis clear I cannot make you see the truth of it on this night. Know this then—'tis your mother who will have both my hide and yours should you pursue this madness," the maid concluded testily. "Mark my words, Esmeraude, this is an ill-fated scheme."

But Esmeraude was not inclined to heed advice in this moment for there was a greater trouble before them. She retraced her steps and counted the rocks anew, but the truth was inescapable. "Célie, our currach is gone!"

"Nay, it cannot be so!"

But it was. And without the small boat they were trapped on the Isle of Mull. Both turned to look back to the hall of the King of the Isles, knowing how readily he could exact his due for the insult rendered to his man. They pivoted and looked across the deceptively narrow stretch of water betwixt the isle and the mainland. In the distance, Esmeraude spotted a dark shadow bobbing insouciantly along.

She swore, knowing that she had not tucked the boat high

enough to be safe from the rising tide. "Oh, 'tis all my own fault!"

"Esmeraude! Such language is unfitting for a lady!"

"But fitting under the circumstance. I will not sit patiently to await the vengeance of the King of the Isles." Or indeed of the Norseman. Esmeraude spoke fiercely and drummed her fingers on her crossed arms as she thought. "I shall swim if need be."

"If you survive such a folly, then I shall throttle you myself!" Célie muttered with equal ferocity. The pair glanced at each other and laughed at their own fierceness. Bickering would serve naught. They sat together on the rocks and watched the waves in frustration.

"There must be a way," Esmeraude declared.

"From the fat to the fire is what my mother would say," the maid said with a shake of her head. "I wager you did not plan on such a challenge as this."

"Nay. But is it not exciting, in a way, Célie? We must resolve our own predicament, as all fortune-seekers and adventurers must do."

"If this is excitement, 'tis a quality I can well live without."

"Not I!" Esmeraude considered the length of the shoreline. "There must be a villager with a boat, or a fisherman who would see us away from here."

"Again, I ask you, for what price will such a man grant your favor?"

Esmeraude waved off this concern. "A fisherman can demand little of me indeed."

The maid snorted, but Esmeraude was looking up and down the coast. There was neither a hint of a dwelling within eyesight, nor a glimmer of lantern light. She recalled Duncan's assertion that the fishermen lived on the ocean side of the island. She cast a longing glance toward their errant curran, which had now disappeared from view.

But not everyone had tallow for a candle or oil for a lamp. There could easily be a dwelling not far away, appearing as one with the rocks for lack of a light. The mist was gathering over the ocean and creeping to the shore, reflecting the moonlight like spun silver. She thought of the elves and faeries of Duncan's tales, the stories that she so loved to hear, and wondered whether wandering into that mist would take them to another land.

"Come, Célie, let us walk up the shoreline away from the king's hall. If we are fortunate, then we shall find some hut or person to aid us."

"Or at least 'twill take the king's men longer to retrieve us," the maid commented darkly.

"Célie, 'twill aid naught to sit and wait for disaster to find us. Let us use our wits to make the most of whatever small advantage we have!"

They walked along the shore then, the maid shooting her charge a bright glance. "You are enjoying this," she accused.

Esmeraude smiled. 'Twould have been futile to deny it when she knew the truth shone in her features. Instead she told Célie one of Duncan's tales, her favorite, that of the knight Tam Lin snatched away from his lady love by the Faerie Queen to serve in her ethereal court. She loved the determination of the mortal lady to win back her beloved and found it a most inspiring tale. She sang it, as Duncan was wont to do, and the tune lent a lightness to their step.

The mist swirled around their ankles, the ocean beat against the rocks, and the moon rolled across the sky as they steadily put the king's hall farther behind them. 'Twas a night not unlike the enchanted night when Tam Lin's lady won his release from the Faerie host.

Esmeraude realized that she was ridiculously happy. She felt as though she alone could shape her own destiny, that she could contrive her own happiness. She had shaken the burden of expectations, however fleeting that might be, and it only increased her desire to live an unconventional life. She knew as she had only guessed before that she would have a great love in her life, though she might have to sacrifice much to hold it.

Esmeraude was well prepared to do so.

She followed her song with two more, then her maid had one, then Esmeraude told another. They sang of elves and sprites and Faerie forges, of houses wrought of moonlight and cobwebs, of enchanted blades and wishing stones and cloaks that might make a person invisible to all. On this night, each tale might have been the blessed truth.

When the lilt of Esmeraude's last song had been carried off by the wind, Célie suddenly clutched the maiden's arm. "Look!" She pointed to a craft somewhat larger than their own had been, riding the evening tide to shore ahead of them.

Esmeraude halted and stared. The boat was silhouetted against the mist as if it were darker than the night itself, and it seemed touched by starlight in a manner not wholly of this world. A man stood alone in its prow, his cloak flaring behind him in the wind. He appeared master of all he surveyed, in Esmeraude's fey mood, a returning champion come to claim his due.

What treasure did this one bring? What lands had he seen? What dragons had he conquered? She had no doubt that they were legion. The moonlight gleamed on what could only be a mail surcoat, revealing his status as a knight.

But no ordinary knight, Esmeraude was certain. Nay, this one was an emissary from Faerie, not unlike the enchanted Tam Lin. She watched the boat draw closer and felt a curious sense fill her, an odd certainty that he was her destiny. Aye, he had been summoned by her desire to be rid of her maidenhead as surely as if she had called to him by his own name.

This, her heart told her with surety, was the man.

The coast was deserted here, wrought of rocks that might have been scattered by giants interspersed with beaches of ivory sand. The sea reflected the moon and the stars, the wind was cool and filled with the scent of salt and shore.

The knight drew closer. Esmeraude's mouth went dry and she urged a dubious Célie farther along the beach. The sea lifted the craft on a great dark wave as they watched and fairly deposited it upon the shore, like a great hand facilitating what should be.

A young boy leapt into the shallows to haul the boat ashore. The knight called to him, his voice melodic, the words tinged with a foreign accent. When a rogue wave pulled the boy down, the knight laughed and waded into the water himself, plucking his squire from the ocean with ease. Esmeraude's heart missed a beat as the knight turned and the moonlight caught at his rugged features.

He was the most handsome man Esmeraude had ever glimpsed. His jaw was square, his profile proud. Starlight glinted in the dark waves of his hair, as if stars dwelt there as readily as within the midnight sky, and she wondered what hue his eyes might be. He could not be mortal, such a man, or if he was, she had never heard tell of the land where such men were bred.

But he was brought by the sea for her alone. Some higher force granted him to her as a gift and Esmeraude had listened too often at the knee of Duncan MacLaren not to understand her part in this unfolding tale.

Ignoring Célie's protest, she leapt over the last scree of rocks, standing tall so that she might be clearly seen against the isle when her knight glanced up.

But he did not. He and the boy hauled the boat onto the sands together. The knight jested with the boy, aiding him so subtly that the young boy seemed convinced that he had brought the craft to safety himself. The knight, whom Esmeraude already thought had a fine character, ruffled the hair of the boy with undisguised affection. They laughed together and roughhoused on the beach, and he looked so masculine a man that she ached to feel his gaze upon her.

If not more.

"Oh, Célie," Esmeraude whispered in awe when her panting maid reached her side atop the rocks. "My mother knew of what she spoke when she said that knights had an unholy allure."

The maid groaned. "Esmeraude! What madness has seized your wits?"

Esmeraude gave her maid no more than a smile.

"Nay!" Célie's eyes rounded with horror and her voice dropped to a hiss. "You would not do as you pledge to do!"

Esmeraude began to climb down the rocks, to be closer to the man who would be her partner this night.

"Not . . . *that*! Not with a knight and a stranger and . . ." Célie sputtered briefly to silence, then began again. Her rebukes were so distant to Esmeraude as to be unheard. The maid seemed to sense as much for she spoke with greater vehemence. "Nay, I forbid you to do this deed. Why, I shall stop you if I must throw myself betwixt you . . ."

But Esmeraude knew what she would do and naught could change her mind. She moved as a maiden snared in a dream from which she desired no awakening. Esmeraude would surrender her chastity to a nameless knight in the moonlight, a man wrought of moonbeams and Faerie dust, a man whom she knew she would never see again.

'Twas perfect. Her heart pounded at her own audacity.

"He is a stranger," she interrupted Célie's tirade with a calm she was far from feeling, "for I know without doubt that he was not among those who came to compete for my hand."

"A man like this has no good reason to be in these parts!"

"Perhaps he has a matter to discuss with the King of the Isles."

"He arrives too far north to seek that court. Nay, he is a scoundrel, fleeing the courts, upon that you may rely! A thief, perhaps a murderer. Esmeraude, you have no means of knowing the character of this man!"

"The sea is capricious, as you well know. Does he look sufficiently familiar with this locale to know its tricks?" Esmeraude shook her head. "And did you not note his manner with his squire? Nay, he is a man of honor, or a knight from Faerie, I care not which. I have chosen him to aid in my quest."

"Esmeraude! We flee that same king whom you believe he may visit. Surely you have not forgotten as much? What if he tells the king of us?"

"Why should he? He will never know my name."

"But . . ."

"We have need of a boat, Célie," Esmeraude said firmly, knowing that only a practical solution would appease and silence the older woman. "The one this knight has brought will suit us very well." She bestowed a confident glance upon her maid, though it cost her dearly to look away from the knight's figure, so lovingly touched by the silvery moonlight. "And if he tells the king of us, 'twill be too late, for we shall have sailed away."

"God in heaven!" Célie passed a hand over her brow in frustration. "You mean to steal the possessions of a knight after you pretend to be a whore? Oh, your mother will be most irked with me! It seems that I do not save you from misfortune despite my good intent."

"Not a whore, Célie, I could not feign such experience." Esmeraude ran her hands over her now tattered and dirty garb. "I shall be a villein, a mere country maid overwhelmed by my first vision of a knight." She smiled and her voice turned soft. "Like an old, old tale in which naught is as it appears to be."

Indeed, 'twould not be that difficult to pretend thus— Esmeraude's mouth was dry at the mere thought of drawing closer to him. How would he kiss her? How would he touch her? How would mating feel? She was terrified at what she might discover, yet at the same time, she tingled in anticipation.

She could not have walked away to save her soul. *This* was adventure!

Célie moaned behind her as Esmeraude strode toward the knight with purpose. She held her chin high and her heart thumped with painful vigor. And when he heard her footsteps and glanced up, she saw that his eyes were as blue as a sunlit sky.

Then he smiled a smile as dazzling as the sun at midday. And Esmeraude knew, she simply knew, that this would come more than aright.

❖

Bayard had had better days.

The current in the narrow stretch of water that lay betwixt Ceinn-beithe and the Isle of Mull had exceeded every warning he had been granted. It was ferocious as the tide rose, and he and Andrew had to strain mightily against it to even keep some semblance of their course. He had feared for a time that they would be swept away and deposited on some nameless shore, on one of the many bays and inlets that he could glimpse from the boat.

That had given him redoubled strength. 'Twas beyond his experience to wage a battle against the elements alone, though he had tasted his mortality before and that oft enough. 'Twas usually a man who stood as his foe, though, and he realized only now how much he relied upon understanding the one who might destroy him.

The sea was capricious in a way that men seldom echoed. She was not a force he understood, though he respected her might. 'Twas doubly galling to know that if they perished, she would draw no satisfaction from what she had wrought. Theirs would be an incidental casualty.

Bayard refused to die incidentally. The prospect gave new strength to his strokes.

The worst was knowing that survival, which seemed a most distant objective, would not be enough. Nay, they were doomed to repeat the journey if he ever meant to see his steeds and his older squire again.

He cried encouragement to Andrew and they raged as one against the strength of the water. Bayard's muscles strained and Andrew was pale with exertion, but they struggled onward, determined to succeed. The land disappeared all around them, naught but the rise and fall of the ink-dark waves on every side.

"Row! Row!" Bayard cried. "We have naught to lose but our all!"

He plunged his oars into the water and found a hidden strength within himself. He felt alive and whole and omnipotent, touched by some power of the divine.

And he knew with terrifying certainty that he would win this battle. Fed by that conviction, he rowed long after Andrew had faltered.

Then, just as suddenly as they had been seized by it, they were past the worst of the current and the rowing became nigh a game in comparison. The isle drew ever closer, if a section of its shore was somewhat distant from their destination.

Andrew shouted in triumph when 'twas clear they would

survive. They laughed as they rowed together with new jubilation, and 'twas as naught to pull the boat ashore. Bayard picked up the boy and swung him around and Andrew laughed heartily as they romped like children on the shore.

"We have need of a draft of ale for a deed well done!" Bayard cried. The rocks cast his words back at him as if they cavorted too.

Andrew laughed anew. "I packed naught but wine, sir."

" 'Twill do, 'twill do. Indeed, I would toast our health with whatsoever comes to hand on this night of nights."

"How far do you think us from the king's hall, sir?" Andrew asked more soberly. "The heat of a fire, some companionship and song would be most welcome after that crossing."

"Aye, 'twould, though I fear 'tis not so close as we might hope." Bayard glanced about them, seeking some hint of their locale, and 'twas then that he saw her.

And he forgot all else.

A maiden of dewy perfection crossed the stone-strewn beach toward them. Her garb was dirty and torn, her flesh was tanned to gold, but she walked with the assurance of one born to privilege. Her face was heart-shaped, her hair a tumble of chestnut curls, her eyes thickly lashed. She was slender for all the ripeness of her curves and his blood quickened at both her charms and her seductive expression.

She unbound her braid and shook out her tresses as she walked, her gaze unswerving from his own, her lips curved in an inviting smile. Bayard's mouth went dry. Andrew whispered something, but he stepped past the boy, captured by the vision of this demoiselle.

To his surprise, a heavy set older woman came into view. She climbed over the rocks with visible effort then trotted after the maiden. She panted with her exertion, her expression stricken.

Bayard knew then with utter certainty who this damsel must be. There could not be two finely bred beauties of roughly an age with him, wandering this isle with an older maid in tow. Bayard's smile widened, for he had not anticipated finding his prize so readily as this.

Nor, indeed, had he thought his intended would be so lovely.

"Greetings, sir," she said when she paused before him, her expression flirtatious. "And welcome to the Isle of Mull."

"I thank you for your greeting." Bayard stepped closer, wondering what she might intend even as he spared a glance to the sky and moon. "But what manner of place is this that a maiden wanders alone in the depth of the night?" He smiled the smile that had coaxed many to his bed and was delighted when she eased closer.

She tapped one fingertip upon his forearm. " 'Tis an isle of magic and myth," she said, an impish gleam lighting her eyes. "An isle upon which the first man to ride the full moon's tide and land successfully ashore is greeted by a willing maid."

Bayard was intrigued by this strange assertion. "A willing maid?"

She placed her small hand on his chest, her cheeks darkening at her boldness even as she did so. He was intrigued by the warring signals she gave—both of seductiveness and innocence. She swallowed and he knew from her uncertainty that she was not so experienced at seduction as she would have him believe.

What did she desire of him?

"Aye, a maid willing to surrender herself fully to a champion from over the seas," she whispered.

He lifted one hand, and felt her tremble as he touched her jaw. "A kiss surely is all that even such an emboldened maid would grant," he murmured.

Her eyes widened but she did not retreat. "Nay," she said, her gaze locked with his, the pulse in her throat hammering against his hand. "She might begin with a kiss, but she would grant her all."

"Why?"

She smiled then, a fetching and mischievous sight. "Because she so wills it, of course. Because she has *chosen*."

Though he desired her, Bayard hesitated to take her at her word, so odd was her claim. He had never heard of such a tradition in any place he traveled and something of her manner told him that she concocted the tale even as she stood before him.

"Chosen?" he echoed and she smiled.

"Aye. Chosen."

And there was all he needed to know. Bayard lifted his hands to frame her face. He doubted she would be sufficiently bold to indeed grant the prize she offered, not on this night, but he saw naught amiss in sharing a full kiss with his intended.

She had chosen him. They would be wed and Montvieux would be his own, his family would be saved. 'Twas ideal and well worth a celebration.

Bayard bent and claimed her lips with tender gallantry. He swallowed her gasp of delight, and felt his own heart race as her lips softened against his own. He lifted her closer without intending to do so, felt the curve of her breasts against his chest and deepened his kiss.

Chapter Three

TO BAYARD'S ASTONISHMENT, HIS KISS WAS NOT DEStined to seal their covenant and end.

Though the lady's touch proved her innocence, her ardor more than compensated any lack of experience. Bayard's own breath caught, his heart halted, then raced madly. Indeed, she was sweet and willing; the combination of her honesty and her eagerness enflamed him.

Bayard's fingers were in her hair before he knew his own intent, his hand at her nape, his other arm wrapped around her waist. He caught her closer, cradling her against him, certain she would back away from the flame she had coaxed to life. But she was undeterred, mimicking his every touch so readily that desire began to cloud his good sense.

"God in heaven," the older maid whispered in horror as the lady kissed Bayard with new vigor.

But 'twas wrong. It took all within Bayard not to roll her to her back right there. He wanted her, as he had not wanted a woman in some time, as if she had cast a cloud of seduction across his shoulders.

He tore his lips from hers with an effort and put a distance betwixt them. They eyed each other, each breathing heavily. Her lips were swollen, her eyes shining. She smiled at him and Bayard thought he might lose every last vestige of honor within himself.

He could not claim her on a rocky beach. He could not rut with her like a savage beast, not before his own squire and her own maid. 'Twas not within him to so dishonor any woman, but most especially not the woman who would be his lady wife.

Bayard steadied his breathing and watched the maiden warily. Her smile broadened and she took a step closer, her hand rising to the tie of her chemise. She flushed at her own audacity, but did not halt.

She had chosen him, and that with so little knowledge of him. The truth of it swelled his heart fit to burst.

Marriage, it seemed suddenly, showed somewhat greater promise than he had hoped.

"The toll I would demand of you is more than a kiss," she teased, her expression provocative, "however artful that kiss might be."

" 'Twould not be appropriate," he argued, hearing desire strain his own words.

" 'Twould be most appropriate. I choose you and I would celebrate that choice. Here and now."

Her smile could make a man dizzy with desire.

Bayard knew that many a couple mated before their nuptials, that many a maiden was sampled by a knight determined to wed her and her alone. And there were many, indeed, who lived as man and wife without the ritual of a church blessing betwixt them. 'Twas not so bold what she proposed, though he was incredulous that victory should come so readily to his hand.

Though he had always been fortunate beyond all. It seemed that even in this, the truth was clear. And he was not a man who would treat her with dishonor—nay, they would stand before a priest and she would be endowed with what was his to grant his lady wife.

"You are certain of this?" he demanded hoarsely.

"More certain than I have been in all my days," she whispered, her eyes shining. "What, indeed, could be more right?" And she slipped her arms shyly around his neck, her expression expectant and pleased.

Bayard had never understood women fully and he certainly did not understand this one. He was, however, a man who understood a strategic advantage and he did not intend to surrender one so willingly offered. He knew enough of women to know that the lady in his arms was more innocent than she pretended, and, indeed, he knew that she was his virginal Esmeraude.

The fact was that if he claimed her maidenhead, then none could contest his claiming of her hand. She would be his bride, and that by her own choice. He could ensure the safety of his family and ease the fears of her own mother.

'Twas too good an opportunity to sacrifice.

Bayard turned to his squire, his decision made. "Andrew, I would have you ensure the boat is high above the tide line and sleep near it lest there be thieves about." Andrew nodded dutifully and ducked away.

Bayard looked at the older maid and smiled kindly. "Madame, I truly doubt that this deed is yours to witness."

She blanched and appealed to her charge. "I think we might also depart, child . . ." she began, granting the demoiselle a hard glance.

The maiden leaned against Bayard's chest, her cheek nigh against his heart. "I am where I shall remain, my dear friend, and you need not fear for me."

The maid's lips worked in silence for a moment.

"She speaks aright. You need not fear for the maiden," Bayard said softly. "I grant you my word of honor that she will not be injured in this."

"She knows not what she does!" The maid's dismay was evident.

"Perhaps not," Bayard said firmly when the maiden might have spoken. "But I do." He held the older woman's gaze and watched understanding dawn there.

"You will treat her with honor, sir?"

Bayard smiled and spoke with conviction. "With all the honor a man of worth grants his lady wife." He arched a brow, willing the older woman to understand, and that woman seemed somewhat reassured. "Upon that you have my pledge."

"Célie, *please*!" the demoiselle entreated and Bayard noted that the maid had a French name. 'Twas another confirmation of what he already knew to be true, for Esmeraude's mother, Eglantine, was of the noble family of Crevy-sur-Seine, a holding southeast of Paris.

The maid, clearly torn, growled acceptance and marched away, though not without several long backward glances, each filled with accusation and concern. The maiden ignored her, turning back to Bayard immediately. Bayard's arms tightened protectively around his intended as she reached up and kissed him with more assurance than she had before.

And he surrendered to the moment fully, tasting her, savoring her, ensuring that she, too, found pleasure in the embrace. When they drew apart, her eyes sparkled and her cheeks were flushed with delight.

Aye, she had chosen him and he would meet every word of his pledge. Not only would he treat her with honor, but he would ensure the lady was not disappointed with her first experience of matters betwixt a man and a woman.

'Twas not a single night without repercussions before them, after all—'twas a lifetime they would share, and on this evening he would lay the foundation for years of mutual pleasure.

'Twas the least he could grant to the woman whose choice of him so readily resolved so much for so many.

※

He was not a knight from Faerie—Esmeraude realized as much in a far corner of her thoughts. At the same time, though, she had a delicious sense of this match being more than the exchanges betwixt unblessed mortals. Aye, 'twas mythic and wondrous and the stuff of the epic tales she loved so much.

Perhaps she had truly stepped into such a tale. There could be no more delicious possibility than that.

Indeed, this knight might as well have come from an immortal realm, for he was not characteristic of her own. His every gesture was filled with confidence, his garb was richer than any she had seen before, he was as alien to her as a man could be.

For he was a *man*, as none of those who had come to court her had been. He made them look callow and uncertain in comparison and Esmeraude knew with all her heart and soul that she would never have been happy with any of those who had called.

This was the manner of man she wanted!

Her knight's kisses were splendid, each more stirring than the last. His every touch stirred her soul and made her heart clamor for more. His kiss was possessive and masterful, both firm and tender, and as unlike the wet offerings of Hamish and Seamus as Esmeraude could imagine. She had chosen her partner aright, there could be no doubt of that.

He scooped her into his arms and carried her away from the stones of the beach, edging into the lush grasses that grew thickly here. He cradled her against him, with one strong arm around her waist as he kissed her again. The rocky outcroppings rose high around them, secluding them from all but one another, the stars above, and the lap of the waves upon the shore.

When she opened her eyes, dizzy from his touch, his cloak was spread across the ground. The silvery fur shone in the light of the moon, looking silky and sensuous. He tipped up her face to his, and she thought he would grant her another thrilling kiss, but his gaze searched hers.

"What is your name?"

"It matters naught."

He smiled then, his lips quirking up in one corner. "And you care naught for mine?"

Esmeraude twined her arms around his neck. "There is but one thing I desire of you, sir, and 'tis not your name."

He chuckled, a deep sound that made something quiver deep inside her. His hand slid from her hip to cup her breast and he watched her as he slid his thumb across her nipple. Even through the thickness of her wool kirtle, his touch made her tingle. She shivered and reached for the tie of her chemise.

"Are you oft so bold?" he asked, amusement not censure in his tone.

"Nay." Esmeraude smiled. "But I thought to try such boldness this night with you."

"There is no shame in a maiden's shyness," he said, making short work of the tie of the chemise. He parted the cloth with a fingertip, baring her breasts to the touch of the wind and his view. Esmeraude felt her eyes widen at the wanton sensation of chill air against her flesh. "Nor is there shame in a lady's desire, if her partner serves her well."

"Do you mean to serve me well?"

"Aye." His eyes twinkled with unexpected mischief and the warmth of his hand cupped her breast. "Though you, my lady fair, may tell me later how well I have done." And he ducked his head.

Esmeraude caught her breath as the warm wet heat of his mouth closed around her nipple, then closed her eyes when his tongue flicked its hardening tip. She heard herself moan and felt herself lean back in his embrace.

She knew not how he loosed the laces at the sides of her kirtle without her awareness of what he did, though she suspected that playful tongue of his did much to distract her. He treated each breast to the same attention, then pushed her kirtle and chemise over her hips, lifting her from the tangle of cloth and setting her upon the fur lining of the cloak.

It felt sinful and pagan to be seated with naught against the night but her stockings and shoes. Esmeraude knew that Célie would be dismayed, but her knight regarded her with much appreciation in his gaze. She kicked off her shoes and stretched out against the cool smoothness of the fur.

She watched as the knight unbuckled his belt and laid it aside with care. He shed his dark tabard, folding it carefully before he lifted his mail hauberk to his waist.

"You must aid me, or I shall have to call Andrew."

Esmeraude scrambled forward, uncertain what precisely she had to do. He leaned forward and instructed her to pull the mail over his head. 'Twas like a shirt fitted too tight to remove readily on one's own, wrought of myriad small metal rings, each sealed to its four neighbors. She did as bidden and it fell into her lap in a clatter, so cold against her flesh that her nipples beaded anew.

He chuckled and shed his own chemise. Esmeraude looked up, fascinated by the differences betwixt them. The hair upon his chest was dark and thickly curled, his own nipples flat, his skin tanned to a deep bronze. He was muscled beyond any of the men who labored bare-backed in Ceinn-beithe's fields in summer. As she laid the weight of the hauberk aside, she could well imagine why. He doffed his boots and joined her on the cloak, clad only in his chausses.

"You shall have to shed those afore the deed is done," she said, hoping she sounded as if she knew more of such intimacy than she did.

He lay back and folded his arms behind his head as he watched her, his eyes gleaming. "Aye, but there is no need for haste. Have you seen a man before?"

"None like you." She was proud that her response was true without revealing her innocence fully, though she doubted that he was deceived.

"Then touch me, at your leisure. We have all the time in eternity together."

Esmeraude thought that one night was rather less than that, but it seemed churlish to argue the matter with him. Instead, she came close and laid one hand upon his arm. His flesh was different from her own—coarser, heavier, warmer. She could feel the corded strength of his muscles as she slid her hand up his arm.

He watched her, his expression unfathomable, and she felt bolder before his stillness. She slid her hands across his shoulders and then down his chest, noting the flat rigidity of his belly, the way the hair grew toward his navel like a dark river.

She flattened her palms against him and moved her hands up to his nipples, running her hands across them, then through the wiry hair upon his chest. When her hands found his shoulders again, she looked up to find his gaze upon her, his eyes darker than they had been before.

"Now me," he murmured. He echoed her every gesture, beginning with one fingertip on her arm. He moved with a deliberation that left a stream of tingles behind that finger as it roved to her shoulder, across her chin, and down her throat.

The warmth of his hand slid down her chest, pausing on the pounding of her heart, turning so that the width of his knuckles slid down to her waist.

Esmeraude felt as if her flesh were enflamed.

He fitted his hands around her waist and drew her closer to him. His lips closed over hers with gentle urgency and his hands slid ever higher. Esmeraude gasped when his palms brushed her nipples, then he closed his hand over her, making circles with his thumbs that made her yearn for something she could not name.

They tumbled down to lie side by side, his hand cupping her jaw as he kissed her over and over again. Esmeraude reached for the tie of his chausses, only to be halted by his chuckle.

"There is no need for haste," he whispered, then ran his tongue around her ear. He kissed her and tickled her there, making her shiver with delight.

"But . . ." Esmeraude tried to loose the lace once more.

"But naught." He caught her hands in one of his and entwined her fingers with his own, stretching her arms over her head. He looked down at her, his expression so filled with admiration that she did not fight him. "You shall have all you desire of me, my lady fair. All I ask of you in exchange is the leisure to enjoy."

His free hand landed on her waist, rising to caress her breast once more. Esmeraude gave a cry of delight as he rolled her nipple between his finger and thumb.

"Are we agreed?" he asked, arching a brow in a way that made him look most diabolical.

"Aye," she whispered breathlessly and saw but a flash of his smile before he bent to nip at her flesh with a deliberation that made her shiver to her toes. She found herself stretching to meet his questing lips, arching back and wriggling against the luxurious fur. He kissed and nibbled at the underside of her breast, the hollow in her throat, the curve beneath her ear. He kissed her temple, her brow, her eyelids, the tip of her nose and finally—just when she thought she could bear it no longer—her lips.

And as he kissed her, his tongue teasing her own, his fingers slipped between her thighs. Esmeraude caught her breath but he whispered to her, easing his fingers even farther and holding her fast as he touched her in a way she had never been touched before.

Heat raced through her from a tender spot that she could not believe she had never known existed. She found herself spreading her legs wider to welcome his touch, matching his kiss with increasing ardor.

She clutched at his shoulders as the tide rose within her, feeling her fingertips dig into his flesh and not caring. Indeed, he smiled down at her, urging her, proud of the storm he summoned within her.

"I want," she managed to say.

"Aye? What do you want?"

"I do not know!"

He grinned as his fingers danced boldly against her. "But you shall have it all the same, my lady fair." He bent and nuzzled her ear, the sensation nigh driving her mad. "I pledge it to you," he growled and she believed him, as she had never believed another before.

She gripped his shoulders tightly, loving the smell of his flesh, the warmth of him leaning over her, wanting desperately whatever it was he meant to give her. The hair upon his chest tickled her breasts, his hand coaxed the fires stoked within her to rage wildly, the tension rose within her to unbearable heights.

It exploded suddenly, like a shooting star blazing across the sky. She arched high and he kissed her soundly, devouring the sound of her startled cry. And when she collapsed against him, trembling, and he rolled to his back with her cradled against his chest, Esmeraude felt the evidence of his own arousal.

"'Tis not done," she guessed, her hand shaking as she pushed the tangle of hair back from her face.

He laughed, and eased her hair behind her ear with a possessive fingertip. His eyes twinkled in a way that made her want to smile. He was so confident, so large, so splendid that for a moment she dreaded that they would never meet again.

She wanted a man like this one. Not this particular one, for 'twas critical to her scheme that they part forever after this night. But one like him would suit her very well. She wanted a man who looked at her as if she were a marvel, one who loved her as if 'twas a deed he had invented, one who had sipped fully from the cup of life and could show her what best to try.

Such a man understood adventure. Indeed, he might have been wrought of it.

Esmeraude resolved that after Airdfinnan, she would go to France. Her mother, after all, spoke often of knights and if they were of this one's ilk, she could well see why. And his words were tinged with the same French accent as her mother's. Aye, 'twas there she would go. 'Twas there she would find a man like this to love her.

Jacqueline would aid her, without doubt. Indeed, Jacqueline had said repeatedly that she wanted to visit Crevy again, ever since her spouse Angus had taken her there several years past. Perhaps Esmeraude could persuade her sister to travel there with her. All this flickered through her mind as the enigmatic marvel of a man watched her with rare intensity, and she wondered whether he could read her very thoughts.

But then he spoke and she knew with relief that he had not.

"Nay, my lady fair," he murmured, the rumble of his voice most enticing against her chest. " 'Tis only just begun."

And Esmeraude leaned down to kiss him, more than willing to learn it all.

He pleasured her twice before he claimed her, for Bayard wanted to ensure that her first mating was a wondrous one for her. She had a rare passion for lovemaking and a hunger for his touch that fired his blood as no woman had in years. Indeed, he wondered fleetingly whether she truly was virginal, but that errant thought was dismissed when he began to ease within her. She was tight and hot, despite the wetness of her, and he knew he would not last overlong.

Perhaps she had kissed many but she had never let a man touch her as he did now. Bayard watched the wonder on her features and knew the truth. He felt a primitive pride that he was the first, that he should show her what delights could be found abed, that he would be her last and her only partner.

Forever. Indeed, he did not sacrifice as much as he had feared in following Margaux's bidding.

Which reminded him of how much there was to be lost. Bayard grasped the closest white garment and shoved it beneath them, doubting he would need proof of this night but unwilling to leave a matter of such importance to chance.

Then she cried out as he entered her fully. He kissed and murmured to her until she returned his kisses with her previous hunger. He eased closer, soothing her, moving so slowly that he thought he might die in this act alone.

When he was within her fully, she shivered and looked up at him, her eyes wide and luminous. Her hair was spread beneath her in a glorious tangle, her lips were swollen from his kisses, and he felt uncommonly blessed that this was the woman he would wed. Indeed, his heart clenched at the sight of her, so beauteous, so trusting.

"Is that all?" she asked softly.

Bayard kept silent, for he did not trust himself not to laugh at her dismay.

Instead, he folded his arms beneath her shoulders, gathered her closer, and kissed her ardently. She sighed and arched against him, and when he moved ever so slightly, she parted her legs yet farther. She inhaled sharply in the way she had that made his blood fairly boil, clutched his shoulders as he rocked his hips and wrapped her legs around him.

Bayard was certain that if he did die of this sweet act, 'twould not be all bad.

Reassured when she moved her hips demandingly against his own, he braced himself above her and moved with powerful deliberation. She clung to him, trembling as she kissed him, and he knew her hunger rose again. She clawed his back as he moved with greater speed, she made incoherent noises, she bit his shoulder when he slid his hand betwixt them and drove her to her climax.

And when she screamed out in her delight, the sight of her drove him to his own. He heard himself roar, heard the cry echo over the hills, and cared for naught but the winsome smile of the thoroughly sated woman beneath him.

He lay down alongside her, his breathing heavy, and caught her fast against his side. Her eyes were closing already, and he pulled the cloak carefully around her, so that she was nestled warmly within it. He touched her cheek, marveling as he listened to the thunder of his heartbeat, the deep rhythm of her breathing.

He felt a new affection for the matter of his own marriage. Bayard had always envisioned himself alone, at war or savoring the bounty of his labors. Even when he agreed to Margaux's demand, he had thought little of the lady he would take to wife. He had thought of men and battles and armaments, of history and legacies, of family and duty.

'Twould be impossible not to think of this lady. Already her smile and her enthusiasm snared him, her desire and her decisiveness intrigued him.

As usual, Fortune had served him well.

When he had recovered himself, Bayard slipped the blood-marked linen from beneath his sated partner. She murmured and rolled over, turning the perfection of her buttocks to his view. He rose reluctantly, tucked the token safely beneath the false bottom of his saddlebag, in case any might seek to steal such proof from him. His experience of Simon had taught him caution.

The lady curled against Bayard immediately when he lay down again and he smiled that she should be both a beauty and passionate abed. Marriage would suit him well—indeed, he might have a son within the year.

That would be better than a man had any right to expect.

Bayard stared at the banner of stars above, his arm tightly around the woman at his side. Truly, he could not believe his good fortune and the marvel of it kept him long awake. When he did finally succumb, he slept the sleep of a man well satisfied with what he had wrought.

Esmeraude could not find her cursed chemise.

Surely it could not have wandered far? But she had prowled the area around the sleeping knight, poked through the garb cast this way and that, and failed to find it. She had found her stockings and both of her shoes—though the second had necessitated a greater hunt, having evidently been cast over his shoulder in the heat of the moment. 'Twas in the deep grasses some half a dozen paces away that she had found it.

But the chemise? What could have come of the wretched garment? She would have expected it to be the most readily found, being woven of fine white linen that would fairly glow in the moonlight.

But she had not caught a glimpse of it. This was vexing indeed, not only because she had to make haste to depart, not only because the wool of her kirtle would scratch her tender flesh without the chemise beneath, but because that chemise bore the sole sample of embroidery Esmeraude had ever troubled herself to finish. She had wrought that chemise with her own needle and embellished it—under protest, 'twas true—and 'twas like a talisman to her.

She was loath to leave without it, but it seemed as if the garment had grown legs of its own and walked away! A more superstitious maid than she might have considered the absence of the chemise to be a portent, an omen that she should not leave the knight's side.

But the sky was lightening and the moon was fleeing and Esmeraude had regained what measure she had of common sense. Her lover was a mere mortal, as revealed by the shadow of whiskers growing upon his chin, and she dared not linger lest he be as inclined as the Norseman to claim her for his own. That she would not risk.

On the other hand, 'twould be most galling to be present when he made it clear that he had had all he wanted of her. Nay, Esmeraude would disappear as surely as her knight had appeared and never again would their paths cross.

Aye, her deflowering had been as marvelous and magical as she had always hoped it might be, and Esmeraude was disinclined to let the sun shine its harsh rays on the memory she would always treasure. 'Twas like a dream that she knew she would savor over and over again. There was not even blood upon the fur lining of his cloak, though she had heard that some maidens did not bleed on their first time.

That she would not be able to prove that her virginity was

gone with such firm evidence was a problem, but Esmeraude would have to resolve that later. Célie might be a reliable witness of her deflowering.

Much cheered, Esmeraude searched again, then tapped her toe and considered the man. 'Twas cursedly difficult to leave his side, though she supposed such an inclination was sentimental and foolish. He might be relieved to find her gone!

His flesh had been warm this morn and her heart had been full, but Esmeraude knew that remaining was fraught with complications. She needed no such complications. She had to leave him, and she would be happy to do so if only she could find her chemise!

She swore through her teeth, then jumped when the knight rolled over. He frowned when his hand closed upon naught and Esmeraude took a step back, not daring to breathe. His scowl deepened and he mumbled something, stretching his arm across the cloak as he sought her.

Esmeraude feared that he would awaken before she could be gone. He might then try to stop her flight. His eyelids fluttered and she knew she had but a heartbeat to act.

She crept closer, rolling his cloak as she went, then whispered to him as she pushed the bundle of cloth and wool into his embrace. Then she stood back and watched, terrified that he would not accept her ruse.

But he murmured and drew it close, evidently mistaking the empty bundle of cloth for one with her within it.

Esmeraude did not imagine 'twould deceive him for long. She had to hasten away! She scurried backward, scanning the area one last time for her chemise with no success. His saddlebags lay some distance away but she could not imagine that the chemise had found its way in there.

He rolled over, muttering something in his sleep and scowling again. Esmeraude dared dally no longer.

Knowing she would not be able to bear the wool directly

against her flesh, she seized his chemise and hauled it over her head. It smelled of his flesh, a most disconcerting fact, and the sleeves were far too long, but she dared not waste another moment. She pulled on her kirtle, knotted her belt, and impatiently shoved her stockings through it. She retrieved her small knife and fled, her shoes in hand and her hair unbound.

At least she did not have to look for Célie.

Though that was hardly a good omen. The maid stood on the beach side of the grasses beyond which they had retreated, her arms akimbo and her expression disapproving.

Esmeraude held a fingertip to her lips, to no avail.

Célie snorted. "I will not be asking how it was, or whether the deed met with your expectations," she huffed. "No doubt the King of Jerusalem himself heard you cry out like a she-cat."

Esmeraude blushed, and was momentarily grateful for the relative darkness. "I had to feign enjoyment," she lied, "otherwise he would have guessed that I was virginal. If his suspicions were roused, we should never be able to steal his boat."

"Ha!" Célie gave Esmeraude a look so knowing that she knew that naught had been hidden from the older woman. "I am surprised you managed to *recall* that we had need of his boat."

Esmeraude stepped past her maid, determined to discuss the matter no further. What was done was done, and she had nary a regret. "We must hasten lest he awaken before we are gone."

"You did not sound like a woman intent upon leaving a man," Célie muttered.

Esmeraude spun to face the maid, hands on her hips. "Would you prefer that it had been horrible for me?"

"I would rather you had been in your marital bed," the

maid snapped. "Then there would be no shame in your finding pleasure with a man."

"Well, I feel no shame."

"Perhaps you should." Célie marched beside her as they began walking toward the boat once more. "Perhaps one day yet you will." She slanted a glance at her charge. "Perhaps we should linger, that you might have no illusions of the way men treat their whores. He might well give you the back of his hand this morn and tell you to be gone."

Esmeraude did feel a twinge of dread at leaving this knight, not only without saying farewell, but also knowing so little about him. It seemed odd to know the shape of him and the smell of him, but not to know his name.

But then, exchanging their names could be dangerous. She forced herself to recall her objective and not look back. 'Twas not as easy as she might have hoped. 'Twould be a marvel, indeed, to love again while the dawn slipped over the horizon. She could imagine how his lips would curve in a slight smile and his eyes would darken with passion as he leaned over her.

And he would kiss her again, very thoroughly, as if it did not matter how long the task took. Esmeraude shivered with delight and felt her flesh heat.

Unless, of course, he kicked her from his makeshift bed with a curse and a slap, then went upon his way.

'Twas better, far better, not to know for certain.

Célie evidently read more of her thoughts than Esmeraude might have preferred. "Why flee this man on this morn?" the maid demanded. "He seems to be wealthy enough and clearly you found naught lacking in his allure."

"Nay, Célie, we must depart."

"He might wed you. He might be the man you seek."

"What foolery!" Esmeraude said sharply, for her own

heart called her a liar. "He was only a means to be rid of my maidenhead."

"You would not have permitted him between your thighs if you believed him to be so little as that."

"I am but a country maid to him. He would not treat me with honor, despite what we have done. Are you not the one always telling me of the lusts of men?"

"You might ask him," the maid countered. "You might ensure that you chose aright." Célie's glance was sly. "You might tell him the truth of who you are."

"After what we have learned since leaving Ceinn-beithe?" Esmeraude shook her head. "Then he could wed me for the prize of Ceinn-beithe alone. Indeed, none would stop him once he made it clear he had claimed my maidenhead, and even if I denied it, a man would be believed before me. Nay, Célie, he must remain a stranger to me. 'Tis for the best that we part this morn forever."

"Even if he might be the suitor you seek?"

Esmeraude gritted her teeth with frustration. "I would have a spouse who loves me for myself alone. A coupling in the dark is no guarantee of that."

"You assume much of this man of whom you know so little."

Esmeraude's lips set stubbornly. "We *leave*, Célie, for my quest and my adventure continues without this man."

The maid might have said more, but Esmeraude headed for the boat, now high above the receding waterline.

Had her own mother not said that love made lovemaking all the more sweet? When she wed the man who held her heart, they would find yet greater pleasure than this, Esmeraude was convinced of it. The very prospect buoyed her; she was certain she had made the right choice. She would not be deceived by her first taste of pleasure, for surely there was more within that cup for her to sip.

The musky scent rising from the knight's chemise seemed to taunt her, weakening her conviction, but she hurried ahead. She and Célie paused as one when they reached the craft and exchanged a glance of frustration. To Esmeraude's dismay, the squire clearly had taken his knight's advice most seriously.

He was fast asleep within the boat she meant to steal.

"What shall we do?" Célie whispered.

Esmeraude rocked the boat with one hand. The boy did not so much as stir. She rocked it more vigorously and he began only to snore in contentment. The women exchanged a glance, then Esmeraude backed away, Célie on her heels. She cast pebbles at the sleeping boy, who seemed oblivious to the assault. When she cast more of them, he rolled over, buried his head beneath his cloak and snored more loudly.

Esmeraude approached the boat cautiously and tried to lift the sleeping boy. He weighed more than she could have imagined. She nodded to her maid, who grasped his feet, but still the two could not lift him.

And he began to move restlessly, dangerously close to awakening and alerting the knight of what they did. Esmeraude glanced over her shoulder, for she heard a stirring that she fancied was her knight awakening.

"The boy sleeps as fast as his master sleeps lightly," she murmured, vexed.

"Then we shall have to remain," Célie pronounced with no small satisfaction. "Trapped betwixt the devil and the sea. That shall teach you to be so bold!"

Esmeraude surveyed the hillock to which the boy had pulled the boat, and noted that the tall grasses surrounding the boat grew almost to the water's edge on the hillock's far side. And they were wet with dew. The tide was retreating, the timing perfect for their departure. 'Twas too good an opportunity to waste!

"Nonsense," Esmeraude said firmly. "We shall take him with us."

And before her maid could protest, she gathered the oars and gave the boat a mighty push down the wet grass. It slipped quite readily and the boy snored contentedly as the boat rocked on its course. Esmeraude heard her maid swear in irritation behind her, but Célie trotted after her and helped her push the boat a moment later.

"We return to Ceinn-beithe," the older woman said with resolve.

Esmeraude cast her maid a sunny smile. "Aye, of course. But only long enough to borrow a palfrey and be rid of the boy. It is too far to walk to Airdfinnan, after all."

"Esmeraude!"

"Do not be foolish, Célie. We shall have need of a steed to reach Airdfinnan before my suitors do."

"God in heaven, but I believe you revel in this," Célie muttered, her own mood most clear.

Esmeraude gave the boat a last shove, then held it as her maid climbed aboard. The knight's squire snored blissfully, untroubled and unaware of the change in his circumstance. Esmeraude imagined the expression upon her knight's face when he awakened to find her gone and smiled broadly. "Aye, Célie, I do. Adventure is as marvelous as I had hoped."

"But the danger—"

"Is part of the price of such a quest, Célie." Esmeraude gauged the tide and began to row into the current. "'Twould be foolish, indeed, if I did not believe the prize to be worth the price. I cannot wait to reach Airdfinnan."

"I can," muttered the maid, but she rowed all the same.

Chapter Four

ESMERAUDE'S ESTIMATION OF BAYARD'S RESPONSE was not too far wrong. He was sorely vexed to find himself alone upon awakening. He stood and glared at the sea, which sparkled merrily as if to defy his temper, and watched a small boat bob farther and farther away.

Three figures were silhouetted within it. In this remote place, they could be none other than the three who had abandoned him here.

That angered him truly. What madness had seized the maiden's wits while he slept? What lack did she perceive in him? And why, for the love of Mary, would she leave him after surrendering so fully to his touch, after *choosing* him to be her spouse?

Perhaps she played some jest upon him, though Bayard was not amused.

Indeed, he feared that she would pay most dearly for her ploy. There was a reason that women should be compliant, especially if they were as compelled as this one to make poor choices when left to their own devices! Bayard recalled his own struggles against the sea the night before and feared for her survival. What would become of his quest then?

Had he won the bride only to lose her to the sea? Had her foolish choice cast his family into peril? He paced and he growled and he worried the matter through.

The fact was, regardless of his concern, that there was naught Bayard could do about the matter. 'Twas clear that the fates had turned sourly against him while he slept. Perhaps he had been too confident of success too soon. Not only was Esmeraude gone, but she had stolen his vessel, ensuring that he could not follow her. Had Andrew accompanied her so that he might inform Bayard of her whereabouts?

Bayard soundly hoped so. 'Twould not be soon that he could lend chase. He donned his garb, seeing immediately that his chemise was gone. Perhaps Andrew had taken it. Bayard did not care particularly: he had greater concerns on this day. He retrieved a clean one from his saddlebags and began to walk south to the distant hall of the King of the Isles. By dint of necessity, he must go to that court and beg, borrow, buy, or steal a vessel. Bayard did not further vex himself by worrying where precisely his bride had gone.

Yet.

He had to walk, having left his horses on the mainland in Michael's care. 'Twas unseasonably sunny and warm, which only increased the apparent burden of his hauberk and armor. Bayard, unaccustomed to walking with all of his gear, trudged stoically toward the south.

He thought of how diligently he would have to teach his bride to obey him, for her own good.

If she survived that crossing. His heart leapt and he glanced over his shoulder to the sea, half expecting to see her waving madly for his aid.

But the sea glinted and sparkled, not a ship upon it as far as he could see. Had she been swept away already? His heart clenched. He wondered then who had brought her to the isle in the first place, finding both encouragement and annoyance in the distinct possibility of another man having aided her.

But who?

❖

Against the odds, Bayard's mood improved considerably upon his arrival at the court of the King of the Isles. All was in confusion. Simon was there, but Bayard was not overly irked since the other knight looked haggard and frustrated. Indeed, Bayard granted the man a confident smile, knowing that he had had the better night of it.

'Twas then he saw that his cousins Nicholas and Connor had also given chase to the maiden, as well as a number of the local men he had seen at Ceinn-beithe. Nicholas looked well, his auburn hair fairly glowing in contrast to the dark blue of his tabard. Connor was as fair as Bayard recalled. The pair were tall and elegantly mannered, joking quietly with each other.

They did not acknowledge him and he did not blame them, but Bayard felt a pang of loss for having chosen to leave his family behind. There was a price to be paid in letting them think the worst of him, but then, they would only believe the truth if they heard it. And they would only listen, 'twas clear, if he first repaired what had gone awry with his own father. He could only do that by admitting that he had been wrong, a confession he would never make.

So Bayard held his tongue and regretted naught.

The suitors clustered closer to the rough chair of the king, though only the two older rival knights approached the king directly.

Simon was nigh double Bayard's age and his golden hair was now touched abundantly with silver. He was tall and strong, a formidable adversary at tourney. He clearly believed that no rule had yet been created to restrain him, undoubtedly a result of being his father's heir and favored child for all his days. There was a harsh line to his lips and a coldness in his gaze that had made Bayard distrust this knight, even before he had learned his instinct to be aright.

Bayard let his smile broaden, simply because he knew 'twould irk the other knight. "Good morning, all."

Simon scowled. "There is naught good about this morn, and naught amusing in this," he snapped by way of greeting. "I fail to see why you might be pleased by her doings."

Bayard bit his tongue, keeping his advantage to himself. "What doings?" he asked innocently.

Simon fairly spat. "Esmeraude fled to the King of the Isles."

"Ah, so she *is* here."

"She was, but no longer!"

"Oh? Has she departed so quickly as that?"

"Fled in the night, the little vixen." Simon scowled, then indicated a large Norseman who seemed to be in even more foul of a temper. A man, perhaps the king himself by his rich garb, berated the Norseman, who listened glumly. "The king had her bound to that man, by some pagan ceremony, but when they retired to consummate the match, she left him trussed, unconscious, and in a room secured from the inside."

"Indeed?" Bayard did not have to feign his surprise. He was impressed with her feat and supposed he should count himself fortunate that the lady had merely left him sleeping.

Then he wondered what the Norseman had done to so deserve this indignity. Anger flared within him. Had his betrothed been abused? Had her flight been an act of bravery or desperation? He glared at the Norseman and the man flinched.

Simon did not note the exchange. "Indeed. She is a troublesome woman, Bayard, and clearly not the manner of wife for you."

This blatant attempt to deflect his interest amused Bayard. "While you believe her the right woman for you?"

"I shall tame her," Simon said with a toss of his fair hair. He smiled coldly. "I have a way of dousing the unnatural fire in such a woman."

"Indeed?" Bayard asked. "How unfortunate a fate that would be for the lady in question."

"What do you mean?"

"She sounds most interesting with her fire." Indeed, he was doubly intrigued by the woman he would wed. Passionate abed and resourceful in dire situations, Esmeraude would suit him very well.

When Simon said naught to that, Bayard smiled coolly and stepped away to bow before the king. They exchanged pleasantries; the king was clearly annoyed. Then Esmeraude's crimes against the partner chosen for her were reviewed. Bayard looked the man up and down, and was impressed anew by this maiden's resourcefulness in eluding such a foe.

"I do not suppose," he asked, "that she left a missive of any kind?"

The king granted him an odd glance. "Howsoever did you know?"

Bayard smiled, pleased that he was gaining an understanding of his intended. "A guess, 'tis all."

The king snapped his fingers and a small man appeared by his side, his manner quiet as so many clerks could be. His fingers were not stained with ink as those of the clerks Bayard knew, but then, there could be precious few books kept in this simple and wild place. The small man produced a scrap of vellum and bowed low before the king.

Simon, who had followed Bayard, leaned forward to reach for the missive. The king struck him across the face for his boldness, the rough expression of authority startling both knights.

"The missive is mine," the king declared through clenched teeth. "I have yet to decide whether its contents are yours to know." Simon stepped back, a red mark upon his handsome features, alarm in his eyes. The clerk gripped the scrap of vellum and blinked in agitation.

Bayard, though equally shocked, said naught. He wondered how he would manage to secure a boat from this barbarian, for he had no desire to linger in this place.

The clerk meanwhile cleared his throat at the king's gesture, and began to read.

> *A ford on a river beckons to me,*
> *That river sprung from the realm of Faerie.*
> *Handfast spurned, a maid yet pure,*
> *I seek a love destined to endure.*

The knights and men gathered there exchanged glances of confusion. Any sense Bayard might have felt that he grew to understand his intended was shattered by her verse.

Where had she gone?

"What river is said to spring from the realm of Faerie?" Simon asked, clearly irritated with Esmeraude's game.

The king smiled coldly. "They all do, if one heeds local legends."

"Are there rivers upon the isle?"

"Of course."

"Then I shall search it from one sea to the other," Simon declared. He granted Bayard an arch glance. "And none shall complete this feat afore me."

But Bayard knew that the maiden had not remained upon the isle. Whatever river she meant to visit was on the mainland or she would not have seized his boat.

He would wager that she had left him to continue to that nameless locale. Perhaps she had not chosen him as victor, after all. Why, then, had she welcomed his touch? Had she not been so obviously clever, he might have assumed her mad. But his Esmeraude was not mad. Nay, there was a greater reason here, he would wager his all upon it. Instead of vexing him, her choice intrigued him.

And redoubled his resolve to win her hand.

But first Bayard would know the number and the strength of his foes. "Does a woman have a right to refuse a hand-fast?" he asked the king instead of answering Simon. He spared a cautious glance at the Norseman who returned his glance morosely.

"Aye, either party can abandon it."

"And once 'tis abandoned? Can your man protest the lady's decision?"

"Nay." The king's lips thinned. "He has been rejected and that is the end of the matter."

"What manner of a vow is this?" Simon demanded.

The king straightened. "A vow that sees to the happiness of both parties and that without a tithe to Rome. 'Tis a pledge for a year and a day, a trial match as it were, before more binding pledges are made between the couple."

"Yet you relied upon such a weak vow to secure her?" Simon asked, incredulous. The king bristled at the knight's audacity and the two men straightened.

"'Tis not the maid he sought to secure, but her legacy," Bayard said, seeing the truth of the matter. "A seed in her belly would have seen the matter resolved."

Simon made to speak but hesitated, then said naught. Bayard wondered whether his desire for Esmeraude was based upon something other than the legacy of Ceinn-beithe.

The king shrugged. "Ceinn-beithe is an old holding and one precious to the folk of the west and the isles. It seemed that 'twould be simple to make it mine own." He eyed the knights warily. "I would welcome the pledged loyalty of any who would win this prize."

"That is a matter to pursue with whosoever claims the

lady's hand," Simon said, his dismissal of the prospect most clear.

The king stepped forward. "This isle is my jurisdiction and no one leaves its shores without my aye or nay. Esmeraude is mine to grant until she departs from Mull and I alone shall decree when that shall be. She has rejected but one man of many in my court. She came to me, and I shall see Ceinn-beithe secured, whatever price must be paid. You shall have your challenge, both of you, for all the men of my court shall seek her as well."

"You have no right!" Simon sputtered. "You were not invited to the Bride Quest. I traveled from afar! I have invested more, far more, than you will ever possess in this madness! You have no right to seize this opportunity from me!"

Bayard saw that Simon had pressed the local king too far, for that man straightened and his face grew ruddy. Bayard took a step back, lest he be implicated in his fellow knight's folly.

"I have every right!" the king roared. "And when Esmeraude enters my court again, I shall see to it that she is claimed fully." He drove his fist into his hand. "She shall be claimed before the entire company to ensure there is no doubt!"

"My estimation of the lady rises with every passing moment," Simon said with a sneer. "She showed much good sense to flee this haven of barbarians."

"Seize him!" the king bellowed.

With startling speed, Simon was restrained by two burly men. He struggled, to no avail. "You cannot do this. You cannot restrain me. I am a knight! I have a quest to pursue!"

"You have obeisance to grant. Perhaps in the morn, you will be more inclined to show respect to your betters." The king's eyes were glittering with anger and Bayard knew he had to think quickly.

The king spun to face him. "And what is your intent?"

Bayard strove to look most troubled. "I fear I shall have to ask your permission to depart the hospitality of your hall and the pleasures of your isle," he said slowly, letting his brow furrow.

"What is this? You retreat already from the prize?" Simon struggled against his captors to ensure that he missed naught. He was unable to hide his glee at the prospect.

The king's eyes narrowed.

Bayard shook his head and lied as well as he was able. "I fear that I must. I lost my squire upon the sea and duty demands that I return to Ceinn-beithe, so that word might be sent to the boy's mother. Also, I grow concerned for the fate of the second squire."

"Where is he?"

"He tends my steeds near Ceinn-beithe." Bayard smiled ruefully for the king. "I fear that the burden of my responsibilities draws me away too soon from your glorious isle, no less the promised delights of Esmeraude."

"I know what it is to be overburdened with duty," the king declared, clearly pleased to have another knight withdrawing from the fray.

"You left your steed with a mere boy!" Simon echoed, incredulous. "You place your trust too easily indeed." He smiled. "But perhaps I may amend the matter for you, Bayard. Borrow *my* ship to run your errand, collect your belongings, then return to the isle. By the time you touch this shore again, I shall no doubt have need of the ship to carry my bride homeward."

The king fixed the other knight with a quelling stare. "You speak above your place yet again," he said coldly, then addressed his guards. "This guest will be ours for two nights afore I so much as look upon his face again."

Simon bellowed in frustration as he was dragged away, but 'twas all for naught. His captors were impassive and efficient.

"Perhaps then he will learn some proper conduct," the king muttered. He then turned a smile upon Bayard, his gaze dwelling on the knight's blades. "How unfortunate that you cannot tarry upon our isle. I shall provide you with an escort to the ship and I would be more than delighted to lend you assistance for your crossing."

"I thank you, sir." Bayard accepted and bowed low, knowing that the escort had naught to do with his comfort. Nay, they would witness his departure to the mainland, and undoubtedly they would come back to the king with Simon's craft.

When he saw the boat, a large, finely crafted vessel, he knew immediately that he had been right.

Indeed, he felt a passing sympathy for Simon as they eased out onto the sparkling water. 'Twas a curious inclination, and truly there had never been a man less deserving of his compassion. He had not seen the last of Simon on this quest, that much was certain.

Indeed, he must use these two days to advantage and secure his intended's hand within his own while Simon was otherwise engaged.

Though first he had to find her. Bayard eyed the length of the convoluted shoreline and felt a rare sense of being overwhelmed. She could have disappeared entirely, she could have been swept away by the tides and lost forever.

And his quest would be lost, through no fault of his own.

But he would not step aside while his goal was snatched from his grasp. Bayard seized his oars and lent his efforts to those of the men of the King of the Isles' court.

When they drew nearer the mainland's shore, he caught a

glimpse of a distant shadow upon the sparkling waves. He looked again, then smiled to himself.

Dame Fortune, 'twas clear, had yet to desert his cause.

❋

Célie did not abandon her theme readily, which meant that Esmeraude argued with her as they rowed. The older woman was slow in aiding her, clearly emphasizing her desire to return to the knight by doing little to put him behind them.

The boy slept through their argument, though Esmeraude could not imagine how. His hair was the brightest hue of red that she had ever seen and a thousand freckles were cast across his nose.

"No man will have you," Célie muttered. "Save the one you leave behind."

"There is no proof of what I have done."

"Ho! There is me and I assure you that I shall tell any man who so much as looks at you what a wanton you have proven yourself to be!"

Esmeraude looked away, well pleased that Célie unwittingly agreed to provide the proof she otherwise lacked.

"And you are mad to go to Airdfinnan," the maid continued.

"Then why do you come with me?"

"Someone has to see to your welfare if you will not have a care for it! You are more like your father than I might have imagined," the maid huffed.

"My father was wondrous," Esmeraude retorted, her loyalty to that man unshaken, although Theobald had died when she was less than two summers of age. Duncan had become her step-father shortly after that, but Esmeraude knew by her tone that Célie did not refer to Duncan. Indeed, she thought the world of Duncan, and though Célie could never be coaxed to speak directly of Theobald, her disapproval of that man had always been evident.

"There was a ruffian," she said sourly now, "bent on doing whatsoever he would with nary a care for the consequences."

"Theobald?"

"Who else?"

Esmeraude halted in surprise, for Célie had never said much of Theobald despite her charge's many pleas that she do so and now she seemed inclined to do so. Esmeraude knew little of the man who had sired her—save that he had died young and that she had adored him while he lived.

And that her mother refused to so much as utter his name. She had always wondered which was the real Theobald, the man of her memories or the man who had spawned her mother's bitterness, though none would speak to her of it.

Until now.

"My father loved me more than any I have ever known," she said carefully.

"Aye, he loved you true enough, for you were of his seed and young enough that he believed you were just like him." Célie shook her head. "I always thought that he was wrong in this, that you shared only his merry manner."

"But?" Esmeraude prompted.

"I long believed that Theobald would have been disappointed if he had lived to see you grow," Célie continued. "For I thought that you did not share his selfish nature. But, of late, you have shown yourself as much a selfish fool as he."

" 'Tis not my wish to injure any other!"

"Nor was it Theobald's." Célie shook a finger at her charge. "But he did so nonetheless. Do you think your mother yearned to leave all she knew and nigh every soul she loved to come to this place and begin anew? Nay! Do you think she yearned to carry her daughters away from her homeland? Nay again! But she had no choice, thanks to Theobald." The maid snorted. " 'Twas his deeds that shamed her before her family and left her without a *denier* to call her own. Your mother sacrificed much so that she did not have to sell her daughters into marriage, for she wished you all to be wed for love. You mock her good intentions in this game."

"You were amenable before . . ."

"Aye, before you sacrificed your maidenhead for whimsy and a night of pleasure. You have wasted an opportunity to find a spouse to love, spurned a chance that any other maid would welcome. And for what? Adventure. Pshaw!" The maid's manner was stern. "I am sorely disappointed in you, Esmeraude, make no mistake, for you have shown your mettle and 'tis of less worth than I had hoped. You shall be fortunate, indeed, if no evil comes of this foolery."

"I do not care if I wed a poor man. I shall wed for love."

"Aye, if you have the choice," the maid said sourly. "I shall be surprised if you do, and yet more surprised if no others pay some price for your folly."

"What would you have me do then?"

"Turn this craft about and wed that knight."

"He thinks me but a peasant maid! You yourself said that he would not wed me."

Célie rolled her eyes. "What other choice have you? You have made a tangle, Esmeraude, and only you can unravel the knot of your deeds."

Esmeraude was chastened, though she still thought her choice made sense. Célie always saw the shadow and not the light, but Esmeraude was convinced that she would find the love of which she dreamed.

Before she could defend herself further, the boy awakened abruptly.

"Ye gods!" he bellowed, leaping to his feet with such haste that the boat rocked dangerously. "We shall all perish!"

"Be still," Esmeraude bade him crossly, having had more than enough of dire warnings this morn.

"Aye, we shall only perish if you capsize our craft," Célie added sternly.

He sat down immediately, though his unease was most clear. "Where is my knight?"

"Sleeping."

The boy glanced at the two grim-faced women. "You must grant me an oar, that I might lend my aid," he insisted. "If I am to die, I shall die fighting, as a tribute to the knight I serve."

"There are no more oars," Esmeraude told him, a fact he surely must already know.

He licked his lips, his gaze flicking over the dancing waves. "Then grant me yours, for I can fight the sea better than a maiden."

Esmeraude laughed and rowed on. She had rowed with Duncan for years and had the strength and knowledge of the sea to show for it. "Is that so?"

She was right about her quest, and she would continue, regardless of Célie's warnings. 'Twas in moments like these that she felt most alive—and least inclined to sit by a fire and embroider, dutifully awaiting the command of a spouse.

This was the adventure she craved. 'Twas true that her journey thus far had been inconvenient for her maid, but Célie always complained of such things. And the men gathered to compete for her hand expected a challenge of some kind. Indeed, this was less of an ordeal for them than warfare.

Nay, Esmeraude could not perceive that any were hurt by her choice.

She eased the boat into the current, as Duncan had taught her, working with it instead of against it. She had chosen the place where they would cross into the fastest flowing waters with care, and was relying upon the outgoing tide to deposit them more or less where they desired upon the opposing shore.

The boy yelped as the current seized the boat, for it spun like a top. The two women lifted their oars and waited. As usual, the water swept them out into the middle of the current, to its fastest course, without so much as a stroke from them.

"We shall perish at sea! We shall be swept away and never seen in Christendom again!" the boy cried, but both women ignored him.

Esmeraude watched the surface of the water carefully, sparing periodic glances to the distant shore. When she judged the moment to be right, she nodded to Célie.

The two women rowed with all their strength to be free of the current. They called encouragement to each other, as the boy watched with wide eyes, then laughed together in triumph when they slipped into the slower-moving waters along the coast. In the moment, their disagreement was forgotten. 'Twas a fair bit of work, but less than fighting the current for the entire width of the strait.

"What did you say afore we crossed the current?" Esmeraude asked the boy archly.

He inclined his head to her. "I beg pardon. 'Tis clear that a maiden can, indeed, row better than I." He sighed. "My knight and I were nearly flung out to sea last evening, and though we battled valiantly, I feared we would not survive. I see now that there is an art to conquering the ocean's current."

"Indeed, there is. You must have endeavored to sail directly across the strait."

"Aye, we did and we struck a fair line, but at a high cost." He dropped his voice, and shivered. " 'Twas terrible. The sea seemed intent upon swallowing us whole."

Esmeraude felt a twinge of pity for him, for it must have startled him to awaken upon the sea once more. He might well have imagined that he was caught within a nightmare. "If you crossed when the tide was fully in motion, then you are most fortunate that you were not carried beyond the isle."

The boy smiled. "My knight is strong beyond all others. And he says oft that Dame Fortune favors him above all others. I did not believe it myself afore I rode with him, but 'tis true enough. He is fortunate beyond compare."

Célie made a muttered comment about ungrateful maidens abandoning Fortune's prizes, but Esmeraude pretended not to hear. Indeed, her heart skipped a beat at the mere mention of the knight.

But she was no more than a local maid as far as this boy was concerned. She had best recall her disguise and ask appropriate questions.

"If you are unfamiliar with these waters, you should have taken a local soul along as a guide," she said, watching the shore.

The boy scoffed. "My knight has no fear for he . . ."

"Is fortunate beyond all," Esmeraude continued, as she navigated their boat closer to the shore below Ceinn-beithe. "So you have said."

"Does your fortunate master have a name?" Célie asked and Esmeraude's heart leapt.

"Bayard is his name, and he has been on crusade with Richard, King of England, and he has battled Saracen and Corsican."

Bayard. Esmeraude's pulse quickened. And he had crusaded to the East! He must have lived countless tales of adventure. No doubt this Bayard rode to Mull on some mission from the king himself, some secret endeavor filled with dire peril.

But she would never see him again. Esmeraude shook her head and forced herself to think sensibly.

To ensure the success of her plan, she had to be rid of the knight's squire. However, her own understanding of the harshness of these lands meant that she could not simply abandon him. She would not be tormented by fears for his survival.

She began to row toward the silhouette of Ceinn-beithe's village, thinking to leave the boy there. "Have you been to Ceinn-beithe?"

"Aye, we halted there and there was much merriment."

"Indeed?" Esmeraude asked as if she knew naught of it. A common maid would surely be anxious for gossip, would she not?

"Aye, knights were invited there to compete for a maiden's hand, but she left a riddle and fled instead."

"Aye? And the men all lent chase?"

"Nay!"

Esmeraude spun to face the boy at this revelation. "Were they not interested in her jest?"

"They had not the chance." He leaned forward, his eyes shining. "There were but two boats to be had and my master bought this smaller one. There was much arguing, for the others did not wish to share the second boat, though 'twas larger, and we left while still they squabbled."

Esmeraude's oar stilled. There were competitors yet lingering at Ceinn-beithe! And if they wished to go to the island, no doubt they would meet her boat on arrival in hopes of claiming it from her. Her ruse would not last long before all who would recognize her there.

She let the boat drift for a moment as she thought. Célie did not look inclined to be helpful, so Esmeraude addressed the boy. "Yet your knight claimed this boat?"

"Aye, and he was not inclined to share."

" 'Tis not very charitable."

" 'Tis not a big boat," the squire observed. "And he departed on a mission of import, not a pilgrimage."

The women's gazes met, though Esmeraude did not ask what business of import the knight had with the King of the Isles.

'Twas better if she knew less of him. "Did your knight make provision as to where you might meet if you were separated?"

"Nay." The squire frowned, then brightened. "But he will have to return to Michael, for Michael is hidden with our steeds."

"Aye? Where would I find Michael?"

"I said he is *hidden*." The boy rolled his eyes that even a peasant maid could be so slow of wit. "I cannot guide you there!"

"Yet I would not abandon you to starve on these wild shores."

"You could take me to Ceinn-beithe."

"And have my boat seized by men anxious to chase a demoiselle?" Esmeraude chose to ignore the fact that 'twas not truly *her* boat. "I should think not!" She slowed the boat with her oar as the boy eyed her stubbornly. "'Tis not so far to shore from here. Leap over the side and swim."

"I cannot swim!"

"Yet I will not take you farther." Indeed, she dared not do so. The sun was already rising high and Esmeraude knew she must hasten. The possibility of suitors yet at Ceinn-beithe meant that 'twas dangerous to linger so close. "Tell me where to find Michael or you shall be left to swim."

"You would not do it," the boy said, challenge bright in his eye.

But Esmeraude was not one to cede to such a challenge. She moved quickly and seized him, holding him over the surface of the water. He kicked and fought but she held fast, even as the boat rocked.

Célie hung on to the sides and looked most grim. "Aye, drown a knight's squire," she muttered. "That will see all come aright in the end."

"Tell me," Esmeraude insisted, looking the boy dead in the eye. She had no intention of dropping him, but he did not need to know as much.

"You are not a common peasant maid!" he charged.

Esmeraude did not answer that. " 'Tis a harsh land we occupy and one that demands difficult choices of those who would survive here." She let her smile broaden. "Like the one before you in this moment. Do you think the water will be cold?"

He glared at her. "I gave my ~~pledge to~~ my knight to keep the secret. No maiden will compel me to break my word."

"Ah, well." Esmeraude sighed and let him drop a little closer to the surface. He squirmed and his eyes widened in fear. "How curious that men and boys are prepared to die for their pledges."

He spared a glance to the water and swallowed visibly. Esmeraude knew his resolve wavered.

"What you must do, if you cannot swim," she suggested amiably, "is float."

"I cannot float, either," he snapped.

"Aye, you can, if you do not fight the water. The current should carry you, oh, not more than a dozen miles past Ceinn-beithe afore casting you ashore." She shrugged. "Or you might be carried out to sea and lost forever. 'Tis difficult to be certain."

The boy's eyes narrowed as he glared at her. " 'Tis over there," he said through gritted teeth, his words nigh inaudible. When she set him back into the boat, his gaze was so clouded with disappointment that Esmeraude felt churlish for compelling him to confide in her.

But not for long.

It seemed that the boy, whose name proved to be Andrew, could not precisely recall the locale of the other boy. At first, Esmeraude believed this to be true, for she knew that even the most familiar land could look so different from the ocean as to be unrecognizable. And evidently the second boy was hidden so that no others could happen upon him or steal the steeds. She had heard tales of the fortunes invested in a fine destrier or warhorse and could not blame the knight for protecting their worth.

But as the sun crested its zenith and still they rowed back and forth, Esmeraude suspected a trick.

"There is another boat crossing from the isle," Célie noted.

"'Tis probably a fishing boat," Esmeraude muttered, then shook a finger at Andrew. "You have not broken your word at all," she said. "You have lied and deceived me." Célie harumphed but Esmeraude ignored her. "Indeed, I shall cast you over the side of the boat here and now . . ."

"Why, there he is!" Andrew cried and pointed to the shore. "I remember that tree."

Having heard all the morn long that he remembered this tree or that stone, Esmeraude was disinclined to believe. But she followed his gesture and looked, startled to find another taller boy standing upon the shore. He waved and shouted a greeting and Andrew shouted back.

Finally! She rowed to the shore, determined to be on her way to Airdfinnan with all haste. Her arms were aching from this morning's labor.

She would sail down the coast again and abandon the boat near Ceinn-beithe. She would tell Andrew this so that Bayard could retrieve his investment. From there, she could borrow a horse and be gone again without anyone knowing she had been home. The horses were grazed in the afternoon and the ostler's boy who so oft accompanied them was inclined to lie in the grass and sleep. Though it often vexed Duncan, that habit would suit her well on this day.

Célie, if she was disinclined to continue on the adventure, could return to Ceinn-beithe, there to sit by the fire and complain. Aye, Esmeraude thought that a most fitting solution to the maid's dissatisfaction.

She was not so immune to the concerns of others as that!

"There!" Esmeraude said, when the boat was close to the shore. "I shall keep the craft here while you jump."

"Oh, I could not jump over the water," Andrew insisted, backing up toward Célie.

"Of course you can jump." Esmeraude's growing impatience showed in her tone. " 'Tis not far."

" 'Tis too far for me." Andrew turned sad eyes upon her. "Unless you would carry me."

"You are too old to be carried like a babe," Esmeraude insisted. "And indeed, I jumped farther than this when I was half your age. Are you no more brave than a small girl?"

"Andrew is afraid, Andrew is afraid," the other boy taunted.

"I am not afraid!" the boy cried, though still he would not leave the boat.

Esmeraude swore and scooped him up into her arms, determined to see the matter resolved quickly. She leapt to the shore and put him down on his feet none too gently. She would have turned back to the boat, happily leaving him there, but he seized her sleeve.

"Oh, I thank you," he said fervently.

Esmeraude tried to shake off his grip. " 'Twas of no consequence. Now, let me be."

"Nay, nay, there is a bond betwixt us now that you have saved my life."

"I did not!"

"You are so modest, 'tis fetching in a maiden," he said and Esmeraude was startled by his sudden charm. "Perhaps you would do a small favor for me, then."

"I have done your favor."

"Nay! You must see my palfrey," he insisted. "She is the finest chestnut in all of France, my master says as much, and she is gentle and she is fleet of foot and"—he heaved a sigh—"and she has need of a name. I would be honored if you would bestow upon her a fitting name."

Esmeraude gritted her teeth, sorely tempted by the prospect of seeing a horse—for she was overly fond of horses—but well aware that time slipped away. Célie folded her arms across her chest, complacent and smug.

"Name her Lightning if she is so fleet," Esmeraude said. She tried to return to her boat, but Michael had managed to step between her and her goal.

"That is no way to name a steed!" Andrew cried. "You must see her first to pick a fitting name, then see whether she likes it. Please! You must come and see her, I beg of you."

'Twas true enough that Esmeraude was curious. Her sister Jacqueline had told her how beauteous the steeds of France could be. Indeed, Jacqueline's spouse, Angus, had a fine destrier as well as a mare from Persia that was graceful beyond belief.

Esmeraude did wonder what manner of horses her knight had.

Surely it could not take long.

"Only for a moment," she said, impulsively claiming the boy's hand. She walked so quickly into the shadow of the woods that he had to trot behind her.

Andrew's palfrey was indeed a lovely beast, far finer than any in her parents' stables. The mare was of deepest brown, its mane and tail nigh black. There was a streak upon its brow, a mark that further justified Esmeraude's suggested name, and it had one white sock. It nuzzled Esmeraude's neck, taking great interest in her hair, and Esmeraude was so enchanted that she forgot her need for haste.

The knight's destrier, too, was a marvel to Esmeraude, being a remarkably large beast of dappled silver and white. Angus's mount was blacker than midnight and she much preferred the hue of this one. The destrier stomped when the three palfreys fetched more of the attention than it evidently thought they should. It stretched its nose out to Esmeraude so inquisitively that she had to scratch its ears, as well.

"His name is Argent," Andrew contributed.

"It seems a most fitting name."

"Michael brushes him. I am only allowed to polish weaponry." Andrew heaved a sigh. "My knight has far too many blades and pieces of armor for my taste. His hauberk is most vexing to coax to a shine, but he says that I do it well."

Esmeraude smiled as the destrier pushed its soft nose into her hand demandingly. "Aye, you do a fine job," she murmured, remembering how the knight's armor had glinted in the moonlight.

All four of the knight's horses were fine creatures, so affectionate and curious that Esmeraude had to greet each in turn. They were well tended and well fed, another good sign of the knight's character.

"Why are there four steeds? Does one carry provisions?" Esmeraude was impressed by the knight's apparent wealth, for such steeds were costly both to acquire and to maintain.

"They all carry provisions of some amount," the boy informed her, obviously pleased that he knew more of such matters than she.

"But does your knight not ride Argent?"

Andrew clicked his tongue. "A destrier is ridden only in battle, at least by any knight who can afford to live properly. 'Tis called a destrier, for the knight leads the warhorse by his right hand, whilst riding another steed."

"Oh." Esmeraude had not known as much.

"Such steeds are wrought so heavily for battle that they tire on long journeys. Argent is better prepared to do his duty when he has traveled with only his saddle upon his back."

'Twas interesting, to learn such a detail, and Esmeraude had no trouble pretending to be an ignorant peasant maid. The horses were marvelous. She was nuzzled and nibbled, and she had her hair bitten, but she loved every moment of it. She was there far longer than she had anticipated.

A sudden splash made her remember her plan to be quickly away.

"Oh, nay, I must depart!" Esmeraude fairly fled back toward Célie and their boat.

"But wait!" Andrew cried, racing behind her. "You have not named my steed!"

"I must hasten! I will be late. You choose her name." Esmeraude plunged through the last veil of the trees and stopped short.

She already was too late.

A knight, *her* knight, had pulled her boat fully onto the shore and tipped it so that it might dry in the sun. The oars were stowed high out of reach and Célie stood back, watching with undisguised satisfaction as Esmeraude took in the scene before her.

Then the knight turned slowly, his smile brightening as he spied her and his eyes turning a deeper hue of blue.

"My lady," he whispered, then blew her a kiss from his fingertips. "Well met."

Chapter Five

SMERAUDE'S HEART BEGAN TO THUNDER AND SHE could not take another step. She heard the splash of oars as the second boat was rowed back toward Mull, but had eyes only for the knight before her.

Perhaps Bayard's mortality was not such a fault, after all. He seemed vibrantly alive this morn, as vital as a dancing flame. He was taller and broader than she had recalled, no less striking in sunlight than in moonlight.

"I did it!" Andrew cried behind her. "I knew you would come, my lord."

A smile touched Bayard's firm lips, though his gaze did not waver from Esmeraude. His words were softly uttered and filled with pleasure, his voice deep. "Aye, Andrew, you did very well."

In the darkest corner of her heart, Esmeraude could not claim to be disappointed to see this knight again. Bayard, crusader and companion of kings, had pursued her.

Bayard. She whispered his name, savoring the taste of it upon her tongue. Bayard had lent chase to her like a hero in an old tale.

His hair was wet and his face was ruddy, and Esmeraude knew that he had rowed hard to come quickly ashore. She could smell the clean tang of his perspiration. 'Twas thrilling to realize that 'twas important to him to pursue her and to do so with such haste. The growth of dark stubble upon his chin made him look wild and unpredictable, a rogue come to claim what he already knew to be his own.

He smiled as if he read her very thoughts, then closed the distance between them with easy strides. His gaze swept over her, leaving heat in its wake, and when he lifted one hand toward her, Esmeraude could not take a breath. Aye, she remembered the sure touch of that hand upon her flesh and tingled in anticipation of another gentle caress.

His fingertip slid along the gathered neck of his chemise, the linen visible above the neckline of her kirtle, his caress leaving no disappointment. Esmeraude inhaled sharply at the heat of his touch and his eyes twinkled as he evidently noted her response.

His hand slipped up her throat, leaving fire in the wake of his touch, and she stood spellbound. His fingertips lingered upon the wild pulse of her heart, then slid into the hair at her nape. He cupped her chin in his hand, a gesture of startling possessiveness yet one that felt perfectly right all the same.

His eyes were blue beyond blue, his smile made her heart race as quickly in sunlight as it had in the deepest night. His dark lashes were so thick and long that many a maid would have been envious of them, yet the crookedness of his smile and the satisfaction in his gaze was all male.

His other hand slipped over her hair in a caress, gently tucked one curl behind her ear, then he cupped her head in his hands. Esmeraude shivered at the familiarity of his touch, and was surprised to find herself with naught to say.

"Why did you leave so abruptly?"

"I thought 'twas better I be gone when you awakened." Esmeraude's words were husky and she felt her face heat.

Bayard shook his head and smiled. "Cover your hair, lady

mine," he whispered, his eyes gleaming, "for you are a maid unclaimed no longer."

Esmeraude knew what he would do but a moment before he did it, and she could think of no better way for them to meet.

Bayard ducked his head and kissed her possessively, blocking both sunlight and reason with his persuasive touch. Célie had named the solution rightly, but for the wrong reason. Aye, Esmeraude and Bayard were destined to be together, like lovers doomed to meet and love for all time. Esmeraude, knowing that her quest had borne the fruit she desired beyond all else, surrendered fully to his embrace.

Just as she had foretold, her heart had known him from the first.

Bayard was hers and hers alone.

❖

Esmeraude's kiss banished Bayard's every doubt. He had seen her uncertainty upon meeting him again, but he was not the manner of man who abandoned women once he had seduced them. To his relief, Esmeraude was hale and she was not angered with him. Indeed, her kiss shook him to his soul, the taste of the salt upon her lips and her very willingness making him inclined to please her once again.

But they would have years for such delights, and time was of the essence this day. He broke their kiss reluctantly, smiled for her, then beckoned to the boys. He gave commands to saddle the horses and pack their bags, even as his lady leaned sweetly against him.

"But where do we go?" she asked.

"To Ceinn-beithe, of course." Bayard spoke crisply, as was his wont. "The nuptials must be arranged with all haste—I should prefer this very afternoon if your mother is amenable—and then we shall have to ride hard to the south." He sighed and frowned, disliking the demands upon his time when he had need of haste to meet the king. "I suppose tomorrow would be the soonest that we might depart . . ."

Esmeraude pulled back in alarm. "But how do you know my mother?"

Bayard smiled and touched her cheek with a reassuring fingertip. "I was introduced to her, of course." Her eyes widened and he hastened to reassure her, assuming that she misunderstood his meaning. He patted her shoulder. "You need not fret about any impropriety. 'Twas all most acceptably done."

The lady, however, was not reassured. She stepped away from his side. "But this means that you know who I am!"

"Of course I know who you are." Bayard chuckled at her astonishment. "You are Esmeraude of Ceinn-beithe, the bride whose hand I was invited to compete to win. And I have won you for you have chosen me and thus we shall be wed. 'Tis as simple as that."

He turned away, determined to make haste. Aye, he would shave and change before they rode to Ceinn-beithe, so that their nuptial vows could be exchanged immediately. Presumably, his lady could change quickly on their arrival at her family home.

But Esmeraude was not prepared to end their conversation so soon. She tugged at his sleeve. "You knew who I was last evening," she said, her words more of an accusation than a question.

Bayard stared at her, unable to determine the reason for her evident dismay. "Aye, of course I did," he agreed carefully.

"But how? How could you have known? I did not name myself, I did not declare myself, I am dressed in garb that is tattered and dirty beyond all!"

Bayard touched her chin with an affectionate fingertip, not minding that she was so innocent as this. "But you walk like a queen, my fair one, and you expect men to notice you. No peasant girl would do as much, and truly there could not have been two noble maidens with a maid in attendance upon that isle last night."

His reasoning explained most clearly in his view, Bayard laid aside his belt. He thought to ask her to turn aside, so that she would not see his bare flesh while he dressed, but then wondered if he made much of naught.

His hesitation only gave the lady the time to poke him hard in the chest. "You *knew*! You knew my name and you took me to your bed apurpose!"

Bayard considered her flashing eyes and could not imagine what irked her so. "Aye." He arched a brow. "You came to my bed willingly, if I recall aright."

"But I thought you were my destined lover."

Bayard chuckled. "And I am. Now, grant me a moment to shave and then we shall share the happy news with your parents."

But Esmeraude stepped into his path and propped her hands upon her hips. "Why?" she demanded.

"Why?" Bayard echoed, not comprehending. He was beginning to understand that this woman would not be a quiet bride, who tended to her needle until she was called.

He supposed he should have been more troubled than he was at the prospect. Truth be told, this Esmeraude was far more interesting than most beauties he had met.

He liked her passion and unpredictability, much to his own surprise. Those traits lent a certain fire to their exchanges, and 'twas not unwelcome.

"Why did you bed me? Why would you wed a stranger so willingly? Do you desire an estate so much as this?"

The prospect seemed to irk her so much that Bayard was nigh tempted to lie. But 'twas not his choice to have lies between himself and his bride even before they were wed.

"Aye," he said gently. "The holding is of particular import

to me." He had not expected her to be pleased, but her eyes flashed in fury.

"Then you will not wed me!"

"Of course I will." His shaving forgotten, Bayard strode after his retreating lady. "I have bedded you and I shall wed you and we shall live upon that estate and you will be as comfortable as ever a woman might be."

"Never!"

Her defiance infuriated him, and though he was not given to shows of temper, Bayard found his voice rising. "Not never, but on this very day, my lovely lady! On this very *afternoon*, you will stand before the priest with me and we shall exchange our vows."

"Nay, I will wed no man to ensure he wins a holding!"

"You will wed me!" he found himself bellowing.

"Nay, I will not!" the lady cried and tossed her hair like a flighty filly. "I will wed no man to fatten his purse."

"But your father offers Ceinn-beithe as your dowry. For what other reason would a man wed you?"

"Oh!" He thought for a moment that Esmeraude might strike him. Her eyes flashed dangerously, then she turned abruptly. She ran but Bayard was fast behind her.

He snatched her shoulders and spun her to face him. "Why would you be wedded, then?" He took a deep breath and held her firmly, though she tried to wriggle free in a most annoying way.

"For love! For naught less than love!"

Bayard blinked, her answer so astounding him that he could not hide his response. Truly he had spent years amidst those who wedded solely for advantage, then had those matches annulled to make another, more advantageous match.

Surely she could not give credence to such whimsy as love?

"This madness is not—" he began, thinking his tone most reasonable under the circumstances.

"Love is not madness," Esmeraude said with heat. "You have asked for my hand and I have declined you. Let me go! I care not what you might say to persuade me."

"But I *do* care to persuade you."

"Then there is but one confession you might make to me," she cried, her chin tilting in challenge.

Bayard regarded her in amazement. "Surely you do not expect some confession of love? We do not know each other . . ." he began firmly, then gasped when she punched him in the nose. His grip loosed for only a moment, though that was time enough for his betrothed to slip away.

"Yet you still would wed me. Your confession, sir, is not sufficiently persuasive." Esmeraude plucked up her skirts and ran.

"What nonsense is this?" Bayard shouted. "Halt!" he cried, but Esmeraude paid him no heed.

Bayard swore as he raced after her. He had never met a more infuriating woman in all his days. He watched her swing into the saddle of one of his palfreys far ahead of him and shouted at the boys to halt her.

But they had no chance. For a heart-stopping moment, Bayard thought Esmeraude mad or inexperienced with horses, and feared to lose her again. Indeed, she clung to the beast's back so easily that she might have been born to the saddle.

"What of Fortune's favor for you, Bayard?" Esmeraude cried in jubilant challenge. She made a striking sight, her hair escaping its bonds, her eyes bright, the steed fully beneath her control. Bayard's desire for her trebled, as did his anger that she denied his will.

The lady was clearly oblivious to his mood.

Esmeraude turned the palfrey and cantered briskly around him, daring him to snatch her from the saddle. Bayard tried, but she anticipated him and expertly directed the steed out of his range at the last moment.

He was more furious than he could ever recall. Indeed, his blood fairly boiled and she, she *enjoyed* what she wrought!

"It seems the lady's smile fades, for you at least," Esmeraude charged cheerfully. "Indeed, I should be the first to encourage Dame Fortune to cast her glance elsewhere, for you have won too much from her indulgence."

"By the piety of Saint Martin de Tours"—Bayard roared—"I shall see you as my wife!"

"Oh, you are angered, sir," she taunted, then clicked her tongue. "Is it because none have ever denied you your will?"

The audacity of her! Passion was one matter but outright defiance quite another, and a much less desirable trait in a wife.

"I am angered because you defy me!" he shouted. "A wife should be biddable and obedient and *submissive* to her lord and husband's will!"

Esmeraude laughed heartily, then blew him a kiss. "You see? I am right and you are wrong. We are ill-suited, after all. Farewell, sir."

And with that, she gathered the reins and urged his own beast to flee from him as swiftly as the wind. Indeed, she cast him an impish smile over one shoulder as the palfrey took the bit in its teeth and galloped.

"I am *not* wrong!" Bayard bellowed, but the lady did not grace his claim with a reply.

Bayard was livid. Aye, he was well aware of his squires watching this travesty of a betrothal. He stormed toward the steed whose reins Michael quietly offered and leapt into the saddle.

Without another word, he lent chase to the madwoman he had pledged to wed. He drove the horse hard in pursuit. His thoughts raced as quickly as the steeds' hooves with the prospect of what he would do to this vexing woman to tame her once he caught her.

He would seduce her a thousand times, taking her to the brink of pleasure then retreating, teasing her with fulfilment until she begged him for release, until she could look upon no man with desire save himself. He would tame her with the passion that defined her, he would make himself the sole possible source of pleasure for her.

The very prospect made his heart pound. He was hard and hot, he took risks with his steed that normally he never would countenance, he rode as if he escaped the bonds of hell.

And still he did not gain upon her.

The horses ran like quicksilver, darting through the woods on sure feet. Esmeraude's earlier departure and her knowledge of these woods proved to be to her advantage. He shouted her name in frustration, then roared that she should at least have a care for the health of the steed.

She ignored him. Indeed, he thought he heard her laugh, as if delighted with some whimsical game.

His blood boiled. Had he ever met a more vexing woman? What had happened to his good fortune that he had been condemned to win the hand of this one? Oh, he would catch her and he would wed her and he would spend a month abed with her if that was what it took to calm her wild spirit. He would persuade her that what he offered was more tangible and more durable than the foolery of love.

But 'twas not to happen this day. To his dismay, Bayard heard the sound of the palfrey's hoofbeats fade, despite his efforts to the contrary.

Before long, he found himself alone in the forest, seething and without a hint as to where his lady had gone. All because he would not lie to her and confess a love he did not and would never feel.

The sole blessing was that he had not had the chance to

confess that 'twas Montvieux he sought to win, not Ceinn-beithe. Had he admitted that, Bayard would have expected a heated response, for women oft did not care to leave their families far behind.

But Esmeraude did not know that detail.

Yet.

That was another battle he might anticipate. Aye, Bayard understood his lady would not leave him wondering about her feelings upon any matter.

He took a deep breath, halted his steed, and glanced over his shoulder. There was one who knew the lady better than he.

He turned about, resolved to seek counsel from the elderly maid. And when he faced Esmeraude again, she would have no chance to surprise him.

At least not afore they were wedded.

The prospect of that nuptial night made Bayard smile in truth.

❈

Dame Fortune—or Fortuna as she had long been known—had been drawn by the mention of her name. She peered down from her lofty perch and shivered slightly in the Scottish mist so unfamiliar to her. Why had men ever left the glorious sun of the Greek isles? She would never understand it. Golden beaches and azure seas, wine and clear skies were a gift of the gods indeed—but men had abandoned such bounty for . . . this.

Fortuna shuddered in distaste. But when she recognized one of many knights upon whom she had smiled, she understood why she had been invoked in this distant place.

The truth of the matter was that Fortuna was feeling somewhat strained. Had she been a mortal woman, she might have concluded that her irritability and exhaustion were the mark of a change in her body, but Fortuna was immortal and

*thus had no body. Oh, she cloaked herself in the appearance
of a body for the sake of courtesy, but 'twas a choice she
made to comply with the old agreement. In point of fact,
there was little reason for so complying, since one did not often encounter mortals in the heavens, which made it much
more difficult to surprise them here.*

*She rather missed spooking the occasional mortal. It
livened up the monotony of timeless existence. Indeed,
Fortuna had always thought retreating to the heavens to be a
bad idea, but one did not argue with Zeus—or at least, one
had not argued with him in those days and survived unscathed.*

*She peeked down and admitted that this knight she had so
often favored did show some similarities to the uncompromis-
ing Zeus. He, too, had always been certain that he was right.*

*Fortuna felt a certain sympathy for the demoiselle's plight,
for men were even more determined in these times to control
a woman's path than they had once been. She sighed, recalling her heyday all too well and regretting its passage.*

*Much had changed in the last thousand years or so. Too
much, in Fortuna's opinion. She held up a hand and scowled
at how insubstantial she was becoming. Fortuna was old-
fashioned, she knew, for she felt compelled to at least take a
peek whenever and wherever she was invoked. But she had
never felt so tired from fulfilling what she perceived as her
obligations.*

*It was true that she was absurdly popular in these times.
Dame Fortune this and Dame Fortune that—the invocations
never stopped. Fortuna rolled her eyes. Mortals!*

*Then there was the matter of her wheel of fortune being
appropriated and adapted by those who would predict the future, by alchemists and gypsies and men generally too bold
to understand where they should not meddle.*

Though she had had a hand in that. Oh, she should never

have confided in Boethius. Fortuna should have known—after all these eons!—that men have to tell what they know.

But what was done was done.

The worst of it was that not only was she overly burdened with responsibilities, but her labor was so very thankless. Men were beginning to think that they alone controlled their futures. Fortuna snorted their folly. This knight was not the only one upon whom she had smiled who insisted that naught existed that he could not hold within his own hands.

It was most annoying. The trouble with such skepticism was that Fortuna could not recall when there had been a ritual slaughter on her behalf, with incense and songs and burning flesh, and feasting and wine.

Such flattery always was bolstering, but it seemed that the Romans had been the last to understand the importance of such doings. Oh, she remembered all too well that the caesars of Rome had kept golden statues of her, that she had been exalted beyond all others.

Fortuna sighed. Those had been the days. She had been everywhere—on vases and jars, represented as statues of grace and beauty. She had burned so radiantly with the power of the faith in her that she could have challenged the sun itself.

She looked at her hand and it flickered faintly, more like a distant star than the sun.

It is the nature of women, both mortal and immortal, to dislike the sense of being taken for granted. Fortuna fell prey to that dissatisfaction in that moment.

Perhaps this knight had won too much too easily and needed to learn some appreciation. Perhaps this woman was precisely the one to teach him. Fortuna had a trick or two of her own to help. The prospect cheered her enormously.

Only when Fortuna sat back on her puff of cloud did she realize that she was not alone. Saint Martin de Tours—or his unearthly representation—*was striding through the clouds toward her.*

Fortuna recognized him, and not only by his halved cloak. She had favored this one time warrior with a smile or two in his time, and in fact, she had been disappointed in his conversion to Christianity after sharing his cloak with a beggar. He had kept the physique of a warrior, even after he became an influential bishop, and was more manly from Fortuna's perspective than these pale celibates who now held the power of the church she loved to loathe. He was from a past era, not one so far past as her own, but Fortuna felt a commonality with Martin all the same.

Indeed, Fortuna might have welcomed Martin warmly had the globe of fire that burned over his head not been far brighter and more substantial than any part of herself. There was a reminder she did not need of how times and mortals were changing.

An educated man, Martin nodded in acknowledgment of Fortuna as he drew near, despite her hauteur. "Invoked again?" he asked with a tired smile, apparently needing no answer. They would not be both in the vicinity otherwise and Fortuna had to admire that he held the same work ethic as she. Martin dropped onto the cloud opposite her and sighed as he shoved a hand through his hair. "'Tis a curse to be so popular."

Fortuna did not note that it seemed to suit him better than she. She could hate him without too much trouble at all.

Instead, she granted him a smile. "I intend to have some vengeance for that."

"How?" Martin was wary, as a good churchman should be of an alluring immortal.

His response was most gratifying. Fortuna adjusted the folds of her Grecian garb of radiant gold and let her confidence shine in her smile. Martin blinked, as if he looked into the sun itself, and she knew she was not so far gone as that. "With a little mischief, of course."

"You would not."

"I most certainly will. There is no one in my pantheon telling me what I must and must not do." *Fortuna lifted her chin, emboldened by the fact that Zeus had faded to a wisp of smoke through his unpopularity.* "We always had a sense of humor, at least. You Christians seem unable to laugh aloud."

Martin granted her a quelling look. "Perhaps 'twas wise to end the sacrifices in your name. Perhaps 'tis good for all men that your power fades."

"Pshaw!" *Fortuna waved him off and peered through the clouds once more, feeling much invigorated by her decision.* "If that were so, they would not call upon me so very much. You and your kind have made more of a mess of the world than ever we did."

Martin fell silent, for he was not a fool, though Fortuna expected he would have more to say once he thought matters through. She liked thoughtful men—their silences gave one ample time to do what one must do, and do it unobstructed.

Fortuna lifted a finger to her lips and made her choice. She flung a little mischief down through the mist, then waited to see the result.

And in this instance, sadly for Bayard de Villonne, Fortuna did not smile.

Célie had no chance to flee. The two squires seemed to understand their knight's plans even without him stating them outright, for they lingered so close to her that she could not take a step without bumping into one or the other of them. Her heart pounded in fear for her own fate and for Esmeraude's.

The knight returned all too soon for her taste, his expression impatient, which was not a surprise given Esmeraude's behavior. He slowed his horse to a walk and drew closer, speaking to her from his saddle. 'Twas undoubtedly meant to intimidate her, and Célie fought to hide how well the tactic worked.

"You know where she has gone," he said smoothly, no hint of anger in his tone.

"Perhaps."

"Then tell me."

Célie shrugged. "Tell me first of your intentions for her."

He smiled and the softening of his features was reassuring. "You are fond of her."

"I have been her maid since she was two summers of age." Célie lifted her chin. "I love her with all her faults and graces as if she were mine own child."

The knight's smile broadened and his eyes twinkled. "We should all be so blessed as to be surrounded by such loyalty," he said with such resolve that Célie believed him. "I fear my lady is so accustomed to your affection that she does not know that matters could be otherwise."

Célie started, for she had oft thought much the same. "She is not a wicked girl, sir. Indeed, her heart is most tender . . ."

"Yet she flees me and risks her own survival. Am I so fearsome as that?"

"She knows not what you desire of her. Indeed, nor do I."

He dismounted and came to stand before Célie. His expression was earnest, his gaze so clear that she nigh believed him afore he spoke a word. "I rode to seek a bride and this alone is my intent. I would wed Esmeraude."

His smile reappeared and the maid decided that this knight was a most attractive man. "I would see her never understand that there is any way to live than surrounded by those who are loyal."

'Twas a sentiment that melted Célie's reservations.

"You know what has passed between Esmeraude and I, madame, and I would have you know that I seek only to do what is right. In my view, the events of last night have made her my lady. Indeed, such incidents only occurred because I believed she had chosen me as victor in this Bride Quest. As you have seen, though, she has spurned my offer for her hand. I ask for your aid in winning her."

"Truly, you will wed her?"

He inclined his head. "You shall have my pledge upon it."

Célie watched as the knight pulled his sword from its scabbard. He held the blade so that the hilt cast a shadow upon the ground, a shadow in the shape of a crucifix. He held her gaze steadily as he spoke, his manner one of appropriate solemnity.

"I swear, by all I hold holy, to wed Esmeraude of Ceinnbeithe, to protect her as my lady wife, to defend her honor, to keep her well, to grant her sons if I am so able. I pledge it to you—" He arched a dark brow in query.

"Célie."

"Célie, as one who holds my lady dear. I swear this to you, with God as my witness." He closed his fist around the reliquary in the hilt, then kissed it.

Célie watched him return the blade to the scabbard and could not help but be impressed. Here was the manner of man Esmeraude needed! Here was a man determined to do right by his lady and to take responsibility for his deeds.

"She left a riddle," the knight said and recounted it by memory. "Where does she mean?"

"Airdfinnan," Célie confessed.

He frowned. "I do not know this place."

"'Tis the abode of her sister Jacqueline and her spouse, Angus MacGillivray. 'Tis not far."

He grimaced, then smiled, his words revealing that he knew

something of Esmeraude already. "Then perhaps 'tis not far enough that the lady can find trouble for herself en route."

Célie laughed, much reassured. "Oh, my lord, Esmeraude could find trouble in two steps without seeking it at all!"

"Then we had best make haste. Would you be so kind as to show me the way?"

"I would be delighted to do so."

The knight smiled, then granted her his hand with much gallantry and helped her climb into the saddle of one of his palfreys. The squires climbed into the saddle of the third steed together and the knight clearly intended to ride his destrier.

He did not release Célie's hand immediately and she looked at him. "Madame, I would appreciate any suggestion you might grant me in banishing my lady's reservations regarding our match."

He looked so concerned that the servant's heart melted. 'Twas not within Célie to say naught when she had an opinion. "She would wed for love alone."

The knight frowned. "And what else?"

"She loves a tale, my lord, more than aught else." Célie sighed. "And she is desirous of adventure before she weds, for she fears a life of monotony and duty above all."

A considering light dawned in the knight's eyes and he looked away, his brow furrowed. "Indeed?" he mused.

"I would have you know, sir, that I favor your suit." Célie took a deep breath. "I wish you success in this endeavor, for I think the match a good one."

His sudden smile was so bright that the maid had to blink. She wondered if she had ever seen a man so confident in all her days.

"I thank you," he said, then gave her fingers a squeeze. "But, madame, 'tis not in my nature to lose."

He released her hand and walked away, then swiftly donned his hauberk and cloak. He mounted his destrier, a

sight that made her old heart sing. Célie could not imagine
how Esmeraude could refuse so finely wrought a man, especially one so determined to win her.

Though Célie knew Esmeraude well enough to guess that
this knight would have more adventure in his courtship of
that demoiselle than he likely anticipated. She smiled, uncommonly glad that she would be witness to his suit.

'Twould make a fine fireside tale for those left waiting at
Ceinn-beithe, on this Célie would willingly wager.

❈

Had her father been as selfish as Célie maintained?

Was Esmeraude truly like him?

The two questions plagued Esmeraude as she rode. The
sound of Bayard's pursuit faded to naught behind her. She
reached a road, then slowed the palfrey to a walk. Esmeraude
glanced over her shoulder in indecision.

Indeed, by abandoning her maid to a knight whose intent
she did not know to see to her own safety, Esmeraude was
selfish. Though she hoped that Bayard would be chivalrous
to Célie, she truly did not know what to expect of him. He
had treated Esmeraude with kindness, but then, he had desired something of Esmeraude.

Célie had no such advantage.

'Twas true that there was little Esmeraude could do if she
returned and found the maid abused by the knight. Not only
was Bayard larger and stronger than she, but he had two
healthy boys in his employ. Seeking him out would only
grant him the chance to force her to wed him.

But she could see to Célie's safety in another way. Bayard
would either return to Ceinn-beithe or he would pursue
Esmeraude. She had left the riddle and he might well solve
it. He would certainly be able to pursue her as far as this road
without difficulty, for the horse had left a broken trail
through the undergrowth.

She would wait for him.

In secret, of course. Aye, 'twas the only way to be certain of Célie's fate. If Bayard and Célie did not appear shortly, then she would retrace her steps. Esmeraude urged the steed onward, then led it beneath the shelter of the trees on one side. She returned to the road and removed all hints of the horse's passing, then joined the steed without leaving a trail herself.

She would follow Bayard if he came and perhaps she could intervene if he meant to abuse Célie. She had been raised in this countryside and did not doubt that she could hide her presence as she covertly trailed behind the knight.

She gripped the reins and stood in silence, the steed sufficiently well trained that it echoed her manner, its only movement the flicking of its ears. Her sole fear was that it would make some acknowledgment of the other horses when they appeared.

Bayard was his name. Was he then Bayard de Villonne, the son of Burke de Villonne? Esmeraude's mother, Eglantine, held Burke in great esteem—perhaps the son shared the father's noble character. The possibility cheered her while she waited.

A short time later, Esmeraude heard the canter of horses' hooves and the sound of a party breaking through the undergrowth to the road. She slipped her hand over the palfrey's muzzle and stroked it softly, praying that the beast would remain silent.

"Which way?" Bayard asked, his voice carrying to her refuge.

The palfrey's ears pricked and it strained its neck toward the road. Esmeraude leaned closer herself for a peek and her heart leapt at the sight of Bayard. He wore his full knightly garb save his helmet and his destrier pranced beneath his weight. The boys rode one of the palfreys behind him, and Célie rode the third. She looked well enough and Esmeraude quickly understood why.

"Airdfinnan lies that way," Célie said firmly. " 'Tis two days' ride, sir."

So the maid had won her own safety by offering to guide Bayard's pursuit of Esmeraude. 'Twas not a bad choice on her part, though Esmeraude did not intend to be found by them.

Nay, she would follow and she would wait. Surely when they made camp, she could steal her maid away and leave this knight in the forest.

He would return to whence he had come then, or at least Esmeraude hoped as much. She waited until they were far down the road, then urged the palfrey from the shadows and lent chase.

They took the road she anticipated and Esmeraude was glad, for it twisted and turned as it climbed the hills to the east of Ceinn-beithe. 'Twas easy for her to remain out of sight and she would be so until at least midday on the morrow. After that, the road ran straight as an arrow to Airdfinnan's gates.

Esmeraude resolved to fret about that when the time came. She took one last glance back from the apex of the hills and smiled at the sight of Ceinn-beithe's village touched by sunlight. It looked so peaceful and her heart swelled with affection for all those she loved there.

Her smile faded when she spied a considerable party departing the village gates. They were numerous and she had no doubt that there was at least one suitor in their number. Did they ride to Airdfinnan or did they surrender the chase?

There was no way of knowing from here and Esmeraude

was not inclined to wait. Nay, she would learn the truth after she was safely at Airdfinnan and whatever suitors lent chase also arrived there.

She had best concoct another riddle while she rode, and to do that, Esmeraude had to decide where she would go next. She dug her heels into the palfrey's side and trailed Bayard's party, considering the possibilities.

Chapter Six

BAYARD WAS WELL AWARE THAT HE WAS BEING PURSUED. Indeed, in the past few years, he had learned to be uncommonly aware of his surroundings. And he knew the rhythm of his own steed's hoofbeats well enough to recognize the missing beast's presence. The palfrey behind them started and stopped, which meant it carried a rider whose dictate it followed.

Bayard knew who that rider must be. Annoyance simmered through him. Why would she flee only to trail him? What manner of feminine game was this? Indeed, a man could readily conclude that she sought to vex him apurpose, perhaps to hold his interest.

His Esmeraude had no need of such a ploy. They rode onward, Bayard setting a pace that he knew his palfrey could readily match, and he pondered the complexities of women.

Or more accurately, of one particular woman.

Once Bayard ceased to be thoroughly irked, he had to admit that he was impressed by her tactics. The other three with him were unaware of the lady's presence, for she kept a goodly distance between them. He glanced back once or twice, but she was always behind a curve of the road. And he only heard the palfrey's hoofbeats when he suddenly halted his own steed.

She was clever, his Esmeraude. Pride warmed him and

dismissed the last of his irritation. A wife of such resource would suit him well. He listened to her progress, glad that he could ensure her safety so readily as this, and even allowing the lady a measure of the adventure she evidently craved. 'Twas harmless to continue thus, for he heard no others upon this rural path.

Perhaps she merely wished to be wooed and courted, as women so often did. Bayard had no argument with that. Indeed, he knew that the finest prizes were those less readily won.

He caught a glimpse of Esmeraude when they paused at midday, though Bayard gave no outward sign of having done so. He "forgot" a satchel of provisions and a wineskin when they packed up to ride again, for his lady had need of sustenance and he knew she had none.

Aye, he was protective of those beneath his hand and he told no lie when he pledged to the maid that he believed Esmeraude to already be his lady.

When dusk fell, they made a camp in a clearing not far from the road. The boys gathered wood and lit a fire, then brushed down the steeds. They had dried meat with which to make a simple stew, bread and cheese and apples, which along with the wine would make a fine repast. The smell of the cooking meat carried through the woods and Bayard noted one slender shadow drawing nearer.

He liked that she had the good sense to not linger too far from the fire. He had heard tell of wolves in these woods and he would lose neither steed nor betrothed.

Indeed, 'twould suit him well if Esmeraude joined their camp for then he would be fully assured of her safety. As he stirred the meat, Bayard knew precisely how he would encourage her to do so.

He had remembered a tale he had heard sung recently in France, a long tale of love and loss. It had come into his thoughts with an abruptness that was not characteristic of his memory, but Bayard was reassured by the timeliness of the idea. 'Twas no doubt a portent of success that he should recall this tale now, when he sought to win a lady with a love of tales.

He could not fail.

※

Esmeraude settled in the woods as close to Bayard's fire as she dared, knowing that the woods were filled with predators on her every side. The palfrey needed no command to remain by her side, its ears flicking.

Esmeraude had one frightening moment shortly after her arrival. The palfrey nickered suddenly, when it clearly spied its usual companions on the far side of the clearing. To Esmeraude's dismay, one of them nickered in return. She feared discovery and rose to cover the palfrey's muzzle to encourage it to silence.

But no one in the camp appeared to notice. They were all occupied with their tasks—the boys gathering wood, Célie aiding with the preparation of a meal, Bayard tethering the beasts and beginning to groom his destrier.

The scent of their meal made her belly growl in protest, but Esmeraude had no intent of making her presence clear. She nestled against a tree, cursed the fact that she was unprepared to spend a night in the woods, then yawned mightily.

Though Esmeraude intended to remain awake, she was more tired than she had hoped. She flushed, even in solitude and shadow, recalling all too readily why she had not slept much the night before. She dozed to the murmured sound of conversation and could not halt herself from slipping into the realm of dreams.

Esmeraude awakened abruptly some time later and blinked in the darkness, disoriented and sleepy. Her heart was skipping, as if she had been startled, and she listened for a hint of what had disturbed her. The horse dozed beside her, evidently untroubled.

Night had fallen fully but she was still alone. It had not been a footfall she had heard, or the snap of a twig, or the growl of a wolf. She saw no eyes glowing in the shadows surrounding her. She eyed the patch of star-filled sky visible through the canopy of trees overhead as she listened carefully.

Naught.

Esmeraude peeked over her shoulder to Bayard's camp. The fire had died down to embers, but she could still discern the silhouettes of the horses on the far side of the small clearing. Célie lay bundled against the night and was clearly lost to dreams. Bayard's squires were nestled together near the horses, their hair tousled. They were also obviously asleep.

Esmeraude caught her breath as she spied the silhouette of the knight. He leaned against a tree on the closest side of the clearing, his back to her. She had no way of knowing whether he slept, dozed, or was wide awake.

Until he cleared his throat. Esmeraude nigh jumped from her skin. To her astonishment, Bayard began to softly sing.

> *There was a knight name of Tristran,*
> *Of wide repute throughout the land.*
> *Trained by faithful Governal,*
> *He soon had no foe left in Gaul.*
> *Seeking love, fame, and fortune all,*
> *He came to the King of Cornwall.*
> *"Take me, King Mark, into your hall*
> *I shall be most loyal of all."*
> *King Mark looked on the noble knight.*
> *"We are blessed you arrive this night.*
> *For we are beset by a giant,*
> *Fearsome, hungered and adamant.*

> *He demands youths, to eat his fill,*
> *Else vows to see each of us killed.*
> *I shudder that this creature came.*
> *Morholt is his most dreaded name."*

Esmeraude shivered in delight. There was something deliciously forbidden about hearing Bayard recount a tale, even while he was unaware of her presence. He sang so softly that she was certain he did so for his own amusement alone.

He had a fine voice, as well. 'Twas rich and deep, and she recalled all too readily how huskily he had whispered sweet words to her. Esmeraude hugged her knees and strained her ears to listen, for his quiet words were not easily overheard. She shivered, noting that the air had taken a new chill.

> *Tristran took this task with a bow,*
> *Proved his intent by solemn vow.*
> *The maidens wept, the old men sighed,*
> *As they watched the bold knight ride,*
> *Faithful Governal by his side.*
> *This knight arrived upon the tide:*
> *He was unlike men they had known—*
> *His armor gleamed, his blade it shone,*
> *His horse was fierce, his face was stern.*
> *"So valiant he," the women cried,*
> *"'Tis more than sad that he must die."*
> *For none believed he would return;*
> *As Morholt's strength they had well learned.*

Esmeraude eased around the trunk of the tree, hoping to better hear what promised to be a most interesting tale. No child raised at the knee of Duncan MacLaren could be immune to the allure of a tale. For Esmeraude, tales were wrought of the adventure she so avidly sought.

She slipped closer, then huddled against the darkness of a

massive tree, where the shadows were deeper. She closed her eyes and listened.

> *Brave Tristran rode out without fear.*
> *How bold was he, his intent clear!*
> *'Twas early morn he left the gate,*
> *And soon he stood before his fate.*
> *The giant slept upon the shore;*
> *The ground trembled as he snored;*
> *As tall as five men he would stand;*
> *A horse he could crush within his hand;*
> *A third eye he had in his brow;*
> *And this it was that opened now.*
> *He saw Tristran and made a shout,*
> *That would have turned most men about.*
> *But Tristran met the monster's glance,*
> *Without a quiver in his stance.*
> *He raised his blade and winked his eye,*
> *"Attack me, Morholt, and you die."*
> *Morholt cried, "I shall prove you wrong!*
> *It is to me this land belongs,*
> *And all her spoils shall be mine own,*
> *Even the youths of that fair town.*
> *I shall eat all whom I desire,*
> *Your attack will but earn my ire.*
> *Know well, Tristran from o'er the seas,*
> *You first will see my belly pleased."*

Esmeraude hugged herself, knowing the tale would come aright but anxious for this Tristran before such a foe all the same. 'Twas a heroic tale and one she had never heard before.

That must be the reason her heart raced so wildly.

'Twas most curious, though. Even though she had drawn

closer, it seemed that Bayard's voice was even fainter than before. No doubt he did not wish to awaken the others, but Esmeraude could not bear to miss a morsel of his tale.

She slipped around this tree and crept yet closer. The palfrey she had stolen snorted and Esmeraude froze, certain Bayard would hear the beast. But he began to sing again, evidently also unaware that the horse stepped heavily in pursuit of Esmeraude.

> *Oh, what dire threat that giant made!*
> *What fear he fed in man and maid.*
> *But Tristran did not hesitate.*
> *'Tis valor which makes a knight great.*
> *He spurred his steed and struck a blow*
> *So harsh the giant did bellow.*
> *The pair fought most ferociously,*
> *But they were matched nigh evenly:*
> *To each wound Tristran did bestow,*
> *The giant matched with another blow.*
> *So terrible was their long fight,*
> *That the townsfolk hid far from sight.*
> *But as the darkness made descent,*
> *Morholt leaned down to make his threat:*
> *"You have valor beyond compare*
> *O Tristran, a knight bold and fair,*
> *I know that when I eat your heart,*
> *I will be stronger than King Mark.*
> *All those children will then be mine,*
> *With leisure too for me to dine."*
> *But while the monster made his claim,*
> *Tristran carefully took his aim.*
> *No sooner had boast passed black lips,*
> *Than Morholt's power was eclipsed.*

For Tristran's blade sank in his eye,
And the monster gave a pained cry.
The eye that was betwixt the pair,
No longer would see foul or fair.
That roar carried to King Mark's hall,
Where townsfolk huddled, one and all.
They climbed the walls in time to see,
Morholt stride back into the sea.

Esmeraude sighed with relief that the fiend was banished, then gasped when the palfrey nibbled on the hair at her nape. The beast's lips tickled, but she dared not laugh and draw attention to herself. She shooed the palfrey away silently and the beast snorted loudly enough to wake the dead.

'Twas cursedly cold and she rubbed her arms, sparing a glance to the sky. The stars were nigh obscured, the sky darkening with clouds driven hard by a wind that had not been blowing moments past.

Before Esmeraude could think much of this abrupt change in the weather, Bayard sang again.

Aye, the giant fled Cornwall's coast,
Cursing both Tristran and his host!
The people then were filled with glee,
For noble Tristran set them free.
They cheered when he rode through the gate,
Their gratitude did not abate!
King Mark embraced the valiant knight,
And showered him with jewels bright.
"Tristran is my favored servant
None in this court are more gallant!
No hope had we of a champion.
Only a knight as brave as a lion,
Could succeed at this great task,
And ensure Morholt gone at last."

The people danced, they ate and drank.
Tristran, they could not fully thank.

Bayard stopped to take a sip of wine. Esmeraude watched his arm and heard him lick his lips. She desperately wanted him to continue, for surely this could not be all of Tristran's adventure.

'Twas not.

But there is much they did not know:
It casts a shadow on my brow.
Three barons there were gathered there,
For Tristran's deed, they did not care.
Their hearts were darkened by envy,
'Twas vengeance soon that they would seek.
They had granted King Mark labor,
But they would not share his favor.
They plotted against brave Tristran,
Even as they praised that bold man.
Worse, Morholt fled across the sea,
To have his wound tended by his niece:
A maiden fair, noble and true,
Iseut of beauty and virtue.
She found a shard of Tristran's blade,
In her uncle's wound and she said,
That she would ensure vengeance paid,
By he who the shard fit his blade.

Oh! A beauteous heroine who inadvertently pledged vengeance upon the noble hero. This was the root of a marvelous tale and could only lead to daunting feats! Esmeraude gripped her hands together tightly and waited with much anxiety, but Bayard halted his song.

She was certain he merely caught his breath, but her impatience grew with every passing moment. She waited and waited, but he sang no more. There was naught but silence from the other side of the wall.

She could not even hear Bayard breathing. He did not appear to move.

Surely he had not fallen asleep, right in the midst of such a story? Had he abandoned his tale, with so much of it unsung?

Esmeraude waited impatiently. Did he sing more softly than before, so softly that she could not hear him from this place?

Esmeraude crept closer, then paused. She strained her ears, but heard not a whisper.

Had he been struck dead? He was uncommonly still and Esmeraude was suddenly concerned. She could not imagine why else he would halt his singing so suddenly.

She should ensure his welfare. Why, regardless of her refusal of his suit, there was no one else to offer aid, if he truly had need of it. Jacqueline's father had choked upon a chicken bone, Esmeraude recalled, because no one had come to his aid soon enough.

Though Bayard did not look to be choking. No doubt he had merely fallen asleep, but Esmeraude had to be certain. She crawled forward as quietly as she could, not wanting to awaken him if he did sleep, and her heart pounded so loudly that she was certain its sound would awaken him. She paused on the other side of the tree upon which he leaned, listened, then took a deep breath and slipped around it.

Then surprise stole Esmeraude's breath away.

Bayard grinned at her, his eyes twinkling merrily. 'Twas clear he had known of her presence and had awaited her appearance. He had shed his armor, for he wore dark chausses and a dark tabard over a white chemise that fairly glowed in the moonlight.

"So 'tis true after all that you cannot resist a tale," he mused.

Esmeraude was embarrassed that she had fallen for his ruse so readily and thus was outraged at him for playing it upon her. "You tricked me!"

"Nay, I merely feared you had been lulled to sleep." The glint in his eye made her doubt any such thing.

"You tricked me apurpose," Esmeraude huffed. "You would mock my affection for tales of daring deeds."

"Nay, I simply did not wish to waste my efforts." Bayard coughed delicately, though his eyes still shone with devilry. "A voice, like a fine instrument, needs to be treated with care."

"You mean only to tease me."

He moved quickly and caught her shoulders in his hands. Their eyes were almost at a level and Esmeraude caught her breath when he brought his face close to her own. His grip was firm but gentle. The moonlight made him look dashing and wicked and Esmeraude's heart leapt painfully that she was in his presence yet again.

'Twould have been far simpler to spurn him if he had not been such a handsome man.

Nay, 'twould have been far simpler if he had not *known* he was such a handsome man. It irked Esmeraude beyond all else that she was susceptible in such a predictable way, and she hoped she could hide her response from him.

Those blue eyes shone though, as if they saw her every secret.

"You liked it well enough when I teased you afore," Bayard murmured.

Esmeraude's face heated with a blush, but she held his gaze defiantly. "Aye, but that time, you did not fail to satisfy."

He chuckled, lifting one hand to snare a tendril of her

loose hair. He wound it around his fingertip, holding her gaze all the while. "And what makes you assume that I shall not do so this time?"

'Twas only with greatest difficulty that Esmeraude feigned indifference. "You shall not touch me again," she insisted. "I have spurned your suit and there is naught to be gained by continuing to court me." She pulled back, as if to retreat into the woods, but he held fast to her hair.

Bayard studied her, his thumb caressing the hair wound round his fingertip. When he spoke, his tone was thoughtful. "Most women who granted their favor to a man would be vexed if he did not pledge to wed them afterward."

"I am not most women."

His smile turned rueful. "Aye, I have discerned this already." He gave her curl a tug, and she found herself leaning closer. "Perhaps I should give you some advice," he whispered, his eyes dancing. "If you wish a man to forget you, then you should not behave in such an inexplicable and fascinating way. I am not alone in enjoying the challenge of a puzzle."

'Twas difficult to argue with him, for had she not deliberately presented a puzzle to her suitors, and that for much the same reason? "But I do not wish *you* to be challenged," she said and his merriment disappeared.

"Whyever not?" he demanded, and Esmeraude could see that he was insulted. He frowned at her. "Which of the others has your preference?"

"Well, none of them," she admitted too quickly. Bayard's smile flashed and she was hasty to amend her confession. "Only because I have not spoken with any of them as yet. You may be certain that I will find the right man for me."

But his smile only widened. "Perhaps you have found him already."

"I think not."

"Why?"

Surely it could hurt naught to tell him? 'Twas an excuse and Esmeraude knew it. Truly though, being alone in the woods had little to recommend it when contrasted with a conversation with Bayard.

In the shadows of the night, when none knew they were together. Esmeraude shivered, knowing that she would prefer a deed more forbidden and adventurous than a mere night's slumber.

Had she not made the same choice the night before?

But this was good sense. Perhaps talking to him would make his unsuitability clear. 'Twas evident that they had wasted little time upon conversation the night before and truly, lust made a poor match.

And he was wondrously warm, as well. She shivered and found herself leaning against his heat before she could stop herself.

She also found herself telling him more than was her original intent. "I will not wed you because you wish to wed me solely to win Ceinn-beithe," she confessed. " 'Tis insulting to be desired for one's dowry alone and I would have more from the man I would wed. A dowry is meant to bless the match already desired, not to be the sole reason for it."

Bayard frowned. "But I have no desire for Ceinn-beithe."

"But you said . . ."

He interrupted her with a dismissive wave. "To be sure, 'tis a fine holding and if it becomes my responsibility as a result of wedding you, then I shall do my best to administer it well, but Ceinn-beithe is *not* the reason I pursue you." He spoke with such vigor that she did not doubt 'twas the truth.

Though still, this did not agree with what he said earlier. "But you spoke of a holding. . . ."

Something flashed in his eyes, then Bayard looked as

resolute and trustworthy as the moment before. And he spoke with uncommon conviction. "Aye, *my* holding, which I will administer with a bride by my side." He smiled as he slipped an arm around her shoulders. "Is it not natural for a man to wish for a wife and sons when he takes his hereditary holding in hand? I wish only for a fine lady to share my good fortune."

Esmeraude stared at him, amazed that she could have so mistaken his meaning. Her heart began to pound with such vigor that she could barely catch her breath. If Bayard did not wish to wed her for Ceinn-beithe, then he was not the man she had feared he was.

"What is your name fully?" she asked.

He smiled. "Bayard de Villonne—knight, crusade, and champion—at your service, my lady fair."

He kissed the side of her neck and Esmeraude closed her eyes as she sighed with delight. Bayard was Burke's son, and clearly had inherited his father's determination to wed the woman he chose.

Which forced her to reconsider Célie's insistence upon this match. Bayard treated her with such gallantry; he recounted tales for her pleasure; he insisted upon ensuring her welfare in a most wondrously protective way. He was alluring and charming. Indeed, he possessed every trait which she had insisted she would have in a spouse, save that he believed he had need of a bride.

Since Esmeraude wanted a man like this knight as her spouse, she supposed 'twas a deficiency she could overlook.

Aye, 'twould be simple to lose her heart to this man.

Perhaps she was already beginning to do so. And surely, he only courted her favor with such diligence because he was smitten with her, as well? Perhaps 'twas naught but male pride that prompted him to deride the promise of love in front of his squires.

"And you would have me be that bride?" Esmeraude asked.

Bayard chuckled and she warmed to her toes. "Aye, you, Esmeraude. You are my betrothed and you will be my lady wife." He kissed the tip of her nose, then rose to lead his errant palfrey to the other horses.

He was gentle, and kind with his horses. Esmeraude liked that. She watched him move with easy grace and her heart thumped. Even if he did not believe in the merits of love, perhaps she could change his thinking.

He had, after all, pursued her. 'Twould seem the winning of her was more important to him than he would readily admit. And he did not seek her dowry, so what other reason might there be? 'Twas small encouragement, but 'twas all Esmeraude needed to convince her that she alone held the key to winning Bayard's heart.

Bayard rubbed the steed's ears and spoke to it, urging it to some feed, then brushed off his hands. He retrieved his cloak and returned to Esmeraude, his eyes gleaming.

"I had thought the best man for me would be one not even seeking a bride," she said.

Bayard's expression turned skeptical as he shook out his fur-lined cloak. "You seek a man already wed then?"

Esmeraude laughed. "Nay, but I desire a man who is not intent upon having a bride as one has other possessions."

His smile made her tingle. "What of a man who sought a bride for the sake of necessity and tradition, but found a treasure instead?" Bayard wrapped the cloak around his shoulders, so that it swirled with a fine flourish. He then squatted down before her, his eyes bright.

"A treasure?"

"A lady of more wit and passion than anticipated, and a beauty as well." He lifted her hand and kissed her palm, his touch making Esmeraude's pulse race. "A treasure most rare and one to be prized above all else. Not all wonders are found when they are sought. Indeed, I have heard it said that the marvels of life cannot be found if actively pursued."

"You seem determined in your suit," Esmeraude said coyly, hoping for a sweet confession to make this moment perfect.

Bayard leaned yet closer, the moonlight glinting upon his hair. His thumb ran across her knuckles in a caress that made her mouth go dry. "Much has passed between us, Esmeraude, and a man of honor must do what is right by his lady fair. Though you left me, I knew 'twas due to a misunderstanding."

"You knew I followed you," Esmeraude guessed.

Bayard's smile broadened. "A man with less training would never have heard your pursuit." He kissed her palm. "You are most clever, my lady."

Esmeraude's pulse echoed in her throat. Oh, she had made a fine choice.

" 'Tis true that I coaxed you closer apurpose." Bayard regarded her warmly. "I heard that you had much affection for a tale, and it seemed a fitting way to see to your safety this night. 'Tis not fitting, Esmeraude, that even a lady upon an adventure should sleep alone and unprotected in the wilderness. As my intended, you are my responsibility and I would ensure your welfare for all our days and nights together."

Esmeraude could think of naught to say to that. Indeed, she quite liked his protectiveness.

Bayard smiled and offered his hand. "Come hither, my Esmeraude," he murmured, heat in his words. "And reward your faithful courtier with a kiss."

Esmeraude could think of no finer way to seal their pledge. She moved into his embrace and touched her lips to Bayard's, loving how possessively his mouth closed over her own. He drew them to their feet without breaking his kiss, then wrapped his cloak securely around her.

When he finally lifted his head, Esmeraude found herself breathless. "I thank you for showing kindness to Célie," she said, wanting to acknowledge his courtesy. "I had hoped you would do so."

"And your trust was not misplaced." Bayard seemed to like that she had expected this of him. " 'Twas she who confided your fondness for tales, for she confessed her own support for my pursuit of you."

That pleased Esmeraude, for Célie knew her well and knew her objectives just as well. The maid's endorsement of Bayard once she knew more of him only increased Esmeraude's certainty in her choice. "Is that why you sing to me?" she teased, hoping again for a sweet confession.

"A man must do what he must to win a lady's regard." Then Bayard began to softly sing once more. Esmeraude sighed contentment, and leaned her cheek against his chest. She closed her eyes, listening to his song and the thrum of his heartbeat.

Indeed, there was much of this man to love.

> *King Mark had need of a fair queen:*
> *He desired a bride with eyes green;*
> *Fair golden locks that fell like waves;*
> *A face that might a man enslave.*
> *He would have a bride true of heart,*
> *Loyal, blessed with love stalwart.*
> *This maid he would cherish and love;*
> *This maid would bear his many sons.*
> *He knew not where to find his match,*
> *But he guessed who best to dispatch.*
> *None other did he trust so well,*
> *As that knight who with him did dwell.*
> *"Tristran," said the king, "Hear my word:*
> *You can see my sweet yearning cured.*

You who are as brethren mine own,
Go find the maid to share my crown!
Spare no distance, turn from no foe,
I care not how far you must go,
But find a maid to hold my heart.
A beauty true, go now, depart!
Return to me with such a bride,
Worthy of sitting by my side,
And I shall see you lack for naught.
Your labors shall not be forgot."

She could imagine that Bayard had been dispatched by his father to find his bride, just as the knight in the song had been dispatched by his liege lord. And Bayard's father, Burke, was said to have been uncommonly diligent in pursuit of the lady who held his heart in thrall, the lady who had become his wife. Esmeraude had heard that tale more times than she could count.

Like father, like son. The thought made her smile.

Bayard kissed her lingeringly between the verses and she knew that this was the man of whom she had dreamed. Aye, he would follow her to the ends of Christendom to make her his own, just like a hero in a *chanson*.

But unlike lovers in a *chanson*, they had resolved their small misunderstanding, rather than losing all to some dire fate. Such foolishness made a better tale than a life. Aye, 'twas the mark of a good match to unravel such confusions.

Esmeraude thought it a good portent that Bayard was not so stubborn as to leave a matter be, and resolved to be as dutiful in this regard as he.

He smiled down at her and sang low.

Tristran rushed forth to do this deed.
He left that day to cross the sea,
Certain this maid would be best found,

Far afield, exotic and proud.
Waves cast him upon Ireland's coast,
Where fearsome dragon made his roost.
What a terror that creature was!
His scales shone brightly like red glass,
His claws were fierce, his teeth yet more,
His breath was fire, his blows were sure.
He attacked Tristran landing there:
His bellow singed the knight's fair hair!
But Tristran showed no fear at all,
He fought the beast at the town walls.
And all the town was there to see,
The savior knight brought by the sea.
He killed the beast before their eyes,
But the dying beast claimed a price.
In his last breath he bit the knight,
His poison felled Tristran that night.

Esmeraude gripped Bayard, fearing the outcome for the knight of his tale. The wind danced through the forest behind them, scattering twigs and rustling the branches. He smiled reassuringly at her.

The people cried and gnashed their teeth,
That Tristran should be trapped in sleep.
They carried him into the town,
And summoned healers of renown.
'Twas thus that Iseut first saw him,
Though Tristran's fate did seem most grim.
She tended him better than all,
For her skill was not at all small.
And as he healed, Iseut could see,
That this man was wrought most finely.
She saw the notch within his blade,
But could not fulfill her pledge made.

She could not avenge her own kin,
Against a man so lacking sin,
That he would battle so for those,
Who could not defeat their own foes.
So well did Iseut tend the knight,
That he awoke in a fortnight.
As soon as he saw her visage,
Then he knew that she was the prize,
Sought by King Mark to be his bride.
And so he sought to win her hand,
For the king of a distant land.

"She healed him," Esmeraude whispered.

"Aye, perhaps even with a kiss as potent as your own." Bayard claimed another kiss, which Esmeraude was only too happy to grant him. 'Twas simply too wondrous to be courted like this, to be kissed within the shelter of his cloak and beneath a starry sky.

"Nay, 'twas with her love," she insisted when they parted. "I am certain they were destined lovers."

Bayard said naught to that but sang again, his gaze locked with her own.

Iseut's parents liked well this thought,
Iseut herself objected naught.
So Tristran made plans to depart,
To escort damsel to King Mark.
Iseut's mother had but one fear:
That her daughter find her spouse dear.
"Take this potion, child of my womb.
Guard it well and savor it soon,
Do so with your betrothed alone,
For it shall make his heart your own.
And your heart shall be held by him,
For it has this magic within."

She sent, too, with Iseut a maid,
Trusted so well, name of Brangain.
Word sent King Mark that all was well,
The townsfolk waved the ship farewell.
Four souls sailed for distant Cornwall,
For there, too, was good Governal.
But on the seas, Brangain did err:
She poured the potion in her care,
For Tristran and Iseut, alas!
Not after Iseut's nuptial mass.
So they two were sorely smitten,
With love that could not be hidden,
And forgetting full the king ahead,
Iseut took Tristran to her bed.

Bayard fell silent, though he arched a brow expectantly.

"Where would we go?" Esmeraude whispered, sparing a glance for the others in the clearing.

Bayard grinned wickedly. "What is amiss with this place?" he whispered, then swept her up into his arms. The generous width of his cloak enfolded them and Esmeraude curled closer to him. The echo of his heartbeat so close to her own and the warmth of him surrounding her made her forget the inclement weather.

His proximity made her forget all but him.

Bayard leaned closer and dropped his voice to a mischievous whisper. "Your maid will hardly be alarmed to find us together in the morn."

'Twas true enough.

His hand slid beneath the hem of her skirts, his fingers making her gasp with delight. "Kiss me, Esmeraude. Let me taste you as you find your pleasure."

Esmeraude felt suddenly shy, though the cloak hid his hands from view. "Here?" she asked, her voice higher than usual. She spared a glance for Célie. As a child, she had been convinced that her vigilant maid saw doings even in her sleep and even now, Esmeraude was not unpersuaded of that.

Bayard leaned closer, a wicked glint in his eyes. "I confess myself surprised by your modesty." He feigned astonishment. "Is it possible that I have lured a demure maid, instead of my adventurous Esmeraude?"

Esmeraude laughed. "But what shall we tell them in the morn?"

He chuckled. "No less than the truth, which they already know. Come, lady mine, welcome me."

His fingers slipped between her thighs again, but Esmeraude's hands fell boldly to the knot of his chausses.

"Not that this night," he whispered with a fleeting frown. "Not here."

Esmeraude offered a wicked smile of her own. "Surely, sir, you do not suggest that I wed a man less adventurous than myself." She untied the laces and slipped her hands around him, her touch silencing his protest before it had begun.

Bayard's eyes shone, their hue bluer than blue. He gasped as Esmeraude straddled him, then he caught her buttocks in his hands and urged her closer. "Know, my Esmeraude, that you have need of naught this night but me," he whispered, then kissed her fully.

Indeed, Esmeraude knew that she would have need of naught for all her days and nights than this knight.

Chapter Seven

THAT EVENING, THERE WERE THOSE AT CEINN-BEITHE less content with their lot than Esmeraude and Bayard. Eglantine did not sleep, though she imagined that Duncan did. She tossed and turned restlessly, unable to think of anything beyond her youngest daughter virtually alone in the wild.

There had been little consolation in realizing that Esmeraude had fled to the King of the Isles. She had always had a faith in that man's goodwill toward her. Eglantine knew that he cared only for his own advantage and feared the worst.

She sighed and rolled over again, trying to be silent yet unable to be still.

"There is naught to be achieved by fretting," Duncan murmured, his words too clear for him to have been sleeping.

Eglantine propped herself up on her elbows and stared down at him. Though their chamber was filled with shadows, she could see the gleam of his eyes. "We should have compelled her to wed someone, anyone! We should have seen to it that she was protected."

" 'Twould have broken her spirit, and truly, Esmeraude's spirit is a rare marvel."

"You cannot agree with what she has done!"

"Nay, I do not." Duncan sat up and donned a chemise with

impatient gestures, his brow furrowed. "But I recognize a matter in which I cannot interfere."

"Cannot or will not? We might have sent men after her. You might have pursued her!"

"To what end?" 'Twas the closest they had come to an argument in years, with Eglantine's accusation hanging between them. Duncan sighed. "Eglantine, fully six men lent chase, most of them knights. They will find her and ensure her welfare."

Eglantine sighed in her turn, then rose from the bed. "If the King of the Isles does not make some trouble for her first."

"Are you not reassured that Célie accompanied her?"

"Some. Are you not worried?"

Duncan smiled slightly. "I am nigh ill with the worrying, my love. And I sent two men to the king's court, to ensure that Esmeraude arrived there safely. But beyond that, little can be done. We have guests aplenty, which precludes our own departure."

Eglantine sighed and paced the chamber, well aware that her spouse's watchful gaze followed her.

"The skill in raising children, I do believe, is in knowing when to save a child from falling and when to let her fall in the hope that she might learn aught of the world."

Eglantine stared grimly at the ceiling, unpersuaded.

"Esmeraude is stubborn, as we both know," Duncan said gently. "I do not think we could have built a prison strong enough to keep her from this course."

"That is no excuse for doing naught."

"We have not done naught. We have raised her to show sense and discipline, we have taught her to hunt, to sail, to ride a horse, to seek aid when she has need of it. We have instilled the best of what we know in her—"

"I am not content to hope for the best," Eglantine snapped, turning upon her spouse. "You place too much credence in good fortune and good thinking! For the love of God, Esmeraude is so impetuous that she is capable of finding trouble in her own chamber!" She turned away from Duncan's considering glance and felt her tears rise.

"You cannot protect her forever, Eglantine," he said softly.

"But I want to," she whispered, and to her dismay, her tears broke at the admission. She caught her breath in a sob, trying to hide her own weakness, but Duncan knew her too well.

He crossed the room to catch her close, holding her fast against his chest. "She will be well, for she is clever. She is with Célie, a paragon of good sense. And she has half a dozen determined men pursuing her, each and every one of whom is noble in his objectives."

" 'Tis not enough!"

" 'Tis all we have. There is naught else to be done now."

"You could go after her!"

"She might not even be at the king's court any longer. And she would not heed me even if she was, as we both know well." Eglantine looked up and Duncan smiled ruefully. "Our Esmeraude is set upon adventure and there is nary an adventure to be found with one's stepfather." He gave her a shake, clearly guessing her next argument. "And even less with one's own mother. Do you not recall what it is to be young and filled with the certainty of one's own immortality?"

"I recall well enough that it is a lie."

"She will not believe you until she discovers the truth of it herself." Duncan kissed Eglantine's brow. "We always knew that Esmeraude would pose a challenge, and we have more than sufficient experience that she will insist upon her own way alone. Should we retrieve her, even if 'twere possible, she would do this again, perhaps without Célie and a bevy of knights. We have done what could be done, now let us pray that all finds a good ending."

Eglantine heaved a sigh and dried her tears. "We should have planned better for this eventuality."

"Ah, and to look back is always to see matters more clearly."

There was a wistfulness in Duncan's tone. Eglantine peered at her spouse and saw the lines of care in his brow. "You are not so confident in this as you would pretend."

He shrugged, then managed a smile. "Is it not my place to reassure my lady's doubts?"

"Even if you share them?"

They smiled at each other for a moment, then embraced tightly. Eglantine buried her face in his shoulder, taking comfort in his solidity and dependability, then raised her face in sudden alarm. "You do not think that this madness might inspire Mhairi to do the same?"

Duncan frowned and said not a word.

"She is always so admiring of Esmeraude and of Esmeraude's boldness." A lump rose in Eglantine's throat. "Even this afternoon, she spoke of how marvelous 'twas to have knights lingering at Ceinn-beithe. God in heaven, we could not lose them both to such folly! Could we?"

Duncan swore, then a gleam lit his eyes. "I fear that your instincts are right. But we can wrest security from this circumstance."

"How?"

Duncan caught her hands in his, his words falling fast. "By challenging those knights who remained to compete for Mhairi's hand. They have complained that they came to tourney, not to chase a damsel through the wilderness."

"But I would have her wed for love!"

"Mhairi is so enthralled with them that I am certain one will win her heart in truth. Think of it, Eglantine! The pageantry will delight all, and it might even ease your worries. And 'twill ensure that these knights do not feel they have traveled so far for naught, which would be diplomatically astute."

"And then Mhairi might have both spouse and champion. Duncan, 'tis a wondrous idea!"

The pair shared a long embrace, then Eglantine pulled back to regard her spouse warmly. "You are a most clever man, and by far the finest father I have had the good fortune to wed." Duncan arched a brow, a smile beginning to curve his lip. "I think such an idea deserves a celebration."

"Aye? And have you any thoughts on the manner of celebration?"

Eglantine wound her arms around her husband's neck, determined to end their talk and end it immediately. She still fretted for Esmeraude, but as always Duncan spoke good sense. There was little she could do now but pray.

And see to it that such folly did not happen again. Aye, Eglantine was more than ready to have the last of her daughters safely wed.

There was one other displeased soul at Ceinn-beithe, one whom none would have expected to be riled. He was more vexed when Eglantine and Duncan made their announcement in Ceinn-beithe's hall the morning after Esmeraude's departure and the knights gathered there cheered at the prospect of a tourney. That Mhairi blushed with evident delight did little to improve his mood.

Well before noon that same day, Finlay MacCormac watched his mother work in their kitchen and brooded. He was typically a cheerful young man, and he thought none noted the change in his mood. He would have been surprised to realize how many commented upon the recent change in him in the village.

But then, he likely would not have cared, for his dissatisfaction consumed him. Finlay lingered at the table, not by deliberate choice, but by some intuitive conviction that Alienor would know what should be done.

If only he knew how to ask for her suggestion without revealing his every thought. 'Twas not easily done with his mother, with her shrewd gaze that seemed most adept at discovering a young man's every secret yearning. He toyed with a mug, driving it across the surface of the heavy table, knowing full well that she flicked more than one interested glance his way.

At thirty-six summers, Alienor was a striking woman, though her son saw none of her charms. No longer the dewy-cheeked maiden she had been upon arriving at Ceinn-beithe, she had been toughened by the life she led here. She was all sinew and lean strength these days, her complexion tanned to a warm gold and her dark hair streaked with bands of silver.

Yet at the same time, Alienor's manner had been softened by marriage, by gain and loss, by merriment and strife. She was much more difficult to rile than once she had been, she had a smile that could warm the coldest heart, and she saw far more than her children wished she did.

Finlay, for his part, knew only that his mother might as well have the Sight, for never was any secret held long in their household. But he lingered all the same, a part of him wanting to be found out so that she might offer a solution.

He stared into the depths of his cup as his father's whistling carried from the smithy beyond the house. They lived well, for Iain's reputation as a silversmith had spread far, and more than one ship that put in at Ceinn-beithe's harbor sought his wares. Finlay knew that his father could wring magic from his forge, and that the silver work he conjured must be touched by the favor of the fey to be as beauteous as it was.

He also knew that he himself could chop wood in his sleep, so much of it was needed in this household.

Their house had been the first built of wattle and daub in Ceinn-beithe and Finlay knew his mother was ferociously proud of that fact, no less than of her favored skillet, brought by her half-sister Jacqueline from Crevy-sur-Seine in distant France. She eased that skillet over the fire as he watched and dropped a bit of fat into it, apparently interested overmuch in its sizzle.

"You had best tell me her name," she said firmly, her back half turned to him. "I shall hear the truth of it soon enough."

Finlay jumped. "Whose name?"

His mother laughed. "The maid who has you sighing when there is wood to be chopped." She nodded satisfaction at the heated fat then dropped lumps of batter into the pan. The smell of their cooking filled the house and made Finlay hungry again.

Alienor shook a finger at him, interpreting his expression rightly. "You will chop that wood afore you eat again, young man. I shall have some labor of you before you eat every morsel in this household."

"Mhairi says 'tis healthy for a man my age to be hungry."

"Mhairi, is it?" His mother's dark brows rose. "And what does that young maiden know of growing boys and men?"

Finlay felt a blush rise from the tips of his toes, for he did not doubt that his mother knew he had answered her earlier question as well. "She has cousins."

"As do you." Alienor cast a quick, knowing glance across the room. Her son's face heated yet further, for Mhairi was his cousin by marriage if not by blood. "So, 'tis Mhairi who has stolen your heart, is it?"

Finlay knew he turned crimson. "Mother!"

She laughed. "Oh, I am embarrassing you, am I? Well, then, you had best be about your labor."

But he did not go and he knew she did not truly expect him to. Indeed, she did not so much as glance over her shoulder before she spoke again.

"I suppose there is no shame in it," she mused. "Though you and Mhairi have been raised as family, in truth there is no blood between you. She is three summers younger than you. Now, what of Mhairi?"

Finlay was tempted to deflect his mother's inquiry, yet more tempted to have her advice. "'Tis not fair! 'Tis not fair that she should be compelled to choose from Esmeraude's leavings! Mhairi is the seed of both Eglantine and Duncan, and as such, *she* should be the heiress to Ceinn-beithe! 'Tis not right that Duncan should overlook his sole child in favor of the daughter of another man."

"'Tis only her legacy that troubles you?" Alienor asked mildly, turning each cake over carefully to cook on the other side.

"Aye," Finlay began, momentarily seeking to hide his feelings, then turned suddenly and pounded his fist upon the table. "Nay! 'Tis more than that! 'Tis not fair to *me*! I have waited, I have been honorable; I thought her too young to be courted and now, *now*, all these men from distant lands with riches and fine manners and tales of valiant deeds shall woo her and win her. 'Tis not fair!"

He folded his arms upon the table and dropped his chin upon his fists, defeated. His voice was small when he continued. "And even if I were to court her now, she would not take note of me among such lavish company. She has barely acknowledged me these past days."

Alienor coaxed the cakes from the skillet in silence, then brought the platter to the table where they steamed before Finlay. She set the skillet carefully aside—though he knew she had more batter—poured another cup of ale, then sat down opposite him.

She smiled as she reached across the board and ran a fingertip down his cheek. "Look at you," she whispered. "A man, indeed, at seventeen, with lovely golden curls and eyes as blue as a summer sky."

"Mother!"

Undeterred, she touched the dimple in his chin and her smile broadened. "You are the image of your father when he and I first met, and I tell you that he stole my heart fair and true."

Finlay straightened. "How?"

His mother's smile turned mysterious. "He made clear his desire for me. He stole a kiss and told me that we were intended for each other. There is naught more tempting to a woman than the love of a man who would honor her above all others."

"I do not think so. Have you looked upon these men who came?"

"Aye, I have, and there is not a one of them who knows aught of Mhairi. There is not a one of them who is smitten with her for the sake of her alone, there is not a one of them who loves her as you do. 'Tis a rare advantage you have in this, Finlay, and one you would be a fool not to exploit."

"But I know not what to do!"

Alienor rolled her eyes. "Then you had best think upon it. There never was a man served his heart's desire while he sat at his mother's board and felt such sorrow for his own poor self." She gave him a hard look, then rose to her feet and returned to her labor. "There are those less fortunate than you in all of Christendom."

"Aye, aye, those with empty bellies and no roof over their heads," Finlay said, repeating a familiar litany. "Those whose parents do not labor hard or do not find success in their endeavors, those whose homelands are less blessed than our own."

"Those who sleep in the churchyard," his mother said

tartly. " 'Tis not every child who lives to see his seventeenth summer, and that hale and hearty."

Finlay met her gaze, knowing full well that she spoke of her third child, the one who would have been his youngest sister. He had been six when that babe came and he had known even then that 'twas not right that its cries did not begin when his mother's ceased. His mother had never ripened with child again, and oft proclaimed that two children—himself and his younger sister Margaret—were more than enough trouble for her.

" 'Tis fine enough to say," Finlay charged, comforted by her stern talk but still not certain of his path. "But there is now to be a tourney two days hence betwixt those men who would win Mhairi's hand. I know not how to compete in such an event and I have no armor, even if I would be a contender."

His mother eyed the fat with concentration but he knew she was deciding what to say to him. When she spoke, her voice was low. "When first we came to Ceinn-beithe, there was an old comrade of Duncan's, filled to the teeth with proverbs. Gillemore is long gone from this earth, though still I hear his grumbling voice hereabouts. He oft said that if you have only got one eye, then look with the eye you have got."

"And what is that to mean?"

"You may have no armor, but you have your wits, Finlay." Alienor flashed him an impish smile. "And from your mother's side, you have gained wits better than most. You have but to use them, and use them with your father's rare persistence."

"Wits are no defense against a knight's armor!"

"Nay, they are a greater one." She dropped batter into the sizzling fat. "I daresay you might win against the mightiest foe, should you put your thinking to that end." She winked at him. "But then, my opinion is biased."

He smiled back at her, much encouraged, then dared her wrath to take two of the cakes she had set on the board to cool. At her cry of mock outrage, his grin widened. "I have need of my strength to chop that wood."

"Oh, your father's audacity and my wits. You are a fearsome foe, indeed, Finlay MacCormac," she teased. "Get away with you and finish your labor this morn afore you forget it completely."

Finlay waved cockily as he ducked out the door, then sharpened his axe with purpose, his thoughts spinning.

His mother spoke aright. Somehow, he had to outwit his competitors for Mhairi's hand, or risk losing her forever. His heart tightened at the prospect of her wedding another.

Nay, he had to do his best to keep her from choosing one of those men. He still might lose her hand, but 'twould be better than losing her for the lack of trying at all.

He made quick work of the woodpile that morn and 'twas not merely his mother's baking that fueled him to greater speed. Aye, with each blow of the axe, Finlay became more resolute.

He could win Mhairi.

Was it not said that the will would find the way?

Chapter Eight

IN OTHER CIRCUMSTANCE, BAYARD MIGHT HAVE BEEN tempted to believe that all was well once again. But his lady had surprised him more than once thus far and he did not believe that she would not do so again.

She was unpredictable, his Esmeraude.

Bayard lay beside her, determined to remain awake even though he was dead tired, and acknowledged that unpredictability was a most intriguing trait. He had always expected marriage to be an obligation, one with its pleasures to be sure, but a duty that would not occupy his thoughts overmuch. He had need of a wife because he had need of sons. 'Twould be a simple arrangement.

And now, he had need of this wife, because he had need of Montvieux, for pledging it to Richard would ensure his family's safety. Simplicity, again.

But little was simple about Esmeraude. Bayard had certainly never anticipated that a single woman would hold his attention so surely as Esmeraude did, certainly not that any woman would do so for the better part of his life. He had anticipated that the price of his insistence upon not wedding for love—as his parents had done—could well be a lack of passion in his nuptial bed. He had expected to seek passion elsewhere. Bayard slanted a glance to his sleeping betrothed and smiled.

Esmeraude had a way of holding his eye and Bayard guessed that might never change. To his own surprise, he was untroubled by this. He liked her passion and fire. And the issue of love was resolved between them, he was certain, his own view much more sensible than her own whimsical ideal. She cuddled against him now, disheveled and flushed, her hair tumbling across his arm and his cloak in glorious disarray.

'Twas quiet in the clearing and Bayard felt more at peace than he had in years. Aye, 'twas no doubt due to how well his scheme came together. Bayard leaned back, contented with what he had wrought, and yawned mightily as he stared at the clouds scuttling overhead.

And felt a pang of guilt. There was no evading the fact that he had told his lady a lie. He knew it should not have concerned him to tell one lie to win Montvieux and ensure that the greater good was served.

But still.

But still.

He had no holding, not as yet, not until Esmeraude wedded him and Margaux knew of those nuptials. And in the strictest sense, Montvieux was not his hereditary estate, though it could be argued that it should have been. Worse, he *did* wed Esmeraude for an estate, though not for humble Ceinnbeithe.

He knew enough of his lady to guess that the distinction would be as naught to her.

Esmeraude need never know the truth of it, Bayard reminded himself firmly. Indeed, they would return to France and she would witness his acceptance of the seal of Montvieux and never know the full tale.

As long as none of his family told her. His heart clenched, though he knew 'twas only the possibility of her spurning him that was worrisome. He stole a glance at her and was less certain of the root of his worry than he might have hoped to be.

Then he had a cheering thought. By the time his family could divulge the truth, Esmeraude might already be ripe with his seed. That deed might have been accomplished this night or last. Though Esmeraude would almost certainly be irked to hear such a revelation, surely no woman would leave her spouse with a babe in her belly.

Would she?

Would any woman leave a life of wealth and comfort such as he could offer at Montvieux for the uncertainty of life beyond its walls? Even if she would do as much herself, surely she would not condemn her child to such a fate?

Bayard eyed his unpredictable betrothed and was not entirely certain. But what choice had he had? It had been clear how upset Esmeraude was to be wed for whatever holding she might bring to her spouse's hand—he had understood that whether 'twas Ceinn-beithe or Montvieux would not matter. Bayard knew she had no objections to his suit otherwise, for she welcomed him between her thighs with uncommon gusto, and he would not lose her over such a detail.

His embrace tightened slightly and the lady eased closer, smiling as she did so. Aye, his lie was an insignificantly small detail, a necessity.

Was it not?

Esmeraude's head placed so trustingly upon his shoulder made Bayard feel like a cur, but he knew he had chosen wisely. They would be wed and they would be wed soon, and they would live happily at Montvieux.

Hopefully. Bayard had best make it a priority to place a babe within his bride's belly, with no regard for counting fingers and whispers if their first child came in haste. The lady, quite to his delight, seemed as intent upon this course as he was himself.

"What happened next?" Esmeraude murmured and he started at the sound of her voice.

Bayard glanced down to find her eyes just barely open, a sliver of sapphire visible between those luxuriant lashes. She had the look of a well-sated cat and he was pleased to be the one responsible for her contentment. He arched a brow, not understanding her question, and when she smiled, he had the impulse to make her cry out in pleasure again.

She propped herself up on her elbow, evidently unaware of how her unfastened chemise gaped open. *His* chemise. His surge of possessive pride surprised Bayard. Her hair spilled over her shoulders, her lips were ruddy and slightly swollen from his kisses. Bayard was certain that the sirens could not have looked more tempting than this.

"Tell me what happened to Tristran and Iseut," Esmeraude said, tapping him with a playful fingertip. "You said that she welcomed him to her bed."

Bayard smiled. "I suspect what happened was much what happened here. I could show you instead, if you prefer."

His lady rolled to her back and laughed under her breath when he followed her, her eyes sparkling. "But I would have the rest of the tale. What happened after that?"

Bayard stole a kiss that quickly took on a heat of its own. "Perhaps they repeated the deed," he murmured.

Esmeraude chuckled, sparing a cautious glance to the others still asleep but not far away. "After the loving, what did they do?" She poked his shoulder. "You must tell me."

"Perhaps you should *persuade* me."

She pounced upon him then, but to his astonishment, she tickled him to win her way. They tumbled across his cloak like playful children, trying to stifle their laughter. Bayard had not been tickled in years. Esmeraude's giggles were the happiest sound he had heard in a long while, and he grinned himself when he discovered that the arches of her feet were particularly sensitive.

He tormented her until she begged for mercy, but when he moved to claim a victorious kiss, she eluded him. She slipped behind him, her fingers between his ribs with alarming speed, and he found himself helpless with laughter in turn.

"Surrender to me, Bayard," she whispered in his ear.

"I surrender!" He gasped out the words even as he squirmed.

"Ooh, a knight surrendering to a mere maiden." Esmeraude laughed. "I shall have need of a witness for none will believe me. Perhaps we should awaken the others."

"I told you . . ." Bayard's claim was never finished, for his intended leapt astride him. She caught his wrists and pinned them to the ground, so pleased with herself that he had no desire to break free.

"Aye, you told me that I had need of naught this night but you," she whispered. She leaned closer, granting him an enticing view of her breasts. "But the truth is that now I have need of the tale only you can share. Will you not share it with me?" She punctuated her request with a kiss that stirred his soul.

"Perhaps you are not so innocent as I believed," he teased when he could speak.

"Perhaps I have had a most diligent teacher," she retorted.

Bayard chuckled until she kissed him again.

"Are you persuaded yet?" she asked pertly.

He shook his head, intrigued at what she might do next. "I can be most determined."

Esmeraude rolled her eyes. "Stubborn is what we call it hereabouts," she chided, then fell upon him in a most delightful way. She kissed his throat, then whispered into his ear so huskily that her breath made him shiver. "But I wager that I am more stubborn than you are, knight of mine."

Hers was a persistence that met little objection from Bayard. Indeed, they loved again with sweet vigor, ignoring the increasing chill in the air. Then they curled within the warmth of his cloak, limbs entangled. The forest around them was filling with a low fog that obscured the undergrowth, as if the clouds that hid the stars had fallen to earth. It suited Bayard well enough, for that fog brought a damp chill that had his lady pressing against him.

He met her expectant gaze then heaved a sigh of mock concession. Bayard ran a fingertip over Esmeraude's cheek, and smiled at the anticipation in her eyes. "I suppose I could tell you more of the tale."

"All of it!"

" 'Tis cursedly long. It could take a lifetime to tell you all of it."

The prospect did not seem to trouble her. "Then tell me a measure more of it now."

So he did.

> The pair loved the journey away,
> Until arrived the fateful day,
> Their vessel sailed into Cornwall.
> King Mark's bride was welcomed by all,
> The King was delighted in truth,
> By Tristran's bringing his pledged due.
> Iseut was garbed in royal red,
> A crown hung o'er the nuptial bed . . .

"Wait!" Esmeraude whispered in horror and pushed away. "Iseut did not wed King Mark, did she?"

Bayard could not understand her dismay. "Certainly she did."

"But she was in love with Tristran!"

"It matters naught. She was pledged to wed King Mark by her own agreement."

Esmeraude sat up fully, more distraught than Bayard thought the matter deserved. 'Twas clear that he and his intended saw this issue differently—and as it involved betrothals and the keeping of a pledge, Bayard thought it necessary that they come to an agreement.

"But that was *before* she loved Tristran," Esmeraude insisted. "Her choice of spouse should change because the inclination of her heart had changed."

This was a truly dangerous premise, to Bayard's thinking, and he spoke even more firmly than was his wont. 'Twas critical to dissuade Esmeraude from her whimsy. Why, by such rationale, she could flee his side at any moment, having found her "love"! Where would that leave his family and his objectives?

"Her heart was of no import," he declared. "She had given her word and her parents had given their approval, so she had no choice but to wed King Mark."

Esmeraude pushed away from him, her lips firm with resolve. "Nay, she had *every* choice. She should have followed her heart. She should have wed Tristran. She should have done whatsoever was necessary to be with her true love in the end."

Bayard sat up in turn, for 'twas clear that the intimacy between them was banished. "Instead of keeping to her sworn word?" he demanded, angered by this suggestion. His patience was run uncommonly thin due to his exhaustion. "Do you suggest that a pledge only be kept when 'tis convenient to do so?"

"She made the wrong choice."

"She made the only acceptable choice."

They glared at each other, each as convinced of their perspective as the other. Then Esmeraude stood up and began to tie the laces on her kirtle with impatient gestures, turning her back to Bayard as she did so.

To be sure, it seemed much colder in the clearing now, though the sky was lightening with the promise of the dawn. Bayard stood and refastened his garments as well, having no impulse to discuss the matter further.

Indeed, he was sorely vexed that his lady did not have the sense to agree with him.

And much worried about the portent of their disagreement over such a key principle.

Esmeraude turned suddenly, facing Bayard anew, her expression one of appeal. "Do you give no credence to love? Do you give no value to the love that she and Tristran found?"

" 'Twas *found*, surely enough. 'Twas the result of the potion they drank, no more." Here was logic with which she could not argue, he was certain, and Bayard was emphatic as a result. " 'Twas destined to last three years and no longer. You cannot break your word for the sake of a madness that will pass!"

Esmeraude smiled. "And because 'twas due to a spell you refuse to trust it? If 'twas genuine love, would you still say that she had chosen rightly?"

'Twas clear what answer she expected him to give, but Bayard shook his head. One lie was sufficient between them. "The sanctity of a pledge is tantamount. Iseut had made a vow and 'twas her responsibility to fulfill it."

Esmeraude's disappointment in him showed. "Even if it made her unhappy?"

Bayard touched her shoulder, hoping to console her. "She could have been happy with King Mark in time. Affection could certainly have grown between them."

Esmeraude looked worried still. "But she did not love him."

"Yet."

Esmeraude rolled her eyes in evident disgust. "She could not fall in love with Mark when she already loved Tristran, Bayard. That is not how love occurs."

"Not in tales, at any rate," he retorted.

"Not in life either. A person has but one true love. Iseut found hers in Tristran and was sorely mistaken to wed King Mark instead."

"Nay, for to do otherwise would be breaking a pledge for the sake of madness."

Esmeraude's eyes widened. "Madness?"

"Aye, love is a fever in the blood, no more than that." The lady took a step back, clearly appalled. Bayard knew that he must speak with temperance to persuade her of her own wrong-thinking, and do so despite his own vexation. "Esmeraude, love is a whimsy for peasants and for fools. No man of sense would place himself in the company of either group."

Esmeraude's color rose, and her consternation was clear. "But I heard tales that your father adored your mother so greatly that he would have no other by his side. All the world knows how he pursued her so ardently, and thus won her hand."

"'Tis indeed true that my father is besotted beyond belief with my mother."

"You make it sound a liability."

"It most certainly is."

Esmeraude's eyes widened and she backed away.

Bayard pursued her, determined to make her see reason. "Make no mistake, my mother is a marvelous woman: a most affectionate mother and a talented lady of the manor. However, my father surrendered much to take her to wife, too much in my view."

"You speak of her as if she were chattel."

Bayard frowned, then shoved a hand through his hair, frustrated that he failed in persuading her of his view. "'Tis not good sense, Esmeraude. His well-known affection for her has been a weakness, one that has proven ripe to be exploited by his foes."

"How?"

Bayard disliked the prospect of more of this discussion but knew that his intended would settle for no fraction of the truth. "Seven years past, a neighbor of ambition desired Villonne. Knowing of my father's affection for my mother, he captured her and swore to kill her if my father did not surrender Villonne in exchange."

Esmeraude's eyes were wide. "Did he do it?"

"Aye, he did," Bayard said bitterly. "Just as he had surrendered Montvieux when my grandmother opposed his intent to wed my mother years past."

"But—"

"But the neighbor, to my father's good fortune, was poorly organized to seize his prize. My father's experience at war stood him in good stead and he recaptured both my mother and Villonne." Bayard shook his head and his tone was dark, for he well recalled his father's disinterest in preserving the estate. "It could have turned the other way."

Esmeraude propped her hands upon her hips. "So, you would discount his valor for it might have cost you an inheritance?"

Bayard gritted his teeth. "'Twas folly to take such a risk! 'Tis a responsibility to hold and defend an estate, and all its residents are dependent upon the lord making choices for the greater good. More than my mother could have perished in her retrieval. The price defied good sense."

"So in the interest of good sense, we should all wed those whom we despise," she said scathingly. "Thus to better preserve our property."

"There is no need to be so extreme," Bayard chided.

"Another woman, one whose hand did not cost my father so dearly, could have been just as fitting a bride. This whimsy of love blinded him and did so more than once."

Esmeraude exhaled in exasperation, but Bayard held up a hand that he might finish. "I vowed long ago not to allow such a weakness to hamper my ambitions. Surely you can see the reasoning in this? Surely you can see that 'tis far safer for all involved to not have this madness called love betwixt them?"

" 'Twould not have been safer for your mother if this neighbor had killed her."

"Aye, if my father's unreasonable affection for her had not been so well known, she would never have been used as a pawn in this game. He would have simply attacked Villonne, and the battle would have been between men, as it should have been. Do you not see the sense of this?"

Esmeraude stared at him, her expression impassive. "Then you will not love your wife?"

" 'Tis a matter of principle. A man of sense can believe in only what he can hold in his hands."

"So you would wed me to win what you can hold in your hands? Or in your bed?"

'Twas clear this did not proceed well. Esmeraude's chin jutted out and fire burned in her eyes, though 'twas not the same flame that had kindled there earlier.

Bayard took a conciliatory step closer, for she was obviously upset, and dropped his voice. "I have no objection to affection blossoming between man and wife over time, but I would never wed for the fleeting folly of love. 'Tis a poor master and one that steers too many men false."

Esmeraude's lips thinned and she looked away, her arms folded across her chest. Bayard thought that she would argue the matter further with him, but was surprised once more.

"If you say as much, then it must be true," she said tightly.

Bayard felt his eyes narrow, for he was skeptical of this sudden change of view, but Esmeraude flashed him a smile that dazzled him.

Was his intended learning to be biddable? 'Twould be a fine change if 'twere so.

If.

Esmeraude inclined her head slightly. "I would speak with Célie, if you will excuse me."

Bayard watched his betrothed with suspicion. "Is aught amiss?"

But the lady merely patted his arm in reassurance, changing moods as quickly as a summer sky. "What would be amiss?" She smiled pertly, and he considered that for all her distinctive qualities, Esmeraude was as much an enigma as other women he had known. "I would assure my maid that I am well after my adventure yesterday, that is all. If you would excuse me."

Esmeraude turned away, leaving Bayard wondering what was in her thoughts. She seemed so outwardly cheerful that he was half-convinced that he made much of naught . . . and yet.

And yet. He rubbed the bridge of his nose, knowing he was too tired from the enthusiasm of their lovemaking and his own lack of sleep these past days to solve this particular riddle now.

At least Esmeraude seemed to have put whatever the trouble was behind her. And he was glad to have made his perspective on matters of duty clear. Perhaps she came to agree with him.

Perhaps she chose to hold her tongue. Bayard watched warily as Esmeraude greeted her maid with good cheer and he was reassured by her manner. Her dismissal of their argument suited Bayard well, for they would have years to discuss such matters.

After they were wed.

Then the boys awakened and questions were asked and tasks had to be assigned and there was so much to be done before their departure that he had no time to fret over his betrothed's moods.

Aye, they could be back at Ceinn-beithe by the evening meal and perhaps exchange their nuptial vows then. Bayard calculated quickly, liking well the prospect of riding out with the morrow's first light to meet the king. He eyed the sky and knew he would be much relieved to have his lady comfortably sheltered before the foul weather that gathered was fully upon them.

To Ceinn-beithe then, and the nuptials he desired above all else. Bayard could not hasten quickly enough.

※

'Twas good that Esmeraude liked a challenge. Indeed, the greatest adventure of her days might lie in winning this knight's heart. He would certainly not surrender it without a fight.

But a man who would sing to coax her closer, a man who teased her and pleasured her, a man who showed such care for all beneath his care was not devoid of a heart. She had a suspicion that Bayard's talk about love was too vehement to be the truth.

Nay, he simply hid his heart safely away. Perhaps it had been wounded once, so dreadfully that he sought to avoid such pain again. She slanted a glance at him and could well imagine that he had no shortage of women seeking his favor.

Clearly, the man had never met her match in determination. Nay, 'twas another sign that they were destined to be together, that she was the woman perfect for him. Esmeraude would not only expose that heart, but convince him to acknowledge its presence and its power. No less than her life's happiness was at stake, after all.

Esmeraude had hoped to discuss her impressions with her maid, who would recall much of knights from her days in France, but that hope proved to be short-lived. Célie embraced her with delight, then proceeded to enumerate all the marvels of Bayard.

But Esmeraude had a dilemma. She was determined to win Bayard's heart and to do so before their nuptials were performed. The difficulty was that she had no idea how to begin. She watched him through her lashes and knew that she had never known a man the like of him.

Bayard would certainly not aid her in this quest.

'Twas then that Esmeraude recalled a pertinent detail. The sole man similar to Bayard she had ever met was wedded to her step-sister, Jacqueline. Only ten years Esmeraude's senior, Jacqueline had not only found love, but married the man in question. Angus was not only a knight and a warrior, like Bayard, but Esmeraude sensed that he had been reluctant to credit love as well.

There was naught for it. She had to seek out Jacqueline's advice. They would have to continue to Airdfinnan.

At home there were only her parents, after all. Duncan, Esmeraude's stepfather and the man who held her mother's heart in thrall, was a poet by his own admission, so her mother's advice would offer no aid in this puzzle. Esmeraude could imagine that Duncan would speak readily of love and its charms, that he would know when that emotion filled his heart and soul. In her experience, he was always quick to express affection, as her brother-in-law Angus was not.

Esmeraude could not, in fact, imagine resolute Angus making sweet confessions at all, regardless of what he felt. Perhaps 'twas not uncommon for a man of war to speak as Bayard did. Certainly, Jacqueline would know the truth—and perhaps supply a key.

"Bayard is such a fine man, Esmeraude," Célie enthused.

"A man of honor, of wealth and chivalrous intent. I know that this knight will make you happy for all your days."

Esmeraude summoned a smile but said naught, her thoughts yet whirling. Would Bayard continue to Airdfinnan willingly?

"Why, you might have a babe of your own in no time at all. And you can be certain that a man who tends to those beneath his care as carefully as this knight will make a fine father."

Célie sighed rapturously. "Babes! Oh, how I adore them. I must confess that I had always hoped that your mother would have a son. Girls are all well and good, and you were a most charming charge, but a boy is special as well." The maid slanted a sly glance at Esmeraude. "Perhaps you will have a son."

"Perhaps." Esmeraude had more pressing matters on her mind than to speculate about what children she and Bayard might have.

Célie tore the loaf of bread with more vigor than the task deserved, her gesture drawing Esmeraude's eye. She then tore it again and again, though the loaf was already in sufficiently small pieces.

Célie's voice dropped as she shredded one piece of the bread to oblivion. "Perhaps you might have need of an old maid who knows a bit about small children," she murmured, then glanced up. "Perhaps, Esmeraude, you might still have need of *me* in your household."

Célie's gaze was bright with hope, her fingers so busy that the bread was nigh in flakes in her lap. When Esmeraude did not respond immediately, the maid spoke in great haste. "I am not too old to be of service, Esmeraude, and I should dearly like to see France's shores once again. At least, I assume that that is where your knight's holding lies. And if you had such a son, I should be able to aid you, I know I should—"

"Célie!" Esmeraude laid a hand on the maid's shoulder, touched that the older woman wished so much to remain with her. She smiled, forgetting her own concerns for the moment. "Of course you may accompany me if 'tis your choice. I had hoped you would, but thought you might prefer to remain here."

Célie closed her eyes and bit her lip, then shook her head. "Nay, Esmeraude. I would prefer to remain with you."

"But you have been here for nigh eighteen years."

"Nay, I have been with *you* for nigh eighteen years." The maid opened her eyes and smiled, her tears threatening to fall. "'Tis no jest that I think of you as my own child, Esmeraude, though we did not meet until you were two. I should be most honored to hold your children upon my lap. I am not so old that I cannot earn my keep, you need not fear for that."

"You need not have fears for earning your keep," Esmeraude scolded softly. "I think of you as my own blood as well, and I know that I should be most pleased to have a familiar face in my household, wherever it may be."

She glanced to Bayard, wondering where his holding was. Truly, the man had a gift for distracting her from matters with which she should be concerned!

The maid nodded, returning to her labor. "'Twill be different in France, upon that you can rely. People are more formal and their homes more grand than what you have known."

"Did he tell you that his holding was in France?"

Célie blinked. "Is it not? I assumed as much."

'Twas a fair assumption, though Esmeraude knew she must find out the truth. "Then you shall be my tutor," she suggested with a smile. "For you will remember what is right and be able to save me from a dire error of protocol." Esmeraude wiped a tear from her maid's cheek. "Fear not, Célie," she said softly. "I shall always have need of you."

"Thank you, Esmeraude!" The maid sniffled. The two exchanged a tight hug then pulled back to regard the shredded bread. 'Twas a rueful mess and the two women began to laugh at the state of it, for there was no way it could be offered to the men as a repast.

"Is aught amiss?" Bayard asked from behind Esmeraude. She turned to find his expression quizzical, his gaze darting between the two women.

"Nay. I simply reassured Célie that I would have her in my company wheresoever I find myself." Esmeraude lifted her chin, wondering whether he would challenge her upon this decision to add to his household. 'Twas made without his endorsement, after all, and she could not guess what he expected of her.

"Fine," Bayard said crisply, his manner dismissive as if the detail was of little import. " 'Twill be a comfort to you to have a familiar face in my hall, no doubt."

He spared a glance to the ruined bread and frowned. "Perhaps we shall wait and eat at midday." He then nodded, his decision made. "Indeed, if we ride very hard, we might make Ceinn-beithe in time to join their midday meal. Come, let us hasten."

"Ceinn-beithe?" Esmeraude echoed, as though surprised. She was not that surprised, in truth. Bayard seemed a man unlikely to dally once his choices were made.

He spared her an incisive glance. "Of course, Ceinn-beithe. Where else should we go?"

"I had thought we rode to Airdfinnan."

"To what purpose?"

"My riddle was intended to lead my suitors there,"

Esmeraude reminded him and smiled. She might win her way with a measure of charm.

Bayard's answering smile was thin. "But you have chosen me as your spouse, thus there is no need to go to Airdfinnan. Indeed, we should be wed at Ceinn-beithe, that your parents may witness the event. 'Tis only courteous, Esmeraude."

Esmeraude straightened at his implication that her manners were lacking. "Is it not courteous to meet those I invited to Airdfinnan?" she asked frostily. "Or to explain to my sister why such men arrive at her gates?"

The tension in Bayard's features eased. "Ah, I see the reason for your concern," he said. " 'Tis most thoughtful of you to worry about such details. I shall dispatch Michael to Airdfinnan with your message and our regrets."

"But—"

Bayard drummed his fingers upon his thigh as he thought, then shook his head briskly. "Nay, that will not suffice. We shall send a runner from Ceinn-beithe with this message, for otherwise we should be obliged to wait too long for Michael's return before our own departure to join the king."

Without waiting for Esmeraude's comment, he gestured to the boys to hurry and turned away. 'Twas clear that Bayard not only expected Esmeraude to agree with him but that she would dutifully follow him. Célie stood and brushed off her skirts, but Esmeraude stood her ground.

She was not a hunting hound, who trotted loyally at its master's heels. This was a matter to be resolved immediately. Indeed, 'twas a matter of principle.

"What if I wished to say farewell to my sister at Airdfinnan?" she demanded.

Bayard's exasperation was thinly veiled when he turned to face her again. "I would be delighted to invite your sister and her family to visit us in France at any time you so desire, but for the moment, I would depart."

"I wish to see her now." Esmeraude braced herself for a fight, folding her arms across her chest. "In truth, I will not wed you without seeing my sister first."

Bayard's eyes flashed, but his tone was temperate. Too temperate, in fact, and Esmeraude knew his irritation with her was rising. She did not care. She wished to discuss this and arrive at a decision together, not be told what she would do. She would not set a precedent now for the rest of her life.

The man had best know that she had opinions of her own, and he had best know it soon.

"Time is of the essence, my Esmeraude. We must meet King Richard before he sails to France, for I should be in his close company. With good fortune, we should arrive in time."

"I had no understanding that you had such obligations."

"I have many such commitments and doubtless you will learn them all in time," he said, his manner indicating that he felt he owed Esmeraude no further explanation. "Let us go immediately, my lady. Your palfrey awaits."

" 'Tis fortunate for your obligations that you won my agreement so quickly," Esmeraude could not help but observe, her tone tart.

Bayard only smiled as he offered her his hand to aid her to mount. "It has long been said that Fortune favored my endeavors," he said, then winked as if a playful manner would take the sting from his authoritative manner.

He was wrong. Esmeraude had never been a particularly biddable woman and she did not take readily to Bayard's easy assumption that she would do whatsoever he desired.

"How sad for you that on this day you must learn how capricious Fortune can be," Esmeraude retorted. She swung into the palfrey's saddle without his aid and looked down at the annoyed knight.

"And what is that to mean?" he demanded, his eyes snapping.

"That I am not chattel, nor am I yours to command. I will see my sister before we depart this land, even if it means that we must ride hard afterward to meet your obligations." She smiled sweetly. "Indeed, if you confided your duties to me, 'twould be far simpler to plan our doings in advance."

"I have no obligation to consult with you. My decisions are made for the entire party!"

"I have no obligation to follow your bidding."

That caught his attention. " 'Tis the place of a wife to cede to her spouse's wishes!" Bayard roared. " 'Tis her duty to do as she is bidden."

Esmeraude laughed lightly. "And men wonder why marriage holds so little appeal for me. I would have not just adventure, but respect from my spouse. Perhaps you have need of a lesson afore we meet a priest."

"You have my respect!"

"Excellent. Then you will take me to Airdfinnan to see my sister, yielding to my desire as a good and loving husband should do."

Bayard seemed at a momentary loss for words.

Esmeraude seized the moment and touched her heels to the steed's side, letting it saunter to the road. "I am going to Airdfinnan," she cried over her shoulder, having no doubt that she provoked him. "Shall I meet you there, or will you ride with me?" She urged her palfrey in the direction of Airdfinnan, knowing full well that Bayard would be fast behind her.

Esmeraude smiled at the sound of his swearing and knew that he would have much to say when he did catch up to her.

She was not disappointed.

Chapter Nine

'TWAS BAD ENOUGH THAT ESMERAUDE INSISTED UPON nonsense and that she defied him openly—before his own squires!—without the added complication of another party approaching.

Bayard was even less pleased that he quickly recognized his brother and cousins among the surrounding escort of squires. Other suitors for Esmeraude's hand were not the people he wished to see, not before this unpredictable lady had sworn herself to him for all eternity.

That she seemed particularly disinclined to do so at this moment only irked Bayard further. He hastened after Esmeraude and laid claim to her palfrey's reins, taking due note of how she flicked her hair over her shoulder, a sign of pending trouble.

The three approaching knights had once been his close friends as well as his cousins and Bayard felt a pang at seeing them. He had once been of their company. Indeed, he had been the instigator of much of the mischief they had made in their younger days. These past five years had driven a wedge between him and them, though the three others clearly remained comrades.

Not that he cared. Nay, he had greater matters in his thoughts.

Bayard took a hard assessment of the three knights, hoping

to convince himself that they could not hold Esmeraude's eye for long. Aye, it behooved a man to know his competition, even when he was nigh certain he had won.

The first was his own brother, Amaury. At eighteen summers of age, Amaury had grown considerably in the years since Bayard had last seen him. He was dark of hair, like Bayard, and possessed their father's ready smile. He wore Villonne's colors proudly and Bayard assumed that his father had chosen Amaury as his heir after Bayard's own departure.

Amaury rode with only one squire, though his armament gleamed, due to both good care and good quality. He had always been quiet, but gracious when called upon. He was no match for Esmeraude, in Bayard's opinion, for she would readily dominate him.

But Villonne was no small prize. If Esmeraude desired comfort and riches to spend as she wished, Villonne and Amaury could keep her well enough, especially as she was accustomed to Ceinn-beithe and its more modest revenues.

Hmm. Bayard turned to assess his cousin Connor. He knew his cousin to be one year younger than Amaury, but if he had not known as much, he would have guessed the age difference between them to be much greater. Amaury was tall, like Bayard and their father—indeed, their mother was tall as well—but Connor was small in comparison.

Connor was only as tall as Amaury's chin, though he was broad of shoulder. He was one to say little but follow a conversation avidly, then make some wry comment that was perfect for the moment. Like his father, he said naught without considering his words well. As a child, he had been the greatest practical joker Bayard had ever known—and had been able to feign innocence so well that he was seldom assumed to be responsible.

His eyes though, a vivid green that made him look like a child of the fey, danced with mischief in those moments and could reveal him to the careful observer. Indeed, Esmeraude with her love of tales and impish manner of her own might find Connor unexpectedly suitable.

Bayard was not as reassured by this exercise as he had hoped to be.

After delaying the matter as long as possible, he considered Nicholas. Nicholas, who believed himself to be heir to Montvieux, whose father believed him to be heir to Montvieux, whose legacy Bayard would steal by winning Esmeraude. Bayard watched his cousin and acknowledged that achieving his ambition would cost another their own.

His success would be Nicholas's loss.

Though it might well save Nicholas's life, he doubted that his cousin would see the matter that way. Nicholas was not qualified to protect the family holding from a king's army and Bayard knew that he alone could prevent Montvieux from being lost. 'Twas he who could ensure that their family legacy endured.

Indeed, 'twas his *duty* to claim Montvieux and protect their legacy before 'twas too late.

A year older than Bayard, Nicholas did not appear as young as the other two knights. He was tall and lean, graced with his father's russet hair and engaging manner. He recounted some tale to his cousins now, his gestures lively and his frequent laughter echoing ahead of the party.

Esmeraude was clearly enchanted. As she gazed upon Nicholas, her eyes sparkled, and her lips were curved in a smile.

Bayard's innards clenched.

If there had ever been a man who would see beyond the lack of virginity in a bride, 'twas Rowan's son. They were a most unconventional family, what with their Venetian connections and uncommon joie de vivre. An unpredictable woman might well prefer such uncommon circumstance and their boisterous household.

It seemed that Bayard would vie with Nicholas over more than the family estate. Bayard took another look at lady and knight, and considered what he might do. He did not intend to lose and needed to make a choice quickly.

"I would ask a favor of you," Bayard said softly. At Esmeraude's enquiring glance, he continued. "I would ask you to not reveal your identity to my cousins and brother."

Esmeraude smiled. "Do you not trust them, sir? Or is it that you do not trust me?"

Bayard's eyes narrowed, for she had not addressed him formally of late. Her eyes were wide with an innocence that he had already learned better than to trust. Rather than vexing him though, Esmeraude's spirit made him long to tame her and his blood quickened with the prospect of how he might do so.

But that would have to wait. "Nay, I do not trust my cousins, not when there is such a prize as your hand involved."

"Then who shall I be, if not myself?"

"Why not continue your ruse, that of being a simple country maid?"

"The ruse that did not fool you?"

Bayard gritted his teeth. "Aye, 'twill do."

"Will it? Will they be readily persuaded that you have claimed such a maid to sate your base desires? Is it a habit of yours?"

Bayard had the definite sense that his intended tried to provoke him. He held her gaze until color rose in her cheeks, but she did not look away.

"I do not know what they think of me, for we have seen naught of each other in five years," he said with a calmness he did not feel. "And I cannot guess what expectation they have of my habits, though 'tis not uncommon for many men to do exactly thus."

"What of you?"

"I have always enjoyed the company of women."

Her eyes flashed for but a moment before her expression was demure once more. "Shall I be a whore or an innocent?"

"Esmeraude!"

"I must know how I am to behave," she said, her tone reasonable though her eyes danced with devilry. "And clearly I must be told by you what to do, as 'tis my *place*. Have I been raped, or seduced? Or did I seduce you? Where did we meet, and when? Truly there are a thousand possibilities, all of which affect . . ."

"Es—" Bayard began to shout her name in frustration, but bit back upon it in time. The other party was nigh within earshot. He took a deep breath and released it slowly.

"My lady," he said, forcing the words through gritted teeth. "I ask only that you do not reveal your name. 'Tis a simple request and if you know not what to say, then I suggest you say naught."

"Aye, I gain the impression that 'twill oft be preferable if I say naught," Esmeraude retorted. "Particularly naught that challenges what you say." She smiled sweetly despite the sharpness of her words, as if she would challenge him to argue with her.

And that was enough.

"What ails you?" Bayard demanded. "I ask only that you keep your name to yourself!" He spared a glance to the rapidly approaching party and found his temper coming to a boil at this most inconvenient moment. "We can argue the matter fully soon enough, but for the moment, do I have your agreement?"

Esmeraude smiled and bowed her head, the image of wifely obedience. "Your will is my command, my lord master."

Aye, she would make some mischief, of that Bayard was certain.

'Twas small consolation that he gained some understanding of this unpredictable temptress. All the same, he wished he had a better idea of what precisely she would do or say to his cousins and brother.

'Twas disconcerting to realize not only how little he knew of this woman he would take to wife, but how greatly she had already challenged his expectations.

He truly did not know what to expect of her. For a man like Bayard, who preferred to hold a situation in the palm of his hand, this was perhaps the most troubling trait his intended could have possessed.

Bayard wished heartily that Dame Fortune would smile upon this exchange, then jumped when he thought he heard a distant echo of feminine laughter. He glanced to the others but they appeared to be oblivious to whatever he had heard.

He truly had need of more sleep. He was dreaming with his eyes open. The winning of this seductress and the press of time had overly strained him. Aye, all would come aright after he and Esmeraude were wed later this day and he slept in his nuptial bed this night.

This time Bayard knew he did not imagine the shout of distant laughter. Indeed, he glanced over his shoulder in search of the sound, but saw naught. Esmeraude gave him a cool smile, as if she knew aught that he did not.

Sleep would heal all of this. Sleep and a quick resolution of his objective.

But first, his cousins and brother had to be dispatched upon their merry way. Bayard closed his eyes briefly and hoped for the best, which did little to ease his concerns.

"Bayard! Surely you do not ride the wrong way," his brother Amaury teased, his features alight with his smile. He clearly interpreted their halted position as a hint that they rode toward Ceinn-beithe.

"Do I?"

"Perhaps he has not solved the riddle rightly," Connor suggested.

"Perhaps 'tis you who have solved it wrongly," Bayard retorted and Nicholas laughed.

"Then pity the lord of Airdfinnan, who is fated to host us all for no reason whatsoever." They chuckled, the horses milling together, and Bayard felt his brother's gaze upon him.

He ignored him. "I will not delay your progress, then," Bayard said smoothly and smiled at the three of them. "For you are no doubt anxious to be upon your way."

"But who is this lovely maiden?" Nicholas teased, sparing a wink for Esmeraude. The lady smiled, then dropped her gaze flirtatiously.

Incredibly, she held her tongue.

"A local maid," Bayard said with forced cheer. "She does not understand French."

"Ah!" Nicholas, undeterred, addressed Esmeraude in some foreign tongue. She laughed, much to Bayard's horror, and replied merrily, her eyes flashing.

It irked him beyond reason that he could not understand this exchange. 'Twas not that his bride laughed with his cousin when she had shown Bayard no such favor this morn, nay, not that! She could not anger him so readily as that!

'Twould have been illogical. 'Twas the rudeness of their conversing in a language that all present did not understand that was the root of it.

"Perhaps you might share the jest," he said coolly.

"It does not translate well," Nicholas said with a shrug.

Bayard felt his grip tighten upon the reins. "I should still like to know of what you speak."

Nicholas's eyes danced. "Afraid that I shall steal the wench who warms your bed, Bayard?"

"Of course not!"

"Wo-ho! He does fear as much!" Amaury began to laugh. "Bayard, you were supposed to ride here to find a bride, not a wench to please you."

"Though she is most pretty," Connor contributed.

"And if Bayard is anxious to keep her fast by his side, she must be amorous as well."

The three of them beamed at Esmeraude and she, curse her, smiled at each of the knights in turn. She granted Bayard a playful smile, then clicked to her palfrey. The steed leapt away from the group and trotted in the wrong direction, toward Airdfinnan, at the maiden's urging.

Esmeraude blew a kiss at Bayard over her shoulder. "Airdfinnan," she murmured playfully.

"Aha! She does choose us!" Nicholas shouted with a glee most inappropriate to Bayard's thinking.

"Ceinn-beithe," he growled, tightening his grip upon the palfrey's reins which slipped through his fingers.

Esmeraude pouted prettily, and had to be aware of how avidly the knights watched her. She came back to Bayard's side, and he guessed from the mischief in her gaze that she was also aware of how vexed he was with her.

But there was a determination in the set of her lips and he knew that she would contrive to go to Airdfinnan, as she desired, with or without him. That he could do naught about the matter, save surrender her to his rivals or cede to her will, did little to improve his mood.

Bayard had never been cornered thus by a woman and he did not care for the change.

Esmeraude laughed, a sound as fetching as fairy bells, and

shook her hair out loose down her back. The glance she cast over her shoulder at the other knights was at the very least encouraging.

If not wanton. Then she turned to him and licked her lips in a most provocative manner. "Airdfinnan?" she whispered, devilry in her expression.

Bayard's anger simmered anew, for he was certain that she had decided to pretend to be a whore purely to vex him. He should have been more disturbed by how readily she provoked him, but his sole response was fury.

"I think she invites us to escort her in your stead," Nicholas mused.

"'Tis but one of her games," Bayard said sternly. "She is oft amorous in the morn—you need not fear that I shall see her sated."

Esmeraude played with the tie of her chemise now—*his* chemise—pouting prettily when 'twas untied. She turned an appealing glance upon the knights, as if she could not manage to fasten the tie again herself, and Bayard glowered at the undoubtedly deliberate display of her creamy cleavage.

Nicholas whistled through his teeth.

"If she was sated, surely she would not be lustful so early in the morn," Connor commented.

"Aye." Nicholas offered his cousin a confident grin. "We could be of aid to you in this!"

"I thank you but I have no need of such assistance. If you would excuse us . . ."

"Oh, he is possessive of her," Amaury teased. "She must indeed be a marvel abed. I recall that Bayard never saved his favors for one maiden alone. He oft said that no one woman could satisfy him."

"I say we let her choose her mate of this morn," Nicholas

suggested, then called something to Esmeraude in that cursed alien tongue again.

The lady laughed and batted her lashes at him.

"If you will forgive me," Bayard interrupted with vigor. "'Tis time we were *all* upon our way." With a curt nod to his cousins and brother, he caught Esmeraude around the waist and hauled her from her saddle.

He planted her before him, and when she settled against him with a purr of satisfaction, his anger changed immediately to desire. Oh, she would be less triumphant when he was done with her. She would not only be sated, but she would be tamed, she would be biddable, and she would wear his ring upon her hand.

And she would be glad of it. He would teach her not to challenge him thus. He gave Argent his spurs and held fast to the lady, riding for Airdfinnan but leaving a distance between them and the other knights.

Bayard would see the matter resolved this very night.

Nay, he would resolve it this *moment*.

❖

Esmeraude watched Bayard's temper rise and conceded that she might have pushed him slightly too far. His eyes blazed with anger and his brow was dark. He held her against him in a relentless grip and showed no signs of halting his destrier. The beast raced unchecked and she was exhilarated to know that she could provoke Bayard to such passion.

She turned to look at him, much encouraged about the prospects for their future, and saw that there was but one matter upon his mind. Her heart leapt.

"Temptress!" he charged, then kissed her with startling vigor. His gloved hand held her captive beneath his embrace, his other arm was locked around her waist. His was a claiming kiss, and Esmeraude was surprised by how exciting she found his possessive touch.

But it still irked her that he expected to command her. He would not easily intimidate her with a kiss, however ardent it might be.

Aye, she would show him what it was to be a temptress.

Esmeraude locked her own hands around Bayard's neck and returned his kiss in every measure. She rubbed her breasts against his chest and locked her fingers into his hair. She slid her tongue between his teeth and kissed him as if she would suck the marrow from his bones.

Bayard swore. Esmeraude felt victorious when he growled beneath her embrace and yet more so when his touch became urgent. She was distantly aware that the other knights hooted and whistled, but Esmeraude had forgotten all but Bayard's kiss. The heat rose between them, her annoyance with his assumptions changing to another passion.

Bayard tore his lips from hers and Esmeraude loved how his eyes blazed brilliant blue. "Witch," he charged, nigh as breathless as she, and Esmeraude laughed aloud.

She felt as she did when she conquered the sea: she felt vibrant and able to conquer whatever lay in her path. That she could conquer this man with a kiss and make him forget all but her was a victory indeed.

Esmeraude stared into his eyes and knew that their desires were as one in this moment. Truly, there was a better use of the heat between them than sharp words.

"You spoke the truth, my lord," Esmeraude confided, her tone wicked. "For I am amorous indeed this morn and will not be readily sated." She stretched to slide her tongue around his ear, then whispered against his flesh. "Do you dare to try?"

Bayard shivered then inhaled sharply. He flicked the merest glance at his squires before staring down at Esmeraude again. Indeed, his gaze simmered. "You win your desire in this, my lady, for we ride for Airdfinnan. Know that 'tis an indulgence upon my part and that I will not accept such defiance in future."

Esmeraude lifted her chin. "I will not wed a man who thinks to own me."

He smiled slowly and her blood heated. "I shall change your thinking," he purred, and his hand rose to cup her breast. "I shall teach you what prize can be yours, my Esmeraude, and you shall be powerless to refuse."

"I invite you to try," she said, her voice breathless though she tried to sound bold.

"Oh, I shall," Bayard whispered. He bent and nuzzled her ear, his expert touch making Esmeraude dizzy. "And I shall begin this very night."

Esmeraude returned his ardent kiss, welcoming its heat. Though he might seek to conquer her with his touch, she would begin her own conquest of his heart. On the morrow, they would reach Airdfinnan and she would have Jacqueline's counsel.

In the interim, she saw no reason to deny herself this pleasure. Aye, this man could be shaped to her expectation, Esmeraude knew it well.

Indeed, she looked forward to the challenge.

❖

The weather worsened as they rode, though the storm clouds that had gathered quickly in their wake that morn stayed behind them. 'Twas as if the storm kept pace with them—a most unusual sensation. The wind was frisky and gusting, but though stray drops of rain splattered upon them at intervals, the storm never broke. Bayard kept expecting the clouds to burst, but they merely hung upon their heels.

He tucked his cloak around Esmeraude and she soon forgot her audacious manner, huddling against him for shelter. There was one good consequence of all of this—the weather was too foul for idle chatter, and that kept his brother and cousins from asking too many questions. Bayard glanced back at one point and his face was stung by the bitter wind that pushed them onward.

Perhaps he sacrificed little in sating the lady's whim in this. He doubted they could have ridden against this wind to return to Ceinn-beithe after all. They made a wretched camp that night, for they could not coax so much as a spark from the wood with the wind dancing wildly about them. They huddled together for warmth, their steeds gathered around them, and shared what bread and cheese they had in virtual silence.

On the second morn, the wind was worse and the sky blacker than black behind them. They saddled up and departed early, the sky only faintly light in the east. There could not have been a one of them who did not anxiously look forward to Airdfinnan's walls.

'Twas early when the sky fell dark, a final rogue streak of orange gracing the western sky. The woods on either side of the road were thick with shadows and the cries of wolves had begun to echo again in the hills. Fog crept through the forest on either side, pressing on the flanks of the road like a silvery wall. The hoofbeats echoed oddly through the stillness and Bayard was uncommonly glad to see the silhouette of Airdfinnan rise ahead of them. Andrew cheered and the other squires took up the cry.

"Airdfinnan," Esmeraude said with undisguised satisfaction. She looped her arms around his neck, looking like some wench he had pillaged in a battle. Her pose irked him, for it made her look like the tavern wench she was not.

He caught her closer, making her catch her breath with the possessiveness of his embrace. "Perhaps 'twill be more easy to persuade you on this night, as 'twas not yesterday," he murmured for her ears alone, then smiled when she shivered.

Then Bayard shed his helmet and left his blade sheathed to show that he came in peace. His cousins and brother glanced quickly to him, then did the same, leaving him wondering what they would have done without his presence.

And then he looked upon Airdfinnan.

The fortress was set upon an isle in the midst of the river Finnan, that isle strategically sited at a fork in a large glen. 'Twas a crossroads of a kind, the glen cutting a course between Skye and points east, the river cutting a path more southwesterly toward Mull.

'Twas among the most impressive fortresses Bayard had seen in this land, though both smaller and younger than Montvieux. The walls of the keep rose directly from the river, the keep filling every increment of the isle. The walls were wrought of heavy cut stones where they met the river, then changed to mud as they rose higher.

There was only one gate and one bridge to the fortress itself, its village sited on the riverbank outside its walls. Though the village was surrounded by palisades, as Ceinnbeithe was, its occupants could certainly retreat to the fortress if need be.

'Twas splendidly defendable and perfectly sited, both of which met with considerable approval from Bayard.

The sentries hailed the party in Norman French, evidently guessing their origin by their garb.

They exchanged greetings and Bayard declared their names and their mission when his companions said naught. 'Twas as if the years had not passed and he was still expected to speak for all of them. But a moment passed before they were beckoned onward.

Bayard heard the sentries whistle as they rode past, then

the cry echoed at the gates. He was not surprised as a result to find a formidable party awaiting them inside the portcullis.

Indeed, he approved of the tactic heartily.

Bayard noted that there was but one single-level structure within the enclosure of those high walls. 'Twas clearly the hall, with a chapel at one end and the solar at the other. The kitchens were beneath thatched roofs between the hall and walls, sensibly sited thus in case of fire; the stables, smithy, and armory were similarly housed.

Bayard spared the keep no more than a cursory survey before looking to the men gathered before him once more. The man who clearly held possession of Airdfinnan stood in their midst, arms folded across his chest. The rich embroidery upon his tabard and the deference of the men surrounding him betrayed his station.

He was armed as Bayard was, the hem of his dark tabard higher than that of the mail hauberk that hung to his knees. His mail coif was pushed back off his head and gathered around his neck. There were spurs on his boots, a sign of his knightly status. His hair was as dark as the night and he wore a patch over one eye that only partly obscured the scar upon his face.

'Twas more than these signs that told Bayard that he had met a man as experienced in battle as he, if not more so. There was a wariness in this man's gaze, a knowledge that could only be won in war. And the lord was surrounded by a party of sentries, as if to emphasize his uncertainty of Bayard's intentions.

Bayard wondered what threat the lord expected to arrive at this hour, or whether he was inclined to anticipate trouble at every turn. Perhaps 'twas the pending inclement weather that prompted such caution—there was an ominous mood emanating from those clouds, one that made a man glance over his shoulder in apprehension.

Bayard dismounted and doffed his gloves, offering his

hand in peace as he stepped forward. "I am Bayard de Villonne, knight and crusader. This is Amaury of Villonne, Connor of Tullymullagh, and Nicholas of Montvieux." His gaze strayed to Esmeraude, who returned his glance boldly and he recalled their ruse. "If this is Airdfinnan, we come here seeking one Esmeraude of Ceinn-beithe."

"Why?" The lord did not move to take Bayard's hand and his French was crisp. His gaze, too, strayed to Esmeraude, though he did not comment upon her presence or reveal her identity.

"I would make her my lady wife."

"As would I," cried Nicholas, and the other two cousins added their assent.

The lord's expression was skeptical. "Perhaps you err. Ceinn-beithe lies to the west and is, I understand, the location of a contest for that lady's hand."

"I know. We have been there. The lady left a riddle to her suitors, to which the answer is clearly Airdfinnan." Bayard recited the riddle and irritation flickered across the lord's features.

"No doubt you will not be the last." He cast a quick glance at Esmeraude that might have made a less bold woman flinch. Esmeraude smiled.

Bayard felt obliged to continue their charade, for the benefit of his companions. "Has Esmeraude arrived at these gates? I am most anxious to see my lady and assure myself of her welfare."

The lord eyed Bayard carefully. "It seems to me that a woman would not flee any man whose suit she intended to accept. If she truly were favorable to your offer, would she not be in your company now?"

Bayard could not fully suppress his smile and he saw a flicker in the lord's eyes. They understood each full well, it seemed.

"It has become clear to me that my lady Esmeraude is inclined to confound expectation." Bayard shook his head as though much tested by this woman. "She was amenable to my suit until I declined her request to visit her sister afore we were wed."

"She was not!" Nicholas said and dismounted, casting his reins at his squire. "You told us naught of this."

"It did not seem to be pertinent." Bayard gritted his teeth against another lie. "I had hoped that she had taken it upon herself to come here of her own volition. Is she here?"

The lord almost smiled, but then his expression turned stern once more. "I am disinclined to grant admission to my hall to any knight come begging at my portal. Grant me a reason why you should be admitted."

"Esmeraude, I believe, concocts a test for the men competing for her hand by granting riddles to them. I had solved them, I thought to her satisfaction, but 'tis clear she still has doubts of me. This is no deterrent, for a lady must be convinced of her choice that she may cling to it once 'tis made."

The lord inclined his head in acknowledgment of that, though he seemed to fight against a smile.

"I intend to see Esmeraude's hand firmly in mine and I shall conquer any obstacle she sets before me in order to see that end achieved."

"As will I," Nicholas interjected.

"And I!" Amaury dismounted and joined them.

"I, as well." Connor then stood there as well.

The lord seemed amused by these declarations. His gaze flicked over the knights, but he did not speak.

"If she is here," Bayard said deliberately, "I would ask your permission to court her favor anew."

The lord studied him carefully. "Airdfinnan lies betwixt two kingdoms and two kings. I cannot trust strangers to be armed within my walls in such circumstance. You will each surrender your weapons and the bridle of your steed to my men, or you will pass beneath the portcullis again and leave Airdfinnan for good."

"But I come to seek a bride!" Nicholas protested.

"'Tis an ill omen to be so distrusted," Connor concurred.

Amaury held his tongue, watching Bayard with bright eyes.

"I fully understand your concerns," Bayard said simply. "But I have no means of knowing whether you will not turn against us once we are bereft of our weapons."

The lord nodded. "Do you pledge that your blade will not be used against me?"

"Nay, I cannot, not without knowing your intent."

The lord's gaze was bright, his tone resolute. "This then is my intent. If you truly court a bride and make no trouble in my hall, then no arms will be used against you. I give you my word of honor." He paused, his steady gaze boring into Bayard's own. "If you lie, though, any one of you, you may rest assured that you will regret your course." He smiled slightly. "Indeed, in such a case I may find a certain pleasure in using your own blade to cut out your black heart."

'Twas the promise of an honorable man and Bayard was not insulted. "I shall have your pledge in exchange for mine."

The lord nodded once. "Each of you, then, choose your course. 'Tis high time the gates were closed against the night."

Bayard did not hesitate. He unbuckled the scabbard from his belt and surrendered his sword to the lord. "I pledge to make no disruption in your hall, to seek the hand of Esmeraude honorably and to depart with her and my possessions alone once my cause is won."

The lord nodded. "And I pledge to inflict no harm upon you, so long as your vow is kept."

A man stepped forward to take Argent's reins. The beast followed willingly, the man telling Bayard that the stallion would see good care. Argent had good instincts for the will of men. Bayard lifted Esmeraude from the beast's saddle, then gave her a gentle push toward the hall, as if she were no more than a tavern wench.

"Perhaps you might find shelter and a meal in the kitchens," he said dismissively, then winked when she glared at him.

Esmeraude tossed her hair over her shoulder and strode away, Célie fast behind her.

He thought the lord stifled a chuckle, but then he offered his hand. "I am Angus MacGillivray, Lord of Airdfinnan. Welcome, Bayard de Villonne." The knights shook hands, then Nicholas stepped forward to echo Bayard's vow.

'Twas not long before all the knights had sworn that they came in peace, that they had been welcomed, and that all the steeds had been led away. The other knights trailed their steeds and their squires, to assure themselves that all was well. Bayard lingered with the lord. 'Twas good to find the company of a man with similar experience to his own and he did not doubt that they would have much else in common.

Angus spoke slowly, a glint of humor in his eye. "I am not certain whether I should encourage your suit or express my reservations. My sister-in-law is a most uncommon woman."

Bayard shook his head. "I know the truth of it."

"How strange that you travel with a wench to seek a bride." The men matched steps and headed toward the hall.

Bayard grinned. "Not so strange when the wench is the bride in disguise."

"I suspected that you knew the truth. I would guess there is a tale in that worthy of Esmeraude." He lifted one hand. "Do not tell me of it. With my sister-in-law, I oft prefer to know less of matters."

"Aye, I am coming to understand that sense."

Angus laughed and clapped Bayard on the back. "You look to be a man in need of a draft of ale. Come to the hall with me."

Chapter Ten

SMERAUDE SIGHED IN CONTENTMENT AS SHE SLIPPED into a hot bath in Airdfinnan's solar, sore after a day and a half of hard riding. Combined with her journey to the King of the Isles, she had been more than four days without a leisurely bath. She had lied to the knights and said that her sister was in service at Airdfinnan, so as to not reveal her identity.

That Bayard had guarded her jealously when they made camp the previous night encouraged her mightily.

There had been a tense moment at the gates of Airdfinnan, when her stern brother-in-law met the party of knights. Esmeraude knew that Angus recognized her immediately, though he said naught until the knights had shared their tale.

A thousand details of hospitality had ensued, for the horses had to be brushed and sheltered. More ale had to be poured and more meat sent to the kitchens. Baths were summoned for the knights and Esmeraude knew that they assumed that she and Célie bathed last in the dirty water. Bayard and Esmeraude were separated, and she wondered how he would continue his suit now.

She could not wait to find out.

Instead of the last water, Esmeraude lay in a lovely bath fragrant with rose petals, by her sister's own dictate. Célie had washed quickly and left for the kitchens, intending to lend assistance, at least by her explanation. Esmeraude knew that her maid went to seek gossip, and no doubt to revel in the glory of bringing new tales from Ceinn-beithe.

Tales of Esmeraude. 'Twas of no import, for Esmeraude meant to make her identity clear when she went to the board this evening. For the moment, she savored the luxury of the hot water. She dozed and might not have noted the opening of the door behind her if a cool draft had not caught her across her shoulders.

"So I am in service to the lord, am I?" Jacqueline demanded cheerfully from behind Esmeraude's tub. "Is that what they say of marriage these days?"

"Close the door! 'Tis cold," Esmeraude cried and her sister laughed as she did so.

"Did you tell them all that I labor upon my back for the man's favor?"

Esmeraude giggled and huddled beneath the water. "I left the matter to their interpretation."

"There is a matter I shall not pursue!" Jacqueline's footsteps grew louder as she approached. "I cannot imagine what brings you to our gates, Esmeraude. I was certain the châtelain spoke wrongly, for you should be occupied with the men summoned by *Maman* to compete for your hand."

"I wished to talk to you, Jacqueline."

"Because you must wed some man or join the cloister? Did you come to me to discover the truth of that life?"

Esmeraude grimaced, though her sister's tone was merry. Jacqueline had intended to join the good sisters of Inveresbeinn until Angus had won her heart. "'Twill be a man for me, upon that you can rely. And indeed, 'tis for that reason that I come to your gates—" She turned to appeal to her sister, then halted in astonishment. "You are pregnant!"

Jacqueline touched her ripe belly as if noting its size for the first time. "Is that what has happened?" she demanded, her eyes dancing with mischief. "I thought 'twas that apple seed I swallowed last summer."

" 'Twas a seed of last summer beyond doubt, but not one of any apple," Esmeraude teased.

Jacqueline laughed and lowered herself carefully to a stool. "Ah, the deeds I do in service to my lord and master."

The playful comment reminded Esmeraude of Bayard and his expectations of a wife, a matter she was not quite ready to discuss. "Do you not have enough children already?" she teased instead.

"There are only the four of them thus far." Jacqueline's features lit as she recounted the graces of her brood. She ticked them off upon her fingers. "Fergus is but nine."

"And the very image of Angus."

"Save that he is unscarred." As always, Jacqueline spoke of Angus's disfigurement calmly, as if it did not trouble her at all. Knowing her gift for seeing the fullness of any soul's character, Esmeraude suspected that such a detail would not. "But he is such a thoughtful boy, I cannot imagine that he will find much trouble in his days."

"He makes sufficient mischief when he sets his mind to it." Esmeraude remembered all too well finding a frog in her bed when her sister's family last visited Ceinn-beithe and how the boy responsible had laughed at her surprise.

Jacqueline laughed. "Aye, and then he feigns innocence with such apparent sincerity. There is more to Fergus than meets the eye, that much is certain."

"While one would never even guess that Annelise is born of the same parents as he." Esmeraude strove to look innocent herself. "At least, I *assume* she has the same father."

"Esmeraude!" Jacqueline laughed as she wagged a finger at her sister. "Only you could contrive such a wicked tale as that." She smiled with affection. "You had best be certain that none think Annelise is *your* child. She is all sparkle and sunshine and charm. And busy! Indeed, she leaves us exhausted merely from watching her antics."

"Has she ceased to grow so quickly?"

"Nay, she is taller than ever, nigh as tall as Fergus though he is two years older than she."

"You should not feed her so well," Esmeraude teased and Jacqueline playfully tossed another chunk of soap into the bath. It splashed, making Esmeraude squeal in surprise, and they laughed together.

"You will be surprised at how tall Ysembel has become this winter as well," Jacqueline continued.

"I think she is the prettiest child that I have ever seen," Esmeraude said firmly. She was fond of her nieces and nephews, and would have loved to have a hundred of them. Indeed, Jacqueline and Angus had a household filled with love of the same ilk she would prefer for herself. Esmeraude splashed in the bath, doubly determined to convince Bayard.

"I am teaching her to embroider, and she has considerable flair with a needle."

"Poor soul," Esmeraude muttered.

"You must ask to see her work—'tis exquisite and she is most proud of herself."

"You know that I have no appreciation for needlework."

Jacqueline chuckled. "Aye, I recall how you hated it. Poor Célie should have been sainted for having to teach you. And my Alina, oh, she has a voice like an angel."

"Does she speak yet?"

"Some. She prefers to sing nonsense and does so all the time." Jacqueline shook her head in bemusement. " 'Tis as if I gave birth to a songbird instead of a child."

"And what shall you bear this time?"

"An apple, of course," Jacqueline said with sparkling eyes. "If a particularly large one." Her smile faded and she leaned closer. "In truth, I care naught for the babe's gender. I would merely have it be hale."

Esmeraude glimpsed the fear in her sister's eyes and reached out, water dripping from her hand. "I would have *you* be hale," she said softly and gripped her sister's fingers. "In all seriousness, Jacqueline, you risk much in bearing so many babes."

"You sound like Angus," Jacqueline said with a rueful smile. "Babes seem a casualty of welcoming my husband to my bed."

" 'Tis not unholy to sleep alone some of the time."

Jacqueline blushed and glanced away. "Nay, but 'tis cold."

'Twas all too easy to understand now what particular kind of heat Jacqueline sought from her spouse. Esmeraude felt her own flush rise, for Esmeraude understood the pleasure that could be found in a man's embrace better than her sister imagined.

What if she bore Bayard's child? Esmeraude straightened in alarm. It could happen, and if it did, 'twould only strengthen Bayard's conviction to wed her regardless of any lack of love between them. But she did not want him to wed her because he thought he had to!

She stood quickly to evade such troubling thoughts, and began to roughly rub herself dry with a length of linen.

"You asked why I came to Airdfinnan," she said briskly. "I wished your counsel."

"Aye? Why do I have the sense that you have made some mischief, perhaps with perilous consequence?"

Esmeraude found herself flushing. "Mine seemed a good idea at the time."

"The worst folly always seems a good idea at some time to you." Jacqueline shook her head, then straightened on her stool, as if sitting in judgment. She showed a startling resemblance to their mother. "But tell me what you have done."

Esmeraude wrapped the linen about herself and folded her arms across her chest. "You will not like the tale."

"Indulge me."

Esmeraude ticked her deeds off on her fingers. "I have embarked upon a quest for a spouse—"

"But *Maman* is hosting a Bride Quest for you!"

"I will not wed a man who desires me only for my dowry," Esmeraude said firmly. "I would be wed for myself first, and have my dowry be, as 'tis intended, a blessing upon the match. I would wed for love, as you have done and as *Maman* intended."

"You might love one of the men summoned for you. No doubt that was *Maman*'s plan."

"No doubt, but it failed."

"And thus you have . . . ?"

Esmeraude indicated her second finger. "I have been handfasted to a Norseman. I have fled that man while yet chaste, leaving him senseless and bound in a locked room." She pursed her lips. "I am rid of my maidenhead. I have stolen a boat and kidnapped a knight's squire. I have stolen a steed, pretended to be a whore, seduced a knight, and fled his side while he slept. I have lied about my identity." Esmeraude narrowed her eyes as she reviewed her recent deeds. "I believe that is the sum of it."

But Jacqueline was still partway through the list. "You are rid of your maidenhead?" she echoed.

"'Twas the source of my woes, Jacqueline, and the reason why the King of the Isles handfasted me to a brute of a man. Its absence gives no man an advantage over me."

One man had an advantage, but Esmeraude chose not to speak of him just yet.

Jacqueline clearly did not share her view. "But, but, to whom did you lose it?"

Esmeraude frowned, knowing that her sister might take Bayard's view of his duty to wed the maid he had sampled first. She was not quite prepared to grant him such an advantage. Not before she knew whether his heart could be won. "It matters naught."

"It most certainly does!"

"Then 'twas given to a dream of a man, a man wrought of the mist of the sea and the dust of the faeries, a man who does not exist in truth. 'Tis gone, Jacqueline, and I will speak no more of it."

"Was it this man's squire you kidnapped?" Jacqueline guessed.

"'Twas not so dreadful as it sounds," Esmeraude admitted, before the gleam in her sister's eyes told her that she had revealed more than she had wished. "The boy was asleep in the boat and I had no choice but to take him with us. I left him with his companion."

"So, you stole this same man's boat as well."

"'Borrowed' is perhaps a better choice of word."

"Borrowed!" Jacqueline shook her head, then looked thoughtful. "And his horse, as well?"

Esmeraude did not answer, though her sister's gaze was cursedly perceptive.

"I do not suppose that he would be the same knight you seduced?" Esmeraude's flush was evidently answer enough to that. Jacqueline sat back and folded her arms across her chest. "So, you have lost your virginity to a knight and fled from him. Would he not wed you?"

"It matters naught!"

"I say it does." Jacqueline dropped her voice, as if they were exchanging secrets abed once again. "What is his name?"

Esmeraude looked away. "I will not divulge it."

"Nonsense!"

"I sought to be rid of the liability of my maidenhead and I chose a stranger for the task. His name is not of any import."

"Then why does it vex you so when I ask? Why did you seduce him and why do you flee him, under disguise as a serving maid?" Jacqueline grinned. "Tell me, Esmeraude. I swear this intriguing tale shall go no further."

"And if I do not share it?"

"You know that I shall uncover the truth without your aid."

Esmeraude realized that Célie would be only too willing to share all the details with Jacqueline. The maid did love to be the bearer of news. Indeed, Célie might already be regaling those in the kitchens with what she had seen. Jacqueline would hear some variant of the truth soon enough.

Indeed, the sole advantage Esmeraude had was in being the one to tell the tale and thus letting the truth reign. Knowing she had lost, she grimaced and sat down upon a stool beside her sister. "If I confide in you, Jacqueline, you must pledge to tell none of what I have said."

"I swear it."

"Then, know that I fear I erred." Esmeraude held up a hand when Jacqueline opened her mouth to comment. "Not in being rid of my maidenhead, for I still think that to have been the wisest course." She sighed. "Each time we love is better than the last. I could not regret a moment of such experience."

"Esmeraude! You mated with him more than once? You still do?" Jacqueline's eyes widened and she leaned so far forward on the stool that Esmeraude feared she might topple off.

"Aye!" Esmeraude nodded, unrepentant, then shook a finger at her sister. "But I fear that I erred in choosing the man to do the deed. Though he was a stranger to me, he knew my name. Indeed, he was seeking me."

"He came for *Maman*'s Bride Quest," Jacqueline breathed.

"Aye, he would wed me, but he believes love a weakness of fools and peasants."

"Oh." Jacqueline sat back, less deterred by this than Esmeraude. "But Angus insisted as much as well, and he was proven wrong."

"He also seeks an obedient wife."

Jacqueline grimaced. "Perhaps you are poorly suited. Do you think he will pursue you here?"

Esmeraude felt herself blush. "He *is* here."

"Which one?" Jacqueline's eyes brightened.

"I should not tell you."

"Then I will guess. The dark-haired one whose gaze fixes upon you."

"How could you know?"

Jacqueline laughed. "How could I not know? He watches you as avidly as a hawk watches its next meal. I think he is not so indifferent as he might have you believe." She clasped her hands together. "Do you mean to make a conquest of his heart?"

"I hope so, but I know not how to begin. You must help me, Jacqueline!"

"You love him."

Esmeraude sighed and closed her eyes. "I have never seen the like of him. He is tall and broad of shoulder, he is handsome, and his eyes are the clearest and deepest blue. He is chivalrous and elegant and says the most marvelous things."

"And is talented abed."

Esmeraude knew she turned crimson, for she belatedly guessed that her sister was teasing her. "A man with such confidence and charm would suit me very well. You must understand, Jacqueline, that I have never met his ilk. *Maman* spoke aright when she said that a knight had a certain allure."

"Aye, she did." The sisters shared a smile. "And I, too, was susceptible to that allure."

"Do you think I might succeed?"

" 'Tis not unlikely. Look how Angus and I found each other, against all odds," Jacqueline said cheerfully. "Love appears when one least expects its presence. Though it must be sought diligently. Such a man will pretend to feel naught long after he knows 'tis not so."

"I am certain that all will be resolved, with your aid," Esmeraude said with a smile, not in the least bit certain of it. "What is most important is that your child arrives healthy and that you are well afterward."

"This babe cannot come soon enough for my taste," Jacqueline muttered. She pushed to her feet. "I shall call a maid to fetch you one of my chemises and a kirtle. That way, yours can be washed for 'tis filthy indeed."

"I thank you."

Jacqueline picked up the chemise and wrinkled her nose, then held out the length of one sleeve questioningly. 'Twas clearly not Esmeraude's own and Jacqueline's eyes widened as she realized whose chemise she must hold. Their gazes met and Esmeraude's cheeks pinkened again.

"His?" Jacqueline hissed.

Esmeraude nodded guiltily, then they giggled like young girls.

"*Maman* would be shocked!"

"Aye!" And they laughed again at the prospect.

When their laughter faded, Jacqueline nodded crisply, once again resembling their mother. "Then 'tis clear you must win this knight and I shall aid you. I shall say this chemise belongs to Angus, so that there will be no chatter in the hall. You shall have one of mine in its stead."

"I thank you." Esmeraude nodded and her sister made to depart. Though all seemed to be resolved, there was yet one question that plagued Esmeraude. She restlessly pleated the linen wrapped about herself between her fingers. Just as her sister made to cross the threshold, she dared to ask for the answer she feared most.

"Jacqueline, do you think me like my papa?" Esmeraude's voice was softer than was typical of her, but Jacqueline heard her all the same.

Her sister glanced back, her expression concerned. "Why?" Then she frowned. "Who has suggested such a thing to you?"

"Célie. She said I was a selfish, impetuous fool, like my papa, and that I would bring injury to those around me, even though I meant no harm." Esmeraude could not hold her sister's gaze. "You must recall him better than I do. Am I like Theobald? What was he like?"

Jacqueline leaned in the doorway and shook her head. "Oh, Theobald. He had a glib tongue and was quick with a fine word, that is what I recall of him. And that he was seldom at Arnelaine after he and *Maman* were wed. She ensured that he was invested with that manor, you know, for he had not a *denier* to his name. 'Twas Uncle Guillaume who granted it to him, and I suppose 'twas the expectation that we should make a modest home there."

"You make it sound as if we did not."

"Theobald much preferred the lively company to be found at court to the quiet pleasures of a rural holding."

"*Maman* must have missed him."

Jacqueline smiled sadly. "*Maman* might have killed him, had he not died of a fever. She was sorely vexed with him, and disappointed that he showed no inclination to tend what he had been granted by her family at her behest."

Esmeraude looked up in surprise. "No one told me of this!"

"You adored him. He was your blood sire, but he is dead." Jacqueline shrugged. "What purpose would be served by tainting your fine memories? 'Twas to you that Theobald showed the best in his character, after all."

"And the worst?"

Jacqueline frowned.

Esmeraude was ready to hear the truth. "Jacqueline, why did we come to Ceinn-beithe?"

"It matters little now."

"It matters a great deal to me. I thought we came because you did not care for your betrothed."

Jacqueline lifted her gaze to meet Esmeraude's across the room. "Aye, 'twas part of it. The greater part, though, was that Theobald gambled all we had and then some. He even lost the seal of Arnelaine, which was not his to lose. And when *Maman* would have bought out my betrothal contract, there was not a coin to be used for any purpose."

Jacqueline sighed. "I think she was embarrassed to face her own brother with what her husband had done in return for Guillaume's kindness. I doubt she knew how distant Ceinn-beithe truly was. Its title was the only thing Theobald did not gamble away and he himself admitted he had not done so because 'twas held to have no value."

Esmeraude looked down at her busy fingers. This was a side of her father that she had not known. 'Twas indeed unattractive that he could tend to his own pleasure at gambling, without a care to the obligations of his family.

"Am I like him?" she asked huskily.

Jacqueline crossed the room with quick steps and gripped her sister's shoulder. "You have his charm and share his delight in the world and its pleasures. You share his impulsive nature, 'tis true." Esmeraude looked up and her sister smiled. "But I cannot believe that you would continue along any course once you knew it injured someone you knew."

"Though I might unwittingly embark upon it." Esmeraude

frowned and propped her chin on her hand. "'Tis scarcely a reassuring comment."

Jacqueline gave her shoulder a squeeze. "If overcoming a weakness can be achieved by any, Esmeraude, it can be done by you. You are fortunate to have our mother's determination, which is more than sufficient strength to temper any weakness of Theobald's." She winked when Esmeraude glanced up at her hopefully. "You will see."

"Why did *Maman* wed such a man?"

Jacqueline smiled sadly. "Because she thought she loved him, of course."

"But if she loved him, how could matters end so badly?" Esmeraude cried in dismay. "I thought love made all come aright?"

"Only if 'tis returned. I suspect that Theobald loved none but himself. You are right to ensure that your love is reciprocated before you wed, for as you see with *Maman* and Duncan, and also with Angus and I, those are the matches blessed with untold happiness." Jacqueline smiled. "Trust me, Esmeraude, you are best to deny this knight until you know the truth of his heart. And even if you love him, if he cannot love you, then you are best without him and his charms."

Esmeraude gripped her sister's hand. "I thank you, for the truth, for your confidence, and for your aid and hospitality."

"You are my sister. What else would I do?" They shared a warm smile, then Jacqueline made her way to the door. She paused on the threshold, her hand pressed into the small of her back, suddenly looking very tired. "Would you do me one service in return?"

"Anything!"

"Speak to these suitors, for they have shown diligence in pursuing you." Jacqueline held up a hand when Esmeraude began to protest. "I thought little good of my Angus when first we met, but time proved my response to be wrong. You cannot tell which man will hold your heart with so little as a glance, regardless of what the old tales say. If I had spurned Angus so quickly as that, I would not know the joy I do now. Esmeraude, please consider the men who have come this far. In the event that your heart leads you astray, you may find love where you least expected it."

"If you suggest as much."

"I do." Jacqueline winked, her happiness easing the signs of her exhaustion. "You might be surprised by what you discover."

Esmeraude inclined her head, doubtful but willing to try. "I will speak to each of them before making a choice. Would it be possible to send word to *Maman*, so that she does not worry that some foul fate has befallen me?"

"Of course." Jacqueline smiled. "You see? Theobald never sent word to any to ease their fears. He cared only for his own concerns. You are not wrought of the same selfishness as he, Esmeraude."

Esmeraude felt reassured by her sister's comment, but keeping this pledge was not all she would do. She thought about Jacqueline's state and decided that she would stay and lend her aid in her sister's household. Esmeraude might have unwittingly invited guests to Airdfinnan's door, but she would do what she could to see that Jacqueline rested so close to her time.

She did not doubt that Angus would be amenable to that plan.

✦

Bayard quickly noted the details of Airdfinnan's hall. 'Twas devoid of windows and hung with rich tapestries. Wall sconces, candles, and braziers filled the large chamber with both welcome heat and a golden glow. A number of trestle tables had been set up and numerous men quaffed ale as they traded tales. Silver chalices gleamed and pottery mugs clinked, while the smell of roasting meat wafted from the kitchens beyond.

There was no sign of the women as yet, though there was a portal on the far wall. That wall looked to be wrought of different stone than the hall's walls and was perhaps of later construction. Bayard assumed that this lord had wrought a separate solar for slumber as so many did in these days.

"Airdfinnan is heavily manned," Bayard commented as he counted the considerable number of men at the board. He added those that accompanied them and those who still walked the walls and was impressed.

The lord slanted him a glance. "A man must defend his treasures if he means to keep them."

'Twas a philosophy that met with much favor from Bayard, though he had no opportunity to comment further. His cousins and brother now returned from the bailey, rubbing their hands together. They sat at the table at the other end of the chamber, and clearly enjoyed themselves greatly. The lord excused himself to make them welcome and no doubt to confirm that the gate was secured.

Bayard enjoyed the ale and the warmth of the hall after the chill ride they had endured. He wondered whether Esmeraude intended to reveal her identity on this night to his brother and cousins and found himself smiling in anticipation of their surprise.

Then someone cleared his throat tentatively from behind him. "Sir?"

Bayard turned to see Michael, Andrew fast behind him. "Aye?"

"If I might be so bold as to make a comment, it seems to me that this lady is perhaps not suited to you, sir."

Bayard watched the boy carefully. "Indeed?"

"Indeed." Michael nodded. "If she wishes so much to evade your hand, there might be a reason for it, which only she knows."

"Or it might be that she plays a game, one intended to find the suitor with the most resolute will."

Michael frowned. " 'Tis true, sir, though I wonder whether a woman who so defies your will would make a fitting bride in the end. Perhaps we should abandon this chase and ride to meet the king instead. This may not prove a victory that can be won, or it may be one with too heavy a price upon it."

Bayard smiled. He was pleased that Michael was beginning to think in a strategic manner, yet the boy did not know all of the details of this quest. "Have you ever known me to abandon a battle simply because it will not be readily won?"

"Nay, sir." Michael shook his head as Andrew watched the exchange with wide eyes.

"And have you ever known me to risk an advantage, like the king's favor, for a prize not worth pursuit?"

"Nay, sir."

"Then know that I do not do as much this time either."

"But sir, never have I known you to pursue a matter beyond reason, either." Michael held his ground beneath Bayard's glare. "Perhaps such a willful lady is not well suited to you. Perhaps 'tis not *logical* to pursue her further."

Bayard was stung by the ring of truth in the boy's words. He had taught him too well. "You are not privy to all the details of this matter, Michael," he said firmly. "Know that no conquest easily won provides such satisfaction as one that tests the fullness of one's wits and resolve."

"Aye, sir."

Bayard smiled at the boys, speaking with his usual confidence. "I do not lose. I *will* not lose in any quest. And this lady shall learn that my resolve is greater than her own. That and that alone will make a fitting bride of her in the end. Now, find yourselves a cup and a place by the fire!"

"Aye, sir." The boys bowed and ran to fetch refreshment, leaving Bayard with his own thoughts.

'Twas true that Esmeraude was not the wife he had expected to win or even to seek in these hills. His Esmeraude was more clever, more complicated, and more stubborn than he had initially understood. It might not be easy to teach her to be compliant with his will, but he found himself remarkably anxious to try.

Aye, he had spoken the truth to his squires. Bayard heartily anticipated the conquest of Esmeraude of Ceinn-beithe. Indeed, he could not recall a battle that had engaged him so much as this. Surely that was a good omen for their match.

He whistled as he signaled for another mug of ale, more than prepared to match wits with this lady once more. He was by far the most fitting suitor for her hand and she had surrendered her maidenhead to him, which gave him a certain advantage. 'Twas true that they did not agree upon every matter, but 'twould have been more troubling otherwise, to his thinking, for 'twas unnatural for two souls to agree in all things.

Clearly, she but tested him. And he was well accustomed to tests.

Still, 'twas irksome that he did not know precisely what to expect of his Esmeraude. He supposed that was what added a spice to the pursuit of her.

Indeed, Michael spoke with a certain truth. Bayard would have abandoned any other woman by this point, knowing that he had done his best to persuade her of the error of her thinking. He might have returned to his grandmother, intent upon persuading her to abandon this whimsical test of his resolve.

But not Esmeraude. 'Twas unthinkable. Bayard guessed

that his urge to win Esmeraude was beginning to go deeper than the challenge set by his grandmother, though he refused to speculate further upon that matter.

Aye, he had need of sleep and a hearty meal, so whimsy claimed his thoughts. 'Twas no more than that.

When the shadows drew long, the far portal opened and children spilled out into the hall, first a dark-haired boy, then a flaxen-haired girl. A smaller girl followed, even as the boy ran to the lord's side. The lord's features softened and he smiled at what were obviously his own children. He stepped forward to greet them, his guest momentarily forgotten.

Bayard deliberately hung back, expecting to see his lady and wanting to savor the moment in some privacy. The lady of the keep was the next to step into the hall. She walked with some difficulty, being ripe with the lord's seed once again. Her skirts were clutched by yet another girl, a dark-haired toddler who seemed shy of the noise of the hall.

The lord moved toward his lady, putting down the boy and picking up the little girl, offering his lady his arm. She leaned heavily upon him, clearly tired, though her smile for him was radiant.

Then Esmeraude stepped into the hall and it seemed to Bayard that the entire hall halted to gaze upon her. He stared himself, grateful for the concealment of the shadows, and studied her, suddenly greedy for every detail about her.

She was more beautiful than he had guessed.

Chapter Eleven

SMERAUDE WAS GARBED AS A NOBLEWOMAN. HER chestnut hair was braided and threaded with ribbons and pearls. She wore a fitted kirtle of a dark blue damask, its hem and cuffs rich with golden embroidery.

The hues emphasized her own coloring, making her hair appear more golden and, no doubt, her eyes more blue. The vibrant crimson embroidery upon her chemise was visible at her neck and again at the hem. When she walked, the deep green of her embroidered leather slippers were visible, as was the yellow of her stockings.

The vivid hues suited her well. Bayard envisioned her in plum and red, in vermilion and green, in gold and deepest red. She sparkled in these colorful garments, like a jewel set among fitting finery, and he knew that he would have to see her garbed so lavishly always. She drew every eye and it suited her to be at the center of attention.

There were roses in her cheeks on this evening and pure mischief in her smile. Though garbed as a noblewoman, she did not assume the demure demeanor of one.

And Bayard did not care. Indeed, he found himself smiling to see that clothing could not change the essence of his Esmeraude. She hovered in the doorway, her gaze fixed upon the knights at the board, and seemed to tap her feet in impatience like a trickster awaiting the last line of his jest.

Bayard smiled, knowing she anticipated the moment her identity would be revealed to the three knights. He acknowledged to himself that 'twas not merely the prospect of winning Montvieux that prompted his interest in this lady.

Esmeraude intrigued him as no other woman had done before.

Bayard liked her passion and her desire for adventure. He liked her quick wits and her determination to influence the rest of her days. He was troubled far less than he had expected that she was not remotely obedient.

Indeed, it made the conquest of her all the more sweet to know that 'twas not easily won. Esmeraude had a way of turning him to her will, of prompting him to anger, of bringing words to his lips that he had not meant to utter. And Esmeraude wished a confession of love beyond all else. 'Twould not be easy to deny her.

But he would not lie to her, not again. One lie was sufficient between them and he would prefer that there were none at all.

'Twas good that Bayard had been well trained to face a challenge and that he had a rare determination to be victorious at any quest he undertook. 'Twould suit him well to have such a lady by his side. He eased to a seat at the back of the hall.

For the moment, he would watch, unobserved. Her gaze flicked over the hall, no doubt seeking him, and consternation touched her features when she did not see him. Bayard smiled into his mug.

She was more than half won.

The lord of Airdfinnan introduced his wife and children to the noble guests, then turned and offered a hand to Esmeraude. "And of course, you must know my wife's sister, Esmeraude of Ceinn-beithe."

Esmeraude smiled and sailed triumphant to the board, even as Amaury choked upon his ale. Connor frowned and Nicholas's eyes were uncommonly wide.

"*You* are Esmeraude?" Nicholas demanded.

Esmeraude took her seat with such perfect poise that Bayard felt a burst of pride. "Of course." She granted them a brilliant smile. "I had said that I would be at Airdfinnan and here I am. I thank you for your accompaniment. One hears that there are oft bandits upon the road." She smiled at the astonished men, searched covertly for Bayard again, then tucked her napkin into her lap.

"But you rode with us and said naught," Connor said darkly. "Indeed, you deliberately deceived us by pretending to be a peasant maid."

"I did not expect you to be so readily tricked." Esmeraude said archly, then smiled as a servant filled a chalice with ale for her. "Indeed, Bayard was not fooled for a moment by my ruse. Is he the sole one in your family with his wits about him?"

Bayard's heart leapt at the sound of his name on her lips. He was delighted that the lady mentioned him with favor. The lord glanced up, evidently recalling the guest he had forgotten in his concern for his wife. He met Bayard's gaze but Bayard shook his head, content to remain unnoticed for the moment.

"Aye, you *rode* with Bayard," Connor muttered, then quaffed his ale. "He always had a desire to be first in all matters."

Nicholas looked alarmed at this innuendo and glanced between Esmeraude and Connor.

"Does this mean that you have spurned my brother?" Amaury demanded.

Esmeraude smiled. "A man who does not believe in the merit of love is not the man for me."

Connor inhaled, his disapproval evident. "Perhaps you should have thought of that afore you coaxed him into the woods."

The silence that descended upon the hall was broken only by the snap of Connor's fingers as he summoned more ale. All on the dais turned to Connor, their expressions either inquiring or condemning.

"What do you mean by this comment?" the lord asked coldly. "Do you cast accusations upon the reputation of a guest at my board?"

"Bayard always had to be *first*," Connor repeated firmly. "And I do not doubt that he has been first in this deed as well."

Esmeraude flushed and her maid, Célie, looked exasperated.

"My cousins may choose for themselves, but I will not court another man's leavings." Connor leveled a cool glance at Esmeraude. "I have always thought that a lady of grace and temperance would come virginal to her nuptial bed."

"The children!" the lady of Airdfinnan cried. She placed her hands over the ears of the toddler even as the color drained from her own face. She sent an imploring glance to the lord, who rose to his feet. Indeed, Bayard took a step forward himself to defend his lady.

But Esmeraude needed the aid of neither of them. She rose, her color high, and urged her brother-in-law aside as she made her way toward Connor. "And you, of course, will be chaste yourself until your own wedding night?"

Connor smiled. "'Tis not your concern what I do and do not do."

"But what I do is yours?"

"'Tis different for a bride."

"Aye? It may be different for the bride you choose, but I would never wed a man who judges women by such a triviality."

" 'Tis hardly a triviality!"

"Nay? But on the morn after the nuptials, 'tis gone either way. And then the couple must make a life together, a marriage dependent upon their character and their strengths, not upon the presence or absence of blood upon the linens."

Connor's lips tightened. "No man of honor weds a whore."

"So, now a woman who is not chaste must be a whore! Surely, sir, there is another choice betwixt the two?"

"Not enough of one to be of import."

Esmeraude leaned toward Connor, her voice low and her eyes dangerously narrow. "There are women, Connor of Tullymullagh, who do not bleed upon the linens of their nuptial bed, though indeed they are virginal. Would you spurn a bride for the sake of a few drops of blood?"

Connor leveled a stare at her. "You lie. And aye, I would."

"Yet men wed widows all the time. How is it that my mother was wed thrice? She bore children in each marriage, therefore could not have been virginal after those first nuptials." Esmeraude lifted her chin in challenge and propped her hands upon her hips. Bayard had the distinct sense that she enjoyed this argument.

And she argued well, this he had to admit.

Connor waved away her objection. "Widows are wedded all the time, though 'tis oft more for their holdings than their person."

"Not true!" Esmeraude protested hotly. "Duncan wed my mother for the love of her!"

"Or was it for the title to Ceinn-beithe?" Connor shook his head. "None can know the heart of any man, only the contents of his own. When I see that a man has wed and won a grand holding, then I cannot trust any such pledge of love."

Esmeraude's expression turned chilly. "So you would suggest that I believe all men come to court me *lie* when they claim to desire me for my own self?"

Connor shrugged. "You should ask one you might count among that company. I court your hand no longer."

"On the basis of a suspicion alone?" the lady demanded.

"I know what I saw."

"You saw naught!"

"I saw enough. Do you confess, then, to surrendering your chastity?" Connor demanded. "Tell us the truth of it, then, and make an argument in your own defense."

The lady of Airdfinnan appeared to hold her breath but Esmeraude's color rose yet further. "I will confess naught to those determined to believe ill of me. Why should I believe that you would grant credit to any truth I might utter?"

Connor snorted and sipped his ale. "For you know the truth will show you no favor. Your reluctance is condemnation enough for me."

"You do not know that!" Esmeraude cried.

"I know what I saw," Connor insisted.

"And what did you see, Connor?" Bayard asked, sauntering forth from the shadows as he did so. "Do tell us all."

Everyone upon the dais as well as those in the hall turned to face Bayard, but he held his cousin's gaze. He arched a brow, as if to dare his cousin to make his accusation openly, but Connor flushed, then buried his nose in his ale.

Bayard glanced to his lady and his heart leapt at her evident joy in seeing him. He knew as he smiled back at her that they would wed shortly indeed.

He strolled across the hall confidently, knowing that a way would be cleared before him. "What you witnessed, Connor, was a kiss of favor bestowed by a lady upon the suitor with whom she was most pleased."

He paused before Esmeraude and bowed low, then took her hand in his and kissed its back. Under the watchful gazes of all, he turned her hand in his, then kissed her palm. She shivered as he folded her fingers over his embrace.

"Lady mine," he said quietly, but not so quietly that the others at the table could not hear, "your beauty challenges the splendor of the heavens this night and your smile is more radiant than the sun itself."

Esmeraude smiled and pulled her hand from his grip. "You probably say as much to all the demoiselles whose hands you court." Her tone was light and teasing, so Bayard could not take offense.

"Nay, Esmeraude, only the one I intend to win." He winked at her and when her smile broadened, he felt a most uncommon surge of relief.

Buoyed, Bayard turned to gesture to the assembly. "Greetings, cousins and brother, and well met. Your argument, Connor, puts me in mind of a tale, one concerned with a knight winning his lady's hand against every adversity."

"Tell it!" cried the oldest of the lord's daughters. She bounced on the bench in evident excitement as the others turned to Bayard inquisitively. "We love to hear tales! Do we not, Aunt Esmeraude?"

"Aye, I have learned that the lady is fond of a tale," Bayard said smoothly. "Let all those suitors gathered here offer compensation to the Lord of Airdfinnan by entertaining his household."

"I have heard the tale that you would tell, and I care naught for it," Esmeraude said with a proud lift of her chin, her mood changing sharply against him.

Bayard smiled. "You have heard but the beginning of the tale, and little of the adventures to follow. I would wager that you will find the continuation of the tale more pleasing than you expect." He saw her indecision and knew 'twas fed by her curiosity.

"We could each tell a tale," Nicholas suggested. "And Esmeraude could choose which one she loved best."

'Twas clear he meant more than the tales themselves. Esmeraude glanced to the other knights, then back to Bayard, her gaze lingering upon him. "Do Tristran and Iseut truly fall in love?" she asked with challenge in her tone. "For otherwise, I do not care to hear it."

Bayard let his smile broaden. "I can tell the tale or not tell the tale. 'Tis your choice, lady mine."

She eyed her very pregnant sister, then nodded once crisply. " 'Tis a good evening to remain at the board and to rest," she said, then put an arm around her sister's shoulders. "If 'tis my bidding that you suitors will follow, then I bid you each to tell a tale that will make my sister smile." Esmeraude turned then to face Bayard, and granted him a knowing smile. "And yours had best improve, sir, if you intend to see me pleased."

"You know that your pleasure is my sole desire," Bayard murmured, meaning more than the pleasure won by a tale.

Esmeraude blushed and laughed lightly, her eyes dancing. Bayard felt a most illogical sense of victory, as if he had won a prize more tremendous than any he had won before. Aye, he dared not lose this contest. Montvieux, after all, hung in the balance.

But as Bayard watched Esmeraude, he knew that Montvieux was not the only prize he desired.

The children were nigh as excited as Esmeraude, though she knew their reasons were different from her own. For them, 'twas a rare treat to have an evening of new tales. Esmeraude found she was impatient with the offerings of the other men, wishing only to hear how Bayard's saga progressed.

Indeed, she thought it a good sign that he was so intent upon winning her favor. Surely a man with no heart, as he claimed to be, would not put himself to so much trouble to charm her? She watched Bayard through her lashes, not wanting him to be so certain of her heart as she. It seemed that there was a thread stretched taut between the two of them, a ripple of awareness that Esmeraude was half-certain all the hall could discern.

It had been gallant of Bayard to pretend that theirs had been naught but a kiss, though his choice had surprised her. Surely the truth would have only strengthened his claim? It intrigued her that he defied her expectation and she was thrilled that he defended her honor.

What else did she not know about this man?

Annelise squeezed onto the bench between Esmeraude and Jacqueline, her expression bright with anticipation. Ysembel and Alina were quick to follow suit, one sitting on each side of the sisters. Fergus remained beside his father, who gave Esmeraude a slow nod of approval. Aye, Jacqueline would have bustled about this night to see to the accommodations of her guests and she was far better simply sitting at the board.

Amaury began to tell a tale and Esmeraude's gaze wandered between the two brothers. She could not help but compare them to each other, for their coloring and features were so similar. Any fool would have known them to be brothers.

But there was something different, for Bayard looked to have sipped from the world's cup of experience. His expression was wary and wry, his eyes glittered with an understanding of both people and events. In comparison, Amaury seemed young and soft, unshaped to manhood as yet, though she knew that she would have found him most handsome had she not met his elder brother first.

Amaury's tale was fair enough, for he told the legend of Melusine. The younger girls were particularly enthralled by this story of faeries good and wicked. Though Esmeraude had heard it oft before, 'twas a fine tale and Amaury recounted it well.

Connor told a thin tale of a ghost at his ancestral estate of Tullymullagh, his disinterest in this contest evident to all. 'Twas clear that he had no desire to seek Esmeraude's favor, but perhaps felt 'twould be a slight to Jacqueline to not participate.

Nicholas recounted a tale that he said he had learned in Venetian from his grandfather. Esmeraude was fascinated by this exotic tale of an immortal doomed to wander in search of his beloved and the salvation only she could grant. There was a tale of lovers true! Surely 'twould sway Bayard to her thinking.

Or not. She could guess naught of his thoughts from his guarded expression.

Then 'twas Bayard's turn. Esmeraude's heart leapt to her throat when he stood. His manner was that of a man with no doubt that he would win. He cleared his throat several times, then bowed to the lady of the manor.

"With your forgiveness, my tale is also one of lovers whose path was fraught with disappointment. Theirs is a fine tale, however, and though I first heard it sung recently in France, 'tis said to have long roots hereabouts. 'Tis the tale of Tristran and Iseut." He glanced toward Esmeraude and her heart thumped. "Would you hear it or shall I think of another?"

Jacqueline smiled and spoke before Esmeraude could do so. "I should love to hear this tale, for 'tis unfamiliar to me by such a name. We have a great fondness in this house for all tales of local origin."

"As my gracious hostess commands, such is my will." Bayard bowed low, then straightened and began to sing.

He sang the verses he had already sung to Esmeraude, addressing them to all of the company and evading her gaze.

But when he came to the part she had yet to hear, he pivoted and caught her gaze, then held it unswervingly as he sang solely for her ears.

Esmeraude was enchanted.

> *The pair loved the journey away,*
> *Until arrived the fateful day,*
> *Their vessel sailed into Cornwall.*
> *King Mark's bride was welcomed by all,*
> *The King was delighted in truth,*
> *By Tristran's bringing his pledged due.*
> *Iseut was garbed in royal red,*
> *A crown hung o'er the nuptial bed.*
> *'Twas not Mark's bride who met him there,*
> *Not Iseut, bride beyond compare:*
> *'Twas Iseut's maid, virgin Brangain,*
> *For Iseut had with Tristran lain.*
> *King Mark never did guess the truth,*
> *For Night allied with Love and Youth.*

Esmeraude was horrified that this Iseut could ask her maid for such a sacrifice, and that the king had been so readily fooled. But what would she do on the night of her nuptials? Would she lie to the man she loved? Or would she deceive him? It seemed that men put more value than she had hoped in the virginity of their brides. Esmeraude belatedly saw the value of her maid's counsel.

Still, she could not regret the pleasure that she and Bayard had shared.

Bayard dropped his voice and the assembly leaned closer to hear the words.

> *Now hear about the dwarf Frocin,*
> *Allied with barons Denoalen,*
> *And Godoine and Ganelon.*

These four had envy for Tristran,
For he was King Mark's favored man.
They saw the lovers meeting when
The King was out upon his lands.
King Mark did not believe their tale,
He refused to credit such detail.
And so they four contrived a plot,
To show the King how he was mocked.
They told him of the lovers' tryst,
An interval he dared not miss.
The pair met oft in the garden,
A quiet spot without warden.
They met beside a small fountain,
Each evening meeting there again,
And there they loved the night away,
Certain the King knew not their game.

Bayard coughed, none too delicately. Esmeraude leaned forward in consternation. 'Twas true that the lovers should not have continued to meet, but surely they could not be discovered? Bayard cleared his throat with an effort, then forced a smile and began to sing again.

King Mark thought he would prove a lie,
By seeing this with his own eye.
He hid himself within a tree,
Above the place they had decreed.
And there he sat as night did fall,
Certain his bride would not be false.
He listened when he heard a sound,
Saw his lady, her hair unbound.
She waited there, her eyes so bright,
He feared his barons spoke aright.
He withdrew further in the leaves,
To wait and see what he would see.

Now, Bayard coughed with a vengeance. He let one of the men thump his back, he accepted a cup of ale, and he coughed again. Every soul in the hall watched him avidly, Esmeraude notwithstanding.

What had the king seen? She knew she would not sleep without knowing the truth. Finally Bayard straightened, holding up a hand and smiling as if he were recovered, and opened his mouth to sing.

But no sound came forth. The company gasped.

Bayard shook his head, as if sorely disappointed, then tried again.

This time his voice came as only the barest and most hoarse whisper. The assembly cried out in dismay and Bayard looked alarmed. Esmeraude began to rise to her feet, fearful that he had injured himself in seeking her favor. This was her fault! Bayard tried one last time, then bowed before the lady of the manor with evident regret.

He made a gesture of helplessness when no apology came forth from his lips.

"But we must know the end of the tale!" Annelise insisted.

Bayard coughed heavily, then gestured to the other suitors, as if inviting one of them to finish the tale for the ladies.

Glances were exchanged and protests were made, for no others here had heard this tale.

Jacqueline smiled prettily. "Can we not implore you to finish? Perhaps after a cup of ale?"

Bayard cleared his throat with tremendous effort, as if valiantly trying to do the lady's bidding, then shook his head with regret. "On the morrow?" he suggested quietly and with obvious effort.

"The morrow!" Annelise echoed. "We have to wait an entire day to know what he saw? You might give us a hint!"

Bayard coughed, then opened his mouth as if to do precisely thus. Not a sound erupted from his lips when he tried to speak.

Esmeraude sat back upon the bench, her sympathy for him much lessened. Aye, she was highly skeptical of how Bayard's voice seemed to come and go. She glared at him and he smiled fleetingly, the glint in his eyes one of pure devilry.

And then she knew.

'Twas a ploy to win a private audience with her! 'Twas a trick he played, no doubt intending that she should rush to tend him, to ply him with healing potions. Oh, he would probably confess that only her kiss could heal him, or some such nonsense.

Esmeraude had no intention of so readily following his will. 'Twas time he learned that she had thoughts of her own.

She stood and granted him a gracious smile. "How unfortunate that your tale could not be completed, though truly a tale of such faithlessness is perhaps unsuitable for my nieces' ears."

Bayard's eyes widened in a most satisfactory way, but there was naught he could say to argue the matter without further undermining his ruse.

"Aye," she said, bestowing a smile upon her nieces in an echo of Bayard's confidence. "You must understand that this Iseut was a particularly selfish woman."

"How so?" Annelise asked.

"She loved Tristran, but wed another. Bayard told me earlier that she fulfilled her duty by wedding her betrothed, but she did not. She deceived her husband, not only on the night of her nuptials, but when she continued to meet with her true love, Tristran. She had the security of marriage and the luxuries of a queen, but never surrendered the affections of her lover. Thus, she was fair to neither man, but saw only to her own desires."

Bayard opened his mouth to argue, but Esmeraude did not let him speak. If he would be mute, let him be mute!

"Nay, nay, do not strain your voice," she chided, not missing how his eyes flashed. Esmeraude shook her head with resolve. "Iseut was wrong. She should have either wed for her love and made whatever sacrifice was required, or she should have foresworn her love and fulfilled her obligation, not only by wedding her betrothed but by remaining true to him."

Bayard stepped forward and raised a hand as if to argue. "But 'twas you who argued that love was the greater power!" he croaked.

"Shhh! Do not injure yourself further on my behalf. 'Tis true that I believe that a man and woman should love each other afore they wed, but 'tis unfair for a woman to wed a man, knowing that another man holds her heart in thrall. I should never be so unfair to the man I wed, nor should I ever be unfaithful."

The men seemed struck to silence by her words, but Esmeraude was not done. She granted them all a sunny smile, so determined was she to prick Bayard's cursed confidence.

"That is why I will not wed a man I do not love. 'Twould not be fair if my true love crossed my path after those nuptial vows were made." She inclined her head regally to her astonished suitor. "I thank you for the reminder, Bayard, for it has bolstered my resolve in my quest for the man who will hold my heart."

There might have been steam rising from the knight's ears, but Esmeraude was not done.

"Perhaps 'tis better that your voice could not sustain the tale," she consoled him, taking the tone one took with an invalid. "I think a tale of faithlessness most unfitting for Angus's daughters and one must, as you well know, be courteous to one's host.

"And now, by the terms of Bayard's own suggestion, I must choose a winner of these tales. Indeed, Nicholas, your tale was offered no true contest."

That man beamed and got quickly to his feet. "And my prize?"

"No less than a kiss," Esmeraude declared. Bayard fumed before her but she did not care. 'Twas time she confirmed that his kisses were not the only ones with the power to awaken her passion.

Yet Esmeraude discovered precisely the opposite.

Though his effort was valiant, Nicholas's kiss made her think of the lips of fishes. Esmeraude even kissed him twice, just to be certain, a move which made every man in the hall hoot. But the only pleasure to be found in Nicholas's kiss was in turning from it to find Bayard glaring at her, his eyes that tumultuous blue.

And 'twas that sight which made her heart leap, not Nicholas' attempt at an ardent embrace.

Aye, her heart had known Bayard from the first. She covertly noted his frustration and wondered whether good might be found in this. It did not seem to Esmeraude that a man who viewed all matters in the cold light of logic would be so very infuriated by her granting a kiss to another.

Fortunately, there were two more suitors here—well, one more, as Connor had lost interest in her charms—and who knew how many more en route. Esmeraude would take her sister's advice—she would talk to and kiss them all. And when more suitors came, she would do the same.

She retired with a smile, certain that she would force Bayard to confess his affection for her in no time at all. Soon enough she would have her heart's own desire and the marriage of which she had long dreamed.

❖

As the company attended Bayard's tale, the storm clouds had closed completely around Airdfinnan's walls. The fortified isle might have been cast adrift in the clouds, isolated from all the mortal world, echoing in the silence of the ages.

The sentries were startled when they changed their shifts, for the fog was nigh impenetrable. Though one could see clear across the bailey from the gates, a man who poked his hand through the portcullis could not see his own fingers for the fog.

More than one man shivered and crossed himself. The gatekeeper barred the great wooden doors that evening without any command from his lord, not content with the protection of the lowered portcullis alone.

What none noted was that a small plant which had long languished in the garden began suddenly to grow. The plant, a gift from the distant south, which had taken poorly to its change of clime, had been assumed dead or close to it for fifty springs. But on this night, it sprouted with unholy vigor and grew as if 'twould compensate for every moment lost.

It climbed the wall with astounding haste, then stretched down the other side. Its length bristled with thorns, each lethal spur the length of a man's hand. When one branch dipped into the river Finnan long before the dawn, the entire plant seemed to sigh with delight. It shimmered brilliant silver—making more than one sentry question his own sight—then grew with even greater speed.

And the mood within Airdfinnan changed slightly during the course of that night. 'Twas as if the fog that surrounded the walls changed the hue of both sunlight and moonlight to flatter those it touched.

Smiles were exchanged in the hall that evening, and more than a few flirtatious glances were cast across the kitchen. Men found the audacity to compliment serving maids and were astonished that the perfect words fell from their lips. Women blushed, many looking more young and soft and desirable than they had in years. The air seemed faintly tinged with an exotic perfume, one that put both men and women in mind of pleasures to be found abed.

And many sought those pleasures as, unbeknownst to all but a few dazzled guards, the vine grew with reckless speed.

By the time the sentries changed shift in the morning's pearly light, the vine had covered the wall behind the garden so thickly that the men could no longer patrol the entire perimeter. It grew no more that morn, though its thorns glistened against the pallor of the fog.

The lord was summoned and he looked long and hard at the plant. He tried to cut it back with his own blade, but it turned the steel away. His men took a step back, more than one certain the plant was a creation of the fey.

"It has long been said the Finnan runs through Faerie," whispered one, the others nodding sagely.

"Nay, 'tis the doing of the lord's mother," muttered another. "'Twas long said that she could cast a spell to turn a man to stone. 'Tis her ghost returned to haunt us all." They argued quietly over this, the company dividing into two camps, each as persuaded of their view as the other.

Angus of Airdfinnan eyed the fog and the vine as if unaware of the dissent. He called for a cold ember, then marked the farthest point of the vine with a black line on the stone.

When he was done, he handed the ember to one of his men. "Mark it all and keep a watch upon it. Tell me the very moment that it grows."

"Is it the fey or your mother?" demanded one man, bolder than the others.

The lord silenced them with a sharp glance, more than one man cringing before him. "Had you any wits at all, you would know 'tis neither." With that, he retired to the company of his lady wife, leaving more questions than answers in his wake.

Chapter Twelve

CEINN-BEITHE, THOUGH UNTOUCHED BY VINES AND witchery and fog, was caught in an uncustomary flurry of activity.

And Mhairi MacLaren stood in the eye of the storm. 'Twas not a familiar place for her, and she saw both advantage and disadvantage within it.

To be sure, she was excited by her father's choice to offer her hand as well as Esmeraude's. 'Twas thrilling to be the center of so much male attention and flattering to have them seeking her favor so ardently. It made her feel like a woman to have the responsibility of choice, and she was very aware that her choice would determine all the rest of her life.

She had not thought much of marriage until recent years, and then she had assumed that her parents would encourage a match with whichever local man of good repute managed to catch her eye. It made sense to Mhairi that Esmeraude, who sparkled more brightly than any maiden she had ever known, would not find a man to suit her close at hand. Mhairi, though, fully expected to fall in love quietly with a man who came courting from nearby.

So, though 'twas not her nature to savor having every eye fixed upon her, for these few days, Mhairi enjoyed the attention. She did not fool herself that 'twould last. Indeed, she made every effort to learn about each man in turn, that she might better assess the shape her life might take by his side.

There was Douglas, a tall man much older than herself and Esmeraude, and one who seemed most intent on imposing his opinions upon others. Esmeraude had found his demands and disapproval most vexing, and Mhairi could see her half-sister's argument in this. Life with Douglas would be filled with recriminations, disapproval, and dour silences. 'Twas true enough that he had a measure of wealth, a home, and a pair of goats, but each moment seemed to bring another disappointment to him.

Mhairi expected that there was a woman somewhere who could make Douglas smile, but neither she nor Esmeraude was that woman. She imagined that his home would be cold and the fare at his board austere, regardless of his fortunes.

Nay, she did not need wealth, but she would enjoy what pleasures came to hand. Life was short enough in itself without making each day an ordeal.

Then there was Alasdair, whom Esmeraude had declared to be too short. He was a lively and jovial man who could readily coax Mhairi to laugh, though he seemed to think of naught but earning the next laugh. Mhairi expected him to prove himself both practical and whimsical, as her father was, but she had yet to see more than his humor. She wondered whether he was always so entertaining, or only when there was a matter at stake, then called herself skeptical.

If she loved Alasdair, he might prove to be most amiable company. If she did not, she suspected his manner would quickly become tedious.

Dour Lars had retired to the corner of the hall, his glum mood surrounding him like a cloud. He had proven to have a taste for ale, which Mhairi did not find attractive, and he did naught but watch her, his baleful gaze making her skin creep.

Nay, Lars was not for her.

The foreign knights were more promising, though Mhairi knew that unfamiliarity increased their allure. Her pulse quickened when one of them strode into the hall in all his finery and she imagined herself as the lady of a marvelous castle, the like of which they only heard of in tales. Aye, there were two of particular interest who did not pursue Esmeraude.

Gabriel was one and he let her ride his destrier, though he held her reins fast in his hand. Mhairi thought him most marvelous with his dark eyes that could be filled with the sparkle of mischievous laughter or as sad as a hound's when she left him for another suitor. He was not so tall, though he was strong, and his hair was dark and curly.

She did not care that he was a younger son or that he had naught but his armor and steed. That alone was rich beyond her wildest dreams. And she liked how he encouraged her to try some new feat—like riding his steed or holding his blade—all the while concerned with ensuring her safety. He spoke of tourneys and winning matches and earning a fortune in the lists, and Mhairi found it all terribly exciting.

She could love Gabriel, given the chance. Mhairi was certain of it. What maiden would not adore such a man?

Kay was so different from Gabriel, yet intriguing all the same. He was fair and quiet, manners exquisite, his eyes a blue so light as to be silver. He said little, but smiled when she spoke to him as if she were witty beyond compare. And he kissed her hand with such elegance that it nigh made Mhairi swoon. His horse was less fine than Gabriel's but still finer than Mhairi's mother's palfreys.

Kay brought Mhairi small tokens each morn when she entered the hall, each presented with a flourish—a shell, a flower, a stone with a vein of shiny quartz. He would point out the charms of each thing with a few words and a warm smile, his eyes lighting when she expressed her gratitude for his thoughtfulness.

Indeed, there was something all too fine about Kay for him to be born of a mortal—Mhairi imagined he was one of the fey, a Faerie prince come to win her hand within his own. He saw beauty in the small things and took stock of his good fortune at frequent intervals. Aye, Kay might be the man for her.

The truth was that Mhairi could not decide on such slim evidence as she had.

To be sure, this matter of courtship was not without its price, for it had altered the former freedom of her days. She had been accustomed to doing whatsoever she desired, without troubling herself much as to what people thought of that. She found it vexing, once in a while, that those carefree days were gone, at least for the moment.

Aye, Mhairi's maid now insisted that her hair be braided perfectly before she entered the hall each morn. Of course, she wanted to look her best, especially because Kay would be waiting for her, but the task took a great deal of time when she was restless to begin her day. By the maid's decree, there was to be no more running barefoot through the grass, or indeed, any running at all.

'Twas not what ladies did. Thus spoke the maid.

Mhairi tried very hard to be a lady, for she was certain that both Kay and Gabriel expected their chosen wife to be one. She wore a circlet and donned stockings and garters each and every day, a change which had been exciting at first but had quickly become an obligation.

There were moments when she longed for the days when she had not had to fret about picking a spouse. In those moments, she could certainly understand Esmeraude's insistence on a small adventure before becoming a wedded woman.

And in those moments, Mhairi found herself wondering what Finlay was doing.

Only when she could not join him did she realize how important their small missions had been to her. He had been a part of her life for as long as she could remember and though she had until recently taken that for granted, now she missed him. Finlay did not care whether her hair was braided or her circlet straight.

Nay, not he. Mhairi smiled in remembrance of their fishing excursions, when she usually hitched up her skirts to wade into the sea and Finlay quite reliably teased her about her skinny legs. She liked it when they raced to the standing stone, or helped with the milking of the goats. She could milk faster than Finlay could and never failed to let him know it, a jest that had oft resulted in a milk war.

Finlay accepted her as she was, not as she was supposed to be. But then, she was becoming a woman and she supposed that the games of her childhood were better left behind her.

Indeed, she was excited about the tourney that her father had suggested. In this event, Mhairi would see the measure of Gabriel and Kay and her heart thrilled that they would meet in combat for her favor. She was dancing with impatience when her mother summoned her to her chamber on the morning of the festivities.

"Aye, *Maman*?" Mhairi hopped from one foot to the other in her desire to rush down to the field and see the knights. She had donned her best kirtle and had let her maid braid her hair in a most intricate fashion.

Eglantine drew a kirtle from the old chest in her chamber and held it up before herself. She smiled at Mhairi across the width of the chamber. "What do you think of this?"

"'Tis beautiful!" Mhairi had never seen the garment before and she crossed the room to examine the rich embroidery upon the hems and cuffs. "You have never worn this," she said with certainty.

Eglantine smiled. "It seemed a frippery unfitting for me."

"But you will wear it this day?"

Eglantine winced and held the dress against herself. "Nay. The bearing of three daughters has thickened my waist too much to show the work to advantage."

Mhairi was not one to be so readily deterred. "Oh, *Maman*, there are laces at the sides. The chemise matches the kirtle so well that none will guess the truth and the green will favor you beautifully . . ."

Her mother bent and kissed her cheek so abruptly that Mhairi was startled to silence. "That is not the real reason that I shall not wear it. 'Twas a gift from your uncle Guillaume, sent after he heard of your birth. He said a new mother needs a luxury to call her own, and though I agreed with him, I chose then to save this garment for you." She tilted her head and smiled at Mhairi. "I was waiting for a special day. Do you think this to be one?"

"Oh, *Maman*!" Mhairi was awed by the softness of the wool, and the splendor of its emerald hue. She looked more closely at the golden embroidery studded with gems and knew she had never seen a garment more magnificent. "Is this how you dressed in France?"

"Sometimes." Her mother flicked a fingertip across Mhairi's nose. "At court, on days of import."

"Like this one."

"Aye. You will choose in these next days the man with whom you will spend most of your life, if indeed one of these men lays claim to your heart."

"I am certain that one will," Mhairi declared, thinking of the two French knights.

Her mother studied her. "I will not have you pressed to make a choice when you would rather not."

"I will not, *Maman*." She spoke so firmly that her mother's fair brow rose.

"Have you a favored suitor?"

"Two, *Maman*, two whom I am certain I could love with all my heart. The difficulty shall be in the choosing, I know it well."

Eglantine smiled. "Then I would have you look your best, and this fine garb will show you to advantage." Her mother laid out a fine chemise and a pair of lacy stockings, then leather slippers dyed a deep green and a golden girdle. She sat on the edge of the bed when she was done, and patted the place next to her. Mhairi sat beside her mother, her gaze trailing to the uncommon finery.

Her mother touched her chin, compelling Mhairi to meet the conviction in her eyes. "You know that I came to this land to grant my daughters the chance to choose their husbands as I could not do for my first nuptials. I also would have you wed for true love, as I did not the second time."

"You chose Duncan for love."

"Aye, I did and there is naught with which I can compare this match. Your father has made me more happy than ever I imagined I might be." She touched Mhairi's cheek. "And you were wrought of a most happy union."

Mhairi blushed.

Eglantine smiled thoughtfully, then stroked Mhairi's hand. "'Twas the strangest thing, for I knew Duncan was different from the first moment we met. My heart seemed to recognize him, though I argued mightily with it in the following weeks and months."

Mhairi shivered with delight. "As if you were meant to be together, as Esmeraude loves to say."

Eglantine nodded with affection, then sobered. "There is no guarantee, Mhairi, that whatever regard you feel will be returned, or even that a match wrought of love will be happy to the end of your days. But I think 'tis better to begin thus, and I think you will know the man best for you if you listen to your heart."

"What of the tourney?"

" 'Tis a way for you to see what manner of men have come before you and no more than that. Men and bards place much faith in the outcome of such tests of valor." Her mother leaned closer and dropped her voice to a fierce whisper as she held Mhairi's gaze. "But if the winner does not compel your heart to sing, Mhairi, then know that I shall support whatsoever choice you make. I shall even support your choice if 'tis none of these men, and I shall do so until my dying breath."

Her mother's determination made Mhairi feel loved as naught else could. "Thank you, *Maman*!" The two embraced tightly, then Eglantine touched the wondrous kirtle with a fingertip.

"Shall we see whether it fits?"

❖

It seemed to Mhairi that the entire village hummed with excitement. Duncan escorted her to the tent pitched upon the field while the villagers watched and whispered. The kirtle seemed to make her taller, as if she walked upon air, and she had the heady knowledge that she looked the best that ever she had.

A tent was set up for them to watch the tourneys. 'Twas an old silk striped tent which had seen finer days, and she knew 'twas a relic of her mother's life in France. 'Twas still uncommonly fine and the fringe around the roof was most splendid to Mhairi's thinking, even if 'twas not in perfect condition any longer. There were two other smaller tents of the same vintage pitched on either side of it, all three open on the side facing the designated tourney field.

Duncan had had his great chair carried out from the hall

and led her to it. Those already gathered under the tents stood for her arrival, as if she were the queen herself.

"Queen for the day," Duncan teased as she was seated, his eyes sparkling when she laughed.

Duncan sat on one side of her and Eglantine on the other. Her half-sister Alienor and her husband, Iain, sat beside Eglantine. A local chieftain, the father of Alasdair, was seated beside Duncan, then a variety of influential villagers and local men clustered behind them all. The perimeter of the field was thick with onlookers to both the left and the right of the tent. All were garbed in their finest and clearly anxious for the festivities to begin.

"'Tis up to you," Duncan whispered.

Mhairi stood up and all fell silent. She clapped her hands and gestured to the horses and men gathered on the far side of the field. "Let the tourneys begin!" she cried and the crowd cheered.

The cook from their own household—who had a booming voice—stepped forward, his chest puffed with importance. "My lady," he said to Mhairi, bowing deeply. "May I introduce the competitors?"

Mhairi inclined her head, then exchanged an excited smile with her mother before she looked to the field again. A pair of boys in bright garb had joined the cook, and she saw that they juggled apples for the amusement of all.

"First upon the field is Douglas MacBain of Moray!" bellowed the cook.

Douglas crossed the field on foot, brandishing his sword. He wore a yellow chemise that fell to his knees. A length of patterned wool was wrapped around his waist. His leather jerkin was laced in the front, his hair was loose, and he carried a round shield.

The crowd roared at the sight of him.

"A valiant warrior, Douglas fought on the side of Angus MacSorley in the battle two years past betwixt the two sons of Somerled for supremacy. Not only is he proven in battle, but Douglas offers his bride a cottage near his family home in Inverness, two goats, and enough wealth to see her in comfort."

The crowd shouted approval as Douglas strode toward Mhairi.

"Inverness!" Eglantine whispered disapprovingly beneath her breath. "Why so far?"

"Because he is a mercenary and unwelcome in closer quarters," Duncan retorted at similar volume. The pair looked at each other over her head and Mhairi knew they wished that they had not been so indiscreet in her presence.

"Not that our opinions should affect your choice," Eglantine said quickly.

Mhairi smiled. "I do not like him, at any rate."

Douglas, unaware of this conversation, bowed deeply before Mhairi. She smiled but granted him no other token of her favor, and his displeasure was more than clear as he walked away.

"Alasdair MacInnes is next . . ." The cook managed to say no more before his voice was drowned out by the cheers of the assembly.

'Twas clear that Alasdair was the popular favorite. His father straightened with pride as Alasdair advanced onto the field. He rode a horse, though rather less expertly than Mhairi herself could ride, and was otherwise dressed much as Douglas.

Alasdair looked more somber today, Mhairi noted, and her heart skipped a little when he halted, bowed, then winked at her. Perhaps he did have Duncan's blend of practicality and mischievousness.

"The son of the chieftain of Clan MacInnes, Alasdair

is heir to a powerful ancient legacy, for as we all know, the blood of Celtic kings runs in his veins. His bride will know no labor of her own hands, for she will live in splendor."

"The splendor of Alasdair's father's house," someone noted wryly in the back of the tent. "Not any luxury gained by his own labors."

The father pivoted, seeking the speaker. "Who spoke thus? 'Tis a fine matter to leave a legacy for one's own son!"

"Not if it means that he is never expected to be a man!" 'Twas a loyal comrade of Duncan's who spoke, a battle-hardened man. "Douglas is a better candidate, for he is proven in matters of war."

"Aye?" retorted the father. "We shall see who is the better man today, for this is the only proof that counts!"

Duncan intervened then, calming the men with a few quiet words. By the time the men had settled and Mhairi looked back to the field, Alasdair had stepped away to join Douglas to one side. She clasped her hands together in delight as a prancing stallion stepped into view.

"Gabriel de Mornay joins us from Normandy, his credentials most impressive," the cook announced. "Be warned, O other competitors, that he has won at tourney in Champagne and also in Languedoc, and he has pledged his winnings of last season and the next two to purchase the abode of his lady's choice."

"If he lives through those seasons," Eglantine amended dryly. Mhairi ignored her mother, so enthralled was she by the knight before her.

Gabriel was garbed in red and white, the matching caparisons fluttering as his horse cantered across the field. His mail gleamed in the sunlight, as did the blade he held before himself. He doffed his helmet with a flourish and leapt from the saddle, dropping to one knee before Mhairi.

Though the sight was impressive and she smiled, her heart had little to say of the knight's presence.

Perhaps such recognition took longer than her mother had implied.

"My lady fair, all I do this day is in your honor."

The crowd sighed as one, necks craning forward as Mhairi stood. Such a romantic gesture deserved an answering one. She had not a sleeve to bestow upon him, but her maid had woven her a circlet of flowers to adorn the silver one on her head. She removed one of the flowers and offered it to him.

At this sign of her favor, Gabriel smiled and the assembly hooted in delight. Applause filled the air, even after he had mounted his horse and ridden to the side to join the other two men.

"And Kay de Pencel has also traveled for this day, for he holds a small manor in Aquitaine."

Eglantine groaned slightly at this detail, though she said naught about distance this time. Kay wore green and gold, and made a sight every measure as rich as Gabriel had. The crowd clapped with enthusiasm as his steed cantered across the field.

"A man long pledged to the service of the Plantagenets, Kay has served as a guardian to the women of that family, escorting them safely through treacherous lands. 'Tis for this service that he won the reward of his holding. He, too, offers a prosperous life to whichever lady takes his hand and one filled with the favor of kings."

Kay also dismounted before Mhairi. He removed his helmet and tucked it beneath his left arm, then pulled off his right glove. He stepped forward and took her hand, pressing a kiss to her knuckles. "If 'tis your will, my lady, I shall win you this day."

Mhairi could not resist his charm, though her heart again had naught to say of the matter. She was prepared to grant it time to decide.

She similarly surrendered a flower to Kay. He smiled warmly, sniffed the bloom, then tucked it carefully into his tabard so that 'twas over his heart. He bowed again and rode away.

Mhairi realized only then that 'twas the same kind of bloom he had brought her just the day before and understood the reason for his warm smile. She sat down again, feeling flustered because she had shown favor to two contestants but knew not how to choose.

Indeed, 'twas irksome that her heart, contrary to her mother's predication, remained silent about the matter.

"Four competitors you see before you—" The cook's summation was interrupted by a cry from the far side of the field.

"Five!" a man shouted. "There will be *five* competitors this day!"

As all turned to look, Finlay dug his heels into the sides of one of Eglantine's palfreys. His fair hair was wild, his face flushed with the awareness that he held every gaze. He rode at a killing pace, though Mhairi saw that he was fully in command of his steed. She was on her feet before she realized what she did, her heart hammering as she noticed that he wore only a leather jerkin and carried only a small knife.

"Fool! You will be killed!" she cried.

He scowled at her as he leapt from his saddle before her and cast down the reins. "Have you no faith in my abilities? Do you not believe that the will can find the way?"

Mhairi stared at him, only now realizing why he was where he was. "You mean to win me?"

"Aye, I do. I waited for you to be old enough to be courted, and this is my reward, but it matters naught. I shall win your hand, Mhairi MacLaren, or I shall die in the trying of it." He met her gaze, his own steely with resolve. "Either way, I shall have no regrets."

Mhairi's heart clenched hard for she feared that Finlay would pay dearly for his choice. She stared at him, knowing he would not take any protest from her in good will.

"But you know naught of such battle," she began, nigh consumed with her fear for him.

Finlay's eyes flashed and he stepped closer. "Do you have so little faith in me as that?"

Mhairi did not know what to say, for the truth was bound to infuriate him. Her heart pounded so hard that she could barely think.

"Do you grant me no token of your favor?" he demanded, his words hot. "Is that how 'twill be? You will favor foreigners and strangers before looking upon the man who loves you wholly and for your own self?"

As he glared at her, furious that she might deny him and that she did not believe he would win, Mhairi knew. Aye, her heart clamored in her breast and she knew with every fiber of her being which man she must choose.

She took off her flower circlet and handed it to him in its entirety, unable to summon a word to her lips. The crowd cheered and shouted and hollered, and Mhairi was vaguely aware of her Aunt Alienor's laughter.

But she was caught by the fire in Finlay's gaze.

Terror rose within her with the realization of what he meant to do. He could be killed! How could this happen, that she could lose him just when she understood his import to her?

Why had her heart been silent so long?

Finlay showed no similar fear. He stepped forward, a

swagger in his step, and bowed that she might slip the flowers around his neck.

"If you mean to fail this foolishness," she whispered, her words uneven, "then you had best die upon the field. For if you survive wounded, Finlay MacCormac, I shall kill you with my own hands."

He chuckled then and she smiled at him. Then he squeezed her hand, his words surprisingly anxious. "Then I have your favor?"

Mhairi leaned forward and kissed his cheek. "My heart is yours, Finlay, for this day and for all time."

"Then I shall win," he said fiercely. "Your choice will be my shield." He looked deeply into her eyes and her mouth went dry. "On that, my Mhairi, you may rely."

But as he turned away, Mhairi was not as certain of his fate as he. Indeed, she feared the worst and clasped her hands tightly together in her lap, terrified that she would lose this treasure that she had never guessed was already within her grasp.

"You could halt the tourney," her mother suggested quietly, obviously guessing the direction of her thoughts. She laid a hand over Mhairi's interlaced fingers.

Mhairi shook her head. "He would despise me for such weakness."

Duncan chuckled at that. "Aye, I suspect he would." He laid his hand over her own and her mother's and gave both an encouraging squeeze. "We shall have to pray that love truly can conquer all."

Mhairi eyed Finlay's competition and was not nearly certain of that. "How long will this endure?" she whispered.

"Three days," Duncan supplied. "Three days, or until there is only one man upon the field, whichever comes first."

Mhairi closed her eyes and swallowed hard, wondering

how she would survive this contest. Curse Finlay! He should have confessed the contents of his heart sooner!

But Mhairi knew that if he had, she would not have understood her own heart. Nay, 'twas his willingness to take a risk to win her that made her see him for the man he was.

She only hoped that she had the chance to savor that new-found understanding.

Chapter Thirteen

FOUR DAYS AFTER HER ARRIVAL AT AIRDFINNAN, Esmeraude was sorely troubled. Though Connor had departed quickly, she could not have been accused of failing to spend time with Amaury or Nicholas. Neither offered a kiss that made her toes tingle, neither's arrival made her heart skip a beat, neither occupied her dreams.

In marked contrast to Bayard, who haunted her every thought. Worse, he seemed to have forgotten that he was at Airdfinnan because he had pursued her there, in order to win her hand. After that first night, he ignored her attempts to stir his jealousy.

This was not good. Esmeraude had spent even more time with both knights.

'Twas to no avail. Bayard brushed his horse, jested with Angus and flirted with the maids.

Esmeraude found herself gritting her teeth; only the occasional wink from her favored knight persuaded her that there was any merit in her actions. Did he tease her? It seemed unlike him, for he had been so solemn before, but truly, she knew little of his nature.

That was even more discomfiting.

Nicholas was charming, but he was also young for his years and somewhat frivolous. He enjoyed a merry tale and a hearty laugh, but confessed readily to boredom with the responsibilities of courts and administrative matters. He delighted in describing the wealth of his hereditary holding, Montvieux, but Esmeraude now knew more of such matters than she had. She could not understand how Montvieux would continue to be prosperous if its lord ignored his responsibilities while he pursued his leisure.

Surely that had been Theobald's error?

When she asked, Nicholas waved away her question, insisting that he and his bride would let their châtelain manage such minor administrative details while they savored life to the fullest.

Hmm. Esmeraude could not restrain herself from asking after Bayard, an initiative which did little to please Nicholas. She learned that Bayard had always been the leader among the cousins, that he had been first to win his spurs despite the fact that Nicholas was a year older, that he had conquered every obstacle before the others and was fiercely competitive. She learned that he had left his home five years past, though Nicholas professed ignorance of the reason, and had joined King Richard's crusade to recapture Jerusalem.

Did Bayard only seek to win her to best his brother and cousins yet again? 'Twas not a reassuring thought—though it could well explain his refusal to speak of love.

When Nicholas had told all he would of his cousin, Esmeraude found her interest in his company waning. Though she knew she was not strictly following her sister's request, Esmeraude cornered Amaury to learn more of his brother. Amaury was charmingly circumspect, saying only that his father and Bayard had disagreed and Bayard had left their family home.

Upon what had they disagreed? Amaury would not say. He knew naught of whatever holding Bayard possessed, nor even the extent and source of his brother's wealth. 'Twas clear that matters were strained between them, though

Amaury would not speak of that either. He assumed, he said, that Bayard had been granted a holding at the behest of his lord king, whom he had served these five years, for the family holding of Villonne was now to be Amaury's own.

On his own behalf, Amaury looked too much like his brother for Esmeraude to appreciate his own merits. 'Twould have been dangerous, indeed, to surrender to his charm, which was considerable. Esmeraude knew that if she wed Amaury, she would see Bayard every time she looked at him, and that would not be fair. She did not dare to imagine the awkwardness of family gatherings in that instance, for 'twould be most odd for one's brother-in-law to know as much of one's body as one's spouse.

'Twas a most vexing circumstance, no less because Célie had predicted such trouble. Esmeraude knew that her plan would have worked beautifully if Bayard truly had been a stranger, or if he would surrender his heart to her. But Bayard being Bayard, he was not inclined to follow Esmeraude's bidding in this or any other matter. Even his own family did not know much more of him than she!

'Twas as if he dared her to ask him directly for details of his life. Indeed, he hovered at the periphery of her vision, watching her efforts with a bemused smile.

But Esmeraude refused to grant him such satisfaction. She hated to feel that she was predictable, that she was falling prey to Bayard's charm just as countless other women—not a one of whom could sate him, according to his cousins—had done.

Would Bayard's interest in her fade once she surrendered fully to him? Was it the competition alone that intrigued him? That was more than plausible and the prospect was far from palatable.

Aye, since the man placed no credence in love, and did not desire her for the prize of Ceinn-beithe, his need to be victorious in every contest was the only motivation Esmeraude could credit for his enthusiasm for winning her.

A wicked part of Esmeraude delighted in vexing Bayard for the first few days of the week, for she knew he had feigned the loss of his voice. No doubt he had hoped to coax her closer, as he had once before by halting his tale at a threshold. She would show him that she was not so biddable as that!

Several times a day, she offered a kiss in exchange for the solving of a riddle, but each time Bayard opened his mouth to grant the answer, she insisted that he remain silent and not strain himself. She knew it irked him mightily that the other two knights won her kisses, but she was mightily irked herself that he had destroyed her perfectly good plan.

Clearly, she had to ignore him and Esmeraude did her best. She played with her nieces and nephews, she surveyed the vine that had suddenly grown on the garden walls along with the rest of the household. 'Twas to no avail. She lay awake each night hearing the endless sounds of lovemaking all around her and burned for Bayard's touch.

She refused to consider how many serving wenches found their way to his bed.

If she truly intended to forget this man, Esmeraude knew that she should flee Airdfinnan and leave her weakness behind. But she could not leave her sister with a company of guests, guests here at Esmeraude's own behest, not when Jacqueline was so close to the arrival of her child. She was snared, as surely as if the thorny vine had grown across the gate itself.

On that fourth night, Esmeraude was determined to give the two knights their due again. But after the meal when all called for a tale, Bayard turned and crooked a finger at Annelise. The girl slipped from her seat and skipped across the floor with determination.

She halted beside Bayard expectantly. "Will you sing your tale on this night?" she demanded, as she had demanded twenty times a day since he had halted. "Will you tell us what the king saw?"

Bayard coughed and touched his throat. "I need a magic wish," he whispered hoarsely, then looked inquiringly at Annelise.

"From me?" she asked, eyes wide.

Bayard nodded.

"But I know naught of magic!"

Bayard arched a brow and rose from the bench. He dropped to one knee before the little girl, and Esmeraude caught her breath at the bright blue of his eyes. He made some mischief, 'twas clear, but Esmeraude could not interrupt any deed that delighted her niece so.

"You need know naught of magic to make it," Jacqueline said in response to her daughter's enquiring glance. "Indeed, you have only to believe that magic can be done. 'Tis oft said that the fervid wish of a maiden can come true when the moon is full."

"Is it?" Annelise eyed the knight. "The fog hides the moon."

Bayard nodded emphatically. " 'Tis full," he whispered. "I know 'tis the time."

Without another moment's hesitation, Annelise placed her fingertips upon his throat. She squeezed her eyes tightly shut and the knight kept his expression solemn.

Jacqueline cast a smile Esmeraude's way and Esmeraude knew that this knight had won her sister's favor by his indulgence of her child. Esmeraude smiled herself when she looked back at her niece, who was pleased with her part in this.

"Then I wish, with all my heart and soul, and all my fingers and toes, and every part of me that can wish, that your voice will return, and your throat will be healed, and you will sing the rest of the tale for us all, right this very moment." Annelise took a deep breath after her lengthy wish and stepped back.

Bayard cleared his throat with more vigor than before. He frowned and coughed a little, then let his voice rumble in his throat. He glanced up at Annelise, as if surprised himself to hear any sound. Annelise gasped and clasped her hands together, clearly holding her breath while she waited. Her eyes were wide and shining. Esmeraude bit back her smile as she watched.

The knight made a tremendous display of gradually regaining his voice, one which delighted all of the children. Esmeraude had not expected him to be so playful and she watched with pleasure.

"Why, why, it has worked!" Bayard finally declared. "My voice is healed, by your own dictate. My lady fair, I thank you!"

Annelise let out a most unladylike hoot when the knight bowed low before her. The assembly cheered and Esmeraude clapped along with many others.

Annelise, however, was concerned with the crux of the matter. "Will you sing now?"

"Of course!" Bayard kissed the child's hand with an elegant flourish. "The wish of the maiden who healed me is mine own command."

Annelise yelled in triumph, a somewhat undignified response but an honest one. She scampered back to her seat at the board and folded her hands together, waiting impatiently for him to begin. She was not the only one who was charmed, for Esmeraude liked this game of Bayard's.

He would make a good father.

Bayard winked suddenly at her, as if he had heard her

thoughts and agreed. Esmeraude caught her breath, surprised anew by the way his glance could make her pulse leap. But 'twas more than that, more than the attraction between them.

She loved Bayard, loved him with all her heart.

Aye, she loved how mischievous he could be, yet how resolute he was in defending what he knew to be right. She loved his honor and his integrity, she loved how determined he was to make her feel like a queen and how he did not seek to change her at all. He was both tender and strong, solemn and humorous, he was clever and an able warrior, he was gallant and he sang with uncommon ardor.

Bayard was all Esmeraude had ever dreamed of finding in a husband. He was, indeed, her destiny and the only man, she suspected, who could ever make her happy.

Save for the issue of his not believing in love. Esmeraude was not one to retreat from a challenge, not when her life's happiness was at stake. The realization of the fullness of her own love only made her more determined to change his thinking.

Indeed, winning this knight's heart for her own might prove to be the greatest adventure of all.

Bayard turned to the company and continued his song.

Esmeraude thought furiously. Surely a man who argued for magic could be persuaded of the merit of love? Esmeraude listened avidly to his song, seeking some hint of Bayard's thoughts in the tale he had chosen.

Bayard sang of the ill-fated couple's meeting in the woods beneath the king's watchful eye. King Mark did not witness any impropriety between the lovers, it turned out, for Iseut had glimpsed his reflection in the pool of the fountain beneath the tree. She then engaged in harmless conversation with Tristran that night and thus fooled her husband into thinking there was naught illicit between them.

The entire company sighed with relief, but this reprieve was not destined to last. Aye, the dwarf Frocin was determined to bring the truth to light and the barons were resolved to discredit Tristran. They persuaded the king to give Tristran an order to carry to King Arthur with first light. They insisted that Tristran would lie one last time with his lady before he left.

Esmeraude bit her lip, knowing 'twas true, and feared that the lovers would now be revealed. Perhaps Bayard favored this tale because the lovers were doomed to misery. Perhaps Bayard meant this to be a lesson in the price of infidelity. Perhaps Bayard meant to show her that the price of love was too high.

How she hated not knowing!

A sentry came into the hall and whispered into Angus's ear. Angus frowned, then murmured an excuse to Jacqueline before he rose and departed. Esmeraude did not pay much attention, as Angus was always leaving the board to ensure the security of his holding. No doubt a raven had landed upon the walls or some such. Esmeraude had interest only in Bayard's tale.

King Mark deliberately left his bed that evening before Tristran's departure, leaving his wife there and his favored courtiers—including Tristran—on their pallets in the chamber. The malicious dwarf spread four *deniers*' worth of flour around the bed, knowing that Tristran's footprints would show. But Tristran had seen this deed and leapt over the flour to woo his lady.

The knight was sorely wounded in the thigh though, and did not note that the wound began to bleed as they loved that night. When the king's footfall echoed on the stair outside the chamber, Tristran leapt over the flour to his own bed. The blood of his wound dripped on the bedlinens and in the flour, revealing his deed to all.

And now discovered, the pair were sentenced to die.

The entire company cried out in consternation, Esmeraude among them. She stood, knowing that here was her chance to glean some of his deeper meaning, and her cheeks warmed when Bayard turned to her.

"This is too cruel a tale," she said. "Though the pair had been adulterous, their crime did not deserve such harsh punishment."

"I but tell the tale. I did not imagine it." Bayard shrugged. "That is a task best left to the bards."

"You could change it!"

"'Twould not be right."

"You could choose another tale."

Annelise cried out at this suggestion, and Bayard's smile broadened. He held Esmeraude's gaze with resolve and his voice dropped low. "Would you truly prefer that I cease this tale now?"

Esmeraude flushed, hating that she was so easily read. "I would not have the children haunted by dreams of their wicked fortune," she said carefully.

"Aye, tell us more!" Annelise entreated.

Bayard blew Esmeraude a kiss. "By my lady's command, I shall continue on the morrow. A voice, like a fine instrument, must be granted good care." And he winked at her, knowing full well that he had captured her curiosity.

He crossed the floor, claimed her hand, and kissed its back. "Dream of me, my Esmeraude," he whispered, a flame that reminded her of their intimacy dancing in his sapphire gaze. "For I know that I shall dream of you."

"Because you love me?" she dared to ask.

Bayard laughed and turned away. "Nay, never that," he said so merrily that she could not take offense. "I but see the good sense of our match."

Esmeraude watched him cross the hall. What a vexing and irresistible man! Indeed, the imprint of Bayard's lips upon her flesh burned all that night, leaving Esmeraude to toss and turn upon her cold pallet and recall Bayard's hands upon her.

Oh, she had to win his heart or die in the attempt!

Célie rose early on the morn after Bayard continued his song, as was her wont. She loved being in the kitchens while the bread was being baked and she enjoyed watching the bustle of a new day begin there.

Truth be told, there was a lightness in her step these days. She was pleased with her charge, for she had never dreamed that Esmeraude could be so adept in the administration of a household. Indeed, the child had never shown the slightest inclination to learn of such duties, and had oft tapped her toe impatiently while her own mother gave her useful advice.

But clearly, Esmeraude simply had need of a motivation. She was deeply fond of Jacqueline, and Jacqueline could not have been more round with child. To help her sister, Esmeraude reviewed meal plans with the cook, checked the weekly inventory with the châtelain, and offered counsel for those hens disinclined to surrender their eggs.

Célie had never guessed that Esmeraude had listened to so much of what she had been told. The maid was proud of the ward she oft considered nigh her own child and did not miss the considering regard of more than one suitor at this display of Esmeraude's organizational skills and good sense.

She did not doubt that Esmeraude would be vexed if she had realized that Bayard de Villonne was most pleased of all. Célie contentedly sipped her ale in the kitchen, certain that he was not only good for Esmeraude but sufficiently stubborn to win both her heart and her hand.

He was a perfect match for her.

By the vigor with which Esmeraude ignored the knight, Célie would have wagered the conquest was nigh completed.

She helped herself to another cup of ale, well content with what she perceived she alone had wrought.

The moment was marred when Rodney, the bald mercenary granted the confidence of the lord of Airdfinnan for reasons Célie could not comprehend, joined her at the board. He harumphed when he discovered that the pitcher of ale was half empty, then poured himself a cup as if 'twas hard won.

"There is plenty left for a temperate soul," Célie said, already prepared for an argument with this one. Whenever she encountered Rodney, he chose to begin a quarrel with her. In Célie's opinion, 'twas a mark of his poor breeding.

"And why would one accept the assessment of an intemperate soul in that?"

Célie straightened. "Do you imply that I drink overmuch?"

"There is naught to imply." Rodney shrugged in that particularly irksome manner he had. "The pitcher is always brought full, 'tis now nigh empty, and you alone sit before it." He looked pointedly to her belly, then met her gaze in challenge. "There seems to be none spilled upon the floor."

"Others were here earlier!"

He nodded as if indulging a child or a woman in her dotage who could not be trusted to recall matters aright. "Of course." He sipped, then licked his lips before slanting a glance her way. "So, is it you who have brought witchery to our hall, or is it your mistress?"

Célie choked on her ale. "What witchery?"

"Look around yourself, woman! Have you not seen the thorned vine that grows from the garden?"

"Vines do grow in gardens," she reminded him coolly.

"Aye, but not vines that have been nigh dead for half a century. 'Tis witchery, naught other than that, which has this vine growing the height of twenty men in a single night."

Célie felt her eyes widen, though she would have dearly

loved to appear insouciant before this particular man. "Truly?"

He snorted. "Do not pretend to know naught of it. I know how women are. You know things, dark things that no man should know. You traffic in secrets, you women, and meddle in the natural ways of the world. 'Tis witchery that makes that vine grow and 'twas witchery that began the very night you and Esmeraude arrived. I at least have sufficient wits about me to see the truth!" He downed his ale and summoned another pitcher.

Célie swirled her ale in her cup and stared down at it, knowing that she would never persuade Rodney to abandon his view. "It grows at night?"

"Aye, while we sit at the board, while your mistress holds court for her suitors. The pattern is most clear."

"When *precisely* does it grow?"

"When that knight sings for her. She must mean to snare him with her wiles. Or perhaps you cast a spell to make him truly wed her."

"Or perhaps he is the one responsible for the witchery."

Rodney laughed long and hard at that; his tanned flesh still crinkled at the corners of his eyes when he finally fell silent and regarded Célie. She was startled to find her old heart skipping a beat. There had always been a vital air about Rodney, and though he spoke roughly, she had never seen him act with cruelty.

"A man of war?" he scoffed. "A crusader and knight? It appears you have drunk more of the ale than even I thought." He leaned closer, dropping his voice to tease her. "Was this your first pitcher or your second?"

Célie recoiled, both from her new awareness of this vexing man and his accusation. "Vile creature! Even if 'twas my *seventh*, a man of decency would not comment upon it."

"Ah, the truth is no friend of women, that much is certain."

Rodney drank with satisfaction, then slanted a knowing glance her way. "But there is a love spell being cast within this hall, and only a soul slow of wit could miss the truth of that."

"I would not have expected you to give credence to a love spell."

"I give credence to what I see and what I hear. What I see is a vine growing at an unholy rate, and what I hear is everybody in this household rutting themselves blind each night." He leaned closer and dropped his voice. " 'Tis not natural, Célie. 'Tis not right."

He arched a brow and a startlingly new awareness sizzled between them. A considering light dawned in his eye, and Célie knew that he had noted the change as well.

What was in this ale? Célie put her cup down on the board and pushed it away.

Rodney shook his head and stood up. "I believe you understand precisely what I mean." He drained his cup and set it down heavily on the board, bracing his hands there as he held Célie's gaze. To her astonishment, she could not look away and she felt the oddest quiver dance over her flesh.

Rodney's voice was softer when he spoke. "If, indeed, you are responsible, Célie, I suggest you halt this madness. My lord is intent on seeing this not only solved but the perpetrator held responsible." He touched her cheek with a rough fingertip, the gesture so fleeting that she might have missed it if she had not been so aware of him. As it was, she tingled. "I would not have you pay too high a price for a prank."

And then he was gone, striding through the kitchens as if he had forgotten her existence. Célie took a deep breath, stunned by her impression that Rodney was behaving protectively toward her.

Surely she was mistaken?

She looked around herself, noticing only now how the cook exchanged amorous glances with one of the scullery maids. A squire pinched a maid's buttocks and they flirted together, disappearing into one of the rooms for dry inventory. A man-at-arms embraced a maid opposite, oblivious to the others in the hall.

Célie, feeling suddenly old and undesirable, left the kitchens, noting with every step that couples cavorted with each other. Kisses and smiles and coy glances seemed to be around every corner, and she even interrupted the lord himself kissing his lady wife.

She trudged out into the silvery light of the morning, cursing the fog that seemed to have enveloped Airdfinnan for good, and accepted aid to climb the walls. The warm glow of the ale seemed to abandon her in the chill of the fog. Célie was not the only one come to see the thorny vine, but she did not know whether she was the only one who shivered at the sight of it.

For she knew as soon as she looked upon it that Rodney was right. 'Twas the product of a spell or some other witchery, for there was an unnatural air about it. Indeed, it seemed to glow with a silvery light.

Célie shivered and turned away, surprised when she bumped directly into another. The man caught her elbows and she inhaled deeply of his scent, tingled, then looked up to find Rodney's assessing gaze upon her.

"Is it yours?" he asked so quietly that no others could hear.

"Nay. I know naught of it." Célie glanced over her shoulder, shivered, and found herself easing closer to Rodney. "God in heaven, but there is something unholy about it." She glanced up at him and smiled, savoring the way his eyes widened in surprise. "How else could its presence have prompted the two of us to agree?"

He laughed then, a hearty laugh that made him look

younger and more vital. "Perhaps you would sit with me for the midday meal," he said with more gallantry than Célie had guessed he possessed.

"Would the presence of a woman not spoil your appetite?" she teased, for Rodney's distrust of women was well known.

He smiled. "Perhaps not on this day."

Célie snorted, then took his elbow. "Then I should take advantage of your moment of weakness. Goodness knows but even such powerful sorcery as this cannot have an enduring power over you."

Rodney laughed aloud once more, making Célie feel young and witty and alluring for the first time in many years. Indeed, why should all the others have pleasure and not she?

She peeked at Rodney and decided she had misjudged him for all these years. He was not an unattractive man and, indeed, this rough gallantry warmed her heart.

Perhaps this night would prove an interesting one.

❖

Bayard was in a more foul mood than ever he had been.

For the first time in all his days, what he desired did not come readily to his hand. It infuriated him that his good fortune should abandon him at this critical juncture, and indeed, he did not know how to proceed. He was impatient with his progress in his suit of Esmeraude, but naught he did seemed to persuade the lady of his merit.

'Twas not as if the other competitors were worthy of her consideration. Though he appreciated that 'twas a great decision to choose a spouse, he thought that Esmeraude embraced the task with too much enthusiasm. The best choice among her suitors was obvious.

But she was barely speaking to him.

Bayard sat in the hall of Airdfinnan after yet another sleepless night and scowled at his cup of ale. He should have taken the simplest course and declared the truth when his cousin challenged Esmeraude's chastity. He should have claimed her as his own by the most ancient claim of a man to a woman and compelled her to wed him. They could have been halfway to the king's port by now.

But unpredictable Esmeraude might not have felt compelled to wed him even after such a revelation. Bayard would have looked like a knave and might have lost any chance of winning her at all.

Still, the days slipped away with relentless speed. The king would undoubtedly be wondering what had happened to Bayard. Perhaps he and his men jested that Bayard had met his match in this almost certainly biddable peasant maid.

Ha. Bayard had another cup of ale to assuage his pride. Esmeraude was far from the demure simpleton they had all expected her to be, and therein lay the problem. She was far more interesting and far more desirable than anticipated.

Aye, Bayard wanted to win her.

And he wanted to win her more desperately than he had wanted a victory in a long time. He could make a reasoned argument for his enthusiasm. Esmeraude was an uncommon woman. Passionate and playful abed, she was also responsible in fulfilling her sister's obligations. She was quick of wit and charming. She was sensible and skilled with children. She was not deferential by any accounting, but he found her spirit far more appealing than he had just a fortnight before.

Indeed, a meek bride would never have quickened his pulse as Esmeraude so readily could. Though Bayard suspected the choice of his bride was made by his grandmother's capriciousness alone, Esmeraude would make a fine lady wife and a gracious mistress of Montvieux. That was why he desired to win her hand, and cared naught for the cost. Though he would never love any woman, 'twould have been most convenient if Esmeraude had loved him so desperately that she could not refuse him.

'Twas annoying beyond all to realize that that must not be the case. The one woman he had to seduce refused to be seduced. Surely his legendary charm had not disappeared at this critical juncture?

But there was no escaping the fact that Esmeraude kissed her other suitors with a most inappropriate ardor and did not kiss him, at least not any longer. Indeed, she ignored Bayard mightily, not sparing him so much as a smile.

Bayard downed his ale, not liking this a whit.

'Twas no consolation that all in this hall seemed smitten with another. Indeed, a man could barely sleep for the sound of others coupling with fearsome enthusiasm. Bayard knew for a fact that Andrew had had his first experience abed here, and understood enough of Michael's smile each morn to not ask for details. He alone seemed to sleep alone each night.

'Twas a novel sensation and not a welcome one. Bayard glared at the portal to the solar and hoped that Esmeraude too lay chaste in her bed each night. She was passionate, though, and his innards clenched at the prospect of another pleasing her while he achieved naught at all.

And the worst of it was this cursed tale he had begun. What had persuaded him that 'twould be a fitting song to court his lady? The truth was that he had thought little of the matter, beyond the fact that the tale was long and that Esmeraude loved tales. He had not expected Esmeraude to seek hints to his own inclinations in the lovers' every action and truly their choices granted him little credit.

This pair cheated and lied and were adulterous, they cared only for their own comfort and indulgence. Knowing Esmeraude's passion for the allure of love, Bayard could not imagine that the revelation that Tristran and Iseut died apart and wed to others would gain him much favor.

But he could not halt the tale, lest he risk offending his host's daughter and thus irritating his host. Bayard drained his cup of ale in frustration and pushed to his feet, impatient for action. In the bailey, he called to his squires, intending to rouse them both for some swordplay. The practice would be good for all of them.

But none heeded his call.

"Andrew!" Bayard shouted in frustration. "Michael!"

He spun, seeking some glimpse of the boys and found only his brother watching him carefully.

"Is it not intriguing," Amaury said softly, "that Esmeraude avoids you as determinedly as you avoid me?"

"I do not avoid you." Bayard cast a glance around the bailey for the errant squires, not wishing to have this discussion now. Doubtless they had learned more about the charms of scullery maids than he would have preferred they know so soon.

"Aye, you do and I would know why." Amaury had a steady gaze that Bayard recalled well enough, even before his younger brother stepped closer. "As your closest kin here and one you have not seen of late, I would have thought we might have become reacquainted. It has been a long five years, Bayard."

"Yet the distance between us is no less now than 'twas when I was in Palestine." Bayard offered a thin smile to his brother. "Make no mistake, I have fond memories of our boyhood together, but too much has been said that cannot be ignored."

"Not between you and I."

"Nay, but the fact that our father and I argued so vehemently, and the fact that you still ride by his side, means that matters can never be as they were between the two of us."

"Surely we can still be cordial."

"We have been cordial. That does not change the truth that we compete for the same demoiselle's hand." Bayard frowned. "Where are those cursed boys?"

He did not anticipate Amaury's soft query.

"Do you not miss us, Bayard?"

Bayard looked back at his brother, then wondered how much he should confess. Guilt coiled in his gut, for he had been fond of his brother and still was. But he had no doubt that whatever he said would be reported to his father by this more dutiful son.

And he had said all he desired to say to his father.

"Aye, I miss what was," Bayard admitted. "But 'tis gone. Harsh words are never forgotten, even when glossed with cordiality. There is naught that any of us can say to return matters to the way they were, and indeed, a part of me could not desire as much. I have seen much and ridden far, and could never regret the experiences of these past five years."

Amaury smiled. "You were always the intrepid one. I would have you tell me of those adventures."

"To what purpose?" Bayard shrugged. "They too are over and done and their details unimportant. 'Twould be just another fantastical tale, spun for your entertainment. What is of import is that those years have wrought of me the man I am now. You have but to look upon me and see all you need to know. That is the legacy of those adventures."

Bayard turned and pointedly looked for the boys. He felt Amaury consider him for a long moment and hoped his brother would tire of this futile exercise.

But Amaury spoke quietly. "I see a man who speaks as if he were older than the years I know him to have seen. You are both more temperate and more resolute than once you were."

Bayard smiled slightly at this assessment, for his affection for Amaury had not faded. He cuffed his brother's shoulder. "And you have grown to manhood without me to wrestle," he said gruffly. "I wager you are tougher to conquer in these days."

"I wager you have learned a new trick or two yourself. And you would have had to, if you intended to best me. 'Tis no longer possible for you to simply grow faster than me." They shared a smile, then Amaury sobered. "Why did you not speak to Father at Ceinn-beithe?"

Bayard looked away. " 'Twas not fitting."

"Not fitting to address your father after five years apart?"

Bayard eyed his brother again. Amaury appeared so young to him, so innocent, so unaware of all the world had to offer. He had been sheltered beneath his father's arm. 'Twas not a bad thing, for he had the confidence of a man certain of his advantage.

But 'twas a false perception, for he had never been tested and Bayard feared what would happen if ever Amaury was tested as he had been. Bayard had tasted death himself more than once after his departure from Villonne, and knew that it had only been the folly of inexperience that nigh cost him his life.

He had always been fortunate—but Amaury had never been so blessed as Bayard. 'Twas Amaury who nicked himself, Amaury who was caught in the rain, Amaury who fell on a step that had been loose for years.

'Twas Amaury whom Bayard had always protected, as an older brother should. Perhaps 'twas that realization which made Bayard say more than might have been his plan.

Chapter Fourteen

"IT WAS NOT FITTING TO CONTINUE AN UNFINISHED ARGU-
ment before a company of friends and family,"
Bayard said crisply. "And truly, we could not have
begun again without finishing what was left unfinished. No
doubt we both have found more arguments to make in favor
of our own side. 'Twas not the reason we were gathered, and
to begin such a dispute would have been an abuse of our
host's hospitality."

Silence stretched between them. On impulse, Bayard drew
his sword and lifted it toward his brother. He smiled. "Come,
Amaury. Show me what you have learned these five years
past. Show me how much more difficult you are to defeat."

A familiar light glinted in Amaury's eyes and he drew his
own blade with grace. "En garde," he murmured and their
blades clashed between them.

Amaury was indeed stronger and quicker, Bayard noted
with pleasure, but not as quick as he. He imagined that his
brother had practiced with an indulgent tutor and deliberately made an unpredictable move.

His blade sang through the air and he nicked Amaury's
tabard. His brother jumped back in alarm. To his credit,
Amaury lunged back into the fray. The ring of the blades at-
tracted observers, including Bayard's errant squires.

From the rumpled and flushed look of them, he knew

where, or at least with whom, they had been. 'Twas galling that Bayard should be the only celibate in this hall.

And by his own choice. Truth be told, there was not a wench in this hall who tempted him though several had tried. Had Esmeraude and her passionate response spoiled him for any other woman?

No wonder he was so intent upon winning her! He parried Amaury's blow and struck harder in retaliation.

"Father was wounded by your decision, I know it," Amaury insisted, his breath coming quickly. "He misses you, though he will not hear your name in the hall of Villonne."

"If 'twere of such import to him, then he might have spoken first to me." Bayard defended himself against a much more forceful thrust and grinned when he cast off the weight of Amaury's blade.

His brother showed definite promise.

"You are the son! 'Tis your duty to show honor to your sire. 'Tis your responsibility to speak first to him, especially as 'twas you who fled his hall."

Bayard shook his head. " 'Tis true that I fled my father's hall with no more than my hauberk, my sword, and my steed. Did he not tell you why?" He caught Amaury's chemise with the tip of his blade in a sudden move that his brother clearly did not anticipate. The strike left a long gash in the linen and a thin line of red along Amaury's flesh. Those gathered to watch gasped and the brothers' gazes met.

Aye, Amaury knew that Bayard could have sorely injured him.

"Because you would not heed him," Amaury retorted.

Bayard snorted at this variant of the truth. " 'Tis true enough, though only part of the tale. I did not heed him because he would have sheltered me, as he has sheltered you."

"I—"

Bayard lunged again and left a cut in Amaury's tabard this

time, directly over his chest. Amaury jumped back in alarm, eyed the gash, then lunged at Bayard again. Their blades clashed time and time again as they fought with greater vigor.

"When a man earns his spurs, Amaury, he assumes the responsibility of knighthood. He can only win that status if he has proven himself to be worthy of it. He must be skilled with his weaponry but he must also have the resolve of a man to do what is just and to see a matter finished."

"I know this," Amaury interjected impatiently, punctuating his claim with a swift strike. "I am a knight."

Bayard darted out of harm's way, though his brother's blade glanced off his hand. "Aye, but your father, *my* father, chooses to ignore this fact. He treats you yet as a child, just as he would have treated me as a child."

"He is protective!"

"He is a fool." Bayard halted his assault for a moment to consider his brother. "I understand that he was forced to make war too young, but in this matter, he corrects his own experience overmuch."

"What do you mean?"

"Like all men, our father grows older, yet his refusal to let his son be a man means that all he yet holds can be lost upon his demise. What do you know of waging war? What do you know of defending what is your own? What do you know of treachery and intrigue and the machinations of greed? What have you learned of swordplay, when your opponent is not a tutor intent upon letting the son of his lord and suzerain win?"

Amaury dove forward, taking advantage of Bayard's pause. Bayard laughed and parried his blow with less ease than before. "Better!" he cried and his brother's smile flashed. "If Father died—and I by no means wish for him to do so—you would take the reins of Villonne as its lord. If another neighbor attacked Mother, as one did seven years past, how would you retrieve her?"

Their blades clashed between the two of them and Bayard leaned closer, holding his brother's gaze even as he held the weight of his sword. "If I came with an army to wrest Villonne from you, would you know what to do to stop me?"

Amaury lowered his blade, clearly shaken by the prospect, and stepped back. His response could be read in the fear flickering in his eyes. "Would you do as much?"

"Nay, I have no desire for Villonne." Bayard gave his brother a minute pause to be relieved, before he continued. "Others will though, Amaury, others with less honor than me. 'Twill be both your prize and your burden to defend."

"I am certain that Father has considered as much and means to grant me experience when I have need of it."

"No man knows when he will die, Amaury." Bayard shook his head. "What if Villonne were assaulted and Father were killed in the defense of it? You would have to decide, over his fallen body, what to do. You would have to make a strategic choice, and that with no time to consider your choice and with grief coursing through your veins."

Amaury opened his mouth and closed it again.

"Could you do it?"

"I pray I shall not have to."

Bayard shook his head, then lifted his blade once more. Their swords clashed with greater vigor and he felt the chill of the air so keenly that he knew his chemise was soaked with perspiration. "Prayers have their place, but experience is a better partner in war. You are a man yet you stand on the cusp of responsibility without the skills to assume it. Though I appreciate that Father wished to protect us from the rigors of his own early years as a knight, I fear he has been overzealous."

" 'Tis disloyal to say as much." Amaury swiped at Bayard's knees.

"Is it?" Bayard leapt aside, then thrust before his brother had gained control of his blade once more. He made another slash in Amaury's tabard, pulling back on the blade so that he drew no blood.

Amaury stared down at the gaping cloth and swallowed.

"And I do not even have a desire to kill you," Bayard muttered. "Do you always say what Father would have you say? Do you always believe what he tells you to believe? His intent is not malicious, but 'tis damaging all the same. Do you desire aught, Amaury, independent of what Father would desire for you?"

"I desire Villonne and a wife, a happy household like our own."

"And so you are here, at Father's dictate, to win the bride he has chosen for you."

Amaury bridled at this. "He merely suggested 'twas a good idea. He does not tell me what to do!"

Bayard did not reply to that, for he knew that his father had a talent for sounding so reasonable that 'twas impossible to argue with him without sounding like a fool. The pair battled anew, both of them breathing heavily as they circled and their blades clanged.

Then Bayard struck a ringing blow upon his brother's sword, driving the blade from Amaury's hand. It fell heavily to the ground and Amaury reached for his knife.

But Bayard rested his blade upon his brother's neck. Amaury froze. He looked up, fear in his eyes, and Bayard realized that his point had finally been made. The group assembled fell silent, clearly uncertain of what Bayard would do.

"Recognize, Amaury, that Father was summoned to just such a bride quest as this by his own father, yet he refused to participate." Bayard took a deep breath. "Father spurned all that his father would have granted him, that he might win the heart of our mother. What came to his hand, what he would bequeath to you now, was what he won through his own skill. He did not desire what would be merely granted to him."

"If you are suggesting that Father is wrong—"

"I am suggesting that you do not wait to be told what it is you desire, but that you seek it yourself. Though our family is divided, I would not see you injured for a lack of foresight, Amaury. I am suggesting that if Father denies you the chance to win the experience you need, just as he denied me, that you leave him and seek it yourself, that you follow his example and perhaps prosper as he has done."

"I could not defy him, as you did!"

Bayard shook his head and stepped away. "Then wait for him to *tell* you to become a man. Perhaps he will do it one day." He sheathed his blade with a smooth gesture, though his brother did not move. "And tell Father that he and I may make amends when he allows you to tourney and to ride to war."

With that, Bayard strode away, his anger simmering. He was surprised to discover that he was shaking. The old anger at his father's protectiveness was still simmering, as was his own protectiveness toward his younger brother.

He was furious that his father had not changed his course over these past years, for he had hoped that his own departure would spur some sort of change. 'Twas he who had always defied his father, and Amaury who accepted what he was told to accept.

Aye, part of Bayard's reason for challenging his father so harshly was to win better training for his brother. He had seen it at the time as granting his father a second chance to train an heir, for Bayard had never doubted that he would win an estate of his own. Villonne, to his thinking, had always been destined for Amaury—good, honest Amaury who made the most of what he was granted and did not yearn for more, as Bayard always had.

Amaury spoke aright—they had always been close. Perhaps the differences between them had allowed them to appreciate each other without the taint of competitiveness. Bayard had kept his brother from many a misstep.

'Twas irksome, indeed, that he had left his family to grant his father a lesson and that lesson had been one his father refused to take. That his father did not see the threat posed to Amaury's future made Bayard want to shout at him anew.

Perhaps he *would* speak to his father again.

Bayard was surprised not only that his fury at his father lingered but that 'twas so intense. He had been certain that his past was left surely behind him, of as much import to him as the tale of another's woes.

'Twas illogical to be so concerned with matters so long behind him.

Perhaps he had not spoken to his father at Ceinn-beithe because he could not have trusted himself to do so in a civilized manner. He might have raged, he might have wept, he most certainly would not have exchanged polite greetings with a bow.

He recognized the same impulse in himself now.

"Andrew! Michael! Hasten yourselves," he shouted, needing only to be away from this place. "We ride on this day!"

But in keeping with Bayard's recent lack of good fortune, Esmeraude herself stepped from the solar as he was riding for the gates. She headed directly into his path, clearly determined to speak with him just when he was in no mood to be persuasive.

Curse Dame Fortune and all her ilk!

"Your eyes are too blue," Esmeraude said with a winsome

smile. "Surely I cannot have riled you already this morn."
She looked as if she had slept well—or loved lustily enough
not to care—and annoyance rolled through Bayard in response.

'Twas unfair that she should torment him, yet be immune
to his own allure!

Though hers was undoubtedly meant to be a teasing comment, Bayard had to force his answering smile. "Save by
your absence."

She regarded him quizzically, her gaze slipping over his
sweat-soaked chemise. No doubt he looked a poor sight for a
man who courted her favor!

Her gaze brightened though, and Bayard knew he did not
imagine the flush that stained her cheeks. He recalled all too
well how she flushed abed and yearned with sudden vigor to
hear her whisper his name as she found her pleasure again.

And again and again and again. The very thought tightened his chausses and made him yet more restless to be
gone. He could not think clearly when she addled his wits
with desire.

"Nay, there is another reason," Esmeraude insisted. "You
are angry or otherwise impassioned."

Clearly his charm was sadly lacking this morn if he could
not even have a compliment accepted. "I have been angry
this morn, but the cause is not of import. If you will excuse
me?" Bayard gathered the reins and gave her a curt nod.

Esmeraude laid a hand upon the bridle and Argent—
wretched, faithless beast!—stilled. "If any matter has angered you, it must be of import. I of all souls should know
that you are difficult to vex."

"I would not have you concern yourself."

She propped a hand upon her hip but did not loose her
hold upon the destrier's harness. "Do you think me too simple of wit to understand matters of men?"

Ah, now he had insulted his lady fair! This morn grew better and better! Bayard hastily tried to make amends. "Nay, I think you most clever and indeed you are uncommonly talented with riddles." Her manner eased slightly, but Bayard knew he would have to tell her more.

Bayard supposed Esmeraude's curiosity was a good portent for his suit and was relieved enough by that to smile slightly for her.

Esmeraude smiled back and he was vastly encouraged.

"If you must know," he confessed quietly, "I am simply vexed to learn that my father has not changed his ways since my departure from his abode."

Esmeraude leaned upon his leg, her curiosity clear. Her fingertip slid along his thigh absently, as if she knew not what she did or how she made him burn for more of her touch. "Was that why you left Villonne, because of him?"

Bayard pursed his lips, then decided he had naught to lose in telling her the truth of it. "We argued, for he refused me the opportunity to ride to war or to tourney."

"Surely any father would do as much."

"Nay, Esmeraude. I had earned my spurs and the station of a knight. He was wrong to deny me the chance to hone my skills on the field."

"But you could have been killed!"

'Twas cheering how the prospect seemed to trouble her. Bayard took her hand in his and let his thumb slide across her knuckles. The lady inhaled quickly and lifted her gaze to his in a way that made his own heart begin to pound. "But without such training, I could have lost much more."

"How so?"

"I was his heir. Imagine if he died and I took his place, yet knew naught of defending what was now my own." Bayard found himself confessing more than he intended. Indeed, the lady was cursedly easy to talk to, for she was keen of wit and seemed to understand his concerns. "Many might have died if the keep was attacked, and lost to another."

"Is that a threat?" Esmeraude watched him carefully. "What happens abroad in these days? Is there peace?"

"I fear that war brews in France, betwixt the King of France and the King of England. They hold many adjacent territories and each is desirous of the rich holdings of the other."

"Like Villonne?"

" 'Tis unaccountably prosperous and near contested lands in Normandy."

"And your father did not train your brother, after you left."

Bayard shook his head. He felt his lips tighten and looked away that she might not read the fullness of his frustration in his eyes.

But Esmeraude seized his hand with her own. "You fret for him."

"How could I not?"

She smiled at him sunnily, a most inappropriate response to his thinking. "Aye, how could you not when you love him so?"

Bayard bristled at the very suggestion. "He is my brother, Esmeraude, there is naught improper between us."

"He is your blood and you fear for him because you love him." Esmeraude shook a playful fingertip at him. "I think there is naught improper about the impulse. 'Tis most honorable for a man to be protective of those he loves."

Bayard regarded her warily. Impulses warred within him, his old instinct for hiding any affection for another warring with the potential of winning favor from his intended.

"Do you intend to speak to your father about the matter?" Esmeraude asked, untroubled by his silence. "Perhaps you could persuade him to reconsider."

"Clearly I cannot." Bayard spoke with undisguised annoyance. "For he has ignored all I said to him five years ago."

"You left to compel your father to do better with Amaury," she whispered with evident delight. "Bayard, that is a most noble impulse, for surely you were his heir afore that. You put aside a prosperous estate for the sake of your brother, then won one for your own elsewhere." She shook her head and smiled at him. "How can you suggest that you do not believe in love?"

" 'Twas reason alone," Bayard insisted. " 'Twas simple good sense. There is no reason for a man to risk death and the loss of his holding for a lack of preparation. My father corrects his own father's error with too much enthusiasm and I merely made the truth of that clear to him."

"Then why are you so angered with him still?"

" 'Tis only sensible to be vexed when one's efforts come to naught."

"And why did you leave Villonne for Amaury then?"

"He is less competitive than I and less ambitious. I knew I would win another holding, and indeed I have, but Amaury is wrought of more gentle matter."

Esmeraude smiled. "You love Amaury and I know it."

" 'Tis only good sense!"

" 'Tis love."

Bayard could not leave the matter be. Truly this discussion proceeded in the wrong direction! "Esmeraude, I would not have you misunderstand. I do not share your faith in the merit of love—"

She laughed at him. "Call it what you will, then." She leaned closer, her eyes twinkling in a most beguiling manner. "But I would bestow a kiss upon a man who loves his brother as much as you do your own."

Before Bayard could decide whether to clarify the matter or accept the kiss he sorely desired, a cry rang out from the gates.

"A guest! A guest arrives!" shouted the herald, then stepped back to let the party pass under the portcullis.

The only man whose presence might have made Bayard's day less promising rode beneath the gates of Airdfinnan, his fair hair swept back from his brow and his steed prancing proudly.

"Simon de Leyrossire," he muttered sourly, without intending to do so, knowing beyond all doubt that his former luck had utterly abandoned him.

"Oh, another knight from France," Esmeraude murmured. She looked far more excited about the prospect than Bayard would have preferred.

"He is a rogue and a scoundrel," he told her darkly. "He cheats and will do whatsoever he can to win his desire. He courts you for some foul reason of his own."

"No doubt because he desires a bride," the lady retorted, then shook a finger at him. "How unlike you to be so ungracious, Bayard." She then turned and smiled at the arriving knight.

Bayard seized her elbow. "You will not go to him!"

"Of course I will. I must greet him in my sister's place." Esmeraude had a stubborn glint in her eye that told Bayard that not only was she provoked but that he would lose if he forbade her to go to Simon.

So he smiled instead and slipped his arm around her waist. He bent low and drew her to her toes, liking how her eyes widened in anticipation. "Then I will have my kiss first, my Esmeraude," he murmured, "and truly it shall be one you do not easily forget."

The lady reached up and pushed a lock of hair back from Bayard's brow, touching him with a possessive ease that made him catch his breath. "Aye, Bayard," she whispered with a seductive smile. "Grant me a kiss that will warm my lonely pallet this night."

Bayard's heart leapt at this confession that she, too, was chaste here at Airdfinnan and hoped 'twas because she yearned for him and him alone. He resolved to put his all into this kiss, to show his intended what she might anticipate if they were wed.

Indeed, 'twas only chivalrous to do his best to grant the lady her favor.

❧

Esmeraude did not truly recall meeting Simon. She was still dizzy from Bayard's demanding kiss when she crossed the bailey and thinking only of how best to win that knight's sweet confession so she might welcome him to her bed again. Bayard himself rode through Airdfinnan's gates with only the most cursory acknowledgment of Simon, the destrier's hoofbeats pounding upon the wooden bridge.

Esmeraude would not soon forget the sight of Bayard when she stepped into the bailey. He had looked vexed and virile, his chemise damp with sweat and clinging to his muscles. His dark hair had been tousled, his expression intent, and Esmeraude had felt a wave of desire so strong that she had clutched the edge of the door lest her knees buckle from beneath her. Bayard was such a vision of masculine grace and vigor that 'twas too easy to recall the deftness of his touch, the grace of his seduction, the vigor of his loving.

No less, to lust for more.

His kiss had only made Esmeraude burn hotter in her desire to have Bayard's strength within her again. She could imagine naught better than seeing the sapphire blaze of his eyes each and every day of her life. She was much cheered by his evident affection for his brother, no less his sacrifice for Amaury and his refusal to call that emotion what it was.

Esmeraude *had* to win Bayard and she knew she would. She would compel him to love her, as never a man had loved a woman before. She would steal the heart he did not even know he possessed, and she would have her every desire fulfilled for all time.

She stood dutifully, if somewhat dazedly, as Angus interrogated his potential guests—for there were four local men riding with Simon—and thought only of Bayard. Esmeraude lifted a hand to tuck an errant curl back into her braid and smelled the tang of Bayard's perspiration upon her flesh. Her mouth went dry at the recollection of their legs tangled together and his fingers sliding over her bare skin.

Lust was not love, Esmeraude knew that, but 'twas a place to begin. 'Twas time she encouraged Bayard again, time she showed him all that he would win in surrendering his heart to her. Her own heart thundered at her audacity. But if she meant to make this man love her, she had to be as bold and confident as he.

Simon, she vaguely noted, was ancient beyond belief, even older than Angus. He was charming to her, perhaps too charming, but 'twould not annoy Esmeraude if his presence continued to prompt Bayard to bestow such splendid kisses upon her.

Indeed, it could only be a good sign that her knight seemed jealous of Simon. Perhaps Bayard already cared more than he would admit!

The prospect put a bounce in Esmeraude's step and one she sorely needed, for the day turned hectic after Bayard's departure from the hall. Jacqueline was in a discomfort which precluded her doing much in the hall, but the suitors who arrived had need of a meal and accommodation. Esmeraude did not see Bayard again, or even hear tell of his return, but she knew he would be back.

A man did not grant such a kiss otherwise. Nor did he make such a lengthy offering to win a lady's favor as the song of Tristran and Iseut if he did not truly wish to win. Bayard's tale echoed in her thoughts all that day, the sound of his voice so close that 'twas as if he whispered it anew in her ear.

There might have been something magical in the song or

in Bayard's voice, for each verse made Esmeraude hungry to hear more. She was tormented by not knowing what had become of the two lovers. She found herself humming its tune as she worked, each scene as vivid in her mind's eye as if she had witnessed it herself. Even knowing that Bayard spun a web around her apurpose did not diminish its power.

Or his allure. Surely 'twas a good omen that he troubled himself to recount such a lengthy tale of love for her favor?

By the evening meal, Esmeraude was more than ready for a merry tale and a stirring kiss from her most ardent suitor.

Esmeraude hastened to the board, but to her chagrin, Bayard was not present. Handsome Calum managed to ensure that he was upon her one side while Simon claimed the other. She smiled at Calum's jests but found him a trying companion compared to Bayard. Jacqueline invited the new arrivals to share a tale with the company after the meal had been served.

Simon demurred, saying that 'twas not the role of a man of war to provide entertainment like a jester or a fool. Indeed, he was so elegantly attired, his squires so quick to cut his meat and wipe his chin, that Esmeraude could not imagine him lifting a finger to do any deed himself.

A moment of awkward silence filled the hall after this pronouncement, then one of the local suitors stepped forward. Robert was as anxious to please as Esmeraude recalled. He told the tale of Angus and Jacqueline of Airdfinnan, that of the couple whose hall they were within.

'Twas a choice which clearly startled Angus and prompted Jacqueline to blush. Esmeraude knew that Robert did not know his host and hostess personally and thus could not have heard the tale from them.

Indeed, Angus called an early halt to the tale, citing the falsity of its details as his reason. Angus glared at Robert as that man retired red-faced from the floor and Esmeraude knew that her earlier decision about this suitor had been accurate.

"Pretentious fool," Calum whispered to Esmeraude.

Simon smirked and sipped his ale, wincing at the taste of it. He had already made his preference for wine clear, and Angus had apologized so elaborately for the absence of wine in his cellars that Esmeraude knew her brother-in-law did not like this new guest in the least.

Perhaps if she did not encourage Simon, he would leave.

The parsimonious Hamish sang a tale of a small Faerie tricked of his hoard of gold. His impressions of the little crooked man made Jacqueline laugh merrily and the children giggle. Applause rang through the hall when he finished and Esmeraude was surprised to see this side of the man who had oft sat silently in Duncan's hall.

But still, the revelation did not change her opinion of him.

"How like him to sing of winning gold undeserved," muttered Calum, the words pitched for Esmeraude's ears alone.

Calum was handsome, 'twas true, though his smile did not prompt much more within Esmeraude than a polite answering smile. He sang an old tale of the lovers for which Ceinn-beithe had won its reputation as a fortunate place to be wed.

Esmeraude had always loved this tale and she was in the midst of cheering it when Bayard stepped into the hall. She halted and stared, despite her intention to greet him coolly. His tan seemed more ruddy and his manner more impatient. He spared her no more than a glance, then his lips set grimly as he took a seat and called for ale.

Esmeraude wondered where he had been, what he was thinking, why he was annoyed with her. Had he changed his thinking about her? He certainly looked disgruntled enough to have done so. She half rose to go to his side before she recalled herself.

"I see that Bayard de Villonne courts you with vigor," Simon mused. "Has he any land to his name these days?"

"He has an estate."

Simon laughed, much to Esmeraude's surprise. "What holding is that? Amaury takes Villonne since Bayard abandoned his father and there is no other holding in Burke de Villonne's possession, not since he lost Montvieux."

Surely Bayard could not have lied to her? Esmeraude knew it could not be so. "He has won another holding by his valor."

"Ah, is it one he holds as yet or one he hopes to hold?" Simon smiled into his cup and his eyes gleamed. "You must be certain to know the truth of what a man offers before you accept him, Esmeraude. Bayard is well known for his conquests of ladies, but I fear there is naught of substance behind his façade of charm."

"He is a knight—"

"Spurs can be bought, for a father's favor or an exchange of land."

"And a crusader—"

"Aye, aye, a member of that fool's company, which failed in their objective."

"I do not understand what you mean."

"Richard did not take Jerusalem from the infidels." Simon spoke to her as if she were a stupid child, a tendency that did little to enchant Esmeraude. "Indeed, he did not so much as try. Twice he approached the Holy City and twice he retreated, being no closer than eight miles from its gates. This is no victory, my dear."

"Bayard is a champion," Esmeraude insisted, though Simon laughed again at this.

"Indeed? Well, I see that our tourney at Tours has been remembered rather differently by the other party." Simon stood and flicked back his cloak, raising his cup to indicate Bayard and interrupting the conversation in the hall. "What ails you, Bayard de Villonne, that you feel so compelled to tell falsehoods to win a maiden's heart? I had long heard that your charm was beyond compare."

Bayard stood, his expression impassive. "I tell no false-hood."

"Where is this estate you claim to hold?"

"The holding comes to me in its own time." Bayard looked most grim. "'Tis premature to speak of it."

Simon laughed. "Because it does not exist or 'tis not assured to be yours! Ask any man in this hall, Esmeraude, and he will tell you of the richness of the Château Leyrossire, which I have held in mine own hand for ten years." He sipped his ale, smiling slightly as chatter broke out in the hall. "And what of your illustrious crusade, Bayard? How do matters fare in the Holy City?"

"You know that 'twas not claimed, for lack of men and power. Indeed, Simon, if you had the courage to sacrifice your leisure time to a great cause, your presence would not have been unwelcome." Bayard sipped his own ale and his gaze turned assessing. "Providing, of course, that you still have an ability to wield a blade. Are you not rather aged to take a young bride, Simon?"

"I am as virile as any man in this hall!"

"And widowed many more times. How many wives have you buried, Simon?"

The older man flushed a dull red. "'Tis not of import."

"I suspect the lady would find your seven brides of great import." Bayard held Esmeraude's gaze, as if he would grant her a warning. What did he know of these wives? "Seven wives in ten years," he mused and Esmeraude gasped at the timing. "Such short lives they lived in your fine château, Simon. Perhaps life there is not so filled with pleasure, after all."

The older man gritted his teeth. "Childbirth is fraught with danger for women, as any fool knows."

Jacqueline caught her breath at this untimely reminder, her hand falling to the ripe curve of her belly.

Angus stood in his turn, his expression most dour. "There

shall be no talk of losses in childbirth in my hall, or you may all leave this very night!"

Bayard inclined his head toward his host in apology and Simon grudgingly did the same. "'Tis odd you should suggest as much, Simon, when the rumor is that not a one of your brides conceived."

"That is a lie!"

"Oh? How many heirs have you?"

"None and you know it well." Simon cast his cup toward a squire—who barely caught it—then leaned upon the board. "But what of your last lie, Bayard de Villonne? What of this tale that you are a champion? I recall the outcome of our tourney at Tours rather differently."

Bayard's eyes narrowed. "Do you?"

"Who won? Tell them all who was the victor of that contest?"

"You did," Bayard said softly. "You won because you cheated."

"There is no proof of that."

"Is there not?" Bayard smiled and sipped his ale, then took his seat. Chatter broke out anew in the hall and Esmeraude wondered what had transpired. Her instinct was to believe Bayard, though she did find it disturbing that he would not name his holding.

Did he truly not have one?

Did she care?

The knight beside Esmeraude fumed silently for a moment, then turned a winning smile upon her. "He lies, as is his wont. Surely you can see the kind of man he is?"

"Aye, I can." Esmeraude watched Bayard, knowing he was angry and guessing why. He was much concerned with fairness and justice and if Simon had cheated to defeat him, 'twas not a deed Bayard would forget.

Simon frowned while Seamus, tall and angular, began his

song. He was blessed with a deep voice that resonated beautifully in the hall. He told a sad tale of a seal turned to woman, then back again, at the price of losing her love, and won a smattering of applause.

Then all in the hall sat forward, Esmeraude as well, remembering where Bayard had halted his tale the night before. Would he tell of the execution of the lovers, or would he offer love a reprieve? Esmeraude had to know, for she believed 'twould tell much of this knight's secret yearnings.

Chapter Fifteen

S ESMERAUDE AND ALL THE COMPANY IN THE HALL listened, Bayard sang of Tristran being brought to the pyre where King Mark intended to burn the lovers alive. That knight deceived his captors by begging for one last chance to pray when they passed a small chapel, one said to have no means of escape.

But Tristran leapt through the small window that faced the sea, daring the drop of the cliffs there. He was saved from dying in the fall by a large flat rock partway down the cliff face. His loyal Governal met him with his armor and his steed and Tristran set out to save his lady fair.

The company applauded this deed with such vigor that Bayard had to wait for silence. Esmeraude was intrigued that the knight evidently thought a lie to escape death was permissible.

A sentry came, as one had the night before, and whispered in Angus's ear. That man excused himself and strode from the hall so quickly that the sentry had to run to match his pace. The company barely glanced up.

For Iseut meanwhile had been led to the pyre, her wrists bleeding from the tightness of her bonds. She was so lovely that all the people mourned her pending death, though the king was not swayed. He would not even heed her pleas for his forgiveness and the company hissed at his coldheartedness. Annelise crept into Esmeraude's lap and clutched her hand in her fear for Iseut. Esmeraude gripped the child's fingers with equal vigor.

Bayard sang that there was a leper, name of Yvain, who had come to the burning with his company of a hundred lepers. When he saw Iseut, he made a gruesome offer to the king. He suggested that a burning would lead to a quick death for the queen. He said that giving her to the lepers for their pleasure would make Iseut wish she was dead a thousand times over, thus prolonging her punishment.

To Esmeraude's horror, the king agreed and surrendered his lady wife to the leper colony. Bayard would have halted there, but the entire assembly roared in protest.

Esmeraude could not be silent, not when Bayard sang of such marital cruelty. Did he think the king had chosen aright? "This is beyond foul!" she cried. "'Tis a shocking travesty of the king's nuptial vows."

"'Tis indeed," Bayard agreed easily, his eyes gleaming.

"'Twas wicked and undeserved and wrong beyond belief! One owes better to one's sworn spouse, do you not agree?"

"Aye. I, too, share your faith in the holiness of a nuptial pledge." Bayard captured her hand, and Esmeraude had a moment's disappointment that he would only bestow a kiss there before he murmured, for her ears alone, "I like it well that we share such convictions, my Esmeraude. 'Tis a good portent for our own match."

He kissed her hand with a proprietary ease that pleased her mightily and made Simon inhale with a hiss.

"Tell me, my Esmeraude," Bayard said. "Is it truly to comment upon the tale that you continue to hail me, or is it my kiss that you seek?"

Esmeraude smiled. "I would bestow far more than a kiss upon the man I favor," she declared, "but only if he proves himself worthy of my love."

"How do I fare?"

Esmeraude liked the competitive light that dawned in his eyes and knew 'twould be good to encourage it. "Well enough," she conceded. "Though only the fate of the lovers will prove the truth of it."

The company fell into rapt silence as soon as Bayard began to sing again. He told of Tristran killing the leper as soon as he reached the forest, thus freeing Iseut only moments after she had been condemned to such hideous penance.

Esmeraude applauded this conquest for love as mightily as all the others gathered there. She could not guess how Bayard could fail to see the merit of love conquering wickedness in this episode. He grinned at her, then told how the lovers had fled into the forest and lived there in exile, content in their love, though they had naught else.

There was a fine sentiment! The company cheered, Esmeraude among them, but Bayard held up a warning finger and they caught their breath as one. That favor was doomed to change, for after two years of living in the forest, the pair chanced to be sleeping one afternoon when the king's hunt brought him near. Esmeraude was not the only one who leaned forward so as to not miss a morsel.

Though discovered by King Mark, the lovers again had Fortune's smile upon them, for they slept clothed and with Tristran's blade between them. This the king interpreted as evidence of their innocence and his own error in condemning them. He traded his blade for Tristran's and his ring for the lady's own. His choice proved his presence to the lovers when they awakened and persuaded them that they were in danger of his wrath.

> To Wales the loving pair did flee,
> Fearful of King Mark's dire decree.
> In Wales they saw the third year pass,
> That the potion was doomed to last.

> *Their love was gone, as quick as that—*
> *And both saw how much life did lack.*
> *The time had come for Tristran to*
> *Return Iseut to spouse she knew,*
> *And put love's madness in the past,*
> *For 'tis an ill that cannot last.*

Esmeraude frowned, much disappointed by this verse. The story lost a certain luster for her then. Indeed, she folded her arms across her chest and glared at Bayard.

Simon chuckled and sipped indulgently of his ale.

Bayard sang on, undeterred. A hermit aided the unhappy couple, suggesting that they never make their intimacy clear to the king, and they followed his advice. Iseut was rejoined with the king amid much rejoicing and Tristran was dispatched to the service of the King of Galloway for a year and a day.

Bayard told how the barons did not rest easy, for they feared that Tristran would take vengeance from them for what he and Iseut had endured at their behest. One last time, they tried to reveal the truth of his wife's infidelity to the king, and King Mark, in his annoyance, told Iseut of this.

Iseut embraced this challenge, telling her spouse that she would welcome the chance to clear her name for all time. She demanded that King Arthur and his valiant knights meet their household at the Perilous Ford, for she would have witnesses of her pledge that could not be contested within King Mark's court.

And to this, both and king and barons agreed.

Bayard halted and Esmeraude was as dismayed as the rest of the company. "How could Iseut prove her innocence when she was guilty?" she demanded.

Bayard spared her a smile. "Show me your favor, Esmeraude, and I shall confess all of the tale this very night."

Esmeraude shook her head. "Nay. I shall not wed a man for the ending of a tale." She held his gaze, daring him to grant her the confession she knew he understood that she desired.

Bayard stared back at her, his eyes a brilliant blue, though he said no more. Esmeraude felt caught by his gaze, and it seemed to her that he would compel her to look within his heart for herself.

"A fine sentiment," Simon said approvingly. "A woman should wed for security and wealth and *honesty*." The two knights exchanged hostile glances.

"I would wed for a tale!" Annelise cried and the company laughed, the moment of tension passing. They returned to their tankards and their gossip and Jacqueline began telling the children that 'twas time they retired.

Bayard sauntered closer, his gaze fixed upon Esmeraude. She felt as if she could not move, could not so much as take a breath. "Would you grant a man a kiss in exchange for a tale?"

He was so certain that he would win that kiss—and worse, that he could change her decision simply with his touch—that Esmeraude was determined to disappoint him, just as he had disappointed her.

" 'Tis a fine idea!" she said and rose to her feet.

Simon cleared his throat. "Perhaps I shall share a tale, after all."

" 'Tis too late for the children," Jacqueline said firmly. "And 'twould be unfair to recount a tale in their absence."

Simon pursed his lips and Bayard's smile widened. He arched a brow at Esmeraude, so certain was he of what gift she would bestow and upon whom she would bestow it.

So Esmeraude stood and gestured to Calum. "Come, Calum, you have won the favor of my kiss for your tale of Ceinn-beithe. 'Twas always a favorite of mine, but you have told it uncommonly well. I have always had a fondness for a tale that rewards true love."

She kissed Calum with gusto, directly beneath Bayard's scowling gaze. Some of the company laughed. Bayard waited, toe tapping, but Esmeraude did not spare him so much as a glance before she turned toward the solar and her cold pallet.

Let Bayard de Villonne think about *that*!

❖

Enough was enough.

Bayard had been patient in granting Esmeraude time to assess her various suitors, having no doubt that she would choose him in the end. He had been chivalrous in defending her virtue before his cousins and brothers.

And for what? That she might grant the favor of her kiss to yet another suitor? That she might smile at Simon, the most untrustworthy man he had ever had the misfortune to meet? Nay! That was not part of Bayard's plan.

'Twas time to make a bold move. He could not afford to linger so long in these lands, waiting upon the assent of a woman who had no logical reason to decline his suit.

'Twas time for Esmeraude to accept him.

This night, his chivalry would banish the last of her resistance. 'Twas risky, what he would do, for it cost him an advantage, but Esmeraude would understand that he trusted her. And trust, all knew, was closely akin to love. 'Twas the closest he could come to the sweet confession she desired.

As Bayard left the hall, he hoped 'twould be enough.

He eyed the way the vine had grown along the walls, stunned by its zealous progress. The lord was on the crest of the wall again, and men were trying valiantly to cut the vine back, all to no avail. It seemed to turn aside their blades, as if wrought of some matter stronger than the stuff of plants.

There was another reason to be gone—that cursed vine

would bar the gates soon enough and there would be naught any man could do about the matter.

Bayard fetched his saddlebags and found what he sought within them, then crossed the bailey. There was one window to the solar, though 'twas set high in the wall. He listened to the sounds carrying from the solar, the snoring of men and maids, the sparkle of a lady's laughter, the richness of a man's chuckle. He heard children mumble sleepily and women sigh. There was an occasional patter of bare feet on stone, followed by a subdued splash of a bucket being put to use.

And of course, the incessant sound of lovemaking. Truly, he had never visited a hall where men and maids made merry with such frequency or such enthusiasm. It did not make his own celibacy any easier to bear.

But that would end on this night.

Gradually, the rustle of activity faded, and only the whisper of deep breathing drifted through the window. Bayard waited. Night sounds filled the bailey of Airdfinnan: the regular pacing of the sentries along the high walls, the muted rush of the river Finnan, the distant hoot of an owl. Bayard stood until the entire keep seemed cloaked in the gossamer of dreams, and then he began to hum.

'Twas the tune of his song of Iseut and Tristran. He hummed it low, daring to hope that Esmeraude was as sleepless as he in this keep. He missed her warmth against him, and these days and nights apart had only made his ache for her touch more keen.

Bayard hummed through a pair of verses to no response, then halted to consider his course. He frowned, then hummed somewhat louder through another verse, knowing he did not imagine a new edge in his voice.

What if Esmeraude refused him for the lack of a confession of love? Women could be whimsical—was this what kept her from accepting him? Would she deny him for the one pledge he could not make?

Simon, he knew well, would lie to win Esmeraude and never think twice of the morality of that. Would she believe him? Would she accept Simon, on the basis of a lie, and refuse Bayard?

Nay! He could not permit that to happen. Bayard hummed more diligently, cradling his gift against his chest. He put every measure of his determination into the music he wrought, and hoped that Esmeraude would answer his summons.

But none came to the window.

He hummed another trio of verses, his gaze fixed upon the dark square of the window. There was not so much as a flutter there, not so much as a whisper of sound.

Esmeraude must be asleep. Bayard frowned and restlessly turned the burden he carried, sparing a glance to the foggy sky as he wondered what to do. He was not accustomed to failure. He dared not hum louder, lest he awaken others. It seemed he wasted his efforts in this, though he had thought it a perfect plan.

He decided to try one last time, then retire himself if his lady did not respond. He turned to address his song to the window again, and his breath caught in his throat.

Esmeraude was there.

Bayard knew he stared, for he had not expected Esmeraude to heed him now. She might have been a vision wrought of the dim luminescence of the fog. He stared, too, because Esmeraude was so lovely that the breath caught within his chest. She had unbound her hair and it shimmered where it fell over her shoulders, the light from the fog making her look ethereal and unreal.

Then she smiled, with all the mischief of his Esmeraude, and Bayard's heart clenched with painful vigor. He strode to the window, intent upon claiming his victory. "I have brought you a gift, my Esmeraude."

"Because I am vexed with you?"

This puzzled him. "Why would you be vexed with me?"

Esmeraude sighed with exasperation. "If I must explain myself, then I shall be doubly vexed."

"You did not care for the tale?"

"I did not care for your conviction that love is an illness from which men and women should be healed."

Bayard smiled with a confidence he did not quite feel. "Ah, but why did Tristran and Iseut still care for each other's futures, if there was no love between them?"

"Perhaps they became friends," Esmeraude retorted coldly. "I thought you regaled me with a tale of true love, once obstructed, then running true."

Bayard considered this, then sang the next verse pitched low, hoping it won her favor.

> But Iseut found that Mark's embrace,
> Tristran's sweet kiss did not replace.
> The old potion meant naught at all,
> For Tristran held her heart in thrall.

Esmeraude clutched the sill. "So she did love him, and he loved her, despite the fading of the potion?"

"They loved to the grave and beyond."

"Then they never were wedded to each other and never found happiness together?"

Bayard shook his head, feeling that the tale suddenly showed a most dire lack. Esmeraude shook her head and made to retreat, as if she despaired of him, and he stepped forward before she disappeared.

"You have not asked what I brought."

Esmeraude regarded him. "There is only one thing I desire of you, Bayard, and that is a confession of love."

Bayard stepped closer and laid claim to her hand. "I will not lie to you, Esmeraude," he said quietly. "I will not pledge that I feel some sentiment that I do not. Indeed, it has oft been said that a man should be measured by his deeds, not by his words."

"What is that to mean?"

"When we met, I had thought 'twould be prudent to have proof of what we shared, lest others might doubt what had passed between us." Bayard removed a white garment from where 'twas tucked beneath his arm and offered it to Esmeraude. "But what has passed between us should remain between us, from that night through to eternity."

He knew the moment that Esmeraude realized that what he held was her errant chemise. "You took it!"

He nodded. "I did not mean to lose you, Esmeraude, and still I do not." He handed her the garment and she clutched it to her chest. "But I would show you that I am not a man to shame you before even your own family. I took your maidenhead and do not deny it, but there is no reason for any other to know that we anticipated the vows that we shall make to each other."

Esmeraude stared at him and said naught. "So, you surrender the proof of your advantage," she mused and he knew it should have sorely troubled him that she understood his thinking so well as that. "Have you abandoned your quest for my hand then?" she asked with alarm. "Is that why you return this?"

"Of course not." He was uncommonly relieved that the lady did not retreat. "But 'tis your garment and graced, I would guess, by your embroidery and it rightfully belongs with you."

She stared at him, her eyes wide. "I thank you."

"And I thank you, my Esmeraude, for choosing me as the man to introduce you to pleasure," he murmured, his gaze unswerving. "I ask you to think upon what is the right choice for you, and, no less, the deeds of a man upon whom you can rely in every instance."

"Is that why you pursue me with such diligence? For the sake of your duty and honor alone?"

" 'Tis no small thing." A smile touched his lips, then faded when the lady did not smile herself. "Use your wits, Esmeraude," he counseled gently. "And choose the man who can best provide the life you desire. I have sufficient wealth to keep you and an estate to call my own. I will defend you with my blade and my body and my word, I will meet you abed with passion, I will raise our children with honor. There is naught else that a woman of good sense might desire of her spouse."

"A woman might desire love of her spouse."

Bayard held her gaze steadily. "But what is the difference, Esmeraude, between the words and the deeds? And which, in the end, is of greater value? I have heard in this hall of your father, who spoke of love and acted with indifference. Is the inverse case not one that will see your future better assured?"

The lady studied him, then leaned out the window until their faces were nigh touching. "Nay, 'twill not. I will not permit you or any other man to break my heart." She kissed his brow, as one would kiss a child, then retreated to the shadows of the solar.

"Esmeraude!" Bayard hissed. There was no reply, and he repeated his call, clutching the sill with his hand.

But his lady was gone. He turned and leaned back against the wall, wondering whether 'twas his competitiveness alone that had him so desperate to win this quest.

Surely it could be naught else?

For the first time in all his days, Bayard forced himself to consider what he would do if he lost. 'Twas not the trial of facing his grandmother that rose in his mind's eye to torment him, nor the fact that he would never hold Montvieux, nor the fear of his family unprepared to defend Montvieux against Richard, nor even the prospect of the king and his companions laughing at Bayard's failure.

'Twas the prospect of living without the sparkle of his Esmeraude that made his innards clench.

And that was a terrifying truth indeed.

✤

Inside the solar and on the other side of the stones that Bayard leaned against, Esmeraude stood with her nose buried in her chemise. She felt no sense of victory in having made a sensible choice, for she knew that she had wounded more than Bayard's pride.

Indeed, as she stood there, Esmeraude realized that he had crossed a threshold this night, for his surrender of the proof of his advantage was not a sensible choice on his part. 'Twas a concession, perhaps a strategic concession, but one that defied good sense.

Was he telling her with his deed how he felt, instead of with his words?

Esmeraude lifted the chemise, savored the mingled scents of leather and horse and a certain man's flesh, and knew what she had to do. She slipped quietly through the solar, crept out the door, and ran across the hall in search of her one true love.

She saw Bayard striding toward the stables, and in her haste to reach him, Esmeraude unwittingly dropped the chemise. She did not return for it, even once she realized what she had done, for she could not delay a moment in pursuing Bayard.

This night she meant to win her heart's desire. This night, she would show him what she offered in full.

✤

Unbeknownst to Esmeraude or Bayard, a certain knight had eavesdropped upon their conversation, greedily listening to every word. He stepped from the shadows now and retrieved the errant chemise, smiling to himself when he saw the distinctive mark of a maiden's blood.

Then Simon de Leyrossire tucked the chemise into his tabard and returned to the hall, wanting very much to whistle in satisfaction but knowing 'twould only reveal his advantage too soon.

Oh, he would enjoy this vengeance, of that there was no doubt.

❀

"Bayard!"

Bayard glanced over his shoulder, uncertain he had heard his name. But Esmeraude ran toward him, her hair flying loose behind her and her feet bare.

And he knew from her jubilant expression that he had finally persuaded her to accept him. He knew not how and he knew not why and he did not care. She came to him! Bayard turned fully and smiled himself, opening his arms to her. She laughed and leapt and he caught her, holding her fast as he turned in place.

"You have decided?" he demanded and the lady looped her arms around his neck.

"There is no choice," she declared then lifted her lips to his.

Bayard kissed her, delighting in her unabashed response. His blood quickened and he held her tighter, his desire nigh taking him to his knees. He lifted his lips from hers, knowing he would be unable to last unless he paced himself, and Esmeraude kicked her feet in dissatisfaction.

"Do you not desire me any longer?"

Bayard laughed beneath his breath. "I have never desired a woman as much as I desire you, my Esmeraude," he admitted. "And each time seems only to redouble the effect of your kiss."

"Aye, 'tis this way for me as well," she whispered. "Is loving always thus?"

"Nay."

She smiled. "Because our match is destined to be." Bayard had no opportunity to argue the matter, for Esmeraude kissed him to silence. She wound her hand into the hair at his nape and drew him closer, the heat of her kiss enflaming him beyond belief.

She demanded pleasure of him this night, and did so with such passion that he knew he had tasted but a mere increment of what she had to offer. They tasted and teased each other, oblivious to whether others watched their ardor. When their kiss ended, they both were breathing heavily and Esmeraude's eyes were filled with stars.

"I want to know every way there is for a man and a woman to love each other," she whispered huskily. "And I choose you, Bayard, to teach me."

He made a mock sigh of concession. "If my lady wills as much, there is naught I can do but agree."

Esmeraude laughed and scanned the bailey. "I would also be alone this night with you. How clean are the stables?"

"There is a goodly abundance of straw there and 'tis warm and dry." Bayard strode in that direction, carrying the lady who would shortly be his wife. "Though one of these nights, my Esmeraude, we shall love in a bed, upon a plump mattress piled with furs, as is right and proper."

Her answering smile made him yearn to kiss her anew. "I predict that the first time we meet abed, my lord, shall be in our nuptial bed, as is proper for any couple."

Bayard laughed, but not for long, for as soon as he stepped into the shadows of the stable, Esmeraude's lips were on his and her hand was under his chemise. Her urgency was infectious and they were both hasty in their responses. He tumbled into the straw and grinned with the realization that he faced yet another sleepless night.

Though this was not one he would regret.

Bayard coaxed his lady to pleasure, reveling in the flush that dawned upon her cheeks and the stars that lit within her eyes. He savored her every sigh as a triumph and felt more of a champion than ever he had when she crested the rise of desire for the third time.

And when Esmeraude arched against him, three words burst from her lips, three words he had never expected to hear, three words that gave him more joy than ever he could have expected.

"I love you," was what she said. Their gazes held until the pleasure consumed her and her lids closed heavily, but still her claim echoed in Bayard's thoughts.

She loved him. Bayard knew 'twas only relief that made his own heart clamor in response, for a wife who loved him would never leave him or betray him.

It could be no more than that.

But Bayard pleasured his lady with all the passion within him. From this night on, he and Esmeraude were as one and naught, to Bayard's thinking, could tear them asunder.

❧

Angus of Airdfinnan did not wish to be disturbed. He had made as much clear to his men, so he willfully ignored the whisper of a sentry in the solar. His wife was curled against him, so ripe that he dreaded the moment this child chose to enter the world. He held her close and knew he was unwilling to sacrifice so much as a moment in her presence, even when she slept, for such moments might prove to be too few.

"My lord!" the sentry whispered again, his voice more urgent.

Angus feigned sleep. His children were tucked into the great bed, nestled beneath the covers on either side of himself and Jacqueline. 'Twas warm and comfortable here, but that was not the reason he would not leave.

The import of his life was here, dozing all around him, in his trusting, happy children and the security of his hall. He was blessed with the happiness he had found without expecting it, happiness wrought by his Jacqueline. 'Twas she who hung the moon and the stars for him and he could not bear to imagine how barren his life would be without her.

The babe stirred and his gut clenched. Aye, Angus was afraid and more afraid than ever he had been. Jacqueline carried such a large child that he feared one of them would not survive its arrival.

Worse, there was naught he could do about the matter, no way he could influence which of them it might be.

He tightened his arm around Jacqueline and kissed her hair, closing his eye when the sentry whispered again.

"I do not need to see it," Angus said flatly. " 'Tis enough that you tell me that it grows again."

"Nay, my lord, 'tis worse than that."

How could it be worse? Angus turned to stare into the darkness where the man stood. "Has it barred the gates?"

"Nay, not quite. But it has grown twice its length this past night alone, and my lord"—the man's voice faltered as if he were incredulous himself—"it has sprouted *leaves*."

Angus swore. He swung from the bed and dressed in haste. He knew enough of magic to recognize its presence, and knew that this vine's growth was linked in some mysterious way to the affair of Esmeraude and Bayard. Though they had arrived separately, there was some bond between them. The vine grew when the knight sang for the damsel, which meant 'twas of his making.

Angus was shocked to see how vigorously the vine had grown the night before and cursed his indulgence of Bayard's song even as he climbed the ladder to the summit of the walls.

Glossy green leaves had indeed erupted over the plant's entire length, making the walls look cloaked in finery. In truth, it looked more lush than it had.

But when Angus bent to examine the vine, his heart stopped cold. Beneath the leaf he examined, he found a bud. Not only did the vine come close to growing over the gates itself, not only did it cloak the walls with its shiny thorns from the bailey to the surface of the river, but now 'twould blossom and scatter seeds everywhere.

The last curse that Angus needed was another of these plants, let alone a thousand of them, all growing in his bailey! He might be able to do naught about the threat to his wife's welfare, but this matter he could see resolved.

Angus set out to find the man responsible for this wizardry, for Bayard alone could put a halt to its progress.

Enough was enough.

Bayard awakened slowly, smiling as he savored the sweet scent of the straw of their bed and the even sweeter perfume of his Esmeraude. She burrowed against him, placing her cold nose against his flesh and making him jump.

"So you are awake," she teased, her eyes sparkling. "I had thought you overtired."

"Aye? And you are not tired? Perhaps I did not please you sufficiently." The lady laughed but Bayard silenced her laughter with a thorough kiss. They parted reluctantly and he studied her flushed cheeks and sparkling eyes.

She loved him. All would now be well.

Bayard thought to celebrate this once more, but a masculine voice cleared at such proximity that both he and Esmeraude jumped.

"Good morning to you," Angus said wryly. "Though I would not intrude on your merriment, there is a matter of greater import that must be addressed."

The lord did not look as if 'twas a cheerful matter. Indeed, he looked more grim than Bayard had ever seen him.

Esmeraude sat up hastily and gathered her chemise before her bare breasts. "Is Jacqueline well?" Her hair hung down the perfection of her bare back in a tangle of curls that Bayard could have spent the day combing to some order.

But Angus passed a hand across his brow and his lips tightened. "Thus far. That is not the sole matter that troubles me this morn." He cocked a finger at Bayard. "You will halt what you have begun and you will do so on this very day."

Bayard sat up in turn. "What have I done?"

The lord beckoned, then turned away. Bayard donned his chemise and chausses hastily, then laced the sides of Esmeraude's kirtle. She looked to him, her gaze full of questions, and he shrugged, for he knew not what the lord meant. He plucked a strand of straw from her tresses, then kissed her brow.

" 'Twill come aright. I shall ensure it," he whispered and she smiled with an ease born of confidence.

"I know."

They left the stables hand in hand and were within a few paces of Angus, who stood stiffly facing the opposite side of the bailey, when a woman's scream rang through the air. Angus straightened and Esmeraude gasped.

"Jacqueline!" she whispered, squeezed Bayard's hand then ran for the hall.

The lord did not move, indeed, he seemed struck to stone. Bayard halted beside him and noted the sudden pallor of his features. "Do you go to the solar as well?"

Angus shook his head. "Nay, my restlessness there only troubles my lady wife. Let us address a matter with an outcome to be determined by the will of men."

He strode away then, and Bayard followed him, noting again how the vine had grown during the night. It cloaked the walls in glossy green leaves now and was a striking sight. "Does this vine grow here every year, or only at intervals?" he asked, hoping to distract the lord from his evident fears. "I have never seen the like of it."

The lord granted him a hostile glance. "'Tis as alien to these parts as the knights who court Esmeraude's hand." He climbed the ladder to the crest of the wall without a backward glance, though he flinched when his wife's cry of pain carried from the hall once again.

Bayard followed, feeling no small measure of confusion.

Angus halted at the boundary of the vine. In fact, 'twould have been impossible to walk farther along the wall, for 'twas thickly adorned with the vegetation. And the leaves hid the vicious thorns upon the plant, making it dangerous to attempt such a feat.

"I am a man who believes in what he sees and what he can hold within his hands," Angus said quietly. "But in my time, I have learned a respect of the unseen."

He turned to face Bayard, his gaze quelling despite the fact that one of his eyes was hidden behind a patch. "I recognize the presence of magic when I see it. This vine is not natural, and its like has never been seen in these parts. Its root was undoubtedly a gift to my mother—as so many of the roots within that garden are—probably from some guest, perhaps a guest from France. I know only that it has *never* flourished here." Angus kicked the vine with his boot, holding Bayard's gaze all the while. "Until you sang for Esmeraude."

Bayard took a step back in horror at the implicit accusation. "Are you accusing me of witchery? I am not responsible for this!"

"Are you not?" Angus seemed unpersuaded. He took a step back and almost smiled. "Then sing, and prove me wrong."

" 'Tis nonsense."

"Prove it."

Bayard glared at the other knight. He stood straight, threw back his head and sang, knowing that he would prove this foolishness wrong.

> *But Iseut found that Mark's embrace,*
> *Tristran's sweet kiss did not replace.*
> *The old potion meant naught at all*
> *For Tristran held her heart in thrall.*

To his horror, the vine sprouted as soon as the first line left his lips. It grew with vigor all the while he sang, twining across Angus's boot and sprouting leaves as it went. Bayard halted, staring at it in astonishment, and the vine halted as well.

This monstrosity was of his own making!

Chapter Sixteen

THIS CANNOT BE!" BAYARD WISHED HIS DENIAL WOULD make it so. He stared at the vine, stunned that he could be responsible for its presence.

"Nonetheless it is," Angus retorted.

"But 'tis illogical. No plant grows in this manner. No song prompts a plant to grow!"

" 'Tis not so devoid of sense as that."

"What is that to mean?"

"Why do you court my sister-in-law?"

Bayard felt his gaze narrow, for he was not prepared to confess his secret to another, not even this knight of such similar experience as his own. "Because I have need of a bride," he said mildly.

"Bah!" Angus kicked the vine. "That would not account for your diligence. Nay, there is another reason for your suit, a greater reason than the mere desire for a wife."

Bayard feared the man knew the truth about Montvieux and Richard, that he might confess it to Esmeraude and destroy the tenuous victory Bayard had won. "You cannot know that."

"Nay, I cannot know your secret desire, but I can look with the eye I have got."

"And what do you see?" Bayard challenged, fully expecting Angus to claim knowledge of Margaux's pledge.

Angus flung out a hand to encompass the range of the vine. "This is conjured by a man's love. Look, how it moves to bar the gate, to keep Esmeraude from departing this hall without accepting you."

Bayard was astounded. "That is madness!"

"Nay, 'tis not. The vine grows when you sing for Esmeraude, it grows when you seek to enchant her with a tale, it grows when you offer the one gift that you believe will persuade her to accept you." Angus shook his head. "Esmeraude's love of tales is well known, Bayard de Villonne, but a song is not sufficient to coax a woman to your side. I would suggest that if winning Esmeraude means as much to you as this that you offer her more than a mere tale."

"What do you mean?"

"Offer yourself." Angus held his gaze for a long moment. "Tell her that you love her. 'Tis that alone that will persuade her." He smiled slightly. "Eglantine has raised her daughters with a healthy esteem for love."

"But I do not love her!"

"Do you not?" Angus surveyed the vine and shook his head. "And I had hoped that you might confess the truth of it to her before we are all sealed within these walls forever."

"I cannot confess what is not true."

"Not true?" Angus smiled. "The vine is a testament to the truth, Bayard." He dropped his voice and let his hand rest on the younger man's shoulder. "There is no weakness in confessing to love a woman. Indeed, you might be surprised at the strength her love can grant you."

"You did not seem strong when Jacqueline cried out," Bayard felt compelled to observe.

The lord's smile faded. "Because I know that all the treasures of my life would be as naught without my Jacqueline. There is naught worse for a warrior than to know that his skills are insufficient to affect any outcome. I cannot aid

Jacqueline in this labor, though I do what I can. The finest midwife I could find is with her now." His manner was so grim that Bayard touched the man's sleeve.

"She has borne four children. Surely this one will arrive without incident."

Angus nodded briefly. "I hope so." Then he slanted an incisive glance at Bayard. "And what would your life be without Esmeraude? Would your riches seem as dust in your hands if she wed another?"

Bayard blinked. Had he not thought much the same just the night before?

Surely he could not love Esmeraude?

The truth hit Bayard like a blow to the chest. Aye, the reason he pursued this woman beyond all rhyme and reason was more than the loving of all her characteristics, more than honor and duty and reason.

He loved *her*.

'Twas a stunning realization, all the more stunning for his long-held determination to never love another. He understood with sudden clarity the desire to have an especial woman by his side that had driven his own father for years. He understood that 'twas unthinkable to wed another, to live out his life without the sparkle of Esmeraude. He had known many women and not one of them had caught him so securely, nor so quickly.

Bayard loved how Esmeraude made merry; he loved how she laughed. He loved the agility of her wits and the passion of her kisses. He loved her hunger for adventure and her willingness to pursue new experiences. He loved her determination to not accept less than her true desire.

Bayard loved Esmeraude. He rolled the thought through his mind, marveling in it, familiarizing himself with it. 'Twas, indeed, an unexpected development. Though he had had his suspicions, he had ignored their portent well.

But what was he to do about the matter?

Angus studied him for a long moment, as if he wondered much the same, until another cry of pain rose from the solar. The other man inhaled sharply, then turned away, gripping Bayard's shoulder before he left. "Pray for my Jacqueline," he whispered, then left Bayard alone upon the crest of the wall.

There was naught he might say to that. Bayard watched the man go, and acknowledged that he spied no weakness in Angus MacGillivray. Indeed, he offered a prayer to the survival of the lady of Airdfinnan, though he was not a man who spent much time upon his knees. He felt battered by the realization of his love, by the fact that he could conjure such sorcery as this vine by the force of his feelings for Esmeraude.

It made no sense, yet made perfect sense. He loved Esmeraude. Bayard frowned, seeing that he was in the same predicament as his father had been. He could not wed Esmeraude without incurring the risks he feared. Yet he could not countenance Esmeraude wedding another, or worse, confront the rest of his life without her.

He turned to pace and halted in horror. Before his eyes, buds unfurled over the length of the vine, one after the other after the other.

The vine knew of his realization.

Bayard's gut chilled. Nay! He loved Esmeraude but none could guess the truth of it! He would not see his own affection used against him, as his father's love for his mother had been used once against their family.

And Bayard remembered suddenly the terror that had passed through their household, the expression upon his father's face, the vulnerability of Villonne that had been shown by his mother's capture. He recalled the sense of vulnerability that had been unfamiliar until that moment, and the fear that they would lose both beloved mother and prosperous holding.

His own vehement pledge to never put himself in a similar position of weakness echoed anew in his ears; he recalled his arguments with his father, his abandonment of his family with so much still left unsaid between them.

There was naught for it. A grim resolve settled within him, a determination to keep his vow and avoid such risk. A pledge of love could never pass Bayard's lips, to the lady herself or any other. He would not grant any man—especially as the kings of France and England postured for war—any knowledge that could be used against him, any whisper that could cost him the holding he would do any deed to hold.

But as he watched, the vine grew buds at an unholy rate, as if invigorated by his decision to deny his love. Nay! It could not betray him!

Bayard drew his blade and hacked at the nearest bud. The vine, which had resisted all attempts to cut it back, surrendered to the blow of Bayard's blade. The cut bud fell lifeless to the stone.

Because the vine was of his own devising.

And if the lord guessed its import, then so would others. Bayard slashed at the new buds with a strength he had not known he possessed, but the vine sprouted three buds for each one he cut. 'Twas as if it would defy Bayard to tell Esmeraude the truth.

Or perhaps it would challenge him to consider the price of not confessing his love to Esmeraude. She had told him of her love and he had not answered in kind, and in the clear light of morning, Bayard knew that this would trouble his lady.

But as long as she aided her sister, he could not make

amends even if he desired to do so. Indeed, if he truly wished to avoid his father's error, he could never make amends.

He sliced through another cluster of buds and they grew back with frightening speed, the vine seemingly compelling him to make a choice. 'Twas whimsy, or madness, and Bayard was sorely troubled by what great sense it made to him in this moment. Indeed, he feared mightily what his life would be without Esmeraude by his side.

But Bayard feared this outward sign of the secret of his heart. He cut back an entire branch of the vine, invigorated when it fell aside lifeless and did not grow back.

He *could* vanquish this menace wrought of his weakness and he would do so. He would not halt until 'twas cut back to the very root itself.

Bayard would not sing, he would not whistle, he would not so much as think about his lady love and perhaps then the vine would not grow back again.

'Twas a feeble hope, but 'twas the only one he had.

※

Within the solar, Esmeraude bathed her sister's brow, wishing there was more she could do to ease her sister's pain. Jacqueline, always sweet of nature, smiled even in this moment. "How goes your quest for the man who will hold your heart captive forever?"

"Jacqueline!" Esmeraude spared a glance for the maids aiding in the delivery, for she knew they listened avidly to every word and would repeat it in the kitchens later. She leaned down and whispered. "I have found him, but there is a small difficulty."

"Aye?"

"He swears he will never love his wife, for 'tis a weakness that can be exploited."

Jacqueline laughed, a most inappropriate response to Esmeraude's thinking. She laughed heartily, then her laughter was cut suddenly short by another contraction. She gasped and Esmeraude gripped her hand tightly, watching the perspiration bead upon her sister's brow as the pain rose within her.

"Very good, my lady," the midwife said with approval. "The babe comes slowly, but it comes." She looked up brightly. "Perhaps 'tis a particularly large child, as your lord suspects."

Jacqueline fell back against the pillows and groaned. She then spoke to Esmeraude as though there had been no interruption in their conversation. "So, Bayard says he will not love—"

"I did not say 'twas Bayard!"

"You did not have to," Jacqueline scolded, then continued. "He says he will not love but he courts you with determination, he sings for you, he charms children for your favor, he hovers diligently near your side, he is daunted by no refusal that passes your lips, and I imagine he steals kisses from you, if not more."

Esmeraude knew her cheeks were flaming red. "Charm and lust are not the same as love."

"But a man's deeds oft speak more clearly of his intent than his words."

"You sound like him." Esmeraude watched her sister carefully, wondering whether she had overheard Bayard's return of the chemise. Jacqueline would make much of that gallantry, Esmeraude was certain!

But Jacqueline leaned back and sighed, wincing as another contraction built within her. "I am glad you are here, and am selfish enough to appreciate whatever has brought you to my side," she whispered, then caught her breath. Jacqueline's grip tightened painfully on Esmeraude's hand and she arched back to release a cry of anguish.

" 'Tis fine, my lady, all is well."

"Angus should be here," Esmeraude said crossly. "Is it not his place to at least witness the result of planting his seed?" Though she spoke with annoyance fed by a sense of helplessness, Esmeraude knew that her sister drew great strength from her spouse's presence.

But Jacqueline laughed under her breath. "His presence is no aid in this time," she said with a rueful smile. "Indeed, his incessant pacing only makes me more fearful than I am."

"But he could hold your hand and whisper assurances to you."

"Angus is a man, and worse, a man of war," Jacqueline said firmly. She opened her eyes and held Esmeraude's gaze. "'Tis his way to solve whatsoever is amiss and to solve it quickly."

"And?"

Jacqueline's lips quirked in reminiscence. "The sole time I allowed him to be with me for the labor, I was half-certain he would cut Fergus from my womb with his own blade, simply to see the matter done and my pain halted. The time it took that child to come into the world pushed him beyond reason." She sighed and smiled, evidently not overly troubled with this trait of her spouse. "'Tis far simpler to let Angus be elsewhere, solving other matters as quickly as is his wont."

"Does he come when 'tis over?"

"I have him summoned when the child is close. He can bear a few moments of my ordeal for the delight of seeing his son or daughter's arrival." Jacqueline caught her breath again and her voice tightened. "Indeed, it gives him uncommon pleasure to be the first to hold his own child, and it gives me as much pleasure to witness his happiness."

Esmeraude guessed that Angus's joy in the arrival of his child was what made the labor easier for Jacqueline. She bathed her sister's brow and held fast to her hand until this contraction passed.

The midwife nodded with satisfaction. "'Tis as though you have done this afore, my lady," she jested and Jacqueline smiled.

Jacqueline turned her bright gaze upon Esmeraude. "Your expectations of men have been colored by Duncan MacLaren."

"And what is that to mean?"

"That our stepfather is an uncommon man."

"Shall I tell Angus that he is common?" Esmeraude teased, pleased when her sister smiled.

"Duncan is a man who speaks readily of the contents of his heart, while men like Angus—and I suspect Bayard—are more reticent in such matters. Duncan is a poet first, while Angus and Bayard are warriors first."

"Does Angus love you?"

Jacqueline's smile was radiant. "Can you doubt it?"

"But has he ever told you as much?"

"Aye, he does so all the time, but that first confession was hard won indeed." Jacqueline smiled in reminiscence. "Indeed, he confessed as much only after he thought he had lost me for all time, after I left him to join the convent." She pressed Esmeraude's hand. "Do not be so quick to accept that whatsoever your Bayard tells you of himself is true. His deeds speak loudest of all in this."

Esmeraude's agreement was cut short by another contraction, then the midwife hooted with victory. "It comes, my lady!"

"You will see, Esmeraude, you will see the truth of it when Bayard witnesses his own child's entry into the world," Jacqueline whispered.

Esmeraude glanced to her in astonishment. "There is naught that says I will see such an event."

"Not if you do not wed the man, 'tis true." Jacqueline smiled, confident of her claim. "But you bear his child, I know it."

Esmeraude's heart leapt. "You cannot know that so soon as this."

"I know it. With my own, I know the moment they are conceived. I cannot explain this, but 'twas this way with Angus's mother and when she died, I seem to have gained her gift." Jacqueline squeezed Esmeraude's fingers. "You bear his child and I would wager my own upon the truth of it."

Bayard's child. Esmeraude gripped her sister's hand, marveling at this, even as Jacqueline labored to bring her own child to light.

The midwife grinned when the contraction passed, though Jacqueline breathed heavily. "I see the head! The child is nigh here, my lady. All is well!"

Jacqueline squeezed Esmeraude's hand so tightly that she almost broke the bones. "Go! Go now and fetch Angus, wheresoever he is. I would not have him miss this moment."

Esmeraude kissed her sister's brow, then ran with all the speed she could muster.

❧

Simon sat in the hall, virtually alone, huddled beneath the expanse of his plainest cloak. He was tired from his furtive observations of the night before, but he did little more than doze. He was in the corner of the hall, wreathed in shadows, and few even noticed his presence in the bustle of activity this day.

Simon sat there and simmered with his newfound hatred of the lord of Airdfinnan. Not one child, but four the man already had, and another came into the world on this very day. Simon should be so lucky as to have a wife so able to bear his seed, instead of the seven barren witches he had wed thus far.

He sat and brooded, toying with the idea of stealing one of this lord's babes and claiming it as his own. Would such savages as lived in this hostile land even note the absence of the child? Would they care?

But there was only one son thus far, a tall and strong lad whose disappearance would be noted. Aye, Simon had seen that the lord favored the boy.

The portal to the solar was flung open even as the lady within screamed in pain, and Esmeraude ran across the hall. She was oblivious to Simon's presence and he did naught to draw attention to himself. Indeed, he considered that this fertile lady of Airdfinnan had a sister, a sister whose womb might be as abundant as her own.

Simon had answered the summons to this bride quest because few fathers would trust their daughters to his hand these days and he had need of another bride. He had hoped that the fullness of rumor had not swept this far afield, but now Simon acknowledged that these barbarian women might have a certain allure.

Fertility was a powerful incentive to a man in desperate need of an heir.

Two serving women hastened from the solar in Esmeraude's wake and Simon huddled more deeply in his cloak. He was thinking of how he should proceed to win Esmeraude himself when the gossip of the women caught his ear.

He listened shamelessly.

"How could you not have heard?" scolded one. The women carried pails of bloody rags and were headed toward the kitchen. "The lady herself said, just as clear as I am saying to you, that her sister was pregnant!"

"Pregnant? But how can that be? Esmeraude is not even wed as yet!"

The first woman laughed. "And what has that to do with the matter? Have you not seen the eyes she has cast at that knight, Bayard de Villonne? And I was not the only one to note that he came to the window of the solar last night to charm her."

"He did?"

"You sleep too much, Berthe, 'tis why you miss all the

meaty tales. And Esmeraude crept from the solar to pursue him, and not only that, but she did not come back all the night long."

"Nay!"

"Aye. There is no mystery about who planted that babe in her belly. You may be certain that the lord of Airdfinnan will ensure that a marriage is made between Esmeraude and Bayard, at least he will if his lady tells him the truth of it. He is a good man, he is, and one who takes care of all his family, as is right and proper."

With that, the women passed out of earshot, but Simon had heard enough to suit him well. He sat up in the empty hall and rubbed his hands together. What better bride for him than a woman already ripe? That Esmeraude would bear Bayard's son to Simon was but an added treat.

Simon rose in haste and strode from the hall, anxious to set his scheme into place. Who knew how long the lady would labor? When she was finished, however, Simon would be poised to depart Airdfinnan with his prize.

Whether Esmeraude was agreeable or not.

❧

Esmeraude was breathless by the time she found Angus in the smithy. He was pacing and looking troubled, paying no attention to the hammering of the smith. "Angus! Jacqueline calls for you!"

Smith, apprentice, and lord looked up in surprise.

"Is she well?" Angus demanded. "Is aught amiss?" He snatched her elbow and strode toward the hall without awaiting her answer. Indeed, he walked so hastily that Esmeraude had to take three steps for each one of his.

"The babe arrives and all seems to be well. Jacqueline would have you present for the last of it."

"Praise be to God," Angus muttered.

Esmeraude shook free of his grip, for she knew she slowed

his pace. "Go," she said, and Angus did not need to be urged twice.

He quickly outpaced her and disappeared into the hall. Esmeraude ran behind, oblivious to the usual bustle of activity in the bailey. Simon bowed to her as she passed him but Esmeraude barely nodded in return. She arrived just in time to see Angus push aside the midwife to reach his wife.

"Jacqueline?" he whispered and the lady smiled for him, then lifted a languid hand.

"Angus, the babe comes," Jacqueline whispered. He crouched beside her, one arm wrapped about her shoulders, his features taut as he whispered encouragement. Jacqueline tensed as another contraction came, then she screamed. 'Twas not easy upon Angus either, Esmeraude realized, but he did his best to let natural forces take their course.

After several contractions more, the midwife shouted and lifted the child free. The babe bellowed with evident health, Jacqueline fell back in relief, and the servants cheered.

Angus reached out and took his child, cradling it against Jacqueline's chest so that she could see it. Esmeraude's vision veiled with tears as he gently cleared the child's face. He disregarded the blood that stained his chemise and the tears that ran down his cheeks.

He lay down beside his wife as the midwife clucked in disapproval of the mess, the child encircled by the two of them. "A son, Jacqueline," he whispered hoarsely. "Another fine son."

"A boy!" Célie cried with pleasure from the cluster of servants.

The babe tipped back his head and wailed, his face turning red with his efforts. Jacqueline smiled and reached up to touch her husband's face. "His name is Ewen," she said softly. "In memory of your brother."

"Jacqueline!" Angus kissed her then, his relief and his love so evident that every woman in the chamber wiped away tears. He offered a finger to the babe, who gripped it firmly, prompting both parents to smile. Their voices dropped to whispers as they examined their new son with evident pride.

"The linens should be cleaned and the babe should be washed," the midwife declared. "The mess should have been cleaned before the lord saw his child. 'Tis improper and inappropriate . . ."

"And 'twill wait a few moments." Esmeraude touched her arm, then drew the curtains round the great bed. "Indeed, the afterbirth has yet to come and there is no need to clean the linens twice."

Whispers and chuckles echoed from behind the drapes and Esmeraude was not the only one who smiled. Though Angus had spoken no words of love, 'twas indeed true that his feelings were clear to all.

Esmeraude heaved a sigh, profoundly grateful that Ewen had shown such haste to arrive and that both babe and mother were well. She lent her aid to the cleaning, her thoughts whirling all the while. Indeed, she surreptitiously touched her own belly in wonderment. Bayard's child! She instinctively knew that Jacqueline was right.

'Twas not her future alone that Esmeraude must consider now. She thought upon her sister's match and how her warrior husband showed the fullness of his heart in his concern for her and his deeds more than by his words.

Esmeraude would wed Bayard, in the faith that he did love her. His confession, she prayed, would come in time. In the interval, she would be content with the honor and passion he showed her.

Esmeraude left the solar, filled with purpose, intent upon telling Bayard of her decision without delay. She smiled to think how pleased he would be.

But Esmeraude had not anticipated that the hall would be uncommonly empty. Most of the women were in the solar and most of the men elsewhere, probably sufficiently far away that they could not hear the lady's screams. She stepped out into the bailey again, noting this time that Simon seemed to be gathering his belongings and his steeds. She started to walk toward the stables, then happened to glance up to see Bayard on the summit of the wall.

He cut back the vine as though 'twas a fearsome foe and she smiled at the progress he had already made. No doubt he did this as a favor for Angus and she deemed it particularly thoughtful of him.

As Esmeraude was debating the merit of interrupting Bayard when he was so intent upon his task, Simon approached her. That knight smiled, looking far too content to be entirely trustworthy, and Esmeraude took a wary step back.

Simon, though, continued toward her undeterred. "I would assume that the lord has a new child."

"Aye, a son," Esmeraude admitted warily. "They have named him Ewen for Angus's brother."

"Such splendid fortune. How sad that I will be unable to linger and give my congratulations."

Simon was leaving! This was fine news indeed. Esmeraude found herself warming to the man, for there was no need to be rude when he was so close to departing. "Sad indeed," she agreed, then smiled. "Godspeed to you then."

"Do you not wonder what compels me to make such a hasty departure?"

Esmeraude felt her smile cool. "What compels you to make such a hasty departure?"

Simon shrugged. "I fear I must attend my own nuptials." He watched her closely, too closely for Esmeraude's taste.

Why would he think that she would care? "Who shall be

your bride?" she asked, more from a sense of duty than any curiosity.

"'Tis premature to speak of it," Simon said smoothly. He turned and gestured to his party, now gathering on the far side of the bailey. "It occurs to me that I have not introduced you to my fine steeds. Perhaps you might like to see them before we ride south."

Esmeraude was always tempted to see horses and 'twas no fault of the beasts that they were owned by Simon. She spared a glance to the walls and reasoned that Bayard had much work yet to do if he meant to cut the vine back fully.

Surely 'twould hurt naught to spend a moment with the horses?

She smiled and took Simon's outstretched hand. "I should be delighted."

❖

Simon let Esmeraude pat the horses and run her fingers over their manes. He was content to grant her time enough to be at ease in his presence before he sprang his trap. His bait had been well chosen, for she was particularly interested in the horses.

And Simon gradually coaxed her farther back toward the surrounding walls of the keep, where the shadows gathered beneath a leaning roof and his plan would be fulfilled. Like most women, Esmeraude was not sufficiently keen of wit to perceive the brilliance of his scheme, or even to notice that he guided her apurpose.

He caught her elbow in his hand and tightened his grip when she might have pulled away. She cast him an enquiring glance, perhaps one tinged with a bit of fear, and Simon felt a thrill of victory. He urged her more deliberately toward the shadows, though she bucked him more openly now.

"Perhaps there is naught to lose in admitting the truth to

you," he mused, feeling a need to boast of his cleverness. "I came to win your hand, Esmeraude, and 'tis clear that now 'tis mine."

Esmeraude tried to free her elbow. "'Tis not clear to me!"

"Ah, then let me explain matters slowly to you, so slowly that even you might understand." Simon spoke deliberately, noting the mutinous set of the lady's lips. "I had a walk in the bailey last evening and could not help but note a certain measure of . . . *activity* in the stables." He arched a fair brow, inviting Esmeraude to guess what he had heard.

She tried to tug her arm from his grip with greater force, but Simon was far stronger than she. "I cannot imagine why such *activity* would be of concern to you. 'Tis not uncommon for a man and a woman to anticipate their nuptial vows thus."

Simon chuckled, well satisfied with what he had learned. "Nay 'tis not uncommon," he agreed easily. "Though 'tis somewhat rare for a man to learn that his wife has borne another man's child."

Esmeraude blinked in confusion. Simon conjured her stained chemise from his tabard and shook it before her, holding it out of her grasp when she tried to snatch it from him.

"Why, look how my claiming of your maidenhead stained the cloth," he mused. "And I, as any sensible man would do, have kept the proof of our dalliance. Do you think I should challenge Bayard in his own hall with the fact that his wife did not come innocent to his nuptial bed, or should I have him summoned to the king's court to confront the truth?"

"'Tis not the truth," Esmeraude argued vehemently. "And you know it well!"

"I may know as much and you may know as much, and Bayard may know as much. But that is not the point, my dear. If

I offer such evidence before a court and insist that your first child is my bastard, do you not think that your child will be surrendered to me?"

"Nay! I will not permit you to claim my child!" Esmeraude tugged her arm fiercely, and this time Simon let her slip from his grip. "No one would heed you! No one would permit this travesty!"

Simon shook his head, amused by her innocence. "You place much credit in the minds of men. Do you truly believe that a woman would be believed, especially one intent upon preserving her reputation and marriage? 'Tis no small thing to be accused of disguising a bastard as a legitimate child, no less of adultery."

"I have not been adulterous! Bayard would defend me."

"Would he? A man cannot be home in his hall all of the time, my dear. I could arrange to visit both your hall and your chamber in his absence. We could cast doubts on his surety without much trouble at all."

She recoiled in horror and quickly glanced about herself for some means of escape. But she was cornered in the shed most effectively, Simon's squires having appeared on all sides. She was clearly frightened and clearly impressed by the thoroughness of his planning.

"What do you mean to do?"

"I mean to wed you."

"I mean to wed Bayard!"

"Ah, then I could discredit you. How long would he keep you if he doubted your integrity?" Simon leaned closer to whisper before she could protest. "Would he believe that I had not known you intimately, when I know the sweet sounds you make abed?" Simon mimicked Esmeraude's cry of pleasure so perfectly that she flushed scarlet. She retreated in horror but Simon pursued her. "How else would a man know this of you, Esmeraude?"

" 'Twould be a lie!" she protested, as though she could not fathom that a man would tell a falsehood to win his greatest desire.

Simon found himself greatly amused. "And what of Bayard's much vaunted sense of honor? Surely this is dependent on having no scandal attached to his name. How much shame would he be prepared to endure to keep you by his side? We know well how much he values the favor of the king. Perhaps he would not enjoy the displeasure of the king in this matter. Perhaps he would cast you aside if you brought infamy to his hall."

"Perhaps he would not!"

"Are you prepared to wager upon that?"

She stared at him, her eyes wide, and Simon knew, he knew, that she was prepared to make that wager. He felt a resounding disappointment, but then, he was always disappointed in women.

He would take her for the child, and after 'twas born, he could be rid of her as well.

Esmeraude did a reasonable task of feigning compliance, but Simon was not fooled. She heaved a sigh and passed a hand over her brow. "You speak aright," she conceded softly. "I could not bear to bring such shame upon his house, nor, indeed, could I bear to lose any child I had borne. What do you desire of me, Simon?"

He seized her elbow. "We shall be wed, of course."

"At Ceinn-beithe?" she asked, clearly hoping for his agreement.

At her family's home, she would have aid in destroying him and his plan. 'Twas irksome that she tried to deceive him for her wits were no match for his own.

'Twas premature for her to guess that he understood the fullness of her treachery though.

Simon smiled, the image of an indulgent suitor, and lied

through his teeth. "If 'tis your desire, my dear, then of course we shall be wed there. We shall depart for Ceinn-beithe this very morn."

Esmeraude smiled, unable to hide her delight. "If we mean to depart, then I must gather my belongings. And I shall have to fetch my maid and say farewell to my sister . . ."

"Oh, nay. We leave immediately, without word, without servants, without farewell."

"But 'twould be rude!"

Simon held Esmeraude's gaze resolutely. "Let us understand each other, my Esmeraude. I shall decide what you will do and when you will do it. You will comply, without protest or argument because 'tis my will and I am your lord. We shall leave immediately, in silence and in secrecy."

The lady's eyes flashed. "You cannot leave Airdfinnan in secrecy for the gate is barred against the strange fog."

"Perhaps 'twas." Simon held up a finger and the unmistakable sound of the portcullis being raised carried to their ears. Esmeraude's eyes widened. "My squire shows great promise, for he accomplishes all he is assigned to do and does so when he is intended to do it. A bright boy indeed. Our party leaves this very moment."

"I must say farewell," Esmeraude insisted. "Indeed, all will know that something is amiss otherwise."

"I doubt that. All know that you are disinclined to fret about others, as was your father."

"I am not like my sire! I will say farewell!" The lady spun and would have marched away, had Simon not been prepared for her defiance. He lifted a finger and the two squires met his gaze. Esmeraude strode past them and they spun silently. One snatched her shoulders and, in the same moment, the other struck her in the back of the head with a blunted hilt.

Esmeraude slumped into the first boy's arms. She was

quickly bound as Simon watched, and tucked into an ornate trunk, one which usually carried his bedding.

'Twas, indeed, fortunate that Simon traveled with all the accoutrements of home, though it made his journeys burdensome. He sorely regretted that he had had to cast the usual contents of this trunk into the river the night before, but one must make compromises to achieve one's ends.

Esmeraude was an expensive prize, there could be no doubt of that, for the bedding had been particularly fine. This bride seemed in particular need of a lesson regarding his authority.

Cheered by the prospect of only enduring her company for eight months more, Simon sent his regrets to the lord of Airdfinnan, who was still in his solar, and prepared to depart with his party for the welcoming walls of Leyrossire. By the time Esmeraude knew he had lied to her about going to Ceinn-beithe, they would be halfway to France.

Perfect. He flicked a glance at the high defensive walls and knew he could not leave without turning one knife in a wound.

"Bayard de Villonne!" Simon cried, and grinned when the knight looked over the crest of stone. "Have you no words of farewell for a departing comrade?"

Chapter Seventeen

THE LAST SOUL IN CHRISTENDOM TO WHOM BAYARD wished to speak was undoubtedly Simon de Leyrossire. All the same, 'twas most intriguing that the man chose to leave now, and most uncharacteristic for him to cede defeat.

Curiosity brought Bayard down to the bailey, his chemise soaked with sweat once again. He eyed Simon's entourage, nigh all packed and mounted in preparation for his journey.

Simon truly did intend to leave.

"I am surprised by your choice," he said by way of greeting.

Simon smiled in that unctuous way he had. "Why? 'Tis more than clear that the lady's hand will be your own."

Bayard found himself wary, for he recalled all too well how untrustworthy this knight could be. "I had no idea that 'twas so evident."

Simon laughed. "I have eyes, Bayard, and ears!" He winked. "And I get no younger, though I should dearly like matters to be otherwise. I have need of a bride soon to ensure that Leyrossire has an heir and therefore I cannot afford to linger overlong in pursuit of one woman in particular."

"There are other women in these parts," Bayard felt compelled to note. "The lord of Ceinn-beithe had another daughter, Mhairi, if you recall."

"Oh, I recall well enough." Simon's manner was remarkably jovial, considering that he had journeyed all this distance for naught. "But this place is too wild for my taste. I yearn for a cup of wine and the luxury of mine own hall."

"I would have thought you to be more troubled by failing to win Esmeraude." Bayard could not understand the other man's mood.

Simon watched an ornate trunk being loaded upon a wagon, and that with no small effort from three squires. Simon watched them avidly and Bayard assumed the trunk was of some value.

The other knight then shook his head. He leaned closer to Bayard, his eyes twinkling in a most uncharacteristic way, and dropped his voice. "In truth, I wonder whether marriage is the choice for me. A wife, as you may not know, can be a tremendous burden."

His hand fell upon the trunk, which clearly was a burden, and stroked the carving on its lid with a gloved hand. "Perhaps I shall indulge myself with mistresses and acknowledge a bastard as my heir instead."

And he began to laugh. Indeed, Simon laughed so hard and so long that he had to wipe away a tear. Bayard stood silently and stared at the other man, who had clearly lost his wits.

Simon recovered himself, apologized, and smiled brightly as he offered Bayard his hand. "Godspeed to you. But then, you have always been blessed with uncommon fortune, have you not?"

Simon seemed to be on the verge of another burst of laughter. Bayard could see naught in the situation to prompt amusement. He shook Simon's hand solemnly and wished the man Godspeed in return, though he lingered long in the bailey, staring after the departing party.

Simon had gone mad. Bayard could think of no other explanation for the man's curious manner. The portcullis closed with a clang and Bayard tipped back his head to survey his progress upon the vine.

It seemed, oddly enough, to be withering even where he had not begun to cut. Aye, the leaves that had so recently burst forth were wilting along its entire length.

He was vanquishing it! It surrendered to his assault, knowing that 'twas defeated. Perhaps his fortune had returned with Simon's departure.

"The lady of Airdfinnan has borne a son," Andrew appeared by his elbow to inform him.

Bayard was momentarily distracted from his urge to see the vine well and truly conquered. "She is well?"

"Aye, they both are well and the babe is both large and hale."

Bayard smiled, knowing that Angus would be relieved. And Esmeraude would undoubtedly be aiding her sister for the better part of this day.

He had best return to the task of removing this cursed vine, particularly if the plant was vulnerable to attack in this moment. Aye, Bayard had learned much of taking advantage of a momentary weakness in his foes.

He climbed the ladder to the summit of the wall, filled with new purpose, and forgot for the moment the madness that had claimed Simon de Leyrossire.

❧

But Bayard vividly recalled the other knight's strange attitude at the board that evening.

Most were gathered when Jacqueline came into the hall, blushing and smiling though she was clearly still tired. She carried her new son as if he were most fragile, and Angus kept an arm fast around her waist to aid her. The household gathered around to peer at the babe. Bayard spared the evidently healthy child a cursory glance, then looked to the portal of the solar with impatience.

There was no one there.

He had not glimpsed Esmeraude all of this day and he was eager to see her. Indeed, he wished to know whether 'twas true that she loved and accepted him. He had bathed and dressed with care for this evening, the conquest of the vine and Esmeraude's pursuit of him the night before feeding his confidence. He meant to ask for her hand before the entire company, so certain was he of her acceptance.

But the lady had to make an appearance for that to occur. Bayard tapped his toe. Where was she? There were plans to make for their nuptials and 'twould not have wounded his pride if she admired his considerable labor in clearing the wall of the vine of thorns.

"Where is Esmeraude?" he demanded finally, interrupting the coos and ahs when no others seemed to note her absence.

Jacqueline glanced up with surprise. "Is she not with you?"

Bayard's gut went cold though he spoke carefully. "I have not seen her all this day. I assumed she was with you."

Now Jacqueline looked as alarmed as he was beginning to feel. She turned to her husband. "I was asleep. I last saw her when she went to summon you."

"Aye. I left her in the bailey, for she urged me to hasten to your side and I did. I assumed she followed."

"She was in the solar when Ewen arrived," contributed the midwife. "I saw her then, but she left shortly afterward."

And none apparently had seen Esmeraude since. Chatter spread through the hall as all speculated and compared their recollections. Bayard felt his confidence ebb, his trepidation grow. He had a sense that a strategic advantage had slipped away from him, though he fought his intuition.

"Perhaps she fled her courtship again," suggested one of the local men who came to court her hand, and Bayard's gut churned.

Aye, Esmeraude had seduced him more than once before and then fled his side. The pattern was not reassuring.

"But there is no riddle," Nicholas observed.

Bayard pivoted to challenge the gatekeeper. "Who left Airdfinnan this day?"

"Only the knight Simon de Leyrossire. And his entourage, of course."

"Is there another means of leaving this keep?"

"Nay," Angus said firmly. "Not a one."

"Could she have departed with Simon?" Nicholas asked. "She seemed to show him her favor at times."

Those gathered broke into excited speculation. Then Jacqueline gasped and lifted her hand to her lips in sudden recollection.

Bayard spun to face her. "What? What do you recall?"

"She wanted to know how to win your heart," the lady confessed softly. She left her spouse's side, then came to lay a hand upon Bayard's sleeve. "I am sorry, but I told her that I only won Angus's confession of love when he thought me lost to him for all time. I never guessed that she would flee your side."

But Bayard knew the truth of it. He had, indeed, lost an opportunity. He had seen a thousand times how one small deed or its lack could change the course of a campaign. 'Twas clear that that was what had happened here. Esmeraude had made her expectation of him most clear, but he, he had been fool enough to not fulfill that desire.

He had cast his suit for her hand into peril by not confessing the contents of his heart. Esmeraude had given him a hundred chances to pledge love to her but he had not done so, even when she tried to prompt him with her own admission.

And now he had lost her. How could he have been such a fool?

But the matter was not resolved! He would pursue her, wherever she had fled, and he would beg for an audience if need be. He would confess his love to her fully and hope desperately that 'twas not too late to set matters to rights.

He would win her.

The question was, where should he begin to seek her?

The apprentice from the smithy rose and cleared his throat. "I heard a woman this morn, arguing with that knight before he left. I was fetching wood for the smith, 'twas after the lord had been called to the solar."

"What did you hear?" Bayard demanded.

"Was it Esmeraude?" asked Jacqueline.

"I could not tell. But 'twas a woman and the knight wanted to wed her." The boy winced. "I did not listen overclose, for it seemed a moment that should be special, if you know what I mean."

"What did she say?" Bayard asked, his heart clenching. Surely she had not turned to *Simon* in lieu of himself?

"She agreed, but only if he would wed her at Ceinn-beithe." The boy shrugged even as horror filled Bayard. "I went back to the smithy with my wood then, as I expected there would be some celebration betwixt them, if you know what I mean."

"Ceinn-beithe!" Bayard whispered, hating his recollection of Esmeraude granting Seamus a kiss for his tale of that place and how fortunate 'twas for nuptials.

He was incredulous, unable to believe that she could meet him abed with such enthusiasm, then accept Simon's proposal. But then, love was of the greatest importance to Esmeraude and he, he had been fool enough to not answer her pledge in kind. She would have been angered with him, perhaps angered enough to act impulsively.

While Simon, Bayard knew all too well, would readily lie to win a victory. He was not a man so noble as to avoid exploiting another's weakness, not when it could be turned to his own favor. Had Simon come upon Esmeraude, despondent over Bayard's lack? If so, Bayard could well imagine that Simon would offer himself to fill the void.

He could not even blame Esmeraude for accepting the other man. Perhaps if love could not be her own, she chose security and wealth instead. He did not imagine that she had believed Simon, for she was more astute than that, but perhaps she saw some gain in the other knight's suit.

Perhaps she meant to make her way to France in Simon's company and there find a more suitable spouse. But the fact was that Simon did not treat women with honor. Esmeraude would not know the tales of Simon raping and abducting more than one of his seven brides, nor even that there were rumors of the untimely demise of several of those women. Bayard doubted that any man in France would permit his daughter to be wooed by Simon de Leyrossire.

In Simon's company, Esmeraude was in dire peril. And 'twas all his fault. Bayard felt suddenly sickened by his failure to protect Esmeraude, no less than by his failure to discern the import of Simon's gloating this morn.

"She did go with Simon!" Rodney asserted with glee. "Trust a woman to make such a choice and tell none of it!"

Célie jabbed her elbow into Rodney's ribs. "Esmeraude would not do as much," she said loyally. "Esmeraude is more responsible than that, and more caring of others. She would have told me. And she would have made her farewells to everyone."

"Did anyone see her depart with him?" Bayard asked. None, it appeared, had done so.

"It was a considerable party," said the stableboy. "A woman could easily have been hidden in their midst."

Especially if her accompanying Simon had not been entirely voluntary.

Perhaps 'twas not too late to set matters aright. Perhaps they were not yet wed, perhaps Esmeraude would listen to a belated pledge from Bayard that came from his heart. Whether she accepted him or not, Bayard could not let her pledge herself to Simon or wed Simon under duress. 'Twas too treacherous, he would see her wed to any other man than the knight who buried far too many wives in quick succession.

Bayard pivoted, his decision made. "Andrew, Michael, we ride in pursuit of the lady."

The boys ran to the stables even as some protested Bayard's departure so late in the day. " 'Tis folly! You will not find shelter before the wolves begin to hunt!" cried one.

"You will become lost in this wretched fog," insisted another.

"Show some sense, boy!" Rodney cried. "The woman has spurned you—'tis no reason to endanger yourself."

"Though it may be folly, I cannot do otherwise," Bayard said firmly. "I cannot rest without knowing for certain that my lady has spurned me, nor without knowing that she is safe in the company of that rogue."

"I will go with you," Célie declared and Bayard had not the heart to refuse her. "I know she loves you and you alone! We shall persuade her to accept you."

"If 'tis not too late." Bayard took the maid's elbow, much encouraged by her endorsement, and headed into the bailey.

He was surprised when footsteps echoed behind him and more surprised when he turned to find Amaury and his squire in pursuit. Nicholas and his squires followed behind, all of them looking determined.

"I will ride with you, Bayard," Amaury said.

"As will I!" cried Nicholas.

"I mean to wed the lady," Bayard felt compelled to remind them both. "I will not countenance any challenge from either of you in this matter. You should know that Esmeraude has confessed her love and her favor to me."

Amaury smiled. "I care not. You are my sole brother and if I can aid you to win your objective, I will do so."

"Aye," Nicholas agreed. "The lady's favor is clear. Once we all rode in unison and took each other's causes as our own." He clapped Bayard on the shoulder, the knights closing ranks around Bayard and Célie. "I would see those days again and I would begin with the retrieval of Bayard's bride."

Bayard was humbled by this show of support from his brother and cousin, support he had never expected to have and which was all the more precious for that.

"I know not what to say. It could be dangerous to make this journey, or it could be a flight of fools."

"Then we are fools with you, Bayard," Amaury said with affection, then gripped Bayard's arm. " 'Tis not so remarkable as that."

"Aye, we have missed you," Nicholas amended. The two knights grinned at Bayard and he felt the fullness of what he had left behind in abandoning his home.

Bayard knew in that moment that he would never accept Montvieux's seal as his own. 'Twas the legacy of Nicholas, by right and by birth, and regardless of his grandmother's will or his own experience, 'twas not his to claim.

Fear danced over his flesh anew, for refusing Montvieux meant that he had naught to his name. He had no home to offer a bride, nor indeed the stability that Esmeraude would favor. He could only hope that he himself and his carefully shielded heart would be sufficient to sate his lady. And he would be disappointing his liege lord, no small matter.

But even that would be as naught if Esmeraude had been injured by Simon. He would defend Montvieux himself for Nicholas against any assault by Richard, if need be, and willingly trade his life for Esmeraude's own.

"We ride!" he roared.

The knights linked arms and strode toward the stables. The squires ran ahead and saddled the destriers in haste, the steeds tossing their heads and snorting as they caught the urgent mood of the men. Other men came from the hall to lend their aid, helping the knights don their hauberks, checking trap and hooves.

In the twinkling of an eye, the steeds were stamping and anxious to run, the knights mounted and their hands upon their hilts. The squires lifted the banners of their knights before the party and the portcullis was opened again. Bayard was startled when the lord's man-at-arms, Rodney, cantered to his side.

"You need not look so surprised," that man said gruffly. "There is not a one of you who know the roads hereabouts. I would not have Duncan MacLaren to answer to regarding the fate of his daughter, upon that you may be certain."

Rodney cast a glance at Célie, who smiled with such pride that the old mercenary's neck flushed crimson.

"Women," Rodney muttered. "A man cannot live with them and cannot live without them." Then he lifted his fist and shouted with impatience. "Away! Let us be away!"

"Aye, let us make haste!" Bayard shouted.

The assembly of Airdfinnan cheered and waved as the horses began to trot. The party dashed beneath the gates, their steeds paired, the wooden bridge echoing soundly with their passing. The horses surged onto the land, tails and caparisons and banners streaming. The villagers of Airdfinnan spilled from their homes at the sound and stared in silent wonder as the party passed.

Rodney lifted a hand and pointed to the right fork in the road ahead. "To Ceinn-beithe!" he cried and the horses thundered in that direction.

They had much time to make up, for Simon had a lead

upon them of the better part of a day. Bayard prayed that the older man's entourage traveled as slowly as such groups often did and urged Argent to greater speed. He led the group even as the fog closed around them like a cloak, careless of the risk to himself in this endeavor.

For there was no telling what peril Esmeraude had already faced this day.

❈

They reached Esmeraude's home at sunset the next night, riding without halt, and not a one of their party had eyes for the glorious hues painting the western sky. The fog had lifted not far from Airdfinnan and they had ridden in clear, dry weather, which had lent speed to their steps. But they had not passed so much as a peasant en route and Rodney insisted the path they took was the sole road to this place.

The bewildered response of Esmeraude's parents told Bayard more than he needed to know.

Simon had not ridden for Ceinn-beithe.

And they had lost precious time.

But if Simon had not come to Ceinn-beithe, then Esmeraude had not departed with him willingly. Bayard had been a fool to not guess the truth sooner. Simon had deceived her somehow, and ridden south, no doubt to France and the security of Leyrossire.

Esmeraude was more endangered than Bayard had guessed. And an entire day had been lost, a day in which any number of crimes could have been committed against his lady.

Dame Fortune had indeed abandoned him! Thoroughly vexed by this uncommon run of poor fortune, Bayard flung down his helm and tipped back his head to roar.

"By Saint Ebrulfus of Bayeux, if this is a penance for my invocation of Dame Fortune, I foreswear her influence!" he cried. "By Saint Trechmor of Carhaix, my lesson is learned!

By—" Lost for the name of another saint, he glanced to Amaury for aid.

"By Saint Stephen of Antioch!" Amaury cried. "We shall find her!"

"By Saint Thomas of Farfa!" added Nicholas. "We shall ensure that she is uninjured." The assembly cheered even as one man stepped forward, his gaze fixed upon Bayard. 'Twas Burke, Bayard's own father, and his expression was more compassionate than Bayard ever recalled it being.

"By Saint Andrew of Baudiment, you shall win Esmeraude as your bride," he softly declared.

Bayard closed the distance between them, astounded by his father's show of support. His father had aged slightly since he had last truly looked at him five years before, but his voice resonated with the confidence he had always shown in his eldest son. And he had the same ability to draw every eye in the hall.

Bayard had missed him, his surety and his counsel, and missed him sorely.

Burke smiled slightly when he stood toe to toe with Bayard. He touched Bayard's shoulder, his voice falling low. "You shall find her, for 'tis your sole desire to do so. You have always had a gift for seeing your own course won."

"Oft at too high a price." Bayard gripped his father's hand. "I owe you many apologies, Father, and there is much we must yet discuss. I would have your forgiveness, for I challenged you rashly many years past."

Burke bowed his head. "There was truth in your accusation. I protected you both too much, fearful to lose you needlessly at war." He shook his head. "In the end, I might have lost you even more needlessly, over harsh words and misunderstandings."

Bayard smiled at his father. " 'Twas an error wrought of love, whereas mine was wrought of folly. On this day, know that I understand far better than once I did the choices you have made."

"Because of Esmeraude?" his father guessed and Bayard nodded.

"Aye." He met his father's gaze and his voice turned hoarse. "Ride with me."

Burke grinned. "I will." Then he pulled his son into a tight embrace.

"We shall return with Esmeraude!" Amaury thrust his fist into the air and the company applauded wildly.

"You had best hasten yourselves," someone declared imperiously. Bayard stiffened in recognition of that voice, even as the company parted before his grandmother. She was more stooped than she had been just weeks before, but still she refused all offers of aid. Margaux of Montvieux hobbled forward on her cane, her incisive glance making even the most intrepid soul step backward.

She halted before Bayard and rapped her cane upon the floor.

"Greetings, *Grandmaman*." Bayard bowed before her, not missing the way his father's eyes narrowed. He might be the only one who knew Margaux's intentions regarding Montvieux, but his father at least was suspicious. "I did not expect you to journey this far."

"Of course I came," she snapped, her eyes cat-bright. "To see you triumph shall be one of the last pleasures of my days."

"You could not have known that Bayard would win Esmeraude's heart," Burke said quietly, as if daring his mother to reveal the truth.

Margaux chortled. "Could I not, then? Could I not? 'Tis said that a man needs only the proper incentive to see a task completed."

Burke glanced to Bayard, who shook his head and turned

away. "My apologies, *Grandmaman*, but we must retrieve Esmeraude with all haste."

"Of course you must," she responded with uncharacteristic gaiety. "I might not live so long in this foul clime and I would see this victory. Hasten yourselves!"

Bayard felt his father's assessing gaze upon him as he stepped back but 'twas not the time to argue this matter. 'Twas of greater import to see Esmeraude safe than to refuse his grandmother and face her recriminations. He would have called for the company to depart immediately, but Eglantine stepped forward, raising her hands for silence.

"You will achieve naught if you depart hungry on tired steeds," she said with firm practicality. "Linger long enough to eat and see your horses refreshed."

"But Esmeraude—" Bayard began to protest.

His lady's mother smiled. "Is more resilient and inventive than yet you know. 'Tis either already too late, or she turns matters to her own advantage." She shook her head. "I would wager upon the latter."

"As would I!" declared Célie, though they did not linger over their meal.

For Bayard knew more of Simon than either of these women. He and his father exchanged a glance of understanding and between the two of them, they hastened the party without making the women more fearful. Duncan declared his intention to join them and Bayard liked that their company would be formidable indeed.

Bayard's mother, Alys, brought the stirrup cup to her spouse and two sons herself, her eyes filled with an awareness of the adversary they faced.

"See him dead," she whispered fiercely as Bayard drank deeply of the herbed mead. She, too, knew Simon's repute. "Not just for Esmeraude but for all the women of Christendom."

Bayard bent to return the cup, then kissed his mother's

brow, easing her frown of concern with a fingertip. "I will," he pledged. "You need have no fear of it."

Alys smiled with pride as Bayard gathered his reins. She blew a kiss to the three men, her figure silhouetted before the entire company as the party departed. Eglantine stepped forward to stand with Alys, the two women's straight figures touched by the silver of the moonlight. The men rode out, their horses galloping from the peninsula of Ceinn-beithe like thunder passing along the road.

And with every step, Bayard feared that he would find Esmeraude too late.

❖

Fortuna regarded the new arrivals upon her cloud with disgust. She had been rather enjoying herself, matching wits and innuendo with Martin and now all these other saints impinged upon the situation. They were radiant, each and every one of them, and greeted Martin with such delight and reverence that her teeth would have ached, had she had any.

Indeed, this might have been a party for all their merriment and shine, not the scene of a lesson being granted to a cocksure knight.

Fortuna turned away from their chatter in disgust, feeling a little less lustrous than she would have preferred. She peered down to watch the knights ride forth and wrapped her arms about herself in undisguised dissatisfaction. She did not like that Bayard had foresworn her, though 'twas more than his newfound favor for saints.

Nay, she had always had an affection for fighting men. She slanted a glance at Martin, now busily debating the arguments for transmogrification with Saint Stephen, and sighed.

"Mortals," she declared to none in particular (and indeed, none listened to her). She mustered her voice and spoke more loudly. "Mortals, 'tis clear, will invoke anyone at all." She cast a scathing glance across the astounded company,

noting only that Martin smiled at her in a decidedly un-saintly manner.

Esmeraude, true to her mother's expectation, had discerned her sole advantage quickly. She had no sooner been released from the trunk than Simon revealed his awareness that she bore a child.

Esmeraude was filled with disgust that he meant to take the child of herself and Bayard for his own. She was determined that he should not succeed, but she knew she must lull him into trusting her if she meant to escape. There was not a doubt in her mind that Bayard would lend chase and she was resolved to be prepared for whatever opportunity he might make.

So she demanded to be able to ride upright for the sake of the babe, and that upon the finest palfrey in Simon's possession. Though she said the beast had the most comfortable saddle, the fact was that 'twould be the fastest if she found an opportunity to flee. Simon had her surrounded each day as she rode, making it impossible to ride at any pace other than the one he set, but Esmeraude had confidence that his distrust would ease.

After all, she pretended to be delighted to be wedding him. She even tolerated his kiss upon her cheek, though if he touched her further, she retreated, citing her fears for the babe.

Esmeraude insisted upon meat twice a day, and a warm pallet in an inn every night. She commandeered a cloak and warm gloves, she called for a hot bath each evening. She hampered their progress with as many delays as she could imagine, even to the point of feigning an unsound stomach several times a day. She spent time then in the woods, pretending to heave even while a good dozen servants milled around her.

Whenever Simon challenged her, she fixed him with a glare and asked whether he intended for her to lose her child.

Her ruse worked, with remarkable consistency. The man knew naught of pregnant women, and wanted that babe hale beyond all else. Clearly Bayard had spoken the truth when he decried Simon's assertion that his wives had died in childbirth.

Esmeraude did not imagine that Simon's solicitous behavior would continue once her babe arrived. Aye, he undoubtedly intended to claim the babe then see that she—having outlived her usefulness—joined the other wives in Leyrossire's churchyard.

She would escape, for herself and for her unborn child.

But Esmeraude was beginning to lose hope by her sixth day in Simon's company. Though she strained her ears, she heard no sounds of pursuit. As she rode surrounded by servants forbidden to talk to her, she had much time to conjure doubts and uncertainties.

And Esmeraude was coming to have a thousand of them. What if she had been but a pleasant diversion for Bayard? What if he had no desire to pursue her, if it required considerable inconvenience to himself? What if he had found another wench to sate him?

What if her declaration of love had done naught but persuade him that she was not the woman for him?

If she was to be left to save herself from Simon's clutches, that man seemed determined to offer no such opportunity. Esmeraude was glum despite the merry sunlight of May that shone upon them. She was despondent when Simon commandeered the hunting lodge of a local lord and sent both his own servants and those in residence to make ready for their night there. She splashed in her bath with disinterest and glared at the trio of maids left to tend her. Simon had told all that pregnancy had made his fiancée quarrelsome so even the local women kept their counsel to themselves.

She was particularly demanding at the board that evening, determined to have some compensation from Simon for the disaster he wrought of her life. "Careful, my love," he whispered beside her. She looked up to find his gaze cold. "Push me overmuch and I shall ensure that you die in the delivery of this child."

Esmeraude lifted her chin and spoke harshly, for she was sorely vexed. "Push me overmuch, my lord, and I shall ensure the child dies rather than surrender it to you."

Simon blanched. "You would not!"

"You know not what I would do to protect mine own," Esmeraude retorted and pushed her trencher aside with force. She would not injure her own child, of course, but she was irked with Simon's control of her fortunes.

"My lord." The resident châtelain appeared before them and bowed low. He was a portly man, tanned from his days at the hunt, and looked kindly. "A troubadour has come to the portal, seeking a meal in exchange for a song. Shall I admit him?"

"Are you accustomed to welcoming troubadours in this distant corner of the world?" Simon asked in surprise.

"Nay." The châtelain shook his head, looking equally surprised. "He is lost, my lord, by his own claim and by his presence here. He seeks Stirling's halls." The company laughed at this, for Stirling was far afield.

"Then perhaps he would make a better fool than troubadour," Simon jested. "He will not make Stirling this night and my lady has a great fondness for a tale. Admit him." He slanted a glance at Esmeraude. "There is no price too large to cajole my lady's sweet temperament."

Esmeraude smiled thinly, though she nigh gasped

moments later when the troubadour straightened from his low bow before Simon. He was dirty and dressed in disreputable garb, but Esmeraude was certain 'twas Andrew.

Bayard's squire.

Which meant that Bayard was near. Esmeraude felt suddenly giddy with expectation. Bayard had come for her and she would soon be in his company again!

She surreptitiously scanned the hall, but caught no glimpse of anyone else she recognized. She felt Simon's gaze upon her and cast him a smile. "Indeed, my lord, you speak aright. My mood improves at merely the prospect of a tale."

Simon's expression turned assessing.

Esmeraude knew she had to allay his suspicion, so she pouted like a spoiled child. "I hope he can sing or I shall be annoyed indeed. 'Tis worse to have no present than one that is less than expected."

"In truth, he looks somewhat familiar," Simon mused.

Esmeraude tried to distract him from such thoughts. She chuckled, then yawned as if mightily disinterested. "They are no better than beggars, these troubadours, and indeed, look much alike in their filth."

" 'Tis true enough." Simon covered her hand with his own. "How pleasant to discover that we agree on some matter."

"We agree as well on the import of my babe," Esmeraude said, smiling sweetly when Simon glanced her way.

"Our child," he corrected quietly. "I will have no doubts cast upon his parentage."

Esmeraude bowed her head, deciding not to provoke him when escape was so close. 'Twas critical that he trust her slightly now, so let him think her demure.

Simon patted her hand, then he flicked his hand at Andrew, indicating he should begin. "You shall feel better soon, my dear."

Andrew had a clear voice, one that resonated like a bell in the rustic hall. "I would sing to you a tale of lovers denied their due," he said, then began Bayard's tale of Tristran and Iseut.

"These two again," Simon muttered and snapped his fingers for more wine.

Andrew took care to recount only those parts of the tale that Simon had not heard Bayard sing at Airdfinnan. He skimmed quickly through the beginning of the lovers' adventures, while Esmeraude sought some message in his tale for her from Bayard.

She found it in the new verses, when Iseut agreed to a trial before King Mark and King Arthur that she did not love Tristran.

> *For though the potion's time was past,*
> *Iseut's true love was doomed to last.*
> *Tristran, too, was smitten fully,*
> *Loved his lady well and truly.*

Esmeraude's heart pounded at this confession, for she knew 'twas Bayard's way of telling her that her regard was returned.

> *The fact remained Iseut would die,*
> *If her spouse caught her in a lie.*
> *Iseut sent word to her Tristran,*
> *Insisting he cede to her plan.*
> *She bade him come to the river,*
> *Where her pledge would be delivered.*
> *A ford there was, called Perilous*
> *Where many feared their steeds to cross.*

Esmeraude recalled very well they had forded a stream this very day and one that had churned quickly down from the hills. Indeed, they had halted early at this dwelling, much to Simon's dissatisfaction, because several in the party had been overwhelmed by the raging river. All had been soaked and tired and in need of a reprieve.

Esmeraude knew that she could find her way back there.

> She bade him garb as a leper,
> And cry for alms like a beggar.
> When those barons three did draw near,
> Tristran told them the way was clear,
> And so their steeds were mired in muck.
> What poor fortune! What sorry luck!
> The men all laughed at their sad plight,
> So Tristran set that debt aright.
> Iseut would not cross mud aboil,
> Lest her fine garments be despoiled.
> She bade the leper lying there,
> Carry her o'er river fair.
> And to the merriment of all,
> Iseut avoided mire and fall.
> She mounted Tristran like a steed,
> Complained mightily of his speed,
> And when she reached the farther side,
> She did not thank him for the ride.
> She then swore on the relics there,
> That King Mark had no knight to fear—
> No man had been between her thighs,
> Save spouse and leper. 'Twas no lie!

The company laughed aloud at Iseut's cleverness and Esmeraude was struck again by Bayard's endorsement of a lie to see the greater good victorious. She did not miss his import.

She turned and plucked Simon's sleeve. "My lord, the meat does not sit well with me." She made a show of discomfort. "The smoke and din does naught to improve my state. If it pleases you, I would retire for the good of the babe."

"I thought the song would amuse you."

Esmeraude grimaced. "Perhaps if his voice were finer, 'twould. As 'tis, the song but makes me more aware of my belly's protest." She waved a hand before her face and hoped she managed to summon a certain pallor. "The smell of this barbaric hall is most troubling."

"Then you must retire, of course. I shall send servants with you. The chamber above has been made ready for us."

Esmeraude shrugged as if indifferent. Indeed, she clutched her belly as she rose. "If you wish it to be so, my lord." She feigned a heave and Simon recoiled.

"Do not be ill upon me!" he cried.

Esmeraude heaved again, just to see him fret about the matter. She managed to summon a bit of spit and took perverse pleasure in letting in land upon his tabard. Simon was immediately distracted, calling for his squires and much agitated about a stain upon the silk.

"My apologies!" Esmeraude cried with a certain glee, pretending with greater vigor that her meal would shortly reappear.

"Be gone!" Simon cried.

Esmeraude fled the hall, those cursed serving women in close pursuit. Andrew, she noted, began to sing another verse.

"My lady, the stairs are this way," said one woman as they left the hall. There were no less than six of them surrounding her and Esmeraude realized she had done a poor job in persuading Simon to trust her.

Though she had no intention of being trapped upon the second floor, Esmeraude found she had little choice. The women herded her up the stairs as if they could read her very thoughts. She found herself tucked into bed, surrounded again by the cursedly vigilant women and wondering how she might best escape.

She had to meet Bayard! She had to get to the ford. 'Twas clearly her part in this rescue. There was one window in the chamber, and Esmeraude noted that 'twas sufficiently large that she might leap through it.

She feigned further discomfort and cried for fresh air, much against the counsel of her guardians. No sooner were the shutters upon the window opened fully than hoofbeats could be heard outside. Two of the women hastened to look, while three others—curse them!—diligently guarded the stairs.

"Thieves!" cried one woman.

"Bandits!" whispered another. They leaned farther out the opening in an attempt to see what transpired.

Or perhaps a distraction wrought by Bayard to allow Esmeraude to escape more readily!

A man shouted from below and the women turned toward the stairs, their fear evident. Esmeraude seized the moment. She leapt from her bed in naught but her chemise. She lunged for the window, shoved the two women out of the way, then leapt through it even as the women cried out behind her.

Esmeraude landed heavily on the ground, for 'twas a longer drop than she had expected and the ground was rocky. Esmeraude was undaunted—she picked up the hem of her chemise and ran into the woods.

"She is escaped!" shouted one, but there was so much din in the hall below that Esmeraude hoped the woman was not heeded. She prayed that none of the women were sufficiently bold to leap after her.

She glanced back and saw the women clustered in the open window, the light from the lantern behind silhouetting them. One cried out, and they turned to face an assault from the stairs.

Esmeraude might have laughed aloud at their plight for

they behaved as witlessly as chickens, but in that moment she tripped over a root. She sprawled into the dirt, landing so heavily that the breath was briefly driven from her. She blinked dazedly, losing precious time in rising to her feet once more.

Only her fear of Simon's retaliation drove her onward. Esmeraude had no doubt that she would have no other opportunity to escape. She had to make the most of this opportunity—for herself and for her child.

Her heart in her throat, Esmeraude headed into the darkness of the woods as quickly as she could. As the shadows of the forest closed around her, she became aware of the realities of her circumstance. She was poorly garbed for such an adventure, without food, without shelter, and in a region she did not know. And Simon's men would pursue her once they vanquished the bandits invading their meal.

Esmeraude hurried onward and hoped with all her heart that she could find the ford again—and that Bayard would reach her in time.

Chapter Eighteen

T BAYARD'S SIGNAL, THE COMPANY OF KNIGHTS BROKE from the darkness of the forest and bore down on the hunting lodge. There was only one door to the structure and the knights surged through that portal with a speed that clearly startled the occupants.

The festivities following the meal ended rather abruptly. Simon's guards were astonished when the "minstrel" drew a blade and felled one of them before they could defend themselves.

"We are besieged!" Simon cried as he drew his blade. The other men leapt to their feet and the battle began. The hall rang with swordplay, and Bayard scanned it even as he fought his way toward Simon.

There was no sign of Esmeraude. He had hoped to reassure her with Andrew's presence, hoped that she would guess he was close at hand and perhaps make her way to a secure corner. But she was not in the hall. Perhaps she had not even heard Andrew.

Perhaps Simon had already killed her.

The prospect made Bayard's heart clench. Filled with fear, he worked his way diligently toward Simon, letting no foe stand in his course. He was determined that this man taste the bite of his own blade and surrender an answer as to the lady's fate. Simon edged toward the stairs at the back of the hall.

Either he meant to flee from some portal Bayard had not glimpsed, or Esmeraude was trapped back there. Bayard increased his pace, cutting down a trio of men before him, then glanced up as Simon disappeared up the stairs.

Simon could not escape him! Bayard bounded after the man, then eased his way cautiously up the dark stairs. There was only a small light coming from above and, knowing his foe, he suspected a trick.

His suspicions proved correct. Near the summit, Bayard parried a sudden strike from an unseen attacker. He fought back, then dashed up the remaining stairs. Simon backed across the sparsely furnished upper chamber, a woman held captive before himself.

She was not Esmeraude. Indeed, there were six women in the chamber, but Esmeraude was not among them.

"Where is Esmeraude? What have you done with her?"

Simon touched his blade to the woman's throat and she gasped. He smiled. "Would you not love to know the truth of it?"

"If you have injured her, I shall see your blood upon my blade."

"Aye? Then why do you not attack, Bayard? Surely you cannot be concerned for the fate of a mere serving wench?"

"Surely you are not so much of a coward that you must hide behind a servant," Bayard taunted. He lifted his blade in challenge. "Cast aside the woman, Simon. A man should not die without battling fairly once in all his days."

"A man should not surrender any advantage he holds."

Bayard laughed. "Ah, then the rumor is true."

"What rumor?"

"That you cannot best me unless you cheat." Bayard

smiled with bravado, determined only to see the serving woman out of this. " 'Tis no wonder that Esmeraude favored me."

"She rode with me!"

Bayard glanced pointedly around the chamber. "But it seems she abandoned you, Simon. She is a passionate woman—were you unable to sate her? Ah, perhaps that is what happened to all your wives. Perhaps they, too, found your capabilities abed to be lacking. Perhaps 'tis not the women who failed to keep their marital due, perhaps they abandoned you."

Simon's eyes flashed and he threw the woman aside with such force that she stumbled. "No woman leaves me!" he cried and dove at Bayard. Their blades clashed, bringing the two men face-to-face. "And no woman leaves my bed unsated," Simon spat. He raised his knee suddenly, but Bayard anticipated his move and flung off the weight of his blade.

"You cannot unman me so readily as that," he taunted, knowing that Simon would battle poorly if he was provoked.

Simon swung his blade toward Bayard's groin with startling speed. He jabbed immediately afterward, backing Bayard toward the stairs once more. Bayard feigned weakness and the women gasped as Simon raised his blade for the kill.

But Bayard slashed at the man's midriff, his blade singing through the air. The blow took the wind from Simon, even though his mail absorbed the weight of the blade. He backed away, and the men circled each other in the small room, the women whispering fearfully as they backed into the corners.

"Where is Esmeraude?" Bayard demanded. He attacked and nicked Simon's jaw.

Simon smiled. "I thought you knew."

Bayard's gut chilled but he parried a blow, following with a quick thrust that sent Simon back against the wall. "Where?" he asked again.

"She agreed to wed me," Simon mused, his breath coming more heavily as they fought. "Perhaps she feared that this estate you will not name could not provide sufficiently for her child."

Bayard missed a step, so surprised was he by this comment, and Simon landed a blow upon his shoulder. "What child?"

Simon began to laugh and fought with newfound vigor. "What estate?" he asked merrily. "It seems that you have met your match in this woman, Bayard de Villonne, a woman who sees all you have to offer and finds it *lacking*." He attacked and Bayard parried, fury rising within him with every stroke.

A child! Any delight Bayard might have felt that Esmeraude would bear his child was destroyed by this man's intent to steal that babe. What had happened to Esmeraude? He understood fully the mixed reaction of Angus to his wife's labor with their son, for he could not imagine that any child would be worth the slightest injury to his lady.

"It seems that she found you similarly lacking, Simon. Indeed, I will willingly relieve you of the *burden* of her." Three quick blows from Bayard left Simon gasping. He thrust again, and caught the hilt of Simon's blade with his own, flicking the sword from the other man's grasp.

It clattered across the floor as the men's gazes held. Bayard smiled and lifted his blade to Simon's throat. The man closed his eyes and even averted his face slightly as he stepped backward in evident fear. He cast the room in shadow as he backed toward the lantern in one corner, his silhouette swallowing the room.

" 'Tis as I long suspected," Bayard mused. "You cannot win a match fairly made."

"I will not lose," Simon whispered. "You do not know where Esmeraude is, and if you kill me, you shall never know."

Bayard hesitated for only a heartbeat at the truth in this. Did Simon know more than he had confessed?

'Twas enough time, though, for Simon to seize the lantern. He flung it across the chamber, the oil spilling as the vessel shattered against the far wall. The flame leapt into the oil and spread with astonishing speed. The wooden walls were old and dry and quickly began to burn as well.

Bayard glanced back to find Simon advancing with his dagger in hand. "I do not lose," he hissed.

"You lost Esmeraude."

"I abandoned her, dead in a ditch, finally sated for all her days and nights." Simon smirked. "My men enjoyed her mightily."

"Nay!" Bayard dove after the other man, fury in his blood. He fought as he had never fought in all his days for he fought for the honor of his lady love. He would permit no man to sully Esmeraude's name with such filth.

He would permit no man to live who could even suggest that Esmeraude had deserved such a fate. The growing flames painted the chamber in bright orange and yellow and the men danced back and forth, oblivious to the fire's peril.

Simon was quickly divested of his blade and he fell to his knees. He seized the hem of Bayard's tabard with desperate fingers. "Would you kill a man defenseless?"

"You are not defenseless so long as you have a viper's tongue in your mouth," Bayard said coldly. "This time, Simon, you lost." And he drove his blade through the other man's throat. Simon made a gurgling sound, then fell lifeless to the floor. Bayard felt no vindication in the deed—'twas but a duty fulfilled to his lady, a pledge to his mother he had seen achieved.

He turned away, fearing that what Simon had said was true and that Esmeraude was lost to him for all time. Though the women had fled to the hall below, the one whom Simon had held captive still lingered there. He wiped his blade and shoved it back into his scabbard, seeing that the flames leapt up the stairs and closed that path to them.

"You saved my life, sir."

" 'Twill be lost if you do not flee this place."

"I could not go, sir, not without knowing that he was finally dead." The woman took a deep breath. "He lied, sir, he lied about your lady."

Bayard crossed the room with haste and peered out the window. 'Twas a long drop but the only chance they had. "Aye?"

"Aye." The woman came to stand beside him. "She leapt from the window. She took advantage of the distraction to see herself freed from him." The woman shuddered. "I could not blame her for that."

"Did he touch her?"

"Nay. She insisted he not do so, for the sake of the child, and he, to his meager credit, did not."

Relief surged through Bayard. And then his heart rose in his throat. Esmeraude had done what she could to protect their child. 'Twas like her to show disregard for her own welfare when she felt passionately about some action to be taken.

Such valor could not go unrewarded.

Bayard noted suddenly how the flames engulfed the wall beside the stairs, the draft from the window fanning them to greater heights. "We, too, shall leap from the window," he insisted, grasping the woman's hand.

But she shrank back. "Nay, sir, I fear heights. I could not."

"You will. Your lingering to tell me of my lady's fate could not win such a poor reward as that." Bayard seized the serving woman around the waist and jumped from the window before she could protest.

She clung to him in terror, but quickly stepped away from

him when they were on the ground. "Perhaps 'twas the song," she said, her eyes still wide from the jump. She clutched Bayard's hand. "Perhaps the tale of those intrepid lovers gave her the strength to defy that wretched man."

" 'Twas my squire who came to sing. I had hoped to reassure Esmeraude with his presence and the implication of mine."

The woman seized his sleeve, her eyes bright. "That is it, then! I noted that the lady brightened when the troubadour sang of the Perilous Ford. We crossed a ford this day, it cannot be far."

"I know it!"

"Perhaps she has gone there. Perhaps she thought you summoned her there."

It made perfect sense to Bayard. He kissed the serving woman's hand in his gratitude, the gesture making her blush, then told her that she would have a home in the household of himself and his lady if she should so desire. He whistled for Argent and rode with all haste through the forest, cutting as direct a path as he could to the ford they had crossed only hours before.

He heard Esmeraude sobbing before he spied her. Bayard dismounted, fearing that some minion of Simon's had found her first and given her cause to weep.

But when he peered through the trees, he saw only Esmeraude. She wore naught but a chemise, that garment glowing white in the moonlight, and her face was buried in her hands as she wept. She looked no more substantial than a wraith and he feared anew that she had been hurt.

"Esmeraude?" he called. "Esmeraude, are you injured?"

She straightened abruptly. "Bayard?"

"Aye, 'tis me. What of you? Are you well?" Concern had put an edge in his voice, and Esmeraude's continuing tears did naught to assure him. "Do not weep, Esmeraude." He strode toward her, disregarding the effect of the water upon his boots, fully expecting her tears to cease.

But Esmeraude ran toward him, her tears falling anew. Bayard caught her in a tight embrace and whispered into her hair. "Are you injured? Who hurt you?"

"None. They did not dare."

Still she wept into his tabard. "You need not fear Simon any longer. I have seen him dead."

"He meant to steal our child, Bayard, *our* child! He meant to claim the babe as his own."

"Aye, I know." Bayard held her close. She had been so sorely frightened by Simon that Bayard half-wished that man had not died so easily. "But he is dead and can trouble you no longer."

This, to his surprise, did not reassure his usually intrepid lady. Perhaps she had been afraid when she arrived here to find no one awaiting her. Perhaps she had feared that he would not come.

"The child," she whispered brokenly.

"Hush, Simon will not threaten the child." Bayard shed his cloak and wrapped it around her, for she was shivering in the cold.

"But Bayard, the child, our child . . ." Her weeping shook her shoulders again and he swept her into his arms, intending to see her warmed before a fire with all haste. 'Twas clear that she had been out in the cold too long and endured too much in Simon's custody.

He carried her back toward Argent, settling her carefully in the saddle before himself. "The child will be well, for you will be well. I shall ensure that you are both warm and hale in no time at all." He gave her a quick squeeze as he touched his heels to Argent's side.

But Esmeraude took a shuddering breath. "But Bayard, I am losing our child. 'Tis too late."

Bayard met her gaze, incredulous, and she lifted her chemise so that he could see the blood upon her thighs. "I fell, I fell hard when I fled from the house," she confessed unevenly. Her tears fell with greater speed. "I wanted only to hasten to you, I wanted to be free of him for the sake of the child. I knew I would have no other chance. But Bayard, oh Bayard, this is too high a price."

She fell against his chest, weeping as if her heart were breaking, and he held her fast as they rode through the shadowy forest. He had a question, one that had to be asked but not when she was so distraught as this. Indeed, its portent might ease her sense of guilt.

When his lady's tears slowed, Bayard bent down to whisper to her. "Esmeraude, it has not been so long since we first lay together. Are you certain you were with child? This might be your courses, no more than that."

"But Jacqueline said that she knew I was with child!"

He shook his head. "She might have been wrong, Esmeraude."

The lady's lips set mutinously. "Do not tell me that 'tis not logical to know such a thing so soon."

Bayard smiled slightly. "Nay, I would not say as much. Who is to know what a mother knows and when she knows it? I would merely have you think upon the matter. Jacqueline might have been wrong, and thus you would have no reason to blame yourself. Or she might have been right, but there was aught amiss with the babe. This might have happened, whether you had fallen or not." He took a deep breath and held her hopeful gaze. "My own mother brought a dead child into the world before myself. I suspect she would tell you that 'tis far easier for all if the babe is lost sooner rather than later."

"I would still mourn the babe."

"Of course. And I would still have you know that Simon was wrong."

"In capturing me?"

"In claiming that I pursued you only for the child. I pursued you and you alone Esmeraude." He looked down into her eyes. "Do not for a moment believe otherwise."

And marvel of marvels, his lady smiled. "I know. I love you, Bayard, and I knew that you would come for me."

He kissed her then, for he could not make an answering pledge. Not yet. Nay, Bayard still believed that words alone offered precious little consolation. 'Twas a man's deeds that spoke the truth of his convictions, and Bayard's declaration would be emphasized by his deed.

Which meant that his pledge must be made at Ceinn-beithe, before the witness of all and after he had confessed all of the truth to his lady. 'Twas only there that he could dispel any doubts that lingered in his lady's heart and ensure that no shadow ever touched their match.

Aye, 'twas not a course without risk. Bayard would offer Esmeraude naught but himself and he could only pray that 'twould be enough.

'Twas nigh a week later that they reached Ceinn-beithe. Though Bayard had been gracious and attentive to her every whim, Esmeraude knew that all was not right between them. He did not come to her bed, he did not even steal kisses from her. 'Twas as if he thought her uncommonly fragile, but even when she teased him that she was hale again, he kept a measure of distance between them.

Bayard did not confess to any tender feelings for her, even after she pledged her own love again, which surprised Esmeraude. All in the company seemed to assume that they were as good as betrothed, save the knight himself.

'Twas clear that her loss of their child had wrought the

change in him. In her darker moments, Esmeraude feared that Jacqueline had told Bayard of the babe and, despite his insistence otherwise, that child had been the sole reason for his retrieval of her. He had told her from the outset that he was a man who guarded what was his own.

Did he not consider her to be his own any longer? Esmeraude ached to know the truth and was astounded by how little difference the answer might make to her own feelings. She loved him and would never love another, regardless of whether her love was returned.

'Twas a terrifying realization.

Did Bayard think her unfit to be his bride now? Did he think her unable to bear him sons, and thus an illogical choice of bride? Esmeraude could not guess. She tried to prompt some sign of affection from him but though he returned what kisses she began, he did not pursue her. She confessed her love for him, though was confused when he only smiled sadly and touched her cheek.

Aye, some change had been wrought in the man she loved and Esmeraude was vexed that she could not name it.

She was more vexed that she apparently could not change it.

There was a great assembly waiting at Ceinn-beithe for them, and much merriment resulted from her safe return. A fine meal had been prepared and ale ran bountifully in the hall. Mhairi and Finlay held hands tightly; the other competitors for Mhairi's hand had returned to France after his victory.

Esmeraude felt her mother's keen gaze upon her as she congratulated her half-sister, but she had no wish to confess the doubts in her heart.

Célie gave Esmeraude a hug so tight that she nigh broke her bones, then touched her charge's cheek. "What is amiss?" she whispered.

Esmeraude shook her head tiredly. "I have merely had more than my share of adventure, Célie."

The maid frowned in concern, but Esmeraude summoned a smile and turned as she was called to the dais.

If Bayard no longer desired her, she did not know what she would do. Aye, the world seemed a dark and dreary place at the prospect of being without Bayard. She realized only now that the married life she had dreaded, one with daily duties such as Jacqueline's, would be most wondrous with a knight like Bayard in her bed each night. No wonder Jacqueline's cheeks were always flushed.

If only she might be so fortunate.

As if he had heard her thoughts, Bayard appeared at her elbow to escort her to her seat. His touch was cool and impersonal and Esmeraude watched him with uncertainty. "Do you not sit with me?" she asked softly when he stepped away, knowing the gazes of all were upon them.

"Not yet."

Bayard melted away into the crowd, leaving Esmeraude feeling alone. She thought to pursue him and demand an explanation for his odd behavior, but Duncan rose in that moment and called for silence.

"Some weeks back, we gathered here for a Bride Quest," he reminded them all, then turned to smile at Esmeraude. "Though the bride in question departed upon a quest of her own. Indeed, Esmeraude was the cause of an adventure that will make a fine tale of the ilk she so favors."

The company laughed, then Duncan lifted his cup of ale. He beamed at the couple with their hands yet entwined. "I am delighted to announce the betrothal of my daughter Mhairi and Finlay MacCormac, a match that has been made in the interim and one with which I am most heartily pleased. May you both live long and be happy together." The company applauded, then drank to the health of Mhairi and Finlay.

"And now, the moment we have all awaited is finally upon us, when the quest we gathered to witness comes to a conclusion." Duncan turned and winked at Esmeraude. "Esmeraude, have you chosen which man has won your hand?"

Esmeraude stood, her mouth uncommonly dry, though she knew full well what she wanted. Perhaps a confession before all would convince Bayard that she was the one for him.

Perhaps there was naught else she could do at this point. "Aye, I have chosen. Indeed, my heart knew him from the very first, though I long neglected its counsel." There was a smattering of laughter at this, for her stubborn nature was well known. "I choose Bayard de Villonne, for I love him as never I thought I might love a man."

The company broke into cheers, and the other knights turned without surprise to offer their congratulations to Bayard. His aged grandmother thumped her cane with vigor, but Bayard did not smile. He stepped forward, lifting up one hand for silence, as he held Esmeraude's gaze.

"The lady does not know all of the truth," he said firmly. "And 'tis only logical that such a great choice as this, one that will shape all of a woman's life, should be made with knowledge of all of the facts."

Esmeraude frowned.

Bayard turned to the murmuring company. "The truth is that I lied to this lady."

The assembly gasped as one and craned their necks to miss no detail. Esmeraude found herself gripping the board, her knuckles turning white. Her mother reached over and placed a hand upon her shoulder. Esmeraude feared that she would be ill.

Bayard could not have lied! Not this knight who placed so much value on honor and duty!

" 'Tis true enough," he asserted as if she had protested audibly. "Esmeraude made it most clear to me that she did not wish to be wed for Ceinn-beithe, or indeed for any holding, but for her own self. This is as is right and good. I have no desire to govern Ceinn-beithe and I told her as much, but here, Esmeraude, here is my lie. I did seek your hand to win a holding. I came upon this Bride Quest because my grandmother pledged to surrender Montvieux to me if I won you."

Bayard heaved a sigh even as Esmeraude's heart hardened into a tight knot. "I had thought that this rich prize would make a fine holding to pledge to the service of my liege lord, King Richard. He is determined to possess it for his own, to thwart the ambitions of his rival, the King of France. I thought myself the only knight in our family capable of defending Montvieux and believed possessing it myself the sole solution. Truly I thought little of cheating my cousin of his due, and even less of the woman I would wed to gain Montvieux. 'Twas not a noble objective." Bayard held her gaze steadily, leaving Esmeraude no chance of doubting that he now told her the truth.

His family exchanged glances of dismay behind him.

"But Montvieux is *my* inheritance!" Nicholas protested.

"And its lord *my* choice!" Rowan, Nicholas's father, glared at Margaux. "You have already granted the seal to me. You have no right to grant it to another."

"And I can rescind my gift, if I so desire," Margaux argued. "You are not my blood, Rowan, and we all know this well. Only Burke is the child of my own womb and only his sons carry the blood of Montvieux in their veins. Though Burke may have spurned what I could have offered him, though he abandoned his rightful legacy, I knew that Bayard would not be such a fool. I knew that Bayard was wrought of the same fortitude as my own father. I knew that he alone should rule Montvieux."

The company whispered at this development. Margaux stood with an effort, bracing her weight upon the cane, and offered a small sack to Bayard. " 'Tis the seal of Montvieux and your own rightful due."

To Esmeraude's dismay, Bayard crossed the floor and took the sack. He opened it and turned the ornate seal in his hand. Surely he did not mean to do this thing?

Then Bayard smiled and shook his head as he dropped it back into the sack. "You are wrong, Margaux," he said softly. " 'Tis not my rightful due, though there was a time when I believed that as much as you." He turned and tossed the small sack toward Nicholas, who snatched it out of the air even in his surprise. " 'Tis yours, Nicholas. Guard our legacy well. Know that if you have need of me, against any foe at your gates, you have but to summon me."

Nicholas turned the seal in his hand. "You would fight even your liege lord?"

"Aye, for blood is thickest." Bayard held his cousin's gaze steadily as Esmeraude watched, then a smile tugged at the corner of his mouth. "And I shall tell him so with all haste, you may be certain of it."

The assembly cheered and some of the tension eased from Esmeraude. Margaux looked sorely displeased, but she tightened her lips and glared at Nicholas. "It seems I shall have to make aught of you, after all," she muttered. Esmeraude did not envy Nicholas his grandmother's tutelage, for she seemed a formidable old crone.

She cared naught for that, though. She looked at Bayard, her pulse fluttering in expectation. "Why do you refuse Montvieux now when I have chosen you?" she asked, needing to hear the truth.

Bayard eyed her steadily. "Because I have learned much these past weeks, and I have learned it from you." He fell silent though, just before he told Esmeraude what she most wanted to hear.

Duncan cleared his throat. "Ceinn-beithe comes to you, if you accept Esmeraude's hand."

Bayard shook his head. "Nay, for that, too, would mean that I wed my lady for my own gain." A smile touched his lips. "I would suggest, with respect, that your own daughter Mhairi and her betrothed would administer this holding quite well."

"Aye!" Finlay cried in such delight that the assembly laughed. He reddened. "I long thought that 'twas Mhairi who should inherit," he said gruffly. "For she is the child of you and Eglantine and thus a true heiress of Ceinn-beithe."

"So she is," Duncan agreed amiably. He glanced to Eglantine, who nodded firmly. "And so it shall be her dowry."

The assembly cheered again, but Bayard walked toward Esmeraude. His eyes were vividly blue, his expression somber. "And so you see, Esmeraude, there is naught binding between us, naught that one might gain in the wedding of the other. There is no child to compel me to wed you with honor, nor to force you to accept me for that child's sake. There is no property to pass upon our pledges to each other, no gain for either of us."

He smiled slightly. "And thus, there can be no doubts between us. I hope that you truly desire what you claimed you did. I would wed you, and that for yourself alone, though I have naught to offer to you in return but myself alone."

Esmeraude's heart was in her throat. "Why?" she whispered.

Bayard smiled and opened his arms to her. "Because I love you, with all my heart and soul. What better reason could a man have to pledge himself to a woman for all time?"

"None!" Esmeraude leapt over the board and ran to him,

laughing as he caught her close and swung her high. He kissed her soundly, even as the company shouted encouragement.

She touched his throat as toasts were made, oblivious to all but Bayard, and felt the thunder of his heart beneath her fingertips. "You feared I would refuse," she whispered in wonderment.

Bayard shrugged, his eyes twinkling with mischief. "I did not know what you would do, though I hoped for the best. You are somewhat unpredictable, my Esmeraude, though that is part of why I love you so."

"I shall never tire of hearing you tell me that," she whispered and Bayard laughed as he caught her closer.

"I shall endeavor to tell you often." Then he sobered. "But Esmeraude, our life may well be the adventure you say you crave. I must ride to meet the king and hope that he will grant me a holding despite my not delivering the holding he sought. Or I can joust in the tourneys and win what I can. We shall find a way." His embrace tightened. "And we shall have children, as many as you desire, upon that you can rely."

Esmeraude smiled at him, well content with what she had won. "We shall have each other, Bayard, and that is enough for me."

The pair kissed with enthusiasm, much to the delight of all, and such was the commotion in the hall that Amaury had difficulties winning silence in the hall.

"I have a wedding gift to offer!" he finally shouted. He lifted a cup in salute to his brother and Esmeraude. "I drink to the health of my brother and his bride, and heartily anticipate repairing the loss of five years apart."

"Hear, hear!" Bayard cried.

"Hear this," Amaury retorted. "Villonne is not rightfully mine, as I am the younger brother of we two. Bayard should be heir and he was heir until he departed our gates five years past. In honor of this day and this betrothal, I relinquish his gift to me and return the legacy of Villonne to his hand."

"But what will you do?" Bayard demanded, his astonishment obvious.

Amaury grinned. "I will ride out to seek my fortune, just as you did. You speak aright, Bayard, for I have lived too sheltered a life. I look upon you and catch a glimpse of all that I might see and all that I might learn. With Father's blessing, I will seek to learn of the world and its ways."

Burke nodded approval and chatter broke out on all sides. The ale was poured anew and the meat was brought, more than one cup raised to the two newly betrothed couples. Esmeraude had never been so happy, though there was one thing that would make this marvelous day complete.

She stood after the meal and clapped to win the attention of all. "I have one request this day for there is one deed that must be done to make all come aright in the end." She gestured to Bayard who smiled indulgently. "I would have my betrothed finish the tale he began in his quest to win my hand."

Bayard kissed her fingertips and rose in turn. "My lady's desire is as mine own," he declared, then gave her hand a squeeze. He took to the floor and sang again the ballad of Tristran and Iseut. He sang long into the night and Esmeraude was not the only one who wept at how close those lovers came to a reunion in the end.

There was not a dry eye in the hall when Bayard ended the tale by turning to Esmeraude and singing a tribute to the power of love.

❈

And even as Bayard sang, far away at Airdfinnan, the vine grew again with enthusiasm over the walls of the keep. It spread all that afternoon and into the evening, the lord keeping a vigilant eye upon it. The fog had cleared days past and 'twas a relief to Angus that he could look over the distance again.

'Twas no relief to him that this cursed vine grew once more.

Jacqueline joined him, their newest son in her arms, as the sun sank in orange glory in the west. The light gilded the fierce thorns of the vine even as its progress suddenly halted.

Angus stared, unable to believe that the growth of the plant had halted. But it grew no more, not so much as the breadth of his thumb. He breathed a sigh of relief.

And then, as they stood there, the vine burst into blossom.

Great red flowers appeared over its entire length, a perfume of unspeakable sweetness flooded the air. Jacqueline took a deep breath of the scent, then cuddled beneath the weight of her husband's arm. Ewen stirred, then dozed anew against his mother's breast, contented for the moment.

Angus stared at the vine, unable to explain its flowering.

"Bayard loves her and he has told her as much," Jacqueline asserted with the same quiet assurance his mother had had in such oddities and their reasons.

"You cannot know as much."

"Aye. I can." Jacqueline smiled up at him. "Because I do."

Angus wryly surveyed the way the vine had stopped just short of the gate, then shrugged. "If his courtship is won, then he will halt his singing at least."

Jacqueline laughed and leaned her head upon his shoulder. "You are happier about this than you would reveal," she chided. " 'Tis perfect, Angus, and I am so glad that Esmeraude is destined to be as happy as we."

The lord of Airdfinnan looked down at his wife's merry smile and found his own lips curving in response. She was right. He was glad that Esmeraude would be happy and that Bayard had won her hand. He bent and kissed Jacqueline, without regard for the sleeping babe and the sentries so close upon the wall.

"I suppose," he mused when he finally lifted his head, "the vine is not such a bad addition to our defenses."

And this time, 'twas Jacqueline who stretched up to kiss him.

Epilogue

T WAS A YEAR AFTER THE THORNED VINE FIRST BLOOMED that seed pods appeared upon it.

Those blood-red blossoms had endured all that spring and people had come from far and wide to look upon the marvel of Airdfinnan's walls. The enchanted vine itself grew no more, much to Angus's relief. It cloaked the great walls as if 'twere armor and made it impossible to surmount those walls without suffering a dire wound.

After Esmeraude and Bayard's nuptials, and after the pair had paused at Airdfinnan en route to France, both flowers and leaves had fallen of one accord. The vine gleamed silver through all the autumn and the winter, as if it had been wrought of pewter.

Jacqueline had thought 'twould change no more, for Esmeraude and Bayard were in France, at Villonne, and almost certainly too far away to affect the plant with their love. And truly, Bayard had his lady's love securely within his grip, as she and Angus had witnessed, so the matter was resolved.

Yet the following spring, instead of leaves or flowers, the vine sprouted pods not unlike those of peas. It proved Jacqueline's expectations wrong and again prompted both speculation in the hall and discontent from Angus. He professed to fear a thousand such vines taking root in his bailey, and swore to see it torn from the walls.

Jacqueline advised him to wait. She had a feeling that there was some detail that would make the vine's behavior clear.

And so there was. At midsummer, when the pods hung black and leathery from the vine, Jacqueline received a missive from Villonne. She smiled at the news of the arrival of Esmeraude's first son and knew instinctively what she had to do.

She plucked one fat pod from the vine and as soon as she had done so, the others shriveled to naught. But it did not matter. Jacqueline rolled the pod into the letter she had written, then summoned Rodney to deliver it to the south.

Aye, this vine had made more than one change. Though he muttered mightily about fulfilling the whims of women, Rodney was more than pleased to ride for Esmeraude's household.

Jacqueline had no doubt that he had a visit to make there of his own.

'Twas September and in the midst of Villonne's harvest when Rodney appeared at Villonne's gates. Célie chided him mightily for some transgression, then filled his ear with nonsense about the splendor of Esmeraude's son before the man could have so much as a cup of ale.

Esmeraude climbed to the solar with the precious gift of Jacqueline's missive. She ran a hand across the elegant handwriting, knowing she would savor every morsel of news within it. Then she touched the dry pod enclosed in the rolled letter, guessing full well what plant 'twas from. The pod sprang open at her slight touch, revealing a row of seeds, each the size of the end of Bayard's thumb.

Esmeraude rose from her seat and leaned out the window of Villonne's tower. Below her stretched the extensive kitchen and apothecary gardens, though she knew that no gardener here had ever known the ilk of this plant.

She closed her eyes and flung the seeds out the window, willing them to fall into good soil and prosper. Esmeraude made a fervent wish that not only her own children but every soul who had the fortune to see the vines that resulted should win their own heart's desire and should be as happy and as blessed as she. She wondered whether plants would grow immediately or whether they would lie dormant in the soil until a man courted his lover true.

Until her son courted whichever lady stole his heart away.

Esmeraude smiled at the thought of little Burke being so grown as to seek a bride. She turned at the sound of her son's cry and spied Bayard carrying the babe to her. No doubt Célie was occupied with Rodney.

Unaware that she watched, Bayard mimicked the way his son's lips worked in anticipation of a meal. Esmeraude chuckled at how undignified he looked and he glanced up, then winked for her alone. His very glance could still warm her to her toes and Esmeraude hoped 'twould always be thus between them.

But how else might matters be? Her knight was known to be uncommonly fortunate, after all, and Esmeraude it seemed had become a part of that luck when she had won his heart for her own.

A woman of sense could have no complaint with that.

Author's Note

There are many versions of the story of Tristan and Iseult—here spelled Tristran and Iseut—each of which has its characteristic elements. I have chosen to use Béroul as a source for Bayard's song, as Béroul is believed to have written his version in the late twelfth century and thus would be contemporary with this story. Béroul's version is considered to be an example of the "primitive" strain of the story, and thus more closely echoing its probable original Celtic roots. I have also echoed Béroul's verse structure of octosyllabic couplets in my composition—as a favored format for romances in Old French, it gives a period flavor even in modern English.

Sadly, only a fragment of Béroul's work is preserved, and that in a thirteenth-century manuscript with many apparent errors on the part of the copyist. Some 4,400 lines of Béroul's poem survive, but beginning only with King Mark eavesdropping on the lovers and ending with the death of the villains. For the remainder of the story recounted here, I have consulted the retelling of Tristan and Iseult by Joseph Bédier, translated by Hilaire Belloc and completed by Paul Rosenfeld for Pantheon Books in 1945.

About the Author

A confessed romantic dreamer, *NYT Extended List* best-selling author Claire Delacroix always wove stories in her mind. Since selling her first in 1992, Claire has written more than twenty romances. Winner of the Colorado Romance Writers' Award of Excellence and nominee for *Romantic Times* Career Achievement in Medieval Romance, Claire has over two million books in print. She also writes contemporary romances as Claire Cross.

Claire lives in Canada with her husband and family.

Write to Claire at:

> Claire Cross/Delacroix
> P.O. Box 699, Station A
> Toronto, Ontario
> CANADA M5W 1G2

Or visit:

> Château Delacroix
> http://www.delacroix.net